THOMAS EIDSON is the author of *St Agnes'*
*Stand*, *All God's Children* and *Hannah's Gift*.
He lives in Boston.

D1440239

Also by Thomas Eidson

*St Agnes' Stand*
*All God's Children*
*Hannah's Gift*

# THOMAS EIDSON

## THE MISSING

HarperCollins*Publishers*

HarperCollins*Publishers*
77–85 Fulham Palace Road,
Hammersmith, London W6 8JB

www.harpercollins.co.uk

First published as *The Last Ride* by
Penguin UK Ltd in 1995

This paperback edition 2003
1 3 5 7 9 8 6 4 2

A catalogue record for this book
is available from the British Library

ISBN 0 00 718173 6

Set in Sabon and Rosewood

Printed and bound in Great Britain by
Clays Ltd, St Ives plc

# FOREWORD

There was once a time and a place called the Wild West . . .

Today, it's easy to think of the old West as ancient history. History it is, but not so ancient. When Custer and the Seventh Cavalry made their infamous "Last Stand" at the Little Bighorn, Alexander Graham Bell had already invented the telephone. And when Geronimo surrendered for the last time to the U.S. government, Harry Truman and Franklin Delano Roosevelt had already been born. My grandmother Rose Eddy—who had her family home burned by Indians on the Fort Sill reservation—used to tell me the Wild West "wasn't more than a hoot and holler away."

Much has been written over the ensuing years about the great saga of the American West—the good as well as the bad. Most of this writing is about the men . . . the cowboys, gunfighters, Indians and lawmen. And they certainly deserve their place in the frontier story. But I've chosen to people my novels with the women who stood by them or stood alone— women who society expected to bear, without protest or whimper, unequal, and oft times ungodly, burdens of pain, labor and sorrow.

Then, as now, women were the caregivers. In the rearing of their children, in the making of their homes and in the defense of their loved ones, they suffered hardship and solitude the men of the frontier never faced and, I suspect, never fully understood. The old West was a man's world . . . made infinitely better by the women who inhabited it.

The great western artist W.H.D. Koerner called these frontier females the "Madonnas of the prairie." Perhaps they were Madonna-like to some. To me, they were simply what women have been since our kind first walked the earth: the soul keepers of mankind, tough mindedly feeding the flame of what it means to be decent human beings. Saints, no. But a goodly number of them were most certainly sainted.

I am greatly privileged to have descended from a long line of these Western women. From my mother, Genevieve, who stood beside my father and watched their wheat farm—and their world—blow away in the Kansas dust of the Great Depression. To my maternal grandmother, Rose, who, after the burning of her family's home by Indians, went on in adulthood to homestead and prove-up 160 acres of Kansas prairie with her sister Ethel. To my paternal grandmother, Hettie Pearl, who raised her three children alone in Liberal, Kansas, after my grandfather Marion Franklin contracted the "white death" (tuberculosis) and left to start a cattle ranch in southern Colorado and die alone so that he wouldn't infect his family with the dread disease. To my great-aunt Olive, a full-blooded Cherokee, who held her family's Kansas homestead together while her husband, Theodore, like so many American men of the West, roamed the country. To my great-grandmother Amanda Elizabeth who in the 1870s raised six sons to manhood in the wilderness that was my great-grandfather William Marshall's cattle ranch on the Cimarron River in Oklahoma.

Maggie Baldwin of *The Missing* (originally published as *The Last Ride*) is kith and kin to these women. First, foremost and forever, she is wife and mother and will do whatever she needs to do to be true to those roles. But she is far more than a dutiful homemaker. She is a woman of great inner strength and conviction. She believes in a Christian God and in giving of herself, around the clock if necessary, to help the poor, the sick and the hurt, who come to the Baldwin ranch for nursing.

But Maggie Baldwin can also be deeply stubborn and unforgiving . . . and sometimes downright unchristian. When her estranged father, whom she hasn't seen in thirty years, a man who abandoned her and her mother for an Apache woman, rides back into her life to die, Maggie wants nothing to do with him. All she can bring herself to say is "He can die somewhere else. He got here, and he can leave the same way."

*The Missing* was written as part of a trilogy of Western novels that I thematically envisioned as faith (*St. Agnes' Stand*), family (*The Missing*) and friends (*All God's Children*). In *The Missing*, Maggie Baldwin learns that a family sometimes grows in unexpected ways.

Importantly, Maggie grows in her own unexpected ways. Throughout the story, her human values—the values of the female of the species—remain instinctively intact. I think it was these qualities in Maggie Baldwin, intuitive qualities shared by so many women on the frontier, that attracted Hollywood to this story.

When *The Missing* was first published I was interviewed about the novel on the radio. In particular, the female interviewer wanted to know if I thought that today's women possessed the same values and strength as the females of the old West. While no expert on the subject, I said it seemed to me that the fundamental meaning of what it is to be human has been cradled in the capable hands of womanhood, and passed from generation to generation, since time out of mind.

As for the self-reliant strength of modern women, I said that I had no way of knowing.

For the next eight years, I didn't give much thought to this question of strength . . . until one chilly night in a lonely canyon in New Mexico during the filming of *The Missing*. I was sitting in a makeshift tent behind the great director, Ron Howard, as he stared at a small screen watching the lovely and talented actress Cate Blanchett acting out a scene . . . again and again. It was a rescue scene in which Ms. Blanchett—Maggie Baldwin—stands off a small group of renegade Apaches so that her children can escape. It was also a rain scene—created by giant sprinklers in the sky—and Ms. Blanchett was soaking wet. In fact, she was the only person on the set who was wet. The rest of us were cold, but dry.

To this day, I'm not certain what those two movie greats— Howard and Blanchett—were working together so diligently to achieve in those many retakes of that small scene. Each performance looked perfect to me. But they continued, like great artists do, to refine and sharpen their work. The artificial rain—rain that was plenty wet and icy to the skin—kept falling, and Ms. Blanchett, her clothing soaked through, kept shivering and acting. Over and over again, the cameras rolled. The hour was late, the desert night freezing cold and everyone tired to the bone. The most physically miserable of us all, I'm certain, was Cate Blanchett. But she carried on— resolutely determined to reach something inside herself as an actress.

As I sat there fighting sleep, the cameras pulled in close on Blanchett's face and I finally saw something new in her eyes—

something hard and stoically determined. And I knew at that moment that Cate Blanchett—as consummate actors do—had *become* Maggie Baldwin. Her children's lives were being threatened and she was going to do whatever it took to protect them. This was more than a shivering actress mouthing lines. This was womanhood protecting our species.

Then, with the cameras still rolling, I heard Ron Howard say, "She's one tough lady." And I knew immediately the answer that I should have given to the radio interviewer eight years before. . . .

# THE MISSING

# CHAPTER
## ONE

Brake Baldwin spotted the horseman as he rode clear of the tamarisk trees. He pulled his spectacles down, watching over the newspaper to see that the stranger was actually coming in, then shoved them back and went on reading. It was late evening, storm clouds gathering in a lowering sky. A poor-will was calling from the hills behind the barn. The sound was off—he didn't know why. The thick-trunked cottonwoods near the creek were blackening in the dusk, night closing over the small valley of the New Mexico ranch.

He returned to the newspaper's headline: PRESIDENT DECLARES WILD WEST DEAD. Amazing. Just like that: it was over. 1886 and gone—a finger snap. Santa Fe was getting ready, the paper said, to celebrate with a parade of modern inventions and a concert in the old Plaza. That should be worth the seeing, he thought.

The bay mare in the pasture whinnied at the stranger's horse, but got no response. Baldwin glanced back up—the rider was moving slowly in the dying light, the wind running hard ahead of the approaching rain. He kept his eyes on him longer this time, noticing something different, but the stormy twilight was too far gone to be good for seeing any distance.

Not liking the tenseness of his shoulders, Baldwin mumbled his grandmother's saying: You weren't born in the woods to be scared by an owl. The man and the horse were coming through the orchard now, the trees singing in the building storm. The animal's head was down and it looked ready to collapse. Behind him, he heard the barn open. Mannito had seen the rider, as well. The old Mexican was nearing seventy-five, but he had the delicate senses of one grown old dodging Mescaleros and Chiricahuas and their Apache brethren. Fortunately, those days were nothing but mean memories. Maybe the newspaper had it right, maybe the Wild West was dead.

He heard another door, and the sound of shutters closing, and knew Maggie was back caring for the woman and her children. She had been going round the clock with these three for days. She wasn't a regular doctor but she had nursed over twenty years, and was better at it than most, running a little infirmary of sorts. Mostly her patients were poor Mexicans like the woman and her kids.

The rider emerged slowly from the shadows and Baldwin focused on him, wanting to smile, but the battered Sharps rifle lying across the saddle kept him somber. Patterns had been tattooed into the stock of the old weapon with brass tacks, Indian style. He tucked the newspaper under his arm, dropping his hand slowly, the reflex surprising him since he hadn't worn a gun in years.

"*Malo*," Mannito whispered. "Bad." The little Mexican, hat in hand against the wind, was squinting through the darkening night at the stranger; then he turned and slipped away into the shadows, most likely gone to get his shotgun, Baldwin figured.

The rancher stood straighter. The rider had stopped his

horse a few yards away, and sat staring at him. "Evening," Baldwin said.

The man nodded. Baldwin's eyes moved slowly over him. He was old, maybe seventies, and big, close to 6'6", deathly lean, but paunching some. Whether white or mixed breed, it was impossible to tell. At one time he must have been built like a range bull—now he was all bones, ridges and valleys. His rough face was burned to umber and looked slapped together with pieces of wet clay that didn't fit just right; the heavy nose had been broken, maybe more than once, and he appeared tired or drunk, or both. His getup was odd: frontier, Indian and Mexican. People had stopped dressing like this forty years ago. Baldwin's eyes went back to the brutal features of the man's face.

A little black-and-white terrier, the size of a good bootjack, was perched on the horse's rump, its fur up against the storm, looking like a circus dog Baldwin had once seen. Without warning, it took a flying leap off the horse, tumbled over the ground and then trotted nervously around the rancher's legs—just out of kicking distance—growling like it weighed a hundred pounds instead of ten.

"He bite?" Baldwin hollered against the increasing roar of the tempest.

The old man nodded again, appearing to Baldwin for a moment like a demon riding in this dark wind. He was wearing a Pawnee medicine shirt made from an eerie blue-colored buckskin and covered with bright golden stars of silk that had been sewn on, and trimmed at the sleeves with a black fringe. A beauty. Gauntlet gloves covered his massive hands and a long black kerchief was clasped tight against his thin neck with a silver ornament; strangest of all, he was bare-legged, wearing a long Apache breechcloth. His body was painfully gaunt. Baldwin chewed on the inside of his lip for a second, wondering who the hell this old bastard was. He looked like he belonged in a Wild West show; everything about him seemed old, as if he and his animals had ridden out of some ancient canyon lost to time.

"I'd rather he didn't bite me."

"Chaco," the stranger said firmly, trapping a cough in his throat.

Lightning flashed in the hills behind them, illuminating the old giant's harsh face for an instant, then thunder rolled slowly across the valley. The little dog had stopped growling when the stranger called his name, and he lifted his leg now where he stood and peed a yellow stream that Baldwin swore was directed at him; then he bolted forward, took one high bound, hit the man's stirrup, twisted, touched momentarily on his thigh, then—with the man leaning out of the way slightly—hopped nimbly back into place on the rump of the horse. It had happened so fast that Baldwin wasn't certain how he had done it.

"Pretty slick."

The old man didn't respond.

Someone lit the lantern in the kitchen of the ranch house and the light from the window made the stranger's holster and cartridge belt sparkle in the night, every inch decorated with rough silver hammered from Mexican coins. He looked seedy and old, but hard, his eyes small and dark, and he was carrying enough hardware to dust half the Mexican army. Baldwin wondered if he was just show. The old man was staring at the kitchen window.

"Join us for supper?" Baldwin called against the wind.

The little gray, her eyes half-closed, jumped at the sound of his voice in the squall. She was old and bony like the man who rode her—an Indian Chickasaw pony, lots of Spanish and not a little wild blood in her veins. She was being followed by a young, claybank-colored mule that nibbled playfully at the old man's stirrup. "Alice," he said, waving the jenny away. Reluctantly, she obeyed. Neat trick, getting a mule to do anything, Baldwin thought.

"Baldwin place?" The old man's words were slurred, but made sense, the voice deep and shaded Indian.

The rancher just watched him, pulling his hat down hard on his head.

"Man on the road told me," the old giant offered, stifling another hard cough that made him wince behind his eyes, and taking a pull on a whiskey bottle.

"Your name?" Baldwin called.

"Samuel Jones."

Baldwin studied him a moment longer, then said, "Brake Baldwin. Those animals could use a feed."

Baldwin turned and started to the barn, knowing Mannito had him covered from inside, and figuring the stranger probably knew it, too. He didn't look like any pilgrim. Not hardly. Baldwin stopped and glanced back at him. He was still staring at the kitchen window, as if hypnotized by the light, his hair and clothes whipping wildly in the gusts.

"Fresh horse tracks in those hills," the old man called, without taking his eyes off the house.

"Probably drifters," Baldwin yelled over the growing gale.

"Eight. None shod." The stranger paused, continuing to stare at the window. "One outrider. Not drifters."

Baldwin felt the tenseness in his shoulders again, shrugging it off, figuring the old man was playing for attention. They had been bothered by Mexican bandits a few years back, and Indians before that. But all had been calm and friendly as of late. He turned and started once more for the barn. The stranger glanced a final time at the window, then clucked the gray forward and followed. It was quieter inside, and somewhere in the dark interior Baldwin could hear Mannito trying to stifle a laugh.

"Is that a Mexican?" the old man asked.

Baldwin watched him for a moment, then said, "The answer is he works for me."

"Then tell him not to laugh at me." The stranger was coughing hard, as though trying to expel something from his lungs; then he began breathing in little gulps like a turkey that had been run in the sun.

"I said he works for me. There'll be no trouble. If that's tough to understand, you can move on."

Mannito stepped from the shadows, carrying his shotgun. Chaco darted for his boots. "*Alto!*" the Mexican boomed. "Halt!" The tiny terrier sat, raising his front paws like he was pleading for his life.

The stranger seemed surprised the dog had quit and he stared at Mannito for a moment, the little man grinning back at him; then he took another long drink from the whiskey bottle he was carrying and walked to the barn window, looking once more at the house. Lightning flashed again, illuminating the gaunt and exaggerated features of the rugged face—the man, Baldwin thought, looking like a candidate for a lynching. Then the southeaster hit, rain slashing hard against the roof and walls.

Baldwin uncinched the Mexican saddle from the belly of the gray, watching the old giant over the horse's back. The saddle was big, with a heavy silver-plated horn and long, hooded, tapaderos stirrups.

"Something interest you?" the rancher asked.

"Just looking."

"It's just a house."

The old man didn't say anything.

"We're used to slick horns in these parts, not Mexican," Baldwin said, running his hands over the finely crafted silver and staring at the Spanish surname etched in the metal.

The stranger turned and watched him for a moment. "The man who owned that gear tried to kill me."

Baldwin looked at him and couldn't tell whether he was bulling, but he knew the old man wasn't Spanish, not even half.

"What happened to him?"

"I was riding with the Chihenne," the stranger said, ignoring the question.

Warm Spring Apaches. That was a new twist—most of the old trail tramps in these parts claimed to have ridden with the outlaws. He let it drop, figuring the old coot wasn't going to tell him if he'd robbed or killed the man anyhow. "Mannito will rub your animals down."

"No. He keeps his hands off them."

Baldwin looked into the man's leathery face, at the small, deeply sunken eyes that appeared in some way like they had seen too much of life. He finished sizing him up slowly, figuring that at one time he could have been real trouble, then said, "Mister, don't start it."

The old giant walked up to the gray and began rubbing her thin back with a fistful of clean straw, the bottle clutched in his other hand. He towered over the little horse.

"No trouble. But I don't want him touching my animals. I don't trust Mexicans."

Baldwin could see his jaw muscles knotting as he worked.

"*Mucho mierda*," Mannito said, turning on his heel and walking off.

"What does that mean?" asked Jones, in a voice that still had the ability to make a person nervous.

"Forget it," Baldwin said.

**B**aldwin watched her in the yellow light of the Rochester lanterns, remembering the newspaper story about the things of the future, the trimmings and fixings of civilizations, and wishing Maggie had them now. She had returned from the infirmary and was at the kitchen stove. From the backside, her slim frame showed fetchingly through the cotton dress, her thick brown hair, shining in the lantern light, was swept to the side and caught in a simple ponytail. A lot of men bragged how beautiful their wives were. Baldwin never had. Maggie possessed such an abundance of God-given attributes that bragging seemed to just carry the point to excess. She was the kind of woman who looked her best in bright sun.

Their two eldest children were looking at him. He finished strapping on his pistol, then held a finger playfully to his lips. The home was soft shadows, mixes of browns and reds, and smelled of burning wood and baking. Maggie and he had hand-hewn it themselves. There was style and comfort to its heavy lines.

Downstairs was one room, big and open two stories—giving the feeling of soaring space. Constructed of unpeeled logs, the heavy walls were caulked with white adobe and decorated with deer heads and Indian blankets. Harp-lanterns hung on heavy chains from the ceiling, their glow creating pleasant yellow pools throughout.

Lily, their seventeen-year-old, had returned a few days earlier from the Salutaire Boarding School for Girls in Denver and was reading in front of the massive stone fireplace, where a pleasant fire burned. He had noticed changes in her. For one, she was fully a woman now. He had seen a package among her things marked the "Peerless Bust Developer"; she dressed fancier and called him "Father" instead of "Dad." And, like all near-grown youngsters, she thought she knew more than she did. But then she had always felt that somehow she'd had a hand in the Creation. He watched her a moment longer. Her mother's great beauty had passed in full measure and that was fortunate because, unlike Maggie, appearances were important to Lily.

James sat at the kitchen table, fidgeting with a model train. He had just come in from riding fence and was still wearing his hat and chaps, his rope coiled on the floor. He was wide-shouldered for fifteen. Baldwin winked at him and tiptoed up behind Maggie, slipping his arms around her waist, his shirt damp from the rain.

She tensed, then smiled. "I knew you were there. Go wash up—supper's ready."

"Geronimo's older brother is joining us."

"Who?"

"A crazy pretend-Indian. Meanest-looking face I've ever seen. And a strange caravan of animals."

She turned back in his arms and smiled up at him. "Not teasing?" After all the summers and winters, her skin was only beginning to show soft lines at the edges of her mouth and under her eyes. Still a great beauty.

"No. Brutal-looking. White. Dressed half-buck. Boasts he once rode with the Chihenne. Looks sick and drinks too much—I suspect he's come for doctoring."

Lily had joined them and stood scrunching up her handsome face, her skin soft and white. It took a tremendous effort to keep it covered from the sun in this country. "White man riding with Apaches—another old liar."

"Lily, it's Sunday," her mother chided; then smiling again, she looked up at her husband. "It'll be fun to have the company."

As fast as it had come, the rain had gone. Jones was sitting on a bale of hay, a frown on his haggard face, and staring at the muzzle of Dorothy Baldwin's shotgun when Baldwin returned to the barn. The little terrier was tugging hard at the girl's pant leg.

"Dot?"

"I caught this Indian. Mister—get your gawddamn dog off

me or I swear I'll shoot him." The young jenny mule was nudging the girl from behind in a friendly way.

Baldwin could hear Mannito snickering in the shadows. He also heard the same two words: "*Mucho mierda.*" The old man heard them, too, casting a glare in the direction of the little Mexican.

"Chaco," Jones wheezed. The dog let go and hopped up on the bale of hay.

"Dot, come here, please," Baldwin said, turning and walking toward the door.

He tried not to smile. The young mule was following Dot like a big dog, pushing her playfully from behind. Eleven years old and a firecracker with copper-colored hair, bright eyes and a sunburned face, Dorothy Baldwin went at life with a vengeance. She was tall and awkward, and looked unlicked. For certain, she would be pretty one day, but for now she was just thin and boyish. She pushed the jenny away with a gentle shove.

"The man is a guest—you don't go pointing loaded guns at just anybody," Baldwin said. "We've had that talk."

"Okay. But he looks dangerous. Have you seen him close?"

"That's no reason to point a cocked gun at a man. Just stay away from him. And watch your language."

The little dog darted into the house ahead of them, sat, and took to looking pitiful, shivering like he was in the middle of a blizzard. Alice the mule would have followed if Dot hadn't stopped her. Maggie started laughing.

Baldwin noticed that Jones had scraped the mud from his clothes, and when he pulled his hat off, it was obvious he had oiled his long hair. He was holding a scraggly bunch of desert flowers in one huge hand, and smelled of whiskey and tobacco, but also of some sweet tonic. A bright-red bandana was tied around his head, Apache-style. He was a fierce-looking desert peacock. And a nervous one. For a second, Baldwin had the feeling he might flee.

Maggie was setting a platter of biscuits on the table and laughing at the little dog when the old man stepped inside. She looked up with a welcoming smile. Then, as her eyes met the stranger's, her face suddenly changed, the smile disappearing. Lily had stepped backward and stood with a hand to her throat.

"Maggie, this is Samuel Jones."

Maggie Baldwin continued to support herself against the table, a crucifix swinging slowly from her neck.

"Maggie?"

She straightened up.

"Ama," the old man said shakily.

Maggie studied his features. Then, in a quiet voice that Baldwin had never heard before, and never wanted to again, she said, "Get him out of this house."

"Maggie?"

"Get him out of this house!"

Samuel Jones left his flowers and fled with his little dog.

At the sound of knocking, Maggie turned toward the open bedroom window, staring out into the darkness and slowly rubbing her hands together as if they hurt. She knew her husband was in the doorway behind her. She didn't turn.

She was remembering things she hadn't thought of in more than twenty-five years, and she didn't like the fact that she was thinking about them now. She rubbed her face, then ran her hands through her hair.

"He's not Indian," Baldwin said.

"I know."

"He called you Ama."

She just shook her head.

Baldwin waited awhile before he spoke again. "Who is he?"

She didn't respond.

"Maggie?"

"I don't want to talk." The words sounded like they hurt.

"Maggie, this is silly."

She turned and looked up into his face. "Please. Don't ever tell me that anything related to that old man is silly."

Jones and Mannito had guns out when Baldwin walked back into the barn. This was becoming a bad habit and Baldwin didn't like it. The Mexican was crouched near the stranger's saddlebags, his ancient scattergun pointed up at the man at an angle guaranteed to separate the top of the body from the bottom; Jones stood with a small silver-plated parlor gun in his huge fist, a brutal scowl on his face. Baldwin was surprised to see the old man carrying a "hideout" gun. He was full of tricks—and though aged and sick, Baldwin sensed he would be tough to take down.

"The Mexican was in my bags," the old man said with a deathly quiet sound. Then he began hacking hard.

"*Bandito*," Mannito remarked.

"None of your funeral," Jones said, trying to catch his breath.

"Put those damn guns down," Baldwin snapped.

Baldwin watched to see where the old man carried the little pistol, but Jones turned away and slipped it into hiding without Baldwin ever spotting where. He was slick. "Mannito—leave us alone."

"*Mucho mierda*," the Mexican called back over his shoulder.

"What does that mean?"

"I don't give a damn what it means," Baldwin paused. "Who are you to my wife?"

The old man ignored him, squatting and repacking the belongings Mannito had pulled from the saddlepack, his backbone and shoulder blades sticking painfully through his shirt, his neck thin and leather-like. There was a raw dignity to him, and Baldwin felt sorry for him. He didn't know why. He knew he wasn't going to tell him anything about Maggie. And for some reason, Baldwin liked that about him.

"You can stay a day or two—just keep away from my family."

Somewhere in the darkness outside, a horse whinnied. Baldwin cut the lantern flame and stepped into the night, wondering at his own sense of misgiving. Something he couldn't describe was triggering a nagging thing in his brain. He heard a hammer cock behind him. Jones had slipped out of the barn, staying back in the deeper shadows of the doorway where he couldn't be seen. Nobody's fool, Baldwin thought. The battered Sharps was resting in the crook of the man's arm, natural like.

Mannito came next, shotgun at the ready, stepping close beside the towering old giant, sharing the shadow. Whatever was bothering him was nibbling at these two as well, he figured. They looked crazy side by side: ill-matched and ancient warriors—pointedly ignoring each other. The old giant's countenance was as fierce-looking as any Baldwin had ever seen. Standing there watching him, Baldwin wondered again if he was just show. He turned back to the darkened pasture.

The big bay had her ears cocked forward, staring out intently toward the night. Her foal was looking in the same direction. Baldwin couldn't see anything, but he was fairly certain there was a strange horse out there somewhere.

"Hello?" he called into the darkness.

Silence.

"Come in and have a hot meal," Baldwin hollered into the night. No reply. But he sensed something out beyond his vision. Maybe a rider, he figured, or maybe just a wild horse.

"They're out there," the old man said, the words sounding ominous.

Mannito nodded.

"Something, anyway," Baldwin said.

The front door to the house opened and Maggie came out carrying her medicine bag. She looked tired and that bothered him because she rarely got sick or worn out. She seemed to hesitate in the light that spilled from the house windows, then stepped off the porch and walked slowly through the shadows toward the one-room adobe sitting some fifty yards behind the big house. To folks in these parts the little building was known as Baldwin's sickroom. Old man Jones turned where he stood and followed her with his eyes. Baldwin couldn't figure him. Or Maggie.

Mannito moved off in the direction of the adobe, and Baldwin knew the little man would wait until Maggie was safely back in the house before he turned in. Jones drifted after him. Baldwin got his rifle, and went for a walk through the darkness. He found nothing.

Maggie had spent the night in the sickroom, and she was kneeling beside the bed of the Mexican woman, trying to get her to take some broth, the woman refusing and turning her head weakly away on the pillow. The morning sun flooded through the door and windows of the adobe, making the room bright and clean-looking, and reflecting off the rows of medicine bottles on the table.

Maggie mopped the woman's brow, stroking her long damp hair for a moment, then moved to the children's beds.

A boy and girl, six or seven years old. They were thin and haggard, burning hot, their ragged clothes drenched with perspiration. She wiped each small face with a damp cloth. Neither were conscious. That frightened her. She had no idea what to do. They wouldn't last long this way, burning with fever. She had seen small children go quickly in this condition.

She fought the panic rising in her breast. She had tried to sweat the illness out of them, starting the small stove in the adobe and closing the windows, but the fever hadn't broken, and their temperatures soared. She had administered laudanum and acetate of lead and bismuth, because, with the diarrhea and the dehydration, the illness had the symptoms of cholera. But there was no relief. And rarely did cholera victims linger, usually dying in a day or two at most. She closed her eyes and rubbed her face, and felt helpless.

Maggie took her Bible and knelt beside the children's bed and read the Twenty-third Psalm out loud, then recited the Lord's Prayer. Exhausted from three days of hard nursing, she slumped into the rocker in the center of the room and fell into a troubled sleep, dreaming of her mother and sister. Drifting until she felt something wrong.

She woke with a start. The clutch of wild desert lilies was standing in a coffee can on the medicine table. Maggie's eyes darted to the bed where the little Mexican boy lay. There was a toy bow decorated with feathers and beads and three small arrows leaning against it. She could tell from the whittle marks on the wood that it was freshly cut. Maggie tensed, sensing someone else in the room with her, and turned toward the little girl's bed. Samuel Jones was bending over the child.

"What are you doing?"

He straightened and held up a little wooden doll for her to see. It was painted in reds and greens and blues. He smiled at her and bent once more over the child. "Hopi Tihus," he said, placing the small wooden figure in the child's hands.

"You don't have any right being in here," Maggie said.

Jones walked over and arranged the lilies in the tin can. He looked almost comical trying to position the delicate stems with his massive hands. Finished, he turned and glanced around the infirmary. "It's nice."

"Please leave."

Dressed in his Indian clout and wearing his blue medicine shirt and string of beads, he looked wild. He nodded and held his hand out toward her. Mannito was standing behind him in the doorway.

"Boil and give the liquid to them, Ama." He was holding a small leather poke.

She tensed at the sound of the name. "Please don't call me that." She waited a moment. "And I don't trust things from you."

He turned and handed the bag to Mannito and left. The little Mexican stepped inside, looking at the contents of the small poke.

"What is it?"

"Cannot tell," he said, pouring some into the palm of his hand. "Dried plants." He squinched his face. "*Insecto* things."

Mannito looked at the children. "*Pobres hijos,*" he said sadly, handing her the small bag. "Poor children."

"You don't think I should give this to them?"

"No harm, *señora,*" he said, turning and leaving.

Outside, Maggie could hear Jones beginning to chant, "Hey-a-a-hey! Hey-a-a-hey!" She looked through the doorway, and saw him sitting cross-legged on the ground, smoking a long Indian pipe, looking very solemn. She closed her eyes and shook her head, and clutched her Bible closer to her as if it were a talisman against the heathen chanting.

⚑

Samuel Jones returned to the barn, staying there through the afternoon and into the dusk of evening. During this time, he worked on his leather, spreading out his saddle, bridle, the mule's pack equipment, boots, gloves, holster and cartridge belts, and cleaning them with rags and small brushes, then rubbing them carefully with saddle oil.

Dot was lying on her belly on top of a bale of oat hay, reading a book and watching him. She had never seen anyone work over equipment with such tedious care and detail, picking the edges and seams clean of dirt with a little pocket blade, massaging the oil deep into the leathers. She was solemnly impressed. Mannito offered him some Mexican oil. Jones shook his head and looked angry. Dot could tell most of the equipment was old, but the care given it had obviously been painstaking and it had weathered the years well, patched and restrung periodically with new rawhide, each piece dark and pliant, like aged objects of art.

When the leather was done, he laid his weapons out on a piece of canvas and began to work on them in the same careful, exacting way—oiling, checking springs and tightening screws, stropping the blades of his various knives, war axes and arrowheads. For a reason she couldn't explain, Dot enjoyed being around him, watching him work. Chaco stayed close to him, leaving him only to visit the old Mexican periodically, but always returning promptly. The pony and the mule stayed close as well—looking like house pets—an oddly loyal bunch of animals.

Dot liked the old horse, a grulla—mouse gray they called her kind of coloring in these parts. Though worn out, pigeon-toed and scrawny, the little animal was a scrapper; the child figured she had to be to tote the tall old man and his heavy silver saddle over these dry lands. And there was something else about her, something like pride, that the child saw deep in the milky pools of her eyes. No crockheaded nag, not in Dot's opinion. Others might jest, but the gray, she thought, was a mighty fine animal. As for Alice the jenny, she was simply divine sweetness; as easygoing and happy a beast as Dot had ever seen, never devious or ornery. But when it came to the little ratter, the girl just calculated he was of no account. Selfish, full of himself and nasty mean.

Dot watched the old man working on his rifle. His rough face still scared her some; but she was getting used to his long silences and took no offense, even when he refused to answer her questions. She hated the hacking coughs that choked his breath off, making him gasp for air in a strangling way; it was the only time he looked out of control, but she was growing accustomed to these spells. He never commented on them; still, she figured, he had something decidedly wrong.

So mesmerized was she by the old man that Dot left the barn only after her mother had clanged the dinner bell impatiently for the third time. Then she rushed her eating until her father told her to slow down. She didn't like the silence at the table. They had always had lively conversations. She wondered how this old man had the power to change the way they talked to one another. It was odd. He was no ordinary person, she decided. She liked that.

Back in the barn, she leaned against a bale of hay, studying him for a while, then started reading her book again. Mannito and her father had begun shoeing horses in the lantern light, the hearth fired and glowing, the barn smelling of burning wood, stock and feeds. It was her favorite place. She loved the sounds, the smells, the activity.

When he had finished putting his weapons away, Jones did something that shocked her; he went to the stall her father had told him he could stay in, and returned with a book in one hand

and his tiny glasses in the other. Dot guessed the book surprised them all, since Mannito and her father stood holding the hoof of a big roan horse up in the air, staring at the old man so long that the animal almost fell over. Jones ignored them, pulling his spectacles onto his harsh face and sitting on a hay bale, soon engrossed in the volume. The longer she watched him, his eyes concentrating behind the little glasses, the more curious she became. He looked strange in his wild Indian outfit studying the pages of the book as if he was sitting in the Santa Fe Public Library. Finally, the curiosity became too much.

"What you reading?"

Jones didn't look up from his page. "A book."

She turned red and started to say something smart about his rudeness, then saw her father smiling at her, and the anger passed. As Mannito went outside into the dark, Baldwin saw him look at the old giant and mutter, "*Mucho mierda,*" again. If Jones heard the words he didn't let on.

"Tie that colt up," Baldwin called after him. "He'll get himself burned in here."

The bay fought them some, worrying about her youngster, tossing her head and dancing, until Baldwin put a half hitch on her nose and tightened it down. She didn't want any part of that and settled nervously into the familiar routine of shoeing. They had positioned her against the side of a stall, and Mannito leaned into her with his shoulder, pushing her weight to the opposite foot, so he could easily lift the one he wanted. He was wiry and agile and moved fast, scraping, cutting and filing, removing excess hoof and shaping what remained, careful not to cut the frog. Then taking the metal horseshoe blanks that they bought from a company in St. Louis, he checked them against the bay's hoof until he had a close fit. Satisfied, he grabbed the shoe with a long pair of tongs and buried it in the hot coals of the hearth, Baldwin pumping the bellows.

Soon the metal was glowing pink and Mannito pulled it out and began to hammer on it with his small sledge. Dot loved the rhythm of the clanging sound, the bouncing of the hammer off the anvil as Mannito worked. He checked the shoe on the hoof again, took another couple of strikes on the metal, then, satisfied, plunged it into a pail of water, the water spitting, steam hissing. Leaning into the horse again, he bent next to her, picked up her hoof, hammer in hand and nails sticking out from his mouth, and quickly hammered the shoe onto the hoof, clipping and filing the ends of the nails off. Baldwin steadied the mare, talking to her, rubbing her ears.

The rancher glanced at Mannito's small back as the Mexican worked. "What does *mucho mierda* mean anyhow?" he asked quietly.

The little man looked up and said, "Much shit, señor."

"Great," Baldwin said. "No more trouble. Okay?"

"Okee, Señor Brake." Mannito grinned.

Baldwin was still holding the bay's head and Mannito was just bending over and pulling the horse's final hoof onto his aproned thigh, when the foal squealed. Not a normal nicker, either, but a shrill-pitched cry of pain and fear.

The bay exploded at the sound, cow-kicking and bucking, sending Mannito sprawling and dragging Baldwin across the barn as he held on to her halter. Dot scrambled up a stack of hay to safety. She looked for the old man. He had disappeared into his stall, returning moments later with his Sharps, and slipping into the night.

"The light," he called back to Baldwin.

The rancher and Mannito followed him into the darkness. It was easy to spot—the grizzled fur standing out in the night against the darker shadows. The wolf had made a pass at the foal's throat but missed, catching the shoulder instead.

"Damn brazen beast," Baldwin said. The animal was disappearing into the shadows, Chaco hot after him. The old man whistled at the little dog and he slid to a halt and raised his leg on a post. Jones bent and put his Sharps through the fence rails, bringing the beaten stock to his shoulder. Baldwin was squinting hard, trying to follow the light smudge of fur streaking away through the shadows of the pasture. He lost it. Thought he saw it again. No. It was too late.

If the old man had wanted a shot, he should have taken a quick one as soon as they walked out of the barn. But Baldwin figured his reflexes were too worn for that. At least he hadn't gotten excited and shot the colt by mistake.

Jones continued to stand bent over, looking down the long, heavy barrel of the old rifle into the night. There was no doubt in Baldwin's mind that the rifle could reach the distance, but there was nothing to see.

"Too fast for us," Baldwin said, trying to ease the old man's embarrassment at not taking a shot. Mannito nodded. Chaco barked pridefully. The old Mexican laughed at him.

"You wouldn't be so jo-fired brave if that wolf stopped running," Dot called to the little dog. She hadn't cared much for him since he'd grabbed her pant leg.

Baldwin was walking toward the trembling foal and the bay, when the Sharps exploded in the blackness, flashing like lightning, the heavy concussion catching the rancher by surprise and causing him to step sideways.

"Lord Almighty—Jones! What are you doing shooting into total dark—"

The single yelp in the far distance caused him to stop talking and turn and face the old man. At that moment, he looked at him differently—would always look at him differently. First the book, then this shot in the dark. He was a strange one, not to be dismissed. Not easily understood. Maybe the shot was pure luck, but something in the way the old man slowly stood and pulled the long, hot cartridge from the breech, slipping it carefully into his belt to be reloaded, said it wasn't. The old giant could handle himself. In fact, at that instant Baldwin wondered whether, even near death, he could kill Jones if he had to. The thought seemed crazy and he wondered why it had come to his mind. But he knew one thing for certain, Jones was dangerous.

"*Madre de Dios!*" was all Mannito could manage. "Mother of God!" He said it over and over.

"Sonofabitch," Dot muttered.

"Dot," Baldwin said sternly.

"Sorry."

"I thought you wore glasses," the rancher said to Jones as the old man turned and started back toward the barn.

"Close up. I see fair at a distance."

"I'd say."

The door to the ranch house opened and Maggie stepped out on the porch, carrying a shotgun. "Brake," she called, peering into the darkness.

"Everything's fine, Maggie. Mr. Jones just shot a wolf."

Maggie didn't reply for a moment. Then she said, "He's good at killing things," and went back inside.

Baldwin watched the side of the man's face, but his expression didn't change. Dot looked confused by her mother's comment, and Baldwin put his hand on her shoulder and squeezed lightly.

**C**arrying lanterns on horseback, Mannito and Baldwin found and finished the hip-shot wolf on the south slope. Twenty more yards and he would have made the tree line and safety. They calculated the shot at a thousand feet. In cracking blackness. Twenty yards to the trees. Studying on it, the rancher knew it hadn't been a luck shot. The old man had

waited until the wolf hit the slope and started the climb—
knowing he would be winded and moving slower, and at
some point would stop to look back at the danger. They always did. When they figured they were safe, they always
stopped and looked back. That was the moment an experi-
enced hunter waited for; and Jones had done just that. But at
night—how had he seen him?

"That old bastard doesn't need a lot of room to dance," he
said to Mannito.

"*Madre de Dios!*" was still all the Mexican could manage
to say about the amazing shot.

# TWO

The two days that Baldwin had said Jones could stay on the place had stretched to four. The rancher wasn't certain why, unless it was that he felt sorry for the old man. He guessed he did. It was early morning on the fourth day, the air cold, mist rising off the watering tanks. Baldwin was leaning on a shovel in the pasture, watching Maggie as she walked slowly from the house toward the western slope. He wondered anew who this old man was, and how he fit in her life. Or didn't fit.

Samuel Jones appeared as good at doctoring as he was at shooting—the two Mexican kids darting over the yard like they had never been sick. Their mother was still bedridden, but improved. Regardless, the old giant's success hadn't softened Maggie. Baldwin had never seen her behave the way she did to Samuel Jones. She was against him from the moment she saw him. It was crazy.

He could see the little picketed enclosure out of the corner of his eye. Maggie's sister, Thelma, and Julia, Mannito's wife, were buried there. And Maggie visited their graves whenever something was bothering her.

Baldwin tightened his grip on the shovel. The old man had

walked out of the barn, moving in his careful strides in Maggie's direction, the mule and the little dog trailing along behind. He was barechested and wearing a battered black cowboy hat, a Sioux breastplate, breechcloth and deerskin boots—a crazy mix. His Indian tales and dress were a hodgepodge of tribes: Pawnee, Apache, Sioux, Navajo. Stiffly old-fashioned and out of touch, Jones might also be losing it a little in the head. And Baldwin knew he drank too much.

Maggie was standing by the picket fence, her head bowed, her Bible held in both hands. If she knew the old man was beside her, she didn't let on. Jones took his hat off and looked down in the same manner. She didn't acknowledge him for a long while. They just stood there, shoulder to shoulder, like a couple about to be hitched, the mule nibbling at the old man's boots. Chaco sat beside Maggie, as if he might be giving her away at the make-believe wedding. The two Mexican kids lined up behind them, the boy with his toy bow and the little girl with the Tihus doll, seemingly sensing that this was a solemn event. Baldwin jumped the creek.

Maggie was talking to the old man now. Moments later, as if they were actors in some strange kind of play, she whirled and slapped his face, the two of them turning and marching away; Maggie to the house, the old man back to the barn.

That was it. Baldwin could accept a lot of things, but when Maggie took to slapping strangers who drank too much, who carried heavy hardware and shot the way the old man did, it was high time to end it.

Baldwin let his eyes adjust to the barn's weak light. Mannito had ridden out with James and Dot to check the calving, turning the stock out before he left. The barn was quiet, shafts of sunlight slanting into the shadows from the open windows, a few flies buzzing lazily in the air. Baldwin glanced around for the man. Nowhere.

"Jones?"

No response. He turned and walked a few paces down the row of stalls. The old man had been sleeping in the last one on fresh straw Mannito had pitched for him. The Mexican had a heart. Interestingly, the two ancient warriors seemed, Baldwin thought, to have struck some sort of truce. Not friends, but willing to coexist in the barn. Baldwin stopped and listened. Chaco was whining.

The old man was sprawled face-first in the stall, the dog lying on top of him and licking the back of his head. Chaco bared his teeth as Baldwin knelt beside the man.

"I'm not going to hurt him, boy."

The little dog growled but didn't move when he felt for Jones's heart. He rolled him over, and Chaco hopped out of the way, continuing to growl beside them. Blood trickled out the side of Jones's mouth. He still had a fair heartbeat and was breathing. Baldwin propped him against a bale of hay, spreading a blue Indian blanket over him, and waited. The little dog sat looking mournful by the old man's side. Baldwin got the feeling that Chaco had witnessed this scene before and didn't like it.

Jones tossed and turned and mumbled for a while. Twice, Baldwin heard him call out, "Yopon." Lost in his own shadow world, Samuel Jones was struggling desperately against something Baldwin couldn't see but sensed.

He was an odd character, Baldwin thought, as he glanced around. Beneath his brutal features there was a certain sensitivity and style. He had dressed the box stall into a home of sorts. There were sacred pahos—colorfully painted prayer sticks, decorated with feathers and kachina-like figures— hanging on the walls. Three Southwest tribes made them: Pueblos, Apaches and Navajos, so he couldn't be sure where these were from. A clutch of dried maize tied with red and blue beads hung next to the pahos. A large parfleche trunk of painted rawhide looked Apache.

He wondered again who this man was, this man Maggie hated. She had never mentioned any living kin. Looking around the stall, Baldwin felt like he was sitting in the sacred hogan of a Zuni or Apache shaman. Was the old man a half-breed? His outfit was an odd collection from different tribes. Lined in a row on a bench sat six full bottles of mescal whiskey. He had arrived at the ranch fully illuminated, and he hadn't quit since. He had the habit. And Baldwin bet he could kick the lid off.

They just looked at each other for a while when Jones came to. The old man sat carefully picking straw from the blue blanket. When he finished, he folded it neatly and stored it in the parfleche trunk. Baldwin watched. The blanket was obviously important to him.

Finally, Baldwin said, "How long have you been like this?"

Samuel Jones didn't try to play games. "Six months, maybe seven."

"Much pain?"

"Some."

"Seen a doctor?"

"Both."

The expression on Baldwin's face said he didn't understand.

"Apache and white."

"And?"

Jones held his hand up in a loose fist, palm toward Baldwin, then dropped it like he was tossing something to the ground. It was the silent language and Baldwin knew this gesture meant "bad." He nodded at the old man, who just watched him and scratched the little dog's head. Chaco looked happy again.

*     *     *

Maggie was sitting in the rocker on the porch, her Bible lying on her lap, her hands squeezing a twisted rag until the knuckles were cream-white. Baldwin stood on the steps and watched her for a moment; then he turned his back and studied the valley. She gazed past him at the sandstone mountains.

"He came to die," he said.

He could feel her eyes on the back of his neck. He turned and looked at her. She was crying without sound, tears running down her cheeks. "Who is he, Maggie? Why did he come here to die?"

"I don't care," she sobbed.

"He traveled hard so he could end it here." He watched her. "Because of you. He calls you Ama. Who is he?"

Maggie seemed to convulse with her crying, her arms wrapped around herself as if she were cold. He held her while she sobbed. When she finally stopped, she walked to the railing and stood looking out at the far mountains.

"Maggie?"

"He's my father." She sounded exhausted.

They sat together on the porch until the sun had leaped the creek and started to drop toward the redstone of the mountains. Lily came out a couple of times, but Baldwin shook his head and she went back inside. Maggie sat with her head clamped between her hands, gazing out across the pasture.

"I want him gone," she said.

"I thought both your parents were dead."

Maggie shook her head slowly. They sat quietly for a while, then she again said, "I want him gone."

"No, Maggie."

"Why?"

"Because he's dying."

"He can die somewhere else. He got here, and he can leave

the same way."

"We can't do that."

"I can."

"No. We can't. And," Baldwin hesitated, "he's going to take his meals in the house."

It was as if he had slapped her face. "I can't have that man in my house. I can't, Brake." She sounded desperate.

Baldwin pulled hard on his cigarette, then blew the smoke out in a long rush. "We have to, Maggie."

"Don't ask that of me, please," she moaned.

"He's your father, Margaret."

She was crying hard again. Her voice sounded controlled when she spoke. "I was ten when he left. Mother was carrying Thelma. We never had much—but we had something. We had an old farm. After he left we lost it all. Mother cleaned for people, washed clothes at night, cooked for the railroad." Baldwin watched her hands—they were twisting and pulling on the washrag until he thought the material would tear.

"She never stopped. She tried to give us something. But we were just drifters, town to town. Always searching for him. Always on some quest that neither Thelma nor I really understood. Never a home. No friends. All we had was the God-awful searching." Maggie looked off into the distance. "I loved him then, used to pray at night for him to come back. I'd pray every night, Brake, until I fell asleep. I thought I could will him to come home. I felt that everything would be okay if he would just return. He never did. And now that he's come, and I see who he is, I know things wouldn't have been okay even if he had."

Maggie tipped her head forward onto her knees. "I think Mother went a little crazy," she said quietly. "She never stopped acting like he was still with her. I used to hear her late at night—talking to him as if he was in the room with her—and I'd be terrified by the sounds. I came to hate him because she couldn't stop loving him. I still do. She just broke and died." She raised her face to him. "That man you're so worried about, Brake, killed my mother. I can't have him here."

She continued to rest her head on her knees for a while. Then she raised it and looked up at her husband. "He took up with an Indian woman. He left me and my mother for an Indian whore." She was sobbing softly. "I can't have him here," she said again.

Baldwin stood watching the cottonwoods moving in the slow breeze, then he looked down at her. She seemed small and childlike, sitting there with her arms encircling her knees, her Bible clutched in one hand.

"We have to do it," he said softly. "This isn't about you and him."

"No? Then who's it about?"

"Our children. That old man is their grandfather."

"So?"

"We can't have them watch us drive him off, near dead the way he is, like he's some scavenger. He's their blood. They have a right to know him—good or bad. You and I don't have a right to stop them." He paused. "And they'll know him in our house."

"Then I'll live in the barn."

Baldwin studied her face and knew she meant it.

Lily had been arguing with her father for the past half hour. Now she was sitting stiffly on the fireplace hearth, sandwiched between her brother and sister, and looking worn out and near tears. Neither Dot nor James had uttered a single word. Not for, or against. Baldwin guessed their awkward quietness was due to learning they were blood relations to Jones. But he knew there was more to it. They were frightened by their mother's sad appearance. She was sitting in a chair a few feet away, preoccupied with seemingly dark thoughts. Normally lively and talkative, her melancholy bothered her younger children more than the news they'd just heard. Still, he figured they'd warm to their new grandfather soon enough.

But glancing at Lily and seeing the cold resolve behind her eyes, he knew she would fight kinship with the old man for a long time. Perhaps forever. Samuel Jones simply didn't fit in her world. Didn't fit at all. Since she was a youngster, Lily had wanted her life to be romantic, like the lives she read about in her magazines. He felt badly for her. But feeling badly wouldn't change what was. Neither would daydreams nor passing fancies. And Jones was blood kin.

Baldwin didn't discount the fact that his eldest daughter had a feeling for the finer things. But he also knew those kinds of people rarely fared well in this wilderness. She had to face reality, not try to wish things into something they weren't.

"He's not my grandfather," she said morosely.

"Yes, he is. And you'll treat him with respect," Baldwin countered firmly.

"Mother?"

Maggie looked up at Lily, but didn't respond. She and Brake had never interfered with each other in the handling of the children. And, upset as she was, Maggie wasn't about to start now.

Brake respectfully gave his wife time to reply; then when he was certain she wasn't, he said to Lily, "You don't need to ask your mother how to behave toward your grandfather. None of you children do."

It was near dark when Dot approached Samuel Jones at the far edge of the cornfield. The full moon was rising, shining over the tall plants and splashing light onto the old man. He looked mysterious in its pallid glow, sitting bare-legged on the ground in a worn yellow buckskin medicine shirt covered with green beads and white porcupine quills, a bright-red blanket wrapped around his waist. He wore Apache boots with their curled-up toes, his hat gone and his long gray hair done up in thick braids covered in soft-looking deerskin; his ears held great brass wire rings. He was shaking a small Navajo rattle in one hand and chanting quietly. Chaco sat beside him. They both seemed to be looking at something in the shadows of the valley. She could smell alcohol on him.

Dot wanted to talk to him, but she felt a little nervous. The old man still had the meanest face she had ever seen. But she was getting used to him. She cleared her throat. Neither he nor his little dog moved. Then suddenly she was feeling strange—like she was being watched. She looked nervously at the expanse of shadows around her, unable to shake the strange sensation. Nothing. But still the unsettling feeling wouldn't leave her. Somewhere off in the darkness something disturbed a flock of tree sparrows and the little birds set up a racket with their constant chirping in the night. Slowly, they settled down. She wondered what had spooked them.

Dot listened for a while, then she shrugged off the feeling of unease and turned back to the old man. He was looking over his shoulder at her. Chaco was showing his teeth, like he was smiling or maybe eating sour grapes.

Dot stepped closer. "Are you really my grandfather?"

"Is that what your mother says?"

"That's what my pa says."

He nodded. "I guess I am."

Dot crossed her arms and scrutinized the side of the old man's face, then turned and studied the young corn plants for a while, cogitating on things in her head. She looked back at him and asked, "What should I call you?"

He didn't answer.

"What do others call you?"

"Jones."

She shook her head. "My pa would make me say 'Mr. Jones' or 'Grandpa Jones.' And that doesn't seem right, us being closely related."

He didn't respond.

"Pa said you once lived with the Sioux."

He nodded.

"What did they call you?"

"Gut eater."

"That's not going to work," she said quickly. She couldn't imagine herself sitting at the dinner table next to Lily and saying, "Gut eater, please pass the gravy." She scratched at an itch and puzzled on the problem for a moment.'

"Maybe just 'Grandpa.' " She paused. "Is that okay?"

He nodded, and Dot nodded in return and grinned. She suddenly enjoyed the thought of calling this wild-looking old man "Grandpa." Something about him, a thing that seemed dangerous and different, made her like being around him and being blood kin. She didn't care what Lily thought.

"Where you from?"

"The mountains."

"Which?"

"Madres of Mexico."

Dot squinted her eyes at him. "You funning me?" She knew Mexico's Madres mountains were a good six hundred miles south. Six hundred miles of dry waste. She marveled that the old gray pony had gone the distance carrying the huge silver-covered saddle and her grandfather.

He reached a big hand and stroked the little dog's back, the hand gnarled and badly busted up.

"You came all this way just to see Ma?" Dot asked, her eyes on the old hand with its liver spots.

"My daughter," he said, as if the words explained everything.

Dot thought for a while, then said, "How come you never came before?"

The old man didn't answer.

They both went to listening to the long-eared owl in the cottonwood near the creek. She hunted the pasture almost every night. Lily had named her Veronica. Crickets were loud in the cool air. Dot tipped her head back and looked up at the stars that seemed close enough to touch, and wiggled her toes in the sand. She loved the ranch.

"If you're Indian, then I'm Indian. Right?"

"I'm Indian—but not blood Indian."

"How can that be?"

He pointed at his chest.

"That's nothing."

The old man didn't reply.

Dot felt that she had won the point. And a moment later, she started in again, feeling more at ease with his brutal features. "Ma says you aren't a Christian."

He stared at the night.

"That true?"

"Once."

Dot studied his face, waiting for him to explain. When he didn't, she said, "I've never known a heathen."

He nodded.

"Why you sitting out here in the dark?"

The old man took a long time to answer, as though deciding whether or not to dismiss her. Finally, he said, "I'm talking to the spirit powers."

"Who's that?" She scrunched up her face and looked as if she thought he might be crazy.

He watched her for a few moments. "If you can't learn about things, then go and leave me be." His voice was firm and deeply serious.

Dot put her hands on her hips and started to sass, then changed her mind and didn't know why. "What are you talking to them about?"

"Things. My things. They are of no importance to you."

She shifted her weight onto one bare foot and placed the other against the inside of her leg, balancing like a flamingo she'd seen in one of her mother's books.

"Where are they?" Dot looked nervously around her, thinking again of the sparrows that had been disturbed at their night roost.

Jones had resumed his chanting and didn't respond. The moon's glow was on him fully now, and he looked like a holy man to her.

Dot squatted down and absentmindedly reached a hand out to touch the little dog. He snapped at her and she jumped back, a drop of blood welling on a finger. She waved the stinging hand in the air and then sucked on the bite. The spell of the moment was gone. "I ought to shoot him," she said angrily. The little dog eyed her back and seemed just as angry.

Jones paid no attention to their squabbling.

Dot stared at the old man for a few moments. He had turned his back to her and was shaking the rattle again.

"Grandpa." Jones didn't turn. "Grandpa. Can you find things?"

He didn't answer.

"With your chanting—can you find things?"

"What things?" he asked finally, not looking at her or stopping the steady shaking of the rattle.

"A cat?"

"How long has he been gone?"

"She. Two weeks."

"That's a long time. Coyotes like white men's cats. I will see whether she still lives."

She looked relieved. "Thanks. Her name is Harriet."

He began to chant and then broke into a rough coughing spell. When he finished he sat catching his breath and staring at the darkness. "Stay out of the hills for a while."

"Why?"

He didn't say anything else. She thought he was mean-looking but funny. She liked the sound of his chanting.

"Will you teach me Indian medicine?"

He looked off across the shadows in a serious way, not angry or annoyed, just quiet and appraising, and was starting to answer, when Maggie's voice cut him off—"No. He will not. He will keep his pagan ways to himself. Or he will leave this ranch."

Jones didn't move.

Dot turned to see her mother standing a few feet away, watching the old man. "Ma, I need to find Harriet."

"You won't find her through Indian magic. You'll just make your soul sick. If you want Harriet, pray to the Lord."

The old giant turned now and stared into Maggie's face, his strange features hard to read. He studied her until she grew more upset.

"If you have something to say, just say it," Maggie challenged.

He shook his head slowly.

She continued to glare at him. "No, go ahead. Please," she said sarcastically, "say whatever you're thinking."

Jones tipped his head down and appeared to be examining the material of his blanket.

"Say it," Maggie said firmly. "Be honest for once."

"Ma?" Dot was squirming.

Jones looked up at his daughter's face, examining her fine features, and seeing something else—her stubbornness—and sensing she wasn't going to stop until he told her what was on his mind. Finally, he said, "I was just thinking about what you told the child."

"What about it?"

He hesitated for a moment, then continued. "That she should pray to the Christian god." He stopped talking and it was apparent he didn't want to continue—felt he had gone too far already. But it was too late.

"Go on," she demanded.

The old man weighed his response carefully, then said, "It won't work, that's all."

"How dare you!" Maggie exploded. "Dot. Go to the house, please."

The two of them watched the girl trotting away. When she was out of earshot, Maggie turned slowly and stared angrily down at him. "Listen. You ran off with some Indian woman. That was your choice and your business. Now you're here. Here because my husband has a good heart. But if you start teaching Dot your heathen beliefs . . ." Maggie stopped and watched his face for a moment. "I'll kill you. I promise."

The old man turned away and stared into the night for a while, before he looked back at her. "It still won't work," he said quietly. "Your god won't find the cat."

"I can reach my God any time I want," she snapped, her voice trembling with anger. She turned and walked off toward the barn.

He began to chant once more, his voice rising in the night air, his eyes following her. He continued the droning singsong long after she was gone, calling on his power to tell him what was causing him to feel this nagging sense of dread. Was it simply a premonition of his coming death? Or was it his inability to accept the fact that Maggie hated him? Somehow he didn't believe it was either.

Jones stopped, convinced he would receive no answer this night. He was struggling to stand, his breath coming in pained gasps, when suddenly his body stiffened, his eyes locking hard on a fleeting vision: a man's face—Indian—a face beyond time and place, floating in the night sky. Then it was gone. The tree sparrows chattered again—then settled back to their roost.

Samuel Jones was shaking.

A couple of hours later, Baldwin saw Jones looking like a lovesick cow, standing in the moonlight and staring in through the barn door at Maggie as she sat reading her Bible in the lantern's glow. She was held in a sort of reverential awe by the old man. It was crazy, but Baldwin understood it better now. Then Mannito had come out of the barn and joined Jones. Neither spoke, two solemn sentries in the night. The mismatched pair standing mutely side by side, straight and stiff, for more than an hour. Then Jones began to chant. And a few minutes later, Mannito had joined the chanting. Two old men, one Indian-in-his-heart, and the other Mexican; two old men standing shoulder to shoulder in the darkness, chanting together like half-mad savages. Baldwin couldn't figure it.

Maggie sat in the barn straw, trying to read a passage from the New Testament in the lantern light, and trying unsuccessfully to block out the sound of the shrill chanting of the old men, ignoring the anger building in her breast. What was Mannito getting involved with him for anyway? Both of them crying in the dark like lunatics. It wasn't like the little Mexican. Maggie pressed her lips together in frustration and watched a mouse scurrying in the shadows by the barn wall. The man had the ability to infect people with his crazy beliefs. She had seen it before.

Maggie tried to ignore the smell of fresh pine drifting in the air. The bough was hanging from the barn's rafters overhead. She shut her eyes. She knew he had done it. He used to do the same thing in their old barn on the farm whenever she and her cousins were going to sleep outside. She was surprised he had remembered. It was piñon-juniper, which meant that he had ridden miles into the high country to find it. It didn't matter. It didn't change anything.

It certainly didn't erase her knowledge of the Indian woman, or his sin against her mother. She imagined the woman with rotting teeth, dirty hair and body lice. Probably not far from the truth. He had left them for pagan vermin. She shook her head.

Maggie worked to shut out the monotonous incantations but couldn't. She clutched harder at her Bible, opening it to where her thumb marked a passage of Luke: "Ask and it will be given you." She had been reading the line over and over, remembering his insult about God not helping. She started to pray, then hesitated.

Maggie rarely asked God for anything. In fact, she couldn't recall ever having done it, except when the children were sick. If she had, she didn't remember receiving anything that resembled a divine response. That last thought bothered her and she closed her eyes and her Bible and squeezed the little book hard. "Dear God. This may seem like a small thing. But I need Your help. I need to prove to Dot that You will help her if she needs You."

Maggie felt silly, ungrateful, asking God for such a thing. She started to open her eyes, but the shrill chanting had increased in volume and she clutched harder at the Bible, her resolve stiffening. "Lord. I need Your help to find Harriet the cat."

The croaking of the grass frogs near the creek was loud in the summer night, as Baldwin entered the barn. Mannito had retired to his room at the back of the cavernous structure. The three children were in the house getting ready for bed. Jones was asleep, or looked to be, wrapped in his Indian blankets on the ground in front of the barn, his faithful little band of animals dozing around him.

Maggie was still sitting on the blanket, still reading her Bible in the lantern's pleasant light, the little lamp making a small hissing sound. The sound wasn't loud enough to block the peaceful noises of the horses in their stalls, their animal warmth rising pleasantly in the cool air. Baldwin felt a slight chill across his shoulders. Something in the darkness beyond the barn door—something that seemed wrong or out of place—was still bothering him. He had tried to figure it, but couldn't and shrugged off the uneasy feeling.

Though Maggie was aware that he was standing before her, she refused to look up from her book. He smiled to himself and settled down on the blanket with a playful groan. She continued reading.

"Why don't you come back to the house?" he said quietly.

She shook her head.

"I asked him if he wanted to sleep inside, but he won't do it."

"He's gone native," she said. "And he's stubborn."

"Oh," he said, grinning. "I'm glad you didn't inherit any of that."

Maggie turned her head and looked at him, and he realized he had said exactly the wrong thing.

"Just joking." He waited for her to say something. When she didn't, he said, "He's sleeping out front. Come on back in."

"I can't." Her voice was soft but firm-sounding.

"Why? He's not there."

"Because if I do, it's like I've accepted him being here. And I won't, Brake. I won't let him have that victory over me."

He watched her from the side for a moment. "This isn't a sporting contest." He paused. "Think of the children."

She tipped her head back to keep her tears from running

and studied the shadows near the rafters of the barn. "I am. They don't know about him. But I do. You wouldn't want me to just forget what happened to my mother."

He studied her for a moment, then cleared his throat and said, "Yes, I would."

Through the thick adobe walls, they heard Jones begin his monotonous chanting. Maggie started to sob hard and Brake put his arms around her and held her tight against him.

"I can't," she cried. "It hurts as if it just happened."

"It's just seeing him again after all those years—you'll get over that."

She shook her head. "Not until he's gone."

He examined her beautiful face in the soft light of the lantern, feeling the warm glow inside him again, and then stretched out on the blanket beside her. "You've got to."

"Why?"

"Because I'm too old to sleep on hard ground during cold nights."

She laughed and cried at the same time, then listened to Jones's soft litany. It was an oddly soothing sound, mixed with the rhythmic shaking of the rattle. A sound that seemed as if it might drift forever in the darkness.

Later that same night, Lily was in her downstairs bedroom brushing her hair and counting the strokes. She brushed 250 times every night, stroking carefully from the roots to the ends of her brown locks to add luster. The house was still and quiet. Her family was asleep upstairs. All but her mother. Lily was proud of her opposing the old man. She felt the stirring of a slight breeze from the open window behind her, the fabric of the curtain ruffling softly.

Unhappily, her thoughts drifted back to Samuel Jones. She wondered what her school friends would think if they knew he was her grandfather. They'd laugh. Pure and simple. She shuddered at the thought. The one good thing about the ranch, perhaps the only good thing, was that it was stuck so far out in this wilderness that her friends would never visit. Would never find out about him. The place was like a tiny dust mote in a vast dirty universe. At least that would keep her schoolmates from accidentally stumbling across Samuel Jones. And she certainly wasn't going to tell them about him. Ever. The old man was an embarrassment.

She studied her fine features in the dresser mirror and tried to figure what her mother would say if she knew about the bustle. She could guess what her father would say—or at least how he'd look at her. He would more than likely make a joke about it. And it wouldn't be funny. She decided not to tell either one of them. She was grown now. Bustles were the fashion rage. She would wear it when she returned to school.

Lily lowered her arms to rest them. She was still watching herself in the mirror when she first got the feeling. It was a tingling sensation on the back of her neck that someone was standing behind her. "Dot," she said. "Don't start sneaking up on me. You know I don't like that."

Lily turned and was surprised to see the room empty. The curtain fluttered slightly in the night breeze. She looked back to the dresser and resumed her strokes. Her eyes moved over the small marble bust of Lord Byron that her roommate had given her on the day they left school. She smiled. Sarah was such a sweet person. Lily stopped, the brush still to her hair, and listened. She could not shake the troubling feeling that someone was behind her. She turned again.

The room was empty. But Lily's eyes were on the window curtain. It was drawn but she had the gnawing sensation that someone was outside. Trembling, she walked over and stood shaking in front of it. She reached out a hand and yanked the curtain back. Nothing but the night and the scolding of a bird in the distance.

## CHAPTER

# THREE

**H**e can find anything, just by dreaming about it. He conjures things," Dot said, exaggerating her talk with her grandfather, and pouring a line of peas out of a pod into the large bowl on the ground in front of her. "Even if it's a tiny diamond buried in a mountain of sand, he can find it. Just like that," she said, snapping her fingers.

"He's a liar and a fool," Lily said.

"You shouldn't talk that way about him," James called back over his shoulder. "He's our grandfather."

"Not mine."

It was late afternoon and the three of them were working in the big vegetable garden down near the creek. The long lines and trellises of dark green plants—hot-weather beans, tomatoes, onions, squashes, Mexican peppers and chard—seemed to overflow the space of the garden, thriving in the heat and bright sunlight of this dry land. Dot wasn't looking at the plants, her thoughts were focused on how Lily was dressed.

That was one of the things Dot admired about her sister.

Dot scrutinized her closely, trying not to let her notice. Lily was wearing a beautiful red mannish-tailored shirtwaist, with padded shoulders and long gigot sleeves that puffed stylishly at the shoulders, and a long black skirt. Her shoes were the new high-buttoned black kidskins. She looked magnificent, Dot thought. Her soft brown hair was done in a Paris style: a chignon on top, with the front hair carried back without parting. It was all the latest from New York and Europe, Lily had told her.

Dot felt her sister was one of the prettiest girls in the world. She and Lily were sitting cross-legged on a blanket shelling peas for the evening meal. James was working nearby opening the irrigation ditches that watered the sprawling rows of plants.

"You heard what Pa said," James continued, shoveling mud out of the first trench and watching the little stream of water snaking its way down through the vegetables.

"And you saw Mother's face," Lily returned. "She didn't look too happy about it. She just wasn't going to fight Father."

"And you are?" James challenged, wiping at a mud smudge on his sunburned cheek.

"No. I'm just not going to accept that man as my grandfather."

"Just because you don't like him, that doesn't mean he isn't our grandpa," Dot said firmly, spilling another line of plump green peas into the bowl sitting between them.

"He can be your grandfather if you want him to be, Dotty Baldwin, but he is not going to be mine. I don't want anything to do with that stinking old man and his Indian ways." She was positioning a lock of her hair as she spoke.

"Better not let Pa catch you talking like that," James warned, shoveling piles of mud into the ditch to cut off the flow of water from the creek.

Lily ignored him and placed her bonnet back on her head, straightening the long satin bow. Dot was mad at her for talking badly about their grandfather. But she liked Lily. Not only was she pretty, she was smart and took chances: like going to Denver to school. Sure she put on airs—but Lily was always good to her. Bought her things, books and pictures, and talked to her like they were equals. She went back to shelling the peas.

James was leaning on his shovel and watching Lily now.

"Why do you wear that dumb hat when the sun is almost down?"

"It's the stylish thing."

"That's crazy."

"You wouldn't understand."

"I would if it made any sense," James said; then he squinted his eyes and stared hard at his older sister's beautiful face.

"What are you looking at?" she asked.

"Nothing," he said quickly, as though trying to hide a secret. A moment later, he sneaked another furtive peek at her.

Lily began to look uncomfortable. "What's wrong?" she asked, running her hand carefully over her soft cheeks.

James shook his head. "It's nothing."

"James, tell me."

"No, really, it's nothing. I'm not even certain."

"Certain about what?" Lily asked, suddenly alarmed.

"Really, I don't think it's anything."

"James Baldwin—tell me!" Lily looked anxious.

"Okay, but don't get mad at me. It's just in this light," he said, squinting again and studying her face from a couple of angles, "I can see your resemblance to Grandfather."

Lily leaped to her feet and stomped off toward the house, wrapping her low flowing dress tight around her legs. James was rolling in laughter on the ground.

"Don't tease Lily," Dot ordered. "And don't joke about Grandpa."

⚑

Jones was sitting quietly at the dinner table, his attention focused on the plate before him. He had only pretended to eat out of politeness. Baldwin studied the distant, haunted look in his eyes, and knew with certainty that the old fellow wouldn't last much longer. He wondered what was going on in his ancient heart. Baldwin sensed he wasn't prepared to go on living but still wasn't quite ready to die, a clock winding down.

Jones wasn't moving at all, just gazing at his plate. He appeared to have receded to some distant place inside his mind, escaping this world. Baldwin didn't blame him. His world had disappeared. The rancher noticed that the little finger on one of the man's huge hands was missing, the hands themselves were badly scarred. They belonged to a man who had fought the earth and its inhabitants hand to hand. Who was this old bastard? And what had his life been like, this man who'd fathered the woman he loved? Somehow tragic. That much he knew.

There were stories here. Not pretty ones. Why had he left his wife and daughters? Was he simply crazy? Baldwin didn't think so. He figured the old giant had known what he was doing, however strange it might seem to others.

Lily was in her mother's chair at the end of the table, wearing a frilly high-collared dress, ignoring the old man, and pouting.

"I'll clear the dishes," James said.

"Before you do, son," Jones said, breathing hard and leaning down and picking up a gunnysack from the floor, "I have things."

He'd seemingly come here with a list of items, and was hurriedly checking them off as though he might not finish. Baldwin figured he was right, Jones didn't have the time. It was a shame.

The old man reached inside the sack, pulling out a pillow-sized parcel covered in brightly colored parfleche. He looked at Lily and held the package out to her. Already uncomfortable, she stood, as though she might turn and run.

"My wife's."

"Grandmother's?" Lily asked, her voice incredulous.

The old man's skin shaded red. "Yopon's," he said quietly.

"No, thanks," Lily said.

"Lily, it's a gift." Baldwin's voice was low and measured.

Lily took the package, her hand shaking, glaring at it, as if even holding it was distasteful.

"What did you get, Lil?" Dot asked excitedly.

As Lily unwrapped the package Baldwin saw the blue blanket he'd seen in the barn and something else. Lily's mouth opened, and she tossed the bundle down in disgust. "What is that?"

"An eagle's claw. The blanket belonged to Yopon," he said solemnly.

"Why would any woman want that rotting thing?" Her face contorted in a grimace.

"Lil—"

"To give her strength," Jones interrupted, "and the ability to flee from danger." He studied Lily's face for a moment. "You may need that someday."

"That's absurd," Lily said, suddenly looking past them all. Baldwin turned, following her gaze, and saw Maggie in the doorway.

"Stop telling these children your Indian lies."

"Margaret," Baldwin said.

She kept her eyes on the old man's face. "Brake, don't. I won't have him filling the children's heads with pagan beliefs, glorifying himself and the devil. He's nothing more than a man who abandoned their mother and grandmother for an Indian squaw. Nothing more than that." She walked to the table and glared down at the old man. "Admit it. You're a blasphemer—a bigamist who loved savages more than your own family."

Samuel Jones stared blindly at his plate as if coldcocked.

"Margaret, that's enough."

Jones held up his hand to silence Baldwin.

"No, it's not," Maggie said. "But I won't interrupt the rest of his great Indian foolery." She climbed the stairs and disappeared into their bedroom, and seconds later, they could hear her crying.

Lily's eyes flashed. "Why don't you just leave? You don't belong here."

"Lily," Baldwin said, "you're not your mother. And I won't have you talking like that in this house."

Lily stalked swiftly away from the table and into her bedroom, slamming the door.

Baldwin fought the urge to go after her; then Mannito sighed loudly and said, "Ahhh, the *señoritas, bonitas* creatures, yes? Beautiful, yes?"

The kindness broke the spell, and the little Mexican and James laughed awkwardly. The old man didn't move. Baldwin helped him from the table. Dot watched him hobble toward the door, and wiped her sleeve across her eyes.

Jones started hacking badly when they stepped into the night air, the sound deep and watery. Baldwin set him in the rocker and moved to the railing. The night was cool and starry. A lone coyote was yipping close to the house. Baldwin stepped down the porch to get a better look. The yipping stopped.

Baldwin waited a second, then said, "Maggie was wrong to—"

"Don't." Jones looked at him sternly. "I don't want to hear bad said about Margaret. She's a fine girl. I'm proud of her. She had every right to say what she did."

Baldwin just nodded.

When Mannito left the house, he paused by Jones and draped the blue blanket over his thin shoulders. "Good night, *viejo*," he said, using the Spanish word for old man.

Jones shrugged him off.

It was after midnight. The fog had come in on the place fast from the creek bottom. Rarely did that happen, but when it did, the air was like a silt-laden river. Mists to lose a soul or a mountain in.

Lily had slowly followed the path to the outhouse behind the infirmary, bringing a candle with her and one of her fashion magazines. The little shack smelled awful, reminding her of all she hated about the ranch. People in cities were using indoor necessaries. She had tried to convince her father to buy one, but he'd only laughed.

She stopped reading and peered at the walls around her. The inside seemed gloomier than usual, the rough-weathered boards wavering eerily in the dim candlelight. She guessed the unnerving sensation came from the haze of fog.

She was wearing a cabriolet bonnet to keep her hair from frizzing in the moisture, but suddenly her hair wasn't important; she felt blinded by the cloth and yanked it off, sitting straighter and holding it in her trembling hand, not sure what was bothering her. She looked down at it, forcing her mind to other thoughts. The hat was a perfect example of what was wrong with this whole wilderness. Her father, and every other man in the territory, called this style a coal scuttle bonnet. No matter how many times she corrected him, it was still a coal scuttle bonnet.

Lily stopped and listened. The first hint of a sound had come to her. Something large. Perhaps a horse. She waited to hear it again, her pulse quickening. Nothing. Just the wind. It had a way of coming off the sandstone cliffs, shrill and crying, hurt and womanish-sounding. She hated it. She went back to her magazine. Then moments later, it was there again: faint footsteps in the night. She sensed them as much as heard them. "Hello? . . . Mannito?" she called. There was no answer.

She started to call out louder, then caught herself. The old man could be trying to scare her. He knew she didn't like him, that she thought he was a fraud. She felt somewhat better, certain it was he.

She turned her head slowly to catch any sound. Nothing. Only the phantom perception of someone moving in the darkness. Lily fought the panic inside her. There was no lock on the door, just a simple wooden latch that could be yanked off with a hard pull, leaving her trapped. She got herself ready.

The night seemed tense with a strange silence. "Father! Mannito!" She listened, knowing she was too far from the thick-walled house and barn to be heard, but hoping her screams would frighten the old man away. She stared at the door, sensing that it was about to be jerked open.

Lily darted out into the wall of dense fog, staying low, instinctively, and driving forward. Something moved in front of her; something dark in the night that grabbed for her and missed.

She ran, twisting and dodging in sheer terror, unaware of where she was running, just doing it, afraid to scream. Then she fell, tumbling into deep sand, realizing that in her panic she'd run away from the house toward the north slope. She crouched, her heart beating a ragged rhythm inside her chest, listening for sound in the darkness that surrounded her.

She waited a long time before she heard them again. Footsteps. He was looking for her. She got down in a tight ball, making herself as small as possible. The soft sound stopped.

Lily fainted when the hand touched her. She did not wake until she was being carried in someone's arms, screaming her way out of a dazed, half-conscious nightmare.

"Granddaughter," Jones said. "Hush."

Baldwin studied the old man. They were standing in the barn, and Lily had just finished accusing Jones of stalking her in the darkness. The night wind was blowing hard beyond the walls. Maggie had her arms around her daughter, holding her close and glaring at her father.

Jones had stripped to his breechcloth and deerskin boots and was rubbing red paint onto his face. He was paying no attention to any of them. The little Mexican watched him closely.

Outside, the wind was working itself into a hard blow, the fog gone. Maggie and her girls stood near the door, in the circle of faint lantern light, as if it gave them some sense of security. The Mexican stepped close to Baldwin.

"What, Mannito?"

The little man turned and looked at the old giant, his face and body covered now by eerie red-and-black designs. "He did nothing, señor. He saved her, perhaps. Nothing more."

"From what?"

Mannito continued watching the old man as he prepared for battle with this thing of the night. "I don't know. I just know this *viejo*, that's all."

Baldwin studied the little Mexican's face for a moment, then nodded. Jones was carrying his bow and arrows and moving for the door now. Lily stumbled away from him, as though she expected him to try to slit her throat. Maggie stood her ground.

"Brake," she called across the shadows, her eyes still on her father's hideous red face, "he tried to frighten Lily."

"Ma, don't say that," Dot pleaded.

Jones stopped in front of them. "Granddaughter. You'll find your cat in five days."

"Poppycock," Maggie snapped.

He slipped silently into the darkness and the stinging sand.

Samuel Jones did not catch the night beast. Nor did they find tracks the following morning, the sandstorm having obliterated any trace. Any trace except for a blurred footprint that looked odd to Jones. Lily's candle and magazine were still in the small shack. Her bonnet was gone. Baldwin thought it had been blown away by the wind. Jones did not. Neither did he figure that the dead sparrow he found lying behind the shack was there naturally.

With the pink smudge of dawn two days later, the gray pony was missing and Jones was stumbling wildly through the barn. The truce was broken. He charged Mannito in the corral, slamming the little man against the wall, pulling his knife and shoving it against the Mexican's throat.

"What did you do with her?" the old man wheezed.

"*Qué?*"

"Don't give me Mexican! My horse—*caballo*—where is she?"

"*No sé*—I don't know."

"You better say unless you want to lose a handful of brains."

"You *loco?* I don't see your horse. She probably died. She's old."

"She better not have!"

Jones threw the little man to the ground and stormed around the corner of the barn, whistling for the old horse. Baldwin and Lily had ridden out early to check the cows in the high valley, while James and Dot had gone for mail at the railhead. Alice the mule was braying in the distance. Jones headed in her direction.

The gray was on her side in the pasture, tongue out, bloating badly, breathing fast and shallow. Sometime during the night, she had broken into the field of dew-covered plants and made a feast of it. Alice was running frantic circles around her, still braying.

The old man moaned from deep inside as he dropped to his knees beside her. Her belly was swollen twice normal size, rising above her backbone on the left flank. He knew she was dying and nothing he could do would save her. He had seen other horses die from the lush green forage of the whites.

The People thought it was the magic of white witches that killed their horses. He knew better. The killer was gas that blew the guts open. It was an ugly death. He didn't want the gray to go through the agony.

He pulled the little pistol from its hiding place and sat next to her, stroking her head, and thinking back over the years they had been together. They had ridden through the worst of his life. She had never let him down. He admired her toughness and loyalty. His throat was tightening and he knew it was more than admiration he felt. The little mare was in terrible pain, panting hard, sweat covering her body.

The Mexican squatted near her middle and placed his hands on the enormous belly and felt around, drumming with his fingertips on the tight skin. Chaco approached the old horse slowly, sniffing her and whining, then he sat beside the

Mexican, shivering. Mannito continued feeling the horse's stomach. Jones watched him. The little man pressed with his hand at a spot between the stifle and the ribs and the gray squealed and tossed her head. Alice darted in and nipped at him. The old Mexican waved her off.

"Leave the horse be!" Jones snarled.

Mannito ignored him, continuing to explore the belly; then he stood and trotted off toward the barn. Chaco followed. When he returned, he was carrying a small wooden box. He squatted and rummaged inside it, pulling out strange-looking metal instruments and setting them to the side, until he finally found what he wanted. It looked like a foot-long hat pin. Jones didn't like the determined look on the old Mexican's face. He cocked the derringer. The gray was suffering enough; he wasn't about to let the Mexican torture her more.

Mannito pulled his hat off, tossing it behind him and rolling up his sleeves. His hair was a dead-white color. Jones was watching him closely.

"Keep your hands off her."

Jones placed the pistol's muzzle against the gray's skull. Mannito dropped to his knees between the animal's legs. She was kicking in her death throes. Alice darted in again, nipping at him. He paid no attention.

Mannito drummed once more with the tips of his bony fingers on the swollen loin, listening for the organs below. Time was running out, he knew. He turned his head toward Jones, concentrating, trying to visualize the critical spot.

Staring up at the old giant, Mannito knew that they were friends, even if Samuel Jones wasn't consciously aware of it. The idea of this friendship with Jones seemed an odd thing to the little Mexican. Nevertheless, he was sure it existed. It didn't matter that Jones had never uttered a single kind word to him. Kind words were nothing. The two of them shared, Mannito knew, far more than words, shared more than just their two long lives. They instinctively understood one another. And understanding, he had always felt, was the foundation of true friendship. The evidence was everywhere. They had both lost their wives, lost most of their children, had lived hard existences, in solitude, far away from their own kind. They were poor men, but men who possessed another kind of wealth: They believed in something far greater than themselves. That was true wealth. These things, Mannito felt, bound them as *amigos*.

As further proof of their friendship, Mannito recalled that since Jones's arrival, the old giant had silently shared the barn work: tossing hay, cleaning stalls and filling water troughs. Mannito greatly respected this about his friend. Though deathly ill, he was no loafer. He was a man of character who mindfully paid his own way. The week before, Mannito had found his burro, Peso, carefully brushed and curried, the animal's hooves cleaned and polished, and its little weathered halter expertly spliced with fresh rawhide. He had thanked Jones. But the old man had simply ignored him. Still, they both knew. Mannito smiled to himself as he stared at Jones, pleased that he recognized these little signs that betrayed their friendship.

From that day forward, Mannito had talked to him whenever they were in the barn. Jones never answered but Mannito sensed that he listened and calculated and weighed the things he said. These one-sided conversations cut the loneliness. He wished Jones had longer to live. Wished that he would acknowledge their friendship.

"I'm warning!" the old man bellowed, pointing the pistol at Mannito and struggling to stand. "You hurt her and I'll splatter you all over this ranch."

Mannito looked back at the old horse. He knew his friend Jones would not shoot him, but he wasn't certain that he wouldn't turn the little gun on himself if they lost the gray.

Mannito's hands were shaking. He had never tried to save a horse with the bloat. The long, thin metal trocar was slippery in his sweating hands.

He looked up at Jones and tried to smile, prayed silently to Jesus' Mother, then leaned forward and plunged the huge pin into the gray's paunch. Jones raised the little pistol; then he heard the loud *shhhhhhishing* and watched in amazement as the mare's belly shrank like a punctured ball.

Even more astonishing was the effect on the old horse. She stopped panting and moaning and lay still on the grass. Minutes later, she struggled to her feet and started to graze again, as if nothing had happened. Jones pulled her away from the wet plants and looked down, stunned, at the little Mexican. Mannito just squatted and grinned up at him, then began to laugh, looking like a small wrinkle-faced monkey, enormously tickled that he had saved the old horse.

"Damn *bueno* thing, right?" the Mexican said, holding up the large pin. "A damn good thing."

Chaco was dancing on his hind legs. Alice was sniffing the gray. Jones nodded, still shocked at the mare's miraculous recovery. Mannito held out his small hand for the rope that was looped around the horse's neck.

"I walk. She needs to move. I watch her. *Muy bueno,*" he said, running his hands over the old pony. "I walk," he said again, sticking his hand closer to Jones.

Jones looked at the man's hand, then his face. He was still stunned.

"I walk," Mannito said once more.

Jones continued to look at him. Finally, he handed him the rope and nodded at the little man again, but didn't speak. It was enough. Mannito understood.

"It was nothing, *viejo.*"

Darkness was falling hard. Baldwin and Lily hadn't returned

from checking the herd in the high pasture. Jones was growing concerned. Baldwin was smart enough. Since the night of the sandstorm, Jones had noticed that he had been wearing his pistol and sticking close to his oldest daughter. But the man wouldn't believe that anyone but a lovestruck cowboy had chased his Lily. Jones had tried to convince him otherwise. So had Mannito. But he wasn't listening. Jones studied the rust-colored mountains surrounding the little valley, hoping the rancher's stubbornness hadn't gotten him and the girl into trouble somewhere out on the trail.

Hardheaded and hard to scare, Baldwin was like most of the men who built things out of this wilderness. That's why the People had such a hard time with them, Jones knew. They did what they had to do to survive. They weren't bad people, just tough and self-reliant. And for the past few days, Brake Baldwin's cows—all the future his family possessed—had been dropping calves, unattended, in this rough country. Some of these animals, the rancher knew, would need his help or they'd die. Therefore, Brake Baldwin had headed for the high pastures, no matter what, and had taken his daughter with him so he could keep a protective eye on her.

Mannito had been left at the house to watch over Maggie. In the rancher's mind, Maggie was safe. Some young cowboy had simply fallen dumbstruck over Lily. The girl certainly had the looks to rattle a man. But Jones didn't have it figured exactly that way. There was more to it, he felt. He just didn't know what it was for sure.

From conversations overheard in the barn, he knew that James and Dot would take the wagon and spend the night in the little railhead town. So that afternoon, after watching the gray to make certain she was truly recovering, and leaving the Mexican with Maggie, he had taken a Baldwin horse and trailed the two youngsters well out onto the desert until he was convinced they were safe. Three times, he rode wide of the wagon's trail by a mile on either side to see that there were no horse tracks following them. Nothing.

Satisfied, he had returned to the ranch, arriving late in the day, his body shot through with a numbing exhaustion. Chaco barked to announce their arrival from his perch on the horse's rump. Maggie was sitting on the porch. She didn't acknowledge him in any way. Mannito was standing hidden in the shadows of the barn, holding the reins of a fresh horse, his ancient shotgun slung across his back. Alice was braying happily.

"*Los niños?*" Mannito asked, mounting the horse he held and pointing toward town. "The children?"

Jones nodded.

"I ride to Señor Brake." He stopped and looked hard into Jones's face and started to say something else, but then seemed to think better of it. Jones could tell he was tense. It was a feeling they shared. Finally, Mannito just smiled and said, "Good night, *viejo.*"

Jones didn't say anything.

Mannito watched him a moment longer, something obviously on his mind, then he turned the horse and began to kick hard for the hills that were fading in the gathering purple dusk.

Jones would have ridden with him, but he didn't want to leave Maggie unguarded. Whatever was wrong might involve her as well. He followed the dark speck of the little Mexican and his galloping horse for a while, trying to figure out what the man had wanted to say to him. He wasn't sure. But he had definitely wanted to say something.

Jones turned and gazed through the deepening shadows at the darkened house. The moon was rising over the rim of the mountain. Maggie was right: he didn't belong here. That's why he had never come before. It wasn't fair to her. Wasn't fair to just walk back into her life after all these years. If he hadn't been dying, he wouldn't have done it. But he was, and he had come to see her one last time. Now he had to move on. Any fool could have guessed how she would feel. He didn't blame her.

Thinking on it, he figured he might return to the heart of old Chihenne country. The thought tugged at something that was hurt inside him. Yopon and he had been there years before. It was the last time they'd been together and free. He found himself retracing their wanderings in his thoughts a lot. He forced himself to stop.

He stood outside the barn, feeling physical pain like a deep boring inside his chest, and turned in a slow circle, studying the darkening trees, the barn, the pastures and the house. He wanted to remember everything here, everything about her, for as long as he could.

He took a pull on the bottle, then left it on the ground, and walked awkwardly toward her, not knowing where to place his hands. He stopped in front of the porch where she sat. Chaco trailed along behind him. Jones watched her for a moment, her eyes gazing past him, then he leaned forward and set a pure white chunk of quartz on the step beside her.

"I found it in the hills. Thought you might like it."

She didn't say anything or look at the stone.

"The Mexican went to find them," he said quietly. "They probably decided to spend the night with the herd, rather than try the hill trails in the dark." Jones knew that hadn't happened. If they were spending the night, it was because something had gone wrong. He had watched them saddling up and saw nothing for making camp; no canvas, no grub sack, no skillets, nothing. He had seen Dot slip the eagle charm into Lily's saddlebag when her sister had gone into the house. The child had a large heart. But then Lily had found it and tossed it angrily to the ground. Dot had retrieved it.

"If they aren't down by morning, I'll go find them," he said, almost as if he was talking to himself. "Then I'll ride on." He turned and looked at her, seeming for a moment to soak her up with his eyes. "I used to think about you," he said quietly. "At night mostly. Where you were, and what you were feeling."

She didn't say anything for a long time, just continued to gaze past him at the hills. When she finally spoke, he was unable to see her face. "I don't need anything from you anymore," she said, her voice sounding tired. "Just go."

He walked slowly past her into the house, deciding to sleep near her tonight so that he could keep an eye out, but also wanting to sleep one night in her home. Chaco sat down beside her.

Maggie contemplated the falling darkness, shutting out all thoughts of the man. She had been praying to God about the cat. Nothing had come to her. She was now convinced it was dead—convinced that was her answer from God. Harriet was lost.

She stood and picked up the quartz rock, studying it for a moment, then tossed it with all her might into the darkness. Chaco scrambled off the porch after it, barking as he ran. A few minutes later, the little dog returned with the rock, dropping it at her feet. She began to cry.

Morning light came grudgingly to the valley of the ranch. Baldwin and the others had not yet ridden down. Jones had awakened early in the darkness, unable to sleep, feeling both the searing pain and something else—something anxious in a place deep inside him. Slowly, he shook it off and crawled stiffly out of his blankets. He had been lying on the floor in the big room of the house, his rifle next to him. Maggie had slept outside on the porch in the rocker. He had listened to the grating sound most of the night. It was silent now. He looked out the window and saw her asleep in the chair. Chaco was lying beside her. Jones sat and watched her for a long time, listening to a white-winged dove calling.

Finally, he forced himself to stop looking at her and wandered slowly through the empty dwelling, moving from room to room, examining the things that he knew or guessed belonged to her, trying to visualize her in these rooms with these objects, sometimes holding them in his hands. He knew he was intruding. But he also knew that the only way he would ever be a part of her life was by this last moment of intrusion. This was his last chance to be alone with her—or at least, alone within her world. That would have to do him. He understood that. She would let him no closer.

It was sitting in the shadows on the dresser in the big bedroom. He studied it, unable to move for a while, adjusting his little glasses on his nose. It was almost a dream to him. He cupped it in his hands, committing it to what he knew was his fading memory. That scared him. He knew that when he left this room, he would never see it again. This was the only time in his life that he had felt the urge to steal. He couldn't do it. Not from her. He had stolen enough from her life.

He let his eyes move slowly over it: a tintype. Maggie, a teenager, and her mother, Susan. He couldn't pull his eyes off her face. She had been a good wife and mother; he felt the familiar remorse and forced his gaze and thoughts along. Why had she never remarried? She had such beauty. He shook his head sadly, knowing the answer too well. It didn't matter. It was over. He could change nothing.

Their two images alone would have been enough to bring the sadness, but there was another person in the tintype: a small brown-haired girl of eight or nine. It was she who shattered whatever rigid structures were left inside his being, so that his emotional world sagged. A bitter-sweet pain coursed through him as he stood before the dresser.

He had never seen her before. He knew only that she had been born after he left, and that she was dead. Seeing her now was both a mysterious gift and a curse. He fought a moaning sound dwelling within him. He had heard that her name was Thelma. His throat tightened. It had been his mother's name. He smiled wistfully: just like Susan to have honored him, even after he had dishonored himself. He kissed the photograph of this child he had never kissed in life, never known.

It was a long time before he could stop looking at her, staring so hard at the small face that her image began to blur. He relived times that he hadn't thought of in a long while. Why had he left, when they had needed him so? He pulled himself up straighter and set the picture back in its place. He knew the answer. He knew he would do it again. He also knew with painful clarity what he had lost. And what he had found. He took his glasses off, then turned and walked out of the room.

He was riding stiffly, he and the gray picking their way carefully up a narrow trail through the pines on the western slope. Chaco was sitting on the pony's rump. Alice ambled along behind with all Jones's worldly possessions strapped to her back. He didn't want to ride anymore. He wanted only to lie down and sleep. He was ready to take the last long trail.

He fingered the old Sharps absently, every once in a while taking a pull on his bottle and turning to look back down at the ranch house. Earlier, he had tried to say goodbye. She hadn't acknowledged him. It was best, he thought. It gave him a chance to look closely at her. He had placed Baldwin's loaded shotgun across her lap. Still, she had not paid him the slightest mind. Not a glance.

He drew a shallow breath and told himself to stop. It was over. He tried to visualize Thelma's small face, vaguely seeing her, the sadness creeping over him. Things were now so different from what he had once believed. Life had seemed so alive, so real and tangible, so easily toted up and carried from place to place. But he realized now it never had been; the things of greatest worth he had never touched.

An aspen, its bark girded by the claws of a bear, stood dying beside the trail, its yellow leaves dropping silently in the breeze. He watched the sunlight shining on the tree, making it look like a sparkling, spiritual thing, the leaves floating in random patterns down toward the earth, drifting away on their separate journeys. At one time, the tree had been a whole thing, unified in life and purpose; now it was disassembling, its different lives dying different deaths, each alone. He felt much like that.

Only superficially had he sensed life's essence, the unseen things which held its true meaning, which throughout the years had touched him like a soft breeze to the skin. Now they were drifting away, leaving him to journey on without them. He was truly alone.

The hills were still, making the sounds of the animals seem loud and intrusive. It didn't matter. If there was trouble ahead, whoever was going to cause it already knew he was coming, and what he was carrying, and from what direction he rode. He thought again of the Indian face—the face he'd seen in the vision in the cornfield two nights earlier—wondering who he was and what he wanted—and why he bothered him so.

He picked up Baldwin's and Lily's trail in the red clay above the pines, then spotted the hoofprints of the old Mexican's horse; the little man was riding to the side so he could read the signs without ruining them. In a couple of places, he could see where Mannito had turned off and sat watching his back trail to see if he was being followed. The Mexican knew some things, Jones figured.

As soon as Jones saw the cactus, he cocked the hammer on

the Sharps, squinting his eyes and studying the path through the broken plants. He sat still and listened. The gray felt tense under him, her ears pitched forward. Chaco whined. He raised a hand to silence him.

The steer had been skinned in some blue bunch grass; its hindquarters were missing. Jones sat squatting next to what was left of the carcass, ignoring the buzzing flies and the stink, while he counted footprints and pulled as much information as he could from their sign. There was a mix of them. All moccasins—badly worn; not a prosperous bunch. He looked for the one who had gone after Lily the night of the sandstorm, some dark echo in his head tugging at him.

He found his glasses and fumbled them onto his face, and leaned down closer over the dusty prints. Different breeds: Chokonen, Chihenne and Mescaleros, all Apaches, but an odd, motley bunch. They didn't figure to fit together.

His eyes, focused now behind the glasses, moved carefully over the tracks. He studied the crisscrossing, the repeated circles, the back-and-forth patterns. He looked up at the sky and tried to visualize each of the men, committing their walk, size, weight and habits to memory. When he felt he had a good picture, he looked back down at the dirt. Then he saw the lone set of footprints and understood why the track had appeared strange to him that night.

Apaches were all dangerous. This one, he sensed, was somehow worse. Jones moved closer, studying the imprint, the right foot turned and dragging some. It wasn't a fresh wound, probably the Apache was lame from birth. He wondered what bothered him about the man. He was big. Short-framed. There were splashes of dust at the front of the tracks indicating the Indian's heaviness. Jones guessed him to be over two hundred pounds.

He reached down and closed his eyes and touched the track softly, reading its telltale characteristics, feeling the disturbances in the earth. The bad feeling stole over him again and he pulled his hand away.

He could smell fire and saw smoke drifting near the crown of an oak. He moved cautiously toward it. A dark shape was swinging grotesquely from a branch in the tree. He stepped closer, trying to stay out of the breeze and the nauseating smell it wafted. The object came into a fuzzy kind of focus: the green cowhide. It had been sewn into a big bag and a fire built under it. Lily's dress was in the dirt next to the fire. "*Bastardos*," he muttered in Mexican, as if the word might reach those who had done this. It was a language the Apaches knew well.

Thick smoke rose and shrouded the hide and made it harder to see; then a breeze came and the smoke cleared, and he saw a small blackened foot protruding from a break in the tightly stitched seam. Staring at that foot and thinking of Lily's grandmother and mother, Jones vowed to find the cripple—and kill him.

He took a deep breath and then held it and slit the stitching of green thongs; the cowhide flaps spread wide, releasing a cloud of putrid-smelling steam, and Jones gagged on it, turning away. Death, in general, had never bothered him much. But this one did.

The body was curled in a tight ball and disfigured to the point where it was almost unrecognizable. Nevertheless, he knew it wasn't Lily. He picked up one side of the cowhide and rolled the corpse onto its back. Mannito. The little Mexican was naked and covered with thousands of tiny puncture holes; but those had not killed him. His death had come from the green cowhide. The fire slowly drying it, shrinking it, until it finally crushed his ribs and suffocated him.

Jones studied the little man's shattered face and felt the bad sense creeping inside his guts. He had never had much truck for Mexicans, but this one had been somehow different. In just a few days, they had come to a silent understanding; and he felt that the Mexican would have honored it. There was something about the little man that he had trusted. He felt pressure building in his chest and he stood quickly. He'd been close to few people during his life. Hard as it was for him to understand, he believed the little man could have been one of them.

Now he was gone. The Lame One and the other Apaches had tortured him to death. Jones felt the beast in him stir and struggled to control it. Killing a man was one thing—torture another. The disrespect of it bothered him.

He brought his pipe from the gray, lit it and squatted in front of the body. He blew smoke over Mannito and sang his death song. It was an honor he would never have guessed he would bestow on a Mexican. For a long while, he sat and watched the body. Mannito had saved the gray, had stood up for him. And Jones knew instinctively the little man had fought to save Lily. Those things counted by Samuel Jones's reckoning.

Jones shifted on his haunches, his eyes moving steadily over the ground. The rancher's tracks weren't anywhere around. He hadn't made it this far.

Chaco sniffed at Mannito's corpse, then flopped down beside it and whined. That surprised him. The dog had seen a lot of death in his nine years of life. He had ignored it. Even children. Ignored it up until this day. Jones blew smoke over the body again to purify it and chanted while Chaco whined. The little Mexican had been different. That was certain.

He moved away from the body and squatted again and smoked, thinking through what had happened here. They had the girl. He figured she was still alive; for a time. Baldwin—probably dead. Most likely they'd ambushed him and Lily, shooting the rancher and grabbing the girl, and then, later, been surprised by Mannito. Somehow they'd caught the little Mexican alive, stripped him naked, put a rope around his chest and dragged him back and forth through the prickly pear. Afterward, with a thousand cactus thorns impaling him, they'd beaten him with clubs and then sewn him up in the hide and hung him from the oak like a giant cocoon.

If he had the tiny man figured right, he hadn't let out a cry. He was different. He deserved better. Jones could see where they had squatted and lounged around, drinking and smoking. Lily had been forced to witness the killing. "*Bastardos,*" he muttered again. The lame Apache had sat off alone, pointed so he could watch her. Jones felt the beast shifting again and fought the urge to ride after them. He had to know more. He was too weak to chase wildly after anything. And they were expecting pursuit. So he would wait.

As Jones sat by the corpse, a large wolf spider scurried over Mannito's body. Spiders were sacred things and he felt this was an omen. "Hear, brother spider—attest my words. I will avenge this man." He hesitated for a moment, then said, "This friend." He stopped talking and stared off into the bright sunlight at the distant hills. He realized now what Mannito had wanted to say to him last night in front of the barn. That they were friends. Jones wiped his mouth in the palm of his hand, looking down at the little body. "I heard you," he said. Then he again looked away and continued his oath. "I will avenge this man. The earth hears me, the spider hears me." Jones blew smoke in the four directions.

Samuel Jones closed his eyes and tried to rest for a moment in the scant shade of a mesquite bush. He was thinking about Lily and her chances, when suddenly the image of the Indian face was before his eyes again, looking so real that he sat bolt upright, clutching at his pistol and squinting at the surrounding brush. Nothing. Jones trembled and stood and walked the scare off. He knew now that it was the face of the Lame One.

Looking down at Mannito's body, he wondered where the small man's clothes were. Then it came to him: They had made Lily put them on. They were about the same size. It could mean only one thing. They didn't plan on killing her, so they had dressed her to ride. Hopefully, they'd keep her alive long enough. For what? His powers had been fading over the months. He had no idea where to start. All he wanted was to lie down and rest. That was all he ever wanted anymore. That, and Maggie's love.

Samuel Jones tracked the rocky ground hard for an hour until he found Baldwin chest-shot and nearly dead a quarter mile from the tree. He rigged a travois to the gray, placed the wounded man on it and started out of the mountains, Mannito's corpse across the mule. Halfway down, he came upon an Apache sprawled in the dirt, nearly decapitated by Mannito's machete. He had been right, the little man had fought hard to defend Lily. He had been a warrior to respect.

## FOUR

**M**aggie did not surprise him. She was dignified and under control, though he knew she was dying inside from the strain. He watched her out of the corner of his eye as she pressed the compress hard against her husband's wound and then wrapped the bandage tightly around his chest. He held the rancher upright on the bed, then together they laid him back carefully on the pillow.

Baldwin was unconscious. But he had a chance, Jones figured. Maggie had not acknowledged him. Not when he rode up to the porch, or even now as they worked side by side. The only word she'd spoken she was again mouthing softly: "Lily." It was an old mantra of mourning that he had heard hundreds of times before in different tongues, but it was always the same. There was nothing he could do to console her.

He watched as she pulled a chair close beside the bed, dragging her medicine bag onto her lap, holding it as if willing its contents to save her husband. He wanted to hold her, comfort her. He had felt this same clawing urge for the past thirty years. But now with her near, it was almost overpowering. Sometimes when he had held one of the other children in his arms when they were small, he had closed his eyes and pretended he was holding her. It had been a self-deception that had made him cry.

He cleared his throat and searched her face. He could still see the child in it that he had seen on that last night, thirty years ago. It was odd—he was an old man about to die, she was a grown woman; they had not seen each other for a lifetime, but still they were lashed together as father and child and no matter what, it would always be that way. He closed his eyes and asked her power to give her comfort.

Jones moved so she would know he was there. "Ama. I will help. I must seek to know them. What they plan," he offered.

She turned and looked at him as if realizing for the first time that he was in the room. "No. Lily and I don't need you. James and Dot went for help. We don't want you." Her words had a faraway sound to them. He left the room.

He came back an hour later, knocking softly on the bedroom door. She didn't answer. Pushing the door open slowly, he studied the profile of her fine face. She had returned to the chair, her eyes on Baldwin. The room's heavy curtains had been pulled against the afternoon light and it was dark and quiet inside. He waited, letting his eyes adjust, then he came in and moved to the foot of the bed, carrying his medicine bundle. Dressed in his tattered yellow medicine shirt and a white breechcloth, he looked every inch an Indian shaman. He stood, letting her get used to his presence.

There was a tattered Bible lying at the foot of the bed. She had been praying her Christian prayers, he knew. He guessed they gave her solace. He looked up through the dim shadows of the room to where a thin ray of sunlight broke through a crack in the curtain. It illuminated a painted cross and a pale-bodied Christ hanging on the wall over the bed, the light making the little figure look alive and agonized in His suffering.

Jones's eyes remained fixed on the small icon. He wondered what and why he had ever believed; he knew that belief had diminished to the point where he felt nothing for the Mexican figurine and the so-called divine moment it represented. He hadn't for years. It was useless for him to even try. He had once—decades before—tried desperately to reach this God, the Thy-Will-Be-Done God, as Yopon had called Him. But nothing happened. No answer came. He had been damned by silence. Jones squared his wide shoulders to the wall and looked away from the wooden form to Maggie.

She hadn't taken her gaze off Baldwin's damp face. The room was quiet save for the watery-sounding breathing of the injured man. Jones spread his medicine objects—the small bird's nest, a turtle-shell, three sacred pebbles, the ears of a coyote—carefully on the floor and lit his calumet and began to chant and blow the purifying smoke over the bed. Still she did not look at him, but stood slowly, holding a broom in her hands, her fists white from the strain, watching the smoke drifting over the feverish face of her husband.

"Please get out," she said in a low voice.

He continued chanting and offering the smoke until she began to beat on him with the broom. He gathered his things as unhurriedly as the blows would allow and left. He was bleeding from a scalp cut. She followed him out of the house, stopping at the porch.

"Take your heathen beliefs and leave." She looked dazed.

Jones dug Mannito's grave in the fenced enclosure and completed his death song. Then he washed the man's broken body. Finished, he returned to the barn and brought back the blue blanket that he had tried to give to Lily. He stood holding it to the side of his face with his eyes closed, as if listening to something it was whispering.

"Yopon," was all he said. He knelt and wrapped it carefully around the dead man, feeling a strange melancholy. For a long time, he and Chaco stood by the open pit; then the little dog moved to the edge and looked down and whined at the blue mound lying at the bottom. After a while, Chaco sat, his back to the grave, and watched the hills. Jones figured his spirit was communing with the Mexican's. They, too, had become friends. He was glad about it. Chaco was wise; therefore the man must have been truly good.

Jones squatted on his haunches and thought about the little Mexican. He cleared his throat and talked to him, tried to answer some of the questions the tiny man had asked when they were living in the barn. He spoke loud so the man could hear his answers.

Afterward, he blew for a long while on his sacred wingbone whistle that was adorned with eagle fluffies, calling to the spirits of the mountains to guide the dead man. Then he filled the earth in—fighting his steady coughing—and made a cross of old wood he found near the barn and drove it into the hard ground. He figured the little man would want that. Done, he said a Christian prayer he remembered, feeling hollow as he spoke the words. He owed the tiny man that much. Then he placed a little food next to the grave for the Mexican's long journey, and a handful of corn for making Tulapi drink. He would have killed the man's horse so that he could ride through the land of the shadows, but the Apaches had stolen it. Jones knelt and put his hand on the fresh mound of earth.

"Good night, *viejo*," he said.

Jones built his sweat lodge next to the creek. It was near evening when he finally finished, and he was exhausted.

He remembered back to the days when he could dogtrot for twenty-five miles through blistering heat, and still have energy to fight. No more. Never again. It was a strange thing, this winding down of life; so natural and so easily accepted.

He stood in front of the brush hut, looking through the darkening twilight toward the small picketed enclosure, something drawing him there. He was curious. For the past few hours, he had been thinking off and on about the small graveyard but didn't know why. He had said goodbye to the Mexican and called for the spirits to guide him. He was finished with that. But there was something else. Slowly, he started walking.

He stared down at it for a long time, fumbling his glasses on. The letters were carved in the weathered wood of the old cross, barely visible. He wondered if he had unconsciously noticed them when he was burying the Mexican, or whether the spirit had sensed his presence in the graveyard and called out to him. It didn't matter. He was here. The meeting had finally taken place. He mouthed the letters: THELMA. Then he lay down on top of her grave and hugged the earth, staying and talking to her, finally forcing himself to stand.

He pulled his tiny glasses off and stood staring down at the ground, stunned that so many years had passed. So many years that the little girl in the tintype was now lost in the earth. Another child gone. He didn't even know how she had died. Or whether she'd ever thought of him. He turned away from the grave. He had to go. It was his granddaughter's only chance.

Later, he built a small fire of mesquite wood in the center of the hut and added stones in a circle around it. When it had burned to hot coals, he brought water from the creek and went inside and pulled the blanket over the doorway and stripped himself naked and squatted, pouring water slowly over the burning stones until stifling clouds of steam were billowing inside the hut. He had one of his bottles and he took a long drink. The heat began to build until it hurt. Jones began his songs of incantation to drive the evil spirits, the poison, from his body and soul . . . encouraging these wrong things to leave him and this hissing place, this place of torment. He poured more water on the stones, chanting, "Hu, Hu, Hu, Hu, Hu." His thoughts drifted to the Lame One. Strangely, he began to visualize a small ring floating in the dim light of the hut. Then it was gone.

They're riding towards Utah Territory," the sheriff said. He was sitting on a big piebald horse, his fleshy face beneath the black fedora heavy and pink-white.

The other men were checking their weapons and saddles and mounting up around him in the ranch yard. Chaco was barking. Maggie sat on her husband's big roan, not listening to the lawman, her eyes fixed on the ground.

The old man was barefooted and barechested, standing with a blanket wrapped around his middle. He had been coughing hard while the sheriff spoke. He stopped and caught his breath and walked around behind the man's horse and stood beside Maggie. Chaco followed. "They will not take her north," he said. The words seemed to drift away on the morning air. Maggie stared blindly at a spot on the ground.

"Christ, Jones, give it a rest. We've been over that same damn ground a thousand times. They took her north. You saw the trail."

Jones ignored the man, moving around Maggie's horse and picking up each hoof, checking to see that the metal shoes were secure. Maggie swayed each time the big roan shifted its weight, but otherwise ignored him. Satisfied, Jones stood and looked up at her. "They will not ride north. They are leading you in that direction. To ambush you. Then they will head in the direction they wish to travel." He paused. "One of the men you follow—" He stopped, uncertain what he wanted to say, knowing only that his thoughts were again on the crippled Apache. Jones stooped and ran his hands over the saddle's cinch. He straightened and trotted off to the barn.

James and Dot watched him from the porch. They both looked deeply worried. Mrs. Abby, a neighbor woman in a clean yellow dress with a white apron, was standing next to the children. She was stout and in her fifties, with a warm, firm way about her. Maggie had sent James for her. Her husband was a horse trader and away on business in Tucson. She had not tried to talk Maggie out of riding with the sheriff. She would have done the same had Lily been hers. Meanwhile, she would stay and take care of Baldwin and the children.

Jones returned with a long strip of rawhide and a pocketknife. He moved Maggie's leg and the stirrup back and uncinched the saddle.

"What are you doing?"

"The stitching is bad. You'll lose the saddle at a hard run."

She watched him for a moment as if she was going to say something, then looked away and let him work. When he was finished, he stood up and put his hand out and touched the roan's shoulder. "Ama—"

Maggie kicked hard at the animal's flanks.

"May your spirit protect you," he called to her.

He had returned to the sweat hut, not done with his purification. Dot was sitting outside, crying. Steam was once again escaping through the cracks of the small structure. Chaco was growling and biting at the girl's boots. Jones tried to ignore the sound of them both and to let his mind drift away to nothingness. "My heart is open. I call on the Great Mystery to cleanse my soul so that I may be ready to hear your voice," he sang.

"Grandpa, why did they have to kill Mannito?"

"He made them."

"I don't understand."

"He tried to save your sister. He killed one of them. He would not have stopped if they had not killed him. He was a brave man."

"But why did he have to die?" She was sobbing softly.

"I do not know. But he was brave and should be honored."

"I loved him a lot." She paused. "I'm scared. My pa is hurt badly and Lily is gone."

He chanted harder, closing his eyes against the heat.

"Everything has changed. It won't ever be the same again." She stopped talking for a while, then said, "Grandpa. It won't ever, will it?"

"No. It will not. You must make it something new. Something good. The Mexican would want that. Make that your gift to him."

"She nodded and stopped crying, and sat thinking. She began to feel upset again.

"How come you didn't go after Lily with Ma and the sheriff?" There was an angry sound in her voice. "And if you're Indian, like you say, how come you didn't catch them? I thought the medicine let you know things." She paused. "You said Harriet was alive and I'd find her."

"I said five days," he called through the steam.

"We'll see," Dot said defiantly. "I don't think your Indian medicine works."

It was silent outside the hut for a few minutes, and then Dot said, "My pa would have gone with them." She sounded like she wanted to cry again. "Lily's your granddaughter."

He began to chant quietly.

It was the last part of morning, two days after Lily's kidnapping, when he heard Chaco growling and sensed someone moving near the hut. He figured it was Dot. Chaco was lying in the sand by his feet, continuing to growl. He opened his eyes slowly against the bright sunlight.

Maggie stood in front of him, studying his face. He returned her gaze, trying to see her as she had been on that last day. He could not. Neither of them found words for a while.

Then she turned her back to him and surveyed the small valley. "The Apaches killed four of the men. They caught one of them at night. He screamed for a long time." She paused. "We found him the next day." She whirled and looked at him, her breath coming in small gasps. "I can't let them have Lily." She sounded desperate.

He nodded.

"The sheriff was killed. The others wouldn't go on."

"Did you see her?"

She shook her head. "But they're heading north. You were wrong."

"No," he said.

She ignored his comment. "We telegraphed the authorities in Arizona, Utah, Colorado, and Texas. And the Army has patrols looking for her." She paused. "We're having a photograph of her copied, and we'll send it to every town we can, offering a reward." She stopped talking and searched his face for a moment. "Will that work?"

"I don't know."

Honest as it was, it wasn't the answer she wanted to hear. "You don't care," she said, the words sounding hopeless. She turned and began walking down the mountain, stumbling and falling, then starting down again, looking to all the world like a sleepwalker.

Samuel Jones sat on the gray pony in front of the ranch house for a long time, before Mrs. Abby noticed him through the kitchen window. She came out onto the porch, drying her hands on a towel, the others following. Maggie had packed that morning to move into the hotel in town so that she could be closer to the telegraph office and the deputy sheriff's reports. Mrs. Abby and a few hands off her ranch would stay with Baldwin and the children.

Maggie stood back in the shadows of the doorway, holding a tray of food. Worried as she was about Lily and her husband, she didn't know how to turn away the sick folks who'd come that day, and she'd spent the morning doctoring and feeding them. Dot stood next to Mrs. Abby on the porch. James stepped down and walked up to the horse. Jones and the old pony looked crazy. He was holding the mule on a tether.

James looked up at him. "I'm going after my sister."

"No. They expect it, and they will kill you slowly in front of her. Stay and care for your family. That is what your father would want." James started to respond, but Jones held up his hand. "If your father does not live—you must be here." Jones handed the mule's tether down to him. "I can't take Alice. She's young; she won't behave."

James took the rope. "I could come with you."

Jones didn't respond.

"Mr. Jones, you should be resting," Mrs. Abby said.

"Nothing has made itself known to me," he replied, as if the woman would know what he meant.

"Where will you go?" she asked. "You are not well."

He looked for Maggie. She was a blur in the shadows before his eyes. "Things lost," Yopon had once told him, "should be left lost." She was right. Still, he wanted desperately to reach his daughter who stood so close.

"If you have no answers—where will you go?" Mrs. Abby asked again.

"To a sacred place. I will seek the answers. There is little time."

"Mr. Jones, I've seen sick men before. You are very ill. You cannot possibly do anything about what has happened. Your body will not let you. Do you understand? We've alerted the Army and the civilian authorities. I've wired my husband in Tucson, and he will be here in a couple of days. Somehow we'll find Lily. All you will do is kill yourself."

They stood quietly scrutinizing each other for a few minutes; then Mrs. Abby looked down at Dot and said, "Child, go wrap that chicken in a cloth and bring it to me."

Mrs. Abby looked at the gray. "Mr. Jones, I don't know horses much, but that animal looks used up. Perhaps you should take mine. You can bring him back when you find the answer you're looking for."

"You are kind. But no. We have grown old," he said, a distant sound in his voice, "but we will ride together."

She nodded at him.

Dot returned and handed the chicken to Mrs. Abby and then went and held the mare's head against her chest, rubbing her ears. The old animal shut her eyes and soon began to snore.

"Grandpa, I don't think she can go very far."

"She'll be fine, child. She would never forgive me if I left her behind."

Something in what he said made good sense and Dot held the gray's head tighter, sad but happy for the old horse.

Jones had always fancied strange outfits, but now he and the pony looked outrageous. The old man was wearing only a black satiny breechcloth, tied at the waist with a long green sash, and his Apache boots. His skin had been covered in a white powder, as though he had rolled in baking flour, then long streaks of red were painted over it, his face completely covered with glistening red pigment. His gray hair was tied in long braids, and a high, bristling porcupine roach, or Pe sa, of the Lakota rode the ridgetop of his skull—from his forehead down to his bony neck—tied in place by two thin strips of rawhide under his chin; and he was wearing his great wire earrings again, and armlets and bracelets of brass.

There were two eagle feathers stuck proudly in the roach. Skinny, old and sick, he still looked frightening. He was holding his beautiful pipestone calumet cradled in a thin arm, the battered Sharps resting across his saddle. Chaco sat on the gray behind the old man, his back to them all, his nose stuck arrogantly into the air. Two small red dots of fresh pigment showed on his little hip.

The bedraggled gray stood with her head drooping against Dot's chest, a bold red handprint on her shoulder and feathers tied throughout her scraggly mane. Half-dead-looking, she had been brushed and curried hard, and was decorated as a war pony of some note. Jones crawled down from the saddle, walked over and held the mule's head against his own for a while, then he whispered something in her ear and went back to the gray.

Mrs. Abby shook her head slowly. "Mr. Jones, it's been a while since we had trouble in these parts; but bad feelings are slow to die. That outfit you're wearing," she looked straight into his face, "could get you into trouble."

"I will not be seen," he replied.

Jones looked past them to where Maggie stood inside the doorway, still holding the tray. Without taking his eyes off her, he reached back into the leather saddlebag and pulled out a small wooden vessel, holding it out toward Mrs. Abby.

"Use these on Baldwin's wound. Soak them in water, then put them over the wound and bind them tight."

"What is it?"

"Ute medicine. Yarrow plant. It is good for bullet wounds." His eyes were still on Maggie. She watched him from the shadows of the house. He fumbled around in the saddlebag again and brought out a small black velvet pouch, worn thin in places, holding it in his hand for a long time, as if weighing whether to part with it. Then he leaned down from his saddle toward Dot and said, "Give this to your mother."

"I want nothing from you," Maggie said from the shadows.

"Open it," he said to Dot, "and take it to your mother."

Dot fumbled awkwardly with the pouch until Mrs. Abby helped her take out a small silver frame. Inside was a tintype and a thin silver chain. Mrs. Abby looked at it and then looked up slowly at him. "Are you sure?"

He nodded, and Mrs. Abby handed it to Dot, who walked over and offered it to her mother. She would not take it.

"It was taken of the three of us, the week before we parted," he said to Maggie. "The necklace was your mother's."

"We didn't part. You ran off. Like now. You're not going to a sacred mountain. You're going to your Indian friends. You're going to let your granddaughter die."

"No, he's not, Ma," Dot moaned, turning away and pressing her lips together tightly, holding the photograph and necklace in both hands as if they were sacred.

"Granddaughter," Jones said to the girl.

She snuffed, then answered, "Yes?"

"Have a good life. Believe. Then you will find the medicine." He watched her for a few moments, then added, "Think of me when the moon is over the corn."

Tears began to well up in Dot's eyes. She turned and ran off the porch, disappearing around the corner of the house. Jones sat watching the spot, as if daydreaming.

"She will always think of you," Mrs. Abby said.

He looked back at the woman as if he had forgotten she was there, and half-smiled, tipping his head, his topnotch swaying menacingly. Slowly, he turned in the saddle toward James. The young man was standing near the porch.

"If you are not going after Lily, tell me," James said.

The old man examined his face for a long while before he answered. "I am your grandfather. I made choices. Wrong ones, perhaps. But choices that a man must make."

"Are you going after Lily?"

"I am going to seek answers about her."

"Will you find her?"

Jones looked back at the shadowy rectangle of the doorway. "Life is not always good. But you must stay and take care of your family. That is important."

"You bastard!" Maggie yelled. She came through the doorway and tossed a coffee cup at Jones, the cup sailing close to his head. He didn't move. "Get off this ranch!"

"Margaret!" Mrs. Abby said, stepping toward her.

Maggie picked up another cup and started to throw it at him.

"Margar—"

"Ma, look." It was Dot's voice. She was trotting toward them from the barn, holding a calico cat in her arms. "She's alive! Grandpa was right! It's the fifth day! Harriet is alive! Grandpa's Indian medicine works! He'll find Lily!"

Maggie looked stunned, moving her eyes from the cat to the old man and back again. She lowered the arm holding the cup as if it were too heavy to hold. He had said five days. She had been keeping track. How had he known?

Jones put his heels to the gray and started at a trot away

from the ranch house. The mule tried to pull away from the hitching post to follow, then began to bray.

"Find her," James yelled at him.

Jones did not turn around. He stopped the gray in front of the picket fence and signed something in the silent language, then kicked the little horse into a trot.

The old pony was wading the creek when Dot caught up with them, her cat clutched in her arms. She ran alongside Jones's stirrup.

"Grandpa," she called up to him.

He didn't look down. He appeared to be contemplating the hills.

"Will my pa live?"

Jones nodded, and Dot grinned through her tears. She was convinced now that he could predict such things with certainty. "I want to help you shoot the men who took Lily."

He put his heels to the gray's flanks and the horse broke into a slow canter. Dot ran harder. "Even though Lily was mean to you, don't hold that against her," she called up to him. "You've got to try and save her."

Jones pulled the horse to a stop and looked down through his red mask of pigment at the panting girl and her cat.

Dot scrutinized the haggard lines of her grandfather's face. She could not read his thoughts, but she was certain in her heart that her mother was wrong about him, that he would try to save her sister. Dot loved him, and believed at that moment that he was invincible. She rubbed the gray's nose with her open palm. The old horse closed her eyes and started to drift off.

Jones began to cough and clucked the horse forward at a walk. Dot fell in beside him. "Grandpa, I want to learn the Indian medicine that will kill men like those who stole Lily."

"Someday I'll come back and teach you. Not to kill. To know and understand. That is more powerful medicine."

"That's a lie, isn't it?" She stopped walking. "You aren't ever coming back, are you?"

The old man, his horse and his dog, all three, continued on, Dot gazing after them. "Grandpa, I love you," she called. "Find Lily."

He kicked the animal into a loping canter. Dot stood watching until he disappeared in the tree line. She was crying and hugging the cat. "Please, Grandpa," she said softly. Alice was braying hard now.

"Find her!" James hollered in the distance.

# CHAPTER

# FIVE

Samuel Jones began to chant again, wondering if the earth and the stones were listening to him and why he continued. Chaco was beside him, the old gray was asleep in the shade of a rocky outcropping. He let his eyes search the parched terrain, his mind drifting elsewhere. He felt the urge to surrender to the sun and the heat.

The land was rugged and barren. Burrobush and grease-wood, and not much else. Sandstone spires rose hundreds of feet from the canyon floor, sculpted through the millenniums by rain and wind. He had traveled three days to arrive in this place, not certain where, knowing only that he had crossed into what the whites called the Pecos of Texas, knowing this from landmarks spotted the day before. Maybe a hundred and fifty miles above the Mexican border, somewhere below the springs at Balmorhea, he knew, because he had come across them at dawn. It was not the sacred place that he had sought. Not even close.

At first, as he had turned and retraced his steps through the hills, going south, then west, doubling back in the canyons, circling one mountain, then another, he had felt confusion, even fear. Then he realized it no longer mattered. His life was ebbing back into the earth. He was slowly being taken, absorbed into those things from whence he had come. It did not matter where this transformation took place. That thought brought him a passing sensation of peace. Chaco was whining in a fitful sleep.

He reached out a hand and laid it gently on the little dog's shoulder, and the terrier quieted down. He had been slowly eating pieces of the chicken that the woman had given him. Nevertheless, he was light-headed and weaker than he had ever been in his life. The sun beat down hard upon him. He needed water but did not want to move. He wanted to be absorbed into the life force now. He was ready.

He slept.

His eyes popped open. Someone was coming toward him, riding slowly through the narrow canyon. Backlighted by the morning sun, he could not see the figure clearly. Was it the cripple? The possibility made his gut tighten. Then he heard Alice bray.

Dot drew up next to him. She had braided her hair and was wearing the moccasins and necklace that Jones had given her a few days before. Jones did not smile.

"Have you found Lily?" Her voice sounded strained. She was watching the old horse sleeping in the shadow of the rocks.

He shook his head. He could tell she was upset, but he couldn't do what she so desperately wanted. She didn't understand. He continued to study her face with his old eyes. He had lived with the People for a long time. He understood determination, tenacity, cruel survival, and sensed the same fibrous cord in the child before him. She was fearless and game. It made him proud of her but also angry. She had no discipline.

"Where are your mother and brother?"

"Home."

"How did you find me?"

"Alice."

The young mule bumped him with her head. Chaco was darting in and out between her legs, barking and spinning in small circles.

"How is your father?"

Dot shot him a nervous, questioning glance. "He's alive. Just like you said. You did say that, didn't you?"

"I did."

"Then why are you asking about him?" she questioned.

"Just asking," he reassured her.

She turned in her saddle and looked around at the tall mountains surrounding the little opening of sand and bushes where they stood. "Is this the sacred mountain?"

"No."

She turned back and looked suspiciously into his face. "You said you were going to find a sacred mountain."

"Yes."

"What happened to it?"

"I couldn't find it."

"Couldn't find it?" she repeated. "Why not?"

He looked up at her for a few moments. "Because I got lost."

"You've got your medicine. You found Harriet."

"No. I told you that she was still alive—that was all. And I no longer have my medicine."

"What happened to it?"

"It's gone."

"Why?"

"You ask too many questions."

"I've got to. I've got to see that you find Lily."

He turned and looked away at the hills. She sat watching the back of his head.

"Grandpa, she'll die," she said, a deep sadness in her voice.

"Child, I can't. I couldn't even find the sacred mountain. I would if I could."

Tears were rolling down her cheeks. "Grandpa, you can't let them have her. I'm scared." She slid off the mule and wrapped her arms around his thin waist. He had to struggle to stay upright.

He loosened her arms and settled down in the sand with her beside him. He began to feel dizzy and put his head in his hands.

"You okay?"

"Just old, child."

He sat up straight and turned to look at her. "I cannot. I have no way. You need to believe that."

She was crying, but not making a sound in the quiet afternoon air.

"I would give you your dream if I could. But nothing comes to me. I don't know where they have taken your sister. I can't find her."

"Then tell me how."

"When you are older."

"Lily doesn't have time for me to be older!"

He didn't respond.

"Please, Grandpa," she sobbed. "At least tell me—let me try."

He looked at the range of blue mountains in the far distance, listening to a bird scratching in dry leaves. Without turning toward her, he said, "It's not as easy as you want it to be, child."

"I don't care. I know there are spirits who will help me find Lily. You told me that."

He looked at her again. Those eyes, they seemed to rush at him. He studied her face before he finally spoke. "The world is not outside, it is in your head . . . inside the one mind of the spirit. All things are within."

She looked confused.

"Life must be affirmed. There are no limits to what the spirits will do for you. If you believe. If you know that all you dream you can do. When you know that—when you truly believe it—when your thoughts are pure, then the spirit will come to you."

"Who is the spirit?"

"I don't know. Only you can know."

"But how?"

"If you believe, it will come to you when you need it."

Suddenly, the heat and tension and fatigue combined to cause Jones to fall asleep where he sat. A woodpecker was steadily excavating a hole in a nearby cactus. Dot watched it for a while; then she, too, slipped into a troubled sleep, hoping to dream.

She did not.


"One day more, one day less," Samuel Jones was mumbling before he awoke. The thought didn't frighten him, but he realized now that he was parceling out the meager supply of hours and days. It had come to that. Lying there staring up at the thin strip of sky above the canyon walls, he knew that once again he had been dreaming about circles.

Jones stretched his body on the sand, the pain slicing through his chest and back. He raised his head and was astonished to see Maggie sitting on her horse a few yards away, her hat pushed back, looking hot and dusty and pretty. Dot was standing beside her.

"You rode in on the mule, you are going to have to ride out on her," she was saying.

"Ma, don't make me."

"There's nothing for you here."

"He's going to find her."

"No, he's not. Dot, he'll break your heart. I believed him, too, when I was your age."

"Yes he is, Ma. He's just trying to conjure up where Lily and those men are. He's Indian. He can do it. Then he's going after her, and I'm going with him."

Samuel Jones struggled to stand up in the sand but couldn't make it. He sat looking at both of them.

"He's white. And there's nothing to his heathenism," Maggie said. "Lily's gone, Dot. We may get her back someday, but we may not. You have to know that."

"No! Grandpa can find her. He found Harriet." Dot had whirled and was staring at him wild-eyed now, her eyes burning into him. He looked away from her toward the hills.

"Why do you tell children lies?" Maggie asked him in a tired voice.

"They aren't lies!" Dot shouted. "Tell her, Grandpa—tell her that you're going to find Lily."

He looked back at the child's face. The eyes. They bored into him in the same way that Maggie's had, three decades earlier, on the morning that he left. He had denied those eyes. He couldn't do it again.

"I'm going to find her."

"Ma—did you hear?"

"Saying doesn't make it so. Now get on the mule."

Dot had collapsed in the sand beside her mother's horse. Maggie got down and took her into her arms and held her for a few minutes, rocking her gently. They were both crying. Jones struggled to his feet and walked unsteadily over to Alice, leading her to where they sat.

"Child, go with your mother," he said. "I will find your sister. That's my word."

"How good has that been over your life?" Maggie asked.

"You think because a cat comes home you have a divine power, don't you? It doesn't work that way."

Jones ignored her. "Your husband will live."

Maggie studied his face for a moment. "You aren't God."

"I have dreamed of it."

"You ought to quit dreaming."

"He will live," Jones repeated.

They mounted their animals. Maggie clucked her horse into a walk, watching him out of the side of her eye, and feeling better about Brake. Even though she didn't believe her father could foresee such things, still the thought gave her hope, and she was desperate for hope of any kind.

Chaco followed them, whining and nipping gently at Alice's heels until they entered the narrow part of the canyon. Then he sat and barked like he was cussing them.

Dot didn't look back.

Sunlight filtered down through the leaves of the old cottonwood, making the creek water dance and sparkle. A foot deep here, and running from the higher altitudes of the brown mountain towering behind it, moving rapidly over smooth stones, it made a pleasing choppy sound—gentle and peaceful—a sound that smothered other noise. Both banks of the creek had wide spots of coarse sand and large rocks. Farther back stood thick stands of desert willow and tamarisk trees, a rich screen that secreted the spot in warm solitude.

Leaves swirled over the surface of the water, collecting like large armadas in the eddies and deeper pools. High overhead, a magpie cursed from the cottonwood, noisy and distracting in the still of the morning.

The boy was playing a game with a wooden sword, launching small stick boats from the shore and then standing up and performing mock fights, swinging the little weapon wildly at imaginary foes. He was seven or eight, thin and freckled, with hair the color of butter. Around his head he had tied a bright green bandana, then secured a longer piece of red scarf around his waist.

The woman was kneeling fifty yards beyond the boy, washing clothes in the creek and draping them to dry over rocks. She was blonde and pretty, her golden hair catching the sunlight, her body lithe and fit-looking under her worn dress. She was singing to herself, the sound drifting peacefully down the creek.

Behind her, far across a green pasture, stood a ranch house. Two Mexicans were working on a fence nearby.

The boy didn't notice the first small boat rounding the bend and capsizing in a swift current between two rocks. It drifted slowly by as he worked on his own. He was getting ready to launch his little craft when the second small vessel came floating around the rocks. Made from a piece of bark with a tall stick stuck in it and a large green leaf skewered sail-like on the stick, it rode high on the water, and looked seaworthy. The boy grinned and glanced upstream to the spot where the creek bent around a large boulder.

"Pa, I thought you had gone to town," the boy called gleefully. He stood and started for the large rock. His mother raised her head and tried to hear what he was saying and then went back to scrubbing.

The boy trotted happily around the boulder, laughing at the game and running straight into the heavy arms of the lame man who had been stalking him. The man tripped him and shoved him into a deep pool of still water near the edge of the creek. The boy struggled, causing the water surface to break, his mouth opening and shutting like a beached fish. He never got a chance to yell.

In minutes, all was still again and the stalker moved to the side of the boulder and carefully looked at the woman. She continued washing. He knew when she finished she would call the boy, and when he didn't answer, she would come to get him. Then he would take her. The horses were tied in the brush upstream.

He turned back toward the water to wait, feeling a deep sense of satisfaction as he watched the yellow hair swirling slowly in the pool. He did not like to take them during the day, but the Other had been demanding. He thought of the girl named Li-Lee. He needed only two more. He had made a pact with the leader of the Apache band. He would provide seven white women to sell in Mexico—and they would give him five hundred cartridges and one of the women. He had chosen Li-Lee.

He waited in the bright sunlight leaning against the boulder, sweating badly beneath his hood. The woman was taking longer than she should have. He did not like it that the Mexicans were so close, or that he did not know where the woman's man was. The Other was prodding him.

He pushed away from the rock and started to check on her again, almost running into a small girl. She must have come from the house. She darted away before he could grab her, hollering and running toward the woman, who stood and yelled. Angry at being foiled, he threw his lance hard into the child's back, whirling and disappearing into the thick brush, the morning air suddenly alive with the woman's screams.

**P**ain blew through Jones's back like a hot bullet. He sat up quickly and rubbed carefully at the hurting. Surprised by its intensity, he half expected to find the stinger of a rock scorpion. But there was nothing. He shook his head to clear it.

Maggie had been right. He had lied his way through life. Now he had done it again—pretended to the one person on earth who believed in him that he was going to do something that he wasn't able to do. Soon, the child would know. He rubbed his hands over his face. What did it really matter?

He forced himself to try to visualize Lily. Where was she? Where were they taking her? Nothing came to him. But he would continue to try. That would be his final gift to his granddaughters.

He took his whiskey and climbed weakly to a ledge overlooking the small enclosure. Chaco trailed along. He shared the last of the chicken with the dog. Then he began to drink. He lit his calumet and blew smoke to the four quarters of the earth, calling to the spirits on his wing-bone whistle, the sound thin and eerie in the small place among the rocks. He sipped more whiskey and began to shake his rattle and chant. A fine mellow numbness slowly seeped through his limbs and into his brain. "Come to me, creator of the vision—I hold out my hands to you. Tell me of things I will never see, but must know. Come, guardian spirit, through the shadows of the canyons."

He was lost deep within his trance. There were no sounds; he saw nothing. He did not see Dot when she returned to the camp in the dark hours of the early morning. He did not see her watering and feeding the gray or feel the heat from the flames of the small warming fire she built in front of him. It had always been thus with him. But now his isolation was even greater. He had no contact with either world. Lost.

He moved through the motions of his medicine trance in rote oblivion, groping for his deerskin drum and tapping it gently in the darkness.

He saw nothing. He did not see Dot mimicking him by taking a long drink of whiskey. He did not hear her gagging as the burning fluid raced down her young throat. She was holding his old battered rattle in her hands and shaking it in a steady rhythm, chanting slowly, "Hu-Hu-Hu-Hu-Hu-Hu . . ." Picking up his prayer fan, she waved it slowly in the cool night air. The breezes it cast were soft and drifted gently into the dark recesses of the mountains.

She watched him carefully out of one squinting eye and tried to do all that he did. The world began to slowly turn around her in a wonderful spinning dance of trees and rocks and night. The red glow of the fire was hypnotic. The old man blew on his bone whistle and called to the spirits of the mountains to come to him. She waved the fan again.

Dot was tossing in a fitful sleep by a large fire in the sandy clearing below where Jones sat on the ledge. Maggie had returned some thirty miles to the camp when she realized Dot was gone, covering most of it at night. She was exhausted and leaned hatless against a large rock, sipping coffee and studying the flames, her durable beauty showing through the dirt and fatigue.

Jones's head was killing him. He struggled slowly down the narrow trail, fighting the sensation of faint and the heavy weakness coursing through his body. No vision had come to him. He had heard Yopon calling his name once. And he had seen his children—lost and wandering in Creation's darkness. Thelma's visage had joined the others, floating in a world of utter blackness. It was a nightmare that haunted him.

He trembled where he stood, looking again at Maggie, but no vision that he understood had made itself known. He had to stop and lean against the rocks before he reached the ground.

He and Maggie stood looking at each other. Her face still contained all of the resentment—she would not forgive.

"Why did you return?" he asked.

"Please," she said sarcastically. "I don't believe you did

this."

"I tried to reach my power."

"Don't you have any decency? You got your granddaughter drunk. She's a child. She believes in you."

"Ma—" Dot was struggling to sit, moaning and holding her head. "I'm feeling bad." She vomited on the sand. Maggie poured water into a handkerchief and cleaned her face, then filled a cup with coffee and put it into her hands.

"Aaaahh. I don't want it. Grandpa—take it."

The old man took the cup.

"When you can ride, we're going home, Dot," Maggie said.

"No." Her eyes were on her grandfather.

"Granddaughter. Others will have to find Lily. We would only wander in the hills and desert looking for her."

"Grandpa?"

"Yes, child?"

"I saw things."

"You saw the beard of the whiskey. You are young, the drink is powerful. You should not have taken it. You do too many things on your own."

She shook her head hard.

"It's easy to be misled. You want this very much. But you must not be confused."

Dot was still staring at him, as though peering through him. Jones studied her face over the rim of the coffee cup. "Because you have seen something doesn't mean it was your power. It isn't that easy."

"I did what you did," Dot mumbled. Her eyes had a funny dazed look to them. "It worked."

"Child," Jones cautioned, "that's only what you think you saw. Some search a lifetime. Some never find it." He studied her eyes.

"Dotty," Maggie said softly.

"Ma, I know where they are."

Maggie shook her head slowly.

Jones continued to watch the child's face. He pulled a tobacco bag out and built a cigarette. Finally he said, "Tell me."

Dot gazed away at the blue mountains and Jones sensed her drifting back, could see her eyes losing focus.

"It's hard—but I—"

He squinted, watching her struggling to put words to the ethereal sensations, and felt for her. Maggie, too, watched her closely.

"Does anything at all come to mind?" he asked.

"A dragonfly. It flew."

"Where?"

"Everywhere. Desert. The river. Mountains. Ohhh," she moaned, "I thought I knew where Lily was."

Maggie started to say something but Jones held his hand over his mouth and she stopped.

"Describe them."

"What?" Dot asked in a dreamy voice.

"The mountains and the river. Tell me about the mountains first." He went to his pack, returning with his calumet and rattle, and squatted next to the fire, filling the bowl and lighting it. He blew smoke over Dot. She coughed and he started hacking hard himself. Chaco lay down beside him, putting his little head on his paws and watching Dot and Maggie suspiciously as the old man struggled for breath.

When he recovered, Jones began to shake the rattle hard, calling in a loud voice, "Now we can start the journey. We come here to this quiet place to look for you. Look down on us. Create for us the vision we seek. . . . Give us the answers we search for and long to know."

Dot moaned.

"This is sacrilege." Maggie clutched her medicine bag and Bible as if they would ward off this evil. She looked confused.

"Dot, let's go."

"I can't," Dot replied, her eyes fixed on the ground. "I know where. I just have to find it again. You've got to let me." Her voice sounded sleepy.

"You don't know where Lily is, child. You just think you do," Maggie said.

He looked at Maggie. "You should leave. I will bring her to you."

"No. If you've harmed her—teaching your pagan things . . ."

"I have not harmed her. I did not wish this for her. It is too difficult for a child. But she is there now, and we must help her understand what she has seen."

Maggie sat down beside her daughter, putting her arms around Dot's shoulders and closing her eyes. "God," she said silently. Maggie held Dot tighter and tried to block out the sound of Jones's voice.

"Granddaughter. The mountains—"

An hour later, Jones rocked back on his haunches, drawing smoke from his long pipe and blowing it over the sleeping child. They had little or nothing to go on. He figured the river was the Rio Grande—but there were hundreds of miles of it slithering snakelike between Texas and Mexico.

Perhaps the desert sand and the rocks were the Castellan badlands. But that, too, was only a guess. He needed more. He thought again of what Dot had said: "It's like a cross." A cross? There was no church along the river that he had ever seen. Graves? His mind leaped ahead and his heart began to beat wildly. Was Lily already dead? Was the child's spirit simply leading him to her grave site?

Dot opened her eyes and stared straight into his face. She was smiling again. He smiled back, his large golden front tooth showing, the entire thing made of yellow metal. Chaco whined. Maggie was biting on her finger.

"I can see Lily riding." Dot dry-heaved, then looked back up at her grandfather. "She'll be there in three days, Grandpa."

"Why do you believe three days?"

"I don't know. I just keep seeing the sun cutting quickly through the sky. Three times." She looked scared. "Grandpa, you've got to believe me!"

"I believe you, child," he said, leaning forward and taking her into his arms.

Maggie moved away.

He squatted in the bright sunlight, hidden in the foothills behind the lonely house, and drew the circle in the sand. It was the third ranch house he had come across that day. This one was right. This woman was right. He had seen her and a man moving around earlier. She would bring a reasonable price. There was no other ranch or town within twenty miles, and the only other humans present were a worker and a small child. He shifted his body slowly, feeling the familiar eagerness in his muscles.

He laid the tuft of blond hair on the ground in front of him with tenderness and circled it carefully with glittering quartz stones, chanting the familiar words. It was good. The Other was free again. Immediately it urged him forward. He resisted. He would wait till dark.

Samuel Jones sat contemplating the cross he had gouged in the sand with a stick, his thoughts suddenly on the lame Apache. He sensed danger again and wondered why. He took a drink of coffee and forced himself to stop brooding over the man. The cross was puzzlement enough for the moment. Fairly certain it was the Rio Grande, he was also pretty sure Dot was talking about the southern Pecos. But where? What cross? Church steeple, grave, crossroads? Nothing distinctive came to mind.

The child's vision had given them three days before the band crossed into Mexico. Three days. Even if they knew where, they were still a hundred miles from the border. More than thirty miles a day through intense heat and rugged terrain if they were to make it. Impossible. The gray wouldn't survive that. She'd try—try with all that was in her—he just didn't figure she'd make it. He probably wouldn't either.

He studied Dot as she lay shivering by the fire under her mother's watchful eye, convinced that she had made contact with the other side, that her visions of the dragonfly, the cross and Lily were absolutely real. For the visions to have come so effortlessly indicated the purity of her great heart. He glanced at Maggie's face. She had a perfect right to the look of agitation in her eyes, he thought. She believed none of it.

Jones ran the stick over the crucifix shape at his feet again. He was squatting on a small rock, his knees up next to his shoulders, a cup of hot coffee in one hand. Suddenly, pain stabbed through his chest and he struggled to stand, spilling the coffee as he rose. His eyes followed the stream of brown fluid down to where it splashed into the tracings of the cross. Annoyed, he started to turn back to the fire, then stopped. The realization seemed to jump at him. That was it. He smiled his golden-tooth smile at Maggie, his reddened face looking beastly.

"I know where Lily will be."

Maggie shook her head. "I'm tired of your Indian fakery. They took Lily north—you're wasting her chances down here." She let her thoughts return to her prayer for Brake and James.

"Where is she, Grandpa?" Dot struggled to sit up. Her forehead was covered with beads of sweat, her hair matted and damp. "What is the cross?"

"A Mexican river that cuts the Rio Grande. The cross is formed by the waters of the two rivers. The cliffs are a mile south of a place called Three Hills. That's where they'll ford the river."

"Hokum," Maggie said.

Dot looked at her grandfather. "I'm going with you."

He lay back on the sand. The fasting, the sweat hut, the long nights of chanting, the alcohol, all of it had come home to roost. The world was spinning before his tired eyes. Then, suddenly, his thoughts were on the Lame One again, the strange fear gnawing like an animal in his mind. The visions were too frequent and too powerful to be ignored any longer. He struggled to his feet and rummaged through his leather packs.

"Child, put this on your face and arms," he said, handing her a small leather sack. Maggie watched them.

"What is it?" Dot asked.

"Red earth."

"Why?"

"To protect you."

"From what?"

Jones hesitated. "Evil."

"What evil?"

"Just do it, or you cannot stay."

Dot opened the poke. Maggie was coming toward them.

"Dot—" she said, her voice firm.

"Do it child, or leave," he said.

"Dot, we don't believe in those kinds of things."

The old man struggled to his feet and took the bag from Dot's hands and rubbed pigment onto her trembling face and down her arms.

"Damn you!" Maggie shouted. "It's enough that you've lost your soul—but you won't teach a heretic's ways to my daughter."

Jones whirled and faced her, his harsh features flashing anger for the first time since he had seen her. Maggie took an involuntary step backward. He shoved the pigment out toward her. "Margaret, put it on," he said.

"I will not. And you, you had better pray for your redemption, and for what you did to Mother."

The words stopped him for a moment. Then he said, "Ama. You may be right, but that changes nothing. Either put this on or leave. I'm certain your faith will survive it."

"I won't."

Jones watched her for a moment and knew that she would not. He returned to the saddlebag and pulled out a necklace of blue stones and a small leather poke and thrust these toward her. "Then put this on and carry the bag in your pocket."

"That's ridiculous," she said, folding her arms. She shook her head. "Black magic."

"Ama. Take the necklace and the bag, or I'll take the child when you sleep and disappear with her. You will not find us."

Maggie turned and looked off into the far distance, biting her lip in anger. She knew he would do what he said. Finally, she turned back and took the things he held and shoved them into her coat pocket.

## SIX

T he stalker stood in the shadows against the side of the
house and watched the woman through the thin crack
in the window curtain. He would wait. He shut his
eyes and listened. The night was silent. He had heard the
child talking earlier, but no one had spoken in the house for a
while. He opened his eyes again and peered at the young
woman through the slice of lantern light. She was preparing
for bed, washing her upper body. She looked relaxed. She had
no idea she was being watched.

He had not heard the man for a while. Perhaps he had
gone to bed; but something inside his head said no. He had
hunted whites for a long time. It was rare for one living in the
wilderness to go to bed without stepping back outside to listen to the night, to check on his stock.

The stalker was leaning half-relaxed against the wall,
when suddenly a stiff wind came down from the hills, tossing
sand and leaves hard against the side of the house. The
woman turned quickly and looked at the window with a startled expression, and he drew back deeper into the darkness.
Then he heard the man's voice again and knew instinctively
that he would be coming out into the night. The stalker

stepped away from the window, moving quickly to where the dog lay in the pooling blood, concealing the animal in the nearby bushes, and then disappearing into the barn's dark stillness.

"Here, Kelsey!" Bob Johnson hollered. He had been calling the dog for the past five minutes. Probably chasing raccoons in the corn again, he figured. Still, he usually came when called. Johnson stepped down off the porch and deeply breathed in the night air, smelling the white flowers of Apache plume and creosote brush. The air was pure and dry. He loved it here. He knew Ethel wasn't all that fond of it. She hated the loneliness. And now with the child growing up, she had a point worth debating. Perhaps they should try to sell out and move closer to a town. Perhaps Colorado. There was good land there, he'd heard. He stretched and looked up at the moon. It was nearly full, with wisps of white clouds passing over it, the black sky blasted with stars. Johnson started back up the steps to the house. Then he stopped, and turned back and faced the barn.

The door was open some, and he could see the dull light from a low-burning lantern; but Hadley, the hired man, hadn't bothered to step outside to see what was going on. That wasn't like him. He was usually so nosy as to be annoying.

Bob Johnson walked to the barn, pulled the door open wider and stopped dead still, his muscles tensing. She was sitting on a bale of hay, her back to him, her head covered with a light blue bonnet. Johnson smiled. Old Hadley was stepping out with a woman, that was why he hadn't responded to the hollering. But where had she come from? There was no wagon outside. She must have ridden in on a horse, but surely the dog would have barked. And the closest town was twenty miles off.

Something didn't square. In all the years Bill Hadley worked here as a hand, the rancher had never seen him say more than hello to a woman. He listened hard. The barn was still and filled with an odd sense of anticipation. Even the animals seemed to be listening. He didn't like it. The woman hadn't moved. The lantern was burning low on the wall in front of her, casting a small gloomy circle of soft light, silhouetting her and making the rest of the barn's interior seem even darker.

Johnson took a slow step forward. "Hadley? Lady?"

The woman didn't move, sitting still as if frozen with fear. He stepped to the side, picking his way through the farm implements, walking slowly toward her. He knew now something was wrong—but what, he had no idea. He picked up his blacksmith's hammer from the anvil and stepped into the soft ring of the lantern's glow and looked at the face under the bonnet. It was Hadley.

His skull had been split in a vicious V. He had been posed—the bonnet tied under his chin, his legs crossed, propped against bales of hay. His chest cavity had been cut open and his heart was gone.

On sudden impulse, Johnson whirled to face the wall of darkness behind him, and took the thrust of the knife deep in his innards. The knife moved fast, relentlessly. His hands opened and shut, the hammer fell; he tried to clench his fists to strike out at the frightening masklike face peering at him from the darkness, but he had no strength. "God," was all he managed to say. He wanted to sit but didn't know how.

The stalker left the barn and moved down the porch as silently as he could, the boards groaning under his weight. He was breathing hard. He leaned close to the curtained window again and peered in. The woman was combing the girl's hair. The child was five or six. She would be worth something, if she didn't cry and cause them trouble. If she did, she would be worth nothing. He stepped to the door and pulled the latch as silently as he could.

"Robert?" the woman called from the bedroom, the voice filled with fear.

He tensed; there would be no surprise. She was suddenly in front of him, the child clutching her waist and a doll, the woman desperately trying to cock and raise a pistol. The child turned and ran frantically for the bedroom. He fired without hesitation, striking the girl in the side, and she collapsed screaming, writhing on the ground, her mother just standing and staring at the source of the blast as if she couldn't possibly comprehend what had happened. Then she dropped her pistol, and sagged spraddle-legged to the floor, gathering her injured child into her lap.

They had been riding without a break since morning. They walked or trotted. Jones set the pace. Maggie and Dot just followed. Often during the trots, he swung down and held on to the saddle horn with one hand, running beside the old horse in a long, turkeylike gait. He was doing so now, and seemed to have more energy—headed somewhere and with a purpose.

The afternoon rays of the desert sun burned into them with a fierceness, but it seemed that nothing would stop the old man and his little horse, and their mad teeth-rattling charge across the landscape. Chaco was balancing up behind. Dot followed on Alice, the red paint bright on her face and arms. The mule kept her head tucked in close behind the old mare's rump. Farther back, as though determined to protest every step, rode Maggie. Clouds of thin dust kicked up, billowing over her, coating her in a muddy film of perspiration.

The land was dry, mostly all sand, alkali flats and greasewood, a place of flash floods and little more. Jones figured they were still sixty miles from the border of Mexico. Forbidding dunes rose like ocean waves in the distance; cactus and creosote were closer by. There were lizards and the occasional roadrunner and lots of colinia warblers in the brush. Every once in a while the horses or the mule kicked up a jackrabbit. Not much else. The terrain was sparse pickings and thirsty. In the distance, in every direction, were tall, barren-looking mountains.

Jones's lungs were hurting, and he was panting hard as he loped along. He desperately missed his energy and stamina. He had slowly reconciled himself to the fact that Maggie would never let him explain. Now he was trying to get used to the exhaustion that enveloped his body and mind.

The gray pony was beginning to fade badly as well, stumbling over small things; the heat, the fatigue and lack of water were taking their toll on her. Dot kicked Alice into a canter and moved up alongside the horse and the old man, slowing the mule to a bone-jarring trot. She looked worried.

At 118 degrees Fahrenheit, Mannito had told her a man exposed to the desert sun could last a day without water. One day. She didn't know how long for horses and mules. Maybe more, maybe less. She gazed off into the distance, watching the air dance in the harsh sunlight, and guessed the temperature to be 115 degrees. She and her mother had a little water left, but the animals hadn't drunk since last night.

"We need water, Grandpa. And we need to let the gray rest."

He didn't respond. He didn't even look at her, just continued jogging beside the gray pony.

"We don't get these animals water, Grandpa, they're going to die on us," she called down to him. Chaco barked at her.

He said something to the horse that she couldn't understand and the gray slowed to a plodding walk, her head lowered close to the ground as though she could no longer carry the burden of its weight. Dot was worried about her. She looked caved in.

The old man stopped walking, and stood squinting at the surrounding hills. He turned slowly in a circle, as though he had no idea Dot and Maggie were sitting a few feet away in the blazing sunlight. Maggie eyed him suspiciously. His face was still red, amazingly dry-looking for a man who had been trotting in the heat next to his animal, off and on for the past four hours. He shaded his eyes and probed a range of mountains. He looked suddenly worried about something.

"Grandpa?"

"I've been here before," he said vaguely.

"Is there water?"

He didn't answer. He left the mare and walked a few yards toward the distant range, a dusty purple in the afternoon haze, and studied it, as if it was something he didn't want to see but couldn't stop his eyes from looking at.

"Which way?" Dot called out to him.

The old man whirled and looked at the mountains behind him, his long arms dangling at his sides as though he had been suddenly stunned by some unseen blow. The lines of his face, around his eyes and mouth, began to shift until there was a strange appearance of panic about him.

Dot kicked the mule and rode up beside him. She reached down and put her hand on his shoulder. "Grandpa, what's wrong?"

"I've been here before," he mumbled again.

"So that's good. Then you know where there's water." She waited a few moments for him to look up at her.

Maggie had ridden up next to Dot and sat staring with narrowed eyes at the old man. "Honey, we've got trouble. He's either heat loco, or just too old and feebleminded. Either way, he has no idea where we are."

Dot shook her head. "No. Grandpa isn't lost. He's just thinking. That's all."

"Child, you can't listen to this old man."

"I'm not. I'm listening to something else."

"What?" her mother asked, wiping her arm across her forehead.

"I'm not sure."

Maggie scrutinized her features for a moment. "The dragonfly?"

"Maybe."

"They don't talk."

Dot didn't reply, turning instead back toward Jones, who continued to scan the distance. "Grandpa, should we go back for water?" The sun beat down on her like a fist.

The old man ignored her. Then suddenly he was striding slowly toward a low brown-colored range of hills, a mile off in the brilliant sunlight, moving as if drawn by some invisible force, drawn against his will. He stopped the old horse and remounted, and headed on toward the brown hills.

"See, he isn't lost," Dot said.

Maggie only shook her head.

The gray went down full on her knees at the mouth of the canyon, Chaco leaping from her rump to the ground and back again in nervous bounds. Jones stood next to her, gazing into the canyon as if he expected a grizzly to come exploding out at any moment. He looked badly shaken, his mouth half-open, his eyes searching the surrounding rocks for some clue that Dot didn't understand.

She crawled down and took the old horse the last of her water, pouring it into the crown of her felt hat and holding the gray's head so she could drink, talking softly to her. When the water was gone Dot stood so that her body gave the old pony's head some shade, and fanned her with her hat. The heat was oppressive, blanketing Dot in sweat.

She looked for signs of water: stains on the canyon walls, clouds of flies, birds coming into the place, any evidence of moisture, but saw nothing that relieved her fears. There was arrowweed and seepwillow, and she knew they liked water, but she also knew their roots could reach down a hundred feet to find it. The old man was still staring into the canyon in his dazed way.

"What's wrong, Grandpa?" she asked, wiping her neck with a kerchief.

He didn't answer. The gray struggled back onto her feet and stood nose to the ground. Dot hugged her. Then a refreshing breeze came flowing out of the canyon, moving like a cool river through the hot air. Alice's ears perked and she put her muzzle out and breathed in deeply, then snorted and started forward. Dot held her back and climbed up in the saddle, smiling and turning toward her mother. "Water!" she yelled.

She could feel it in the cool currents flowing around her. All three of the mounts were moving at an eager trot down the canyon. Dot reined Alice to a walk and Maggie fell in next to her. Riderless, the gray pony went rushing ahead of them, Chaco balancing and barking frantically as they passed. Dot looked around at the old man. He was gazing in a stupefied way at the soaring palisades of sandstone that formed the massive canyon, deeply troubled by something.

"Grandpa, come on," she called.

It was a beautiful place. Bold cliffs with China-blue sky above, the air moist and laden with the smell of plants and, deeper in, the sounds of birds and wind through leaves. Dot saw pickleweed and salicornia, surefire signs of surface water, and knew they wouldn't die of thirst. At least not here.

Worlds away from the harsh desert that lay beyond its mouth, the canyon was filled with fine willows and cotton-woods, a coarse carpeting of rich tobosa grass blanketing the floor, and in clear places Dot could see deer tracks. It was lovely. Mexican poppies, Arizona jewels and blackfooted daisies. A hidden paradise.

Dot looked over her shoulder again. The old man was not following. "Grandpa!" she hollered. He did not respond. "I'll come back for you."

Dot's breath reversed in her throat when she came around a bend in the canyon and saw the wagons. Maggie yanked the roan to a halt, the animal fighting her to be at the water. Alice was dancing as well. Dot reined her in hard.

"Ma?"

"It happened long ago."

The canyon was silent. Maggie rode forward, Dot following, unable to take her eyes off the wagons. There were six of them, their canvas tops tattered and torn from long years in the sun. Nothing moved.

Dot crawled slowly off the mule and walked hesitantly toward the wagons. She saw skeletons on the seats, under the wagon beds, behind rocks that hadn't shielded them. Still clothed, though the garments were nothing but rotting fragments. Men had died clutching weapons. Women clutched children. The oxen had been shot in their traces—their huge, sun-bleached backbones and rib cages exposed. Dot moved slowly down the line, her breath coming in hard little jerks.

"How come no one buried them?"

"We're the first to find them."

Dot sat down hard next to something in the sand and began to rock back and forth, moaning. Maggie walked over to her. She was sitting beside the remains of a small girl, maybe five or six, her red dress almost covered by the sands, a decomposing doll still clutched in the bones of her fingers. Dot reached a trembling hand and touched the fabric, then pulled away as if it had bitten her. Maggie knelt and held her, listening to a soft echoing sound floating on the wind of the canyon—the wind crying as it had on the day her mother died. The whispers of lost dreams, she thought.

"Ma, why?"

"Indians," Maggie said, as if the word alone were an explanation.

Dot struggled to her feet and went to the nearest wagon and pulled a rusty shovel off the side, returning to the child. She began to dig.

Maggie didn't say anything. She was looking at the wagons. Dot sensed that something was wrong and stopped digging, following her mother's gaze to where her grandfather sat cross-legged on the ground near the last wagon, smoking his calumet and chanting loudly. Every so often he would set the pipe down and shake his Navajo rattle. Then he broke into a low wailing death song that spread chills over Dot's hot skin.

Maggie started walking in a slow and determined way toward the old man. Dot followed.

"Ma?"

She didn't answer, just continued walking until she stopped directly in front of Jones. He had stripped to his breechcloth and moccasins and was talking to himself in a tongue Dot didn't recognize. He looked delirious.

Standing hatless under the harsh June sun, Maggie squinted at him as he offered the purifying smoke and sang the emigrants' death song. When she finally spoke, it was with a voice her daughter had never heard before.

"You were here."

Jones stopped chanting and stared directly ahead as if considering her words.

"You were here, weren't you? Isn't that what you said?" Maggie's voice was rising. "That you'd been here before."

The old man sat mutely on the sand.

"Grandpa?"

He began to chant again.

"You were here! You helped slaughter these people!" Maggie pulled her pistol and pointed it at him. "You're celebrating your damn Indian victory!"

"Ma, don't," Dot pleaded. She looked desperately at Jones. "Grandpa, tell her. Tell her that you don't know anything about what happened here. Tell her that you just found this place by accident."

The old man looked up at her with a dazed expression.

"Grandpa?"

He continued to look blindly into her face, as if he were looking through it to something in the sky beyond. Then he cleared his throat and said, "I was here."

The explosion stunned Dot for a moment. She couldn't move, couldn't see him clearly through the cloud of smoke. "Ma, don't!" she yelled. The old man was still sitting up. Dot dropped to her knees beside him, afraid to look. "Grandpa? Are you hit?"

"No. Move away."

Dot looked up angrily at her mother. "You tried to shoot him! Why? He's just sun-sick."

Jones was struggling to stand, then settled back down on the sand, his eyes looking haunted.

Maggie turned and started walking slowly back toward the animals, her shoulders slumped. Jones was chanting softly now, his eyes moving over the canyon. Chaco sat by his side, trembling in the hot sunlight.

"No," Dot said.

Maggie sat in the shade of the canyon wall, still holding her pistol and still watching him, but the fight had seeped out of her. For a moment, she had wanted to destroy him. Then, as much as she hated what he'd done to her mother and these people, she knew she couldn't bring herself to do it.

Somewhere inside she was feeling things she didn't want to

acknowledge. Whatever these feelings were they disoriented her badly, stirring within her like a creature slipping the bonds of sleep. She looked back at him, drawn again in a curious way to this old man.

Fighting these emotions, Maggie struggled hard to think of reasons why she still hated him. Hated his Indian ways. She let her mind drift, her thoughts turning back eleven years to the day they lost Thelma and Mannito's wife, Julia. She trembled.

The Apaches had come out of the hills at early morning. Brake and Mannito were off in the high valley branding calves. The three women had gotten up at dawn, and Thelma and Julia were taking turns milking the cow in the front pasture. Maggie winced. They shot them there, killed them for no reason.

She looked quickly about her, as if seeking an escape from the memory she'd unleashed. But there was no escape. She could still see them turning to run in the morning sunlight, their arms suddenly flying forward like they were tumblers in a circus. Maggie peered sadly at the sandstone walls surrounding her.

She would go to her grave loathing Indians. Those who'd stolen Lily. The woman. All of them. And her father wasn't any better. He'd chosen their ways. A man of free will. And someday, Maggie knew, he would have to answer to his Maker.

She looked up at the thin blue sky above the canyon. "God. I know You exist. Help me. Help me find Lily. And help me know what I should do about him. Please."

Maggie listened to the wind, hoping to hear a celestial voice. There was nothing. Then she remembered the necklace and the little bag he had given her to ward off his mad demons. She squirmed and pulled these from her pocket, burying them quickly in the sand, wondering if they'd belonged to his Indian whore. It didn't matter. But perhaps they were the reason that God had not answered her. She asked forgiveness for having carried them, then prayed again for something that would tell her where to find Lily.

The old man was finishing his ritualistic walk through the wagons, holding a small ceremony at each, blowing sacred smoke, singing and chanting. Maggie hadn't stopped watching him. "No bond exists between us," she said silently, as though to still the new sensations sifting like winds through her. As a further antidote, she continued to think about the things she disliked about him.

She hated his moralizing hypocrisy. Here he was, crying his pagan incantations over his victims' bones. Nor were these people the only things he'd killed and then mourned. There was her mother, for one. And long ago, Maggie knew, something had died deep inside of her because of him. Something that she desperately needed to feel whole. He had let it suffer, then die. Now there was just the awful sense of longing inside her.

Evening was on the canyon when Dot returned. Her face and arms were still covered with the red pigment and she looked exhausted. She ignored them both and went and pulled some green tufts of grass and took these to the gray. Then she picked up the rusted shovel and began to work again on the little girl's grave, a determined look on her face.

Jones went to where she knelt, his shadow falling across her. "I have sung their death songs," he said quietly. "It is enough."

Dot stopped digging and stared into the small hole in the sand for a moment, then she slowly raised her head until she was glaring up at him. "You don't have a right. No right at all to say anything about them!"

"We must find Lily."

She shook her head.

"There's little time."

"I don't believe you anymore."

"Then believe the dragonfly."

"Ma is right. That's poppycock."

Jones studied her for a moment. "Because of it we know where Lily is. We have one, perhaps two days. After that she will disappear into Mexico."

Dot stiffened but showed no sign that she was going to answer him.

"I need your power. Your sister needs you."

Dot just shook her head, staring down at the new grave. Jones watched her for a few moments, then mounted the gray.

Samuel Jones rode slowly into the desolate canyon. White-eyed vireos were calling their evening song from the mesquite thickets. He had ridden alone most of his life, but never this alone, never before this sense of dark solitude.

Suddenly, his thoughts were on the lame Apache and a small white girl-child he didn't know. Had never seen. All he knew for certain was that the child was badly injured. Maybe dead. He didn't know how he knew—the thought was just there in his head. His throat tightened. Was his mind, as it faded, playing tricks? Was he only remembering what had happened here in this canyon so long ago? No. He was not a man to use age or death as excuses. He was thinking of the cripple and a white girl-child and something desperate. Something that had already happened. He was certain of it.

A feeling of helplessness engulfed him—thoughts of the man driving him to distraction. Then Lily's face seemed to float in a strange circle of light before his eyes. He blinked and abruptly the beautiful visage and the glowing circle disappeared. He kicked the old gray into a trot.

\*    \*    \*

They dug only shallow graves in the sand for the smallest of the children. Even so, it was dark when they were finally done, and Dot was gasping and moaning. It had nothing to do with being tired, only with the fact that she had to let out the awful feelings trapped inside her.

They knelt and Maggie squinted her eyes in the deepening shadows of the night and read a passage from her Bible. Afterward, Dot wearily stood and peered down at her: her mother's skin alabasterlike, her features resembling those of the Roman goddesses Dot had looked at a thousand times in the stereoscope at home. Beautiful and strong and dignified. Maggie was covered with sweat and dirt and looked exhausted. Dot loved her. Even though Maggie didn't believe in the vision, Dot knew she would not abandon her or the search.

"Thank you."

Maggie smiled. "You've got a good heart. Never let go of it."

They drank again, then Maggie washed and changed into fresh clothes. Afterward, they let Alice and the roan at the water, watching them sucking up the liquid, their sides and bellies filling out until they looked like they might burst. Dot wouldn't remove the red pigment. Maggie didn't push.

"We should be home in three or four days."

Dot was standing next to Alice, rubbing the mule's ears. "I can't," she said.

Maggie just sat staring at the sand.

Jones's trail led deep into the wild and beautiful canyon for many miles. Then it turned sharply into a narrow slit in the red sandstone and began to climb into higher mountains. When there was enough moonlight to see, they visually followed the gray's hoofprints in the dirt. But it wasn't necessary. Alice had the scent and she was frantically unraveling the trail like a hound.

They continued even after the moon was lost behind dark clouds, making it impossible to see much. Alice trudging on, smelling and snorting her way along, her walk sure and steady, Dot confident in her ability to cipher the trail in the vast pool of blackness that surrounded them.

They had left the mountains and were moving now through rolling hills and sand dunes. Dot could make out the shapes of mesquite trees and little Harvard oaks. Though riding knee to knee, she and her mother hadn't spoken in a while when Dot turned and looked at her.

"He's headed for the river," Dot said softly. "Lily is out there. Grandpa knows that spot I described and that's where he's going."

Maggie didn't respond.

The horses had been walking through bladder sage and the cool night air was pungent with the spicy smell of the plants. The moon behind clouds, all chance of seeing any distance was gone. Probing the darkness, Dot figured there must be water close by since she could make out the shadowy shapes of cottonwoods against the skyline. The trees reminded her of home and her thoughts flew painfully to her father, Mannito and Lily. Two of them lost.

She pushed the sadness away and remembered things that she and Lily used to do. Though six years older, her sister had always had time for her: playing stick games or dolls, puppets or learning verses, dress up or just talking. If something was bothering her, she went to Lily. Now she was gone.

The horses moved steadily toward the vague shapes of the trees. She peered at the surrounding brush. Fluff grass and iodine bush. Poor grazing. They had been searching for feed for their animals for the past couple of hours. Maggie shifted in her saddle and Dot looked at her.

"What will they do to her?"

The question seemed to stun Maggie, and she stared at the neck of her horse for a few moments, then dismounted. "Let's let these animals graze for a while." She pulled out Brake's silver pocket watch, pretending to check the time, studying the small photograph of her and Brake, and trembling hard. Dot continued to watch her face.

"Ma, why won't you tell me?"

"I don't want to tell you things I don't want to know myself," Maggie said, squatting and setting the watch down on a small rock, then tipping her head back to stare at the heavens.

"You have to tell me."

Maggie looked at her again, then sucked in her breath. "Maybe sell her."

"Like a slave?"

Maggie nodded.

"Why?"

Maggie didn't say anything.

"Ma?" Dot's voice sounded frightened.

Maggie looked back down at the sand, shaking her head.

"Ma?"

"To breed."

"I don't understand."

Maggie shook her head. "Just to breed."

"Will they hurt her?"

Maggie stood quickly and walked away from her daughter, fighting off the scream clawing out of her throat. She had forgotten the timepiece.

Dot watched the animals grazing for a long time. The thought of breeding made her sick. They had to get to Lily before it happened.

They were sitting near their animals out on the sandy flat when a noise from the cottonwoods drifted to them. The roan and the mule perked their ears sharply and watched the dark shadows at the edge of the tree line. Maggie and Dot froze, then slowly rose to their knees and looked under the belly of the horse in the direction of the sound.

"See anything?"

"I've got a fix on the spot," Maggie said softly, "but I can't see anything. You?" She stood and slipped her rifle quietly out of the saddle scabbard beneath her stirrup.

"No."

"Good chance they don't know we're here. Let's keep it that way. Tighten the cinches while I keep watch. No noise. Then let's get out of here."

Dot stood and fumbled nervously in her saddlebag for a moment, finally pulling out something small and dirty-looking, and clutching it in her hand.

"What's that?"

Dot hesitated. "An eagle claw Grandpa gave Lily. It helps a person run from danger."

Maggie didn't say anything immediately. She just continued to scrutinize the dark silhouettes of the trees in the distance; then she turned her head and looked through the darkness at her daughter, waiting until their eyes met before she spoke. "Toss that thing away," she said firmly. "Now. Before you harm yourself."

The stalker had left the captive and her hurt child sitting in a cruel position on the horse, a slipknot drawn tight around the woman's neck, the rope snubbed down hard so that she was forced to ride bent over the girl, or choke. Then he'd bound her wrists together so tightly she could no longer feel her hands; the straps secured to the saddle horn by line left just slack enough so she could still hold her child. Barely hold her.

The woman was desperate. She'd tried pleading with him, but each time he'd struck at her or kicked her horse hard in the flank, making the animal buck. She'd stopped trying, fearful that she would drop her child. She knew if she did, he would leave her behind to die.

She couldn't let her die. The child was whimpering now and the woman began to sing in a dazed voice, wondering why her husband had not come back from the barn.

The Apache squatted awkwardly on his deformed leg and investigated the place where he'd heard talking. His medicine was good: even in the darkness, the little watch shined. He picked it up and struck a match and studied the image of the man and woman, his heart beating faster, sensing he'd seen them both before. Then the match died and he wasn't certain. Something about their faces. Something. He tensed, his thoughts flying to the old giant.

Quickly, he hobbled over the sand, scouring the ground in ever-widening circles. He found nothing to indicate that the thin one was nearby; his thoughts returned to the people in the spirit-image, striking another match and looking at their faces. Why had they brought him thoughts of the old ones? He didn't know. Frustrated, he looked up and watched the woman struggling to hold her wounded child, and felt better.

**M**aggie and Dot had been riding hard for several hours when the smudge of yellow firelight in the trees ahead brought them up sharply. Dot sensed Alice hunching up for a bray and she leaped off and grabbed the mule's nose.

"Don't you dare," she whispered into the animal's ear. "We've got no idea who that is. You aren't careful, Alice, you could be steak before morning comes."

Maggie dismounted and pulled her pistol, squinting at the light and listening. "More than one voice," she said.

"Grandpa's one."

"How do you know?"

"Alice is quivering. She does that whenever she gets near him. He must have made camp with someone." She paused. "But that doesn't seem much like him." There was a worried sound in her voice.

"That's what I'm thinking," Maggie said.

They led the horse and mule back up the trail almost a mile, hobbling and halter-tying them in a stand of willows, far enough away so even if Alice brayed to wake snakes, the sound wouldn't reach the campfire. Convinced it was a white man's fire, Maggie made Dot scrub the red pigment from her face and arms. Then they went carefully back, the smear of yellow light still wavering softly, menacingly, through the tall trees, the voices rising and falling among the shadows. Maggie took the lead, her pistol drawn.

Samuel Jones was sitting on the gray, his arms bound tightly behind his back. He was still wearing his breechcloth, breastplate and Lakota topnotch. Most of the paint on his face and body had been smudged off, but there was enough left that he still looked like something wild and beastly. The old mare was tied to a tree and asleep. Chaco was sitting behind the old man, growling every once in a while. A dozen white men were standing around a big fire, arguing.

"Hang him."

"Burn him!" another shouted.

Dot started running. "That's my grandpa!"

The men in the circle froze for a moment, then exploded, jumping and tumbling for cover. They stared in stunned surprise at the angry young girl standing before them. Chaco growled at her. "Grandpa, are you okay?"

The old man turned and looked at her, and nodded.

"What the hell are you doing out here?" one of the men asked.

"Looking for my grandpa," she said, the words sounding like a challenge.

The men looked from her to Jones. One of them, a big, well-used barrel of a man with a red beard, walked over to her. "That's your grandpa?" he said, winking to the others.

"That's right."

Surprised by her answer, the man said, "Naw, that old man is Indian."

Dot stepped back as if getting ready to charge. "He's my grandpa. He isn't really Indian. He just thinks he is. Let him go." Dot was trying to figure if she should point her shotgun at them, when she caught movement from the side of her eye.

"Let him go," Maggie repeated softly, her pistol pointed square at the chest of the man in front of Dot. Her hat was hanging around her neck by a string, her long brown hair flowing to her shoulders. Looking at her, Dot realized again how much she loved her. How she could always count on her and her great strength. Her grandfather was watching them.

"Who are you?" the man asked.

"I'm this child's mother. And that's her grandfather."

The men stared suspiciously at them, a few turning to look at the old man sitting still and silent on the Indian pony, then back at Maggie and Dot. They didn't buy it. It seemed impossible.

"Maybe they just don't like hangings, Henry," someone called from back in the pack.

"I don't," Maggie returned. "Specially my kin." She paused. "And I'll kill anybody who tries it."

"This old man is a damn Indian. Look at him. He's no kin of yours," the man called Henry snorted. "What's your game?"

Focused hard on the men, neither Dot nor Maggie noticed Jones's warning with his eyes. Suddenly, it was over. Two men had crept up behind them and made a grab, disarming them, and shoving them into a sitting position.

"Get your hands off!" Maggie said fiercely.

"Lady, who the hell are you and what are you doing?" the red-bearded man asked, uncorking a pint of whiskey and taking a drink. "We're legal. Deputized to kill hostiles."

Maggie glared up at him. "My name is Margaret Baldwin and this is my daughter. My husband ranches in New Mexico. My oldest girl was kidnapped a week ago and we've been trying to get her back. Now let us go!"

"And this is your father?"

Maggie nodded.

"Why is he dressed like a goddamn heathen if he's white? Or are you half-breed?"

"I'm full white and so is he." She paused. "He's just eccentric, that's all."

"Eccentric, hell!" somebody yelled.

"Which part of New Mexico?" a tall, thin man asked.

"Chimayo."

"Then why ain't Sheriff Bob Wills hunting your daughter?" the man continued, studying her face as though he didn't believe her.

Maggie stood and brushed off her pants. "He was killed trying."

"Wills is dead?" the red-bearded man asked.

"Ambushed by the Indians who took my girl and shot my husband."

"Hey, Henry," someone shouted. "This is that do-gooder ranch woman who doctors all the curs and misfits up that way. Hell, she's just trying to save this one."

"That true?"

"That I doctor people? Yes. But this man is still my father."

"And these hostiles are heading south with your girl?"

Maggie glanced at Jones. He was still watching her, but with no visible emotion. She was feeling the odd stirrings again.

"Lady, I asked you a question."

Maggie nodded at the man. "They're riding south."

"I don't believe Cochise here is part of the family tree," somebody yelled. "He don't look like any mail-order Indian." The men laughed. "He's a damn Sioux dog soldier—or maybe a sodomite!" A small crowd of them had moved over to surround the gray and Jones. The old man ignored them.

Dot couldn't take her eyes off him, biting at her lower lip as she watched his weathered face and small dark eyes. He looked peaceful. She wondered why she still cared about him after seeing those people in the canyon. It didn't matter why. She just did. She was scared for his life. These men were drunk and angry. She remembered Mrs. Abby's warning about the way he was dressed. All he had said was: "I won't be seen." But he had been. She guessed his medicine had gone bad like he said. He hadn't lied about that.

"You men Texans?" Maggie asked to keep them talking. "There hasn't been Indian trouble in these parts for a while, so why arrest my father?"

"Lady, you're fooling with us or you missed some important news. Apaches jumped the reservation a couple of weeks ago, headed for Mexico. We were just heading down to be of help when we cut their trail. Been tracking them hard for three days now. Should catch them tomorrow, or the next day."

For a brief moment, Maggie calculated the odds that these men were tracking the same Apaches who'd taken Lily. It wasn't probable. Then somebody tossed a rope over a tree limb.

"Let him go!" Dot screamed.

"You ever killed a white?" a man with dirty yellow hair yelled up at Jones. The old man ignored him.

"Gawdammit, say something!" The man slashed at Jones's shoulder with a riding whip, drawing blood. Chaco stood trembling for a moment, then took a flying leap off the gray, tackling the man's boots and causing him to dance. Finally the man caught the little dog in the middle, kicking him hard into the chaparral. The little terrier didn't come back out of the bushes.

"Leave them alone!" Dot squealed. Someone was holding her from behind and she was kicking backward at him and struggling to free herself. Maggie was fighting with another man.

They had a noose around Jones's neck now.

"I'm asking you again," the yellow-haired man wheezed. "You ever killed a white man?"

"No, he hasn't," Maggie shouted.

"I ain't asking you, strumpet-bitch."

Jones turned slowly and looked down at the man with a stare that—though he was near death and a slap-on-the-gray's-rump away from being hung—looked menacing.

He dropped his voice a notch. "Don't ever talk to her like that again." Maggie's eyes went to her father's face.

The man spit at him. "What you going to do?"

Jones didn't answer immediately, he just gazed into the man's eyes until he got uncomfortable and averted his stare and turned away. "You ever speak to her like that again," he repeated, "I'll split you from your navel to your nose."

The crowd laughed, appreciating the remark all the more knowing it had come from a condemned man. The yellow-haired man's skin reddened. "Let's hang him!" he screamed.

"Then get them out of here," Jones said quietly, nodding toward his daughter and granddaughter.

"Now, that we agree with!" somebody joked.

The men began marching Maggie and Dot out of the camp, both of them screaming and fighting.

"I'm Indian," Dot yelled back at them. "Hang me, too!"

Maggie jerked her shoulders free and stood looking at her

father, emotions flooding over her. All movement and sound seemed to stop, her body shuddering with the thought that he would be gone in a few minutes. They forced her away.

She tried to glimpse him through the trees, but couldn't. Sounds were returning to her. People were moving again, and she was remembering how proud she had once been of him. But the sense of pride was gone. Only a sense of longing remained.

The old man yanked himself around hard, looking for her, and the gray startled and jumped, the men grabbing and holding the pony still. "Whoa, you old bastard. We got to do this right. We don't want you choking and spitting, biting off your tongue, and pissing on us. Clean snap, that's only fair."

Jones was paying no attention to them, his eyes searching the darkness for Maggie. But she was gone.

Maggie stopped struggling and let the man shove her through the darkness, hurriedly tugging on one of her riding gloves as she moved. She waited. Waited until the grip on her shoulders relaxed some. Then waited again. She'd only get one chance. Then it happened, the man holding her glanced over his shoulder toward the campsite. It was her only chance. She stopped abruptly, the man bumping into her, raised her boot and stomped hard on his foot, then whirled and slammed a knee up into his groin.

The man was overweight and he exhaled hard and moaned, doubling at the waist. Maggie quickly judged the distance and stepped back—dropped her shoulder, shifted her weight onto her right foot, took aim and swung her gloved fist with everything she had in her 120 pounds. Swinging all the way through his head, the way Brake had taught her. Her knuckles smashed with a painful jolt against the man's temple. The man seemed to hang suspended in the air for a moment, then stumbled forward, sagging to his knees. Upright, but coldcocked. Maggie grabbed his pistol and darted frantically back toward her father.

"What the hell are you men doing?" a voice called somewhere ahead of her.

Maggie ran through the milling crowd and grabbed the gray's bridle, holding the horse steady, and waving the pistol at the men around her.

"You were to wait in El Paso," the new arrival said to the men. "What happened?"

Maggie took a better grip on the gray and Dot scrambled up behind her grandfather and pulled the noose off.

"You okay, Grandpa?"

The reply was faint, but strangely unafraid. "Fine, child."

"We thought you'd never quit that faro game, John," somebody said to the new man. "So we just drifted south. We knew you'd catch up."

Maggie saw him standing near the edge of the crowd. He was short-legged and mule-hipped, wearing a black bowler on top of a soft-looking face. Impeccably neat, but somewhere far this side of impressive. Still, the anger in his eyes held her.

"Just drifted south to hang a man without a trial?"

Nobody answered, the tone of the man's voice didn't encourage it. He worked his way through the crowd and stood staring at Maggie, tipping his bowler. She turned and pointed at Jones.

"That's my father."

The man looked at Jones and then back at her, and grinned.

"Your father?" the man asked. He was dressed oddly to be hunting Indians in the wilderness: a three-piece business suit, collar and tie. The suit had fancy pearl buttons that caught her eye. Maggie didn't see a pistol, but she glimpsed a marshal's badge on his vest.

She nodded again.

The marshal glanced up at Dot sitting behind the old man.

She was ready to fight. "Your grandfather, I assume?"

"Yes. And you shouldn't be treating him like this. He hasn't done anything. And one of them," she added, pointing angrily at the blond, "hurt his dog."

"That so?"

"Jesuspriest, John. Because a half-Indian kid and a pretty woman tell us we got to let an Indian go, we gotta do it?"

The marshal ignored the remark. "You men leave these folks alone."

He looked back up at Jones and burst out laughing. The old man was pointedly ignoring him. The lawman stood in front of the gray, grinning and scratching her ears. Finally he said, "Samuel, you look like a damn turkey with a porcupine humping its head in that outfit." Then he paused and looked at Maggie and Dot. "How many wives you got?"

Maggie looked uncomfortable. Jones didn't respond.

"I know an Indian one," the marshal continued. "Now it looks pretty certain you have a white one."

He pulled a pocketknife and cut the ropes off Jones. Then he stopped laughing and stood studying the old man.

"You don't look so good."

Jones glanced down at him. "Which Apaches jumped?"

"Stay out of that or the boys will lynch you. And I'll help them." He turned and started toward the fire.

Jones stared at the man's back. "Is he with them?" he persisted.

The marshal stopped and turned around. "I don't know, but you stay out of it. Hear? It doesn't matter. If he is, then he made the choice. And he'll have to pay." The marshal studied Jones for a moment longer, his face betraying a feeling of compassion, then he turned and walked to the fire.

Dot and Jones crawled down and combed the brush for the little terrier. They found him unconscious and bleeding from his mouth. Jones picked him up carefully, then remounted and clucked the gray over to the yellow-haired man and said, "Rifle."

"I got to give it to him?" the man asked the marshal.

"Yes."

Jones checked the battered Sharps as if it were a fine watch, then looked back down at the man and said, "My dog dies, I'll be back for you."

The man lunged. Jones brought his foot up fast and caught the charging figure square in the throat, the man crumpling to the ground and gasping frantically for breath, the vinegar gone. Dot had seen fights before, but none finished as sweet as this.

The marshal was drinking coffee and grinning up at Samuel Jones. Then he said to the men, "Leave Mr. Jones alone before somebody gets killed." He looked at Maggie. "Come eat. And let's talk about your lost daughter."

Jones was sitting quietly on the gray, his huge hands resting on the big silver saddle horn, his attention focused on the sand next to the horse. Maggie and Dot were listening to the marshal. The lawman had been encouraging Maggie to stay with the posse, promising to search for Lily. He got up and walked over to where an Indian sat alone on a rock. The two men talked for a while. Their tracker, Maggie figured. Navajo, from the look of his necklaces and stone earrings.

When the lawman returned, he said, "Mequecito says we're tracking Apaches. And he's good at ciphering." The man looked at Maggie. "You stay, we'll find your girl—and you'll be safer with us than riding around the hills in the dark. Even with that old man as your guide."

Maggie detected respect for her father in the marshal's comment and wondered how he knew him. She watched as the Navajo and Jones stood talking, then glanced back at the marshal. "My daughter isn't with them," she said. "You're following another group."

"They'll bunch sooner or later," the marshal said, building a cigarette. "Always do. Scatter like wolves, then come back together. Slick as quicksilver."

Dot moved closer to her mother. "Ma, we have to go with Grandpa," she whispered. "He'll find Lily."

"If Lily's down here," Maggie said, keeping her voice low, "which I still doubt, these men will find her long before your grandfather ever will."

"Please, Ma."

Maggie stood up and dusted off her pants. "Let me think on it, marshal."

An hour later, Jones was still sitting on the old gray, looking reluctant to leave. Maggie and Dot were near the fire, resting against some rocks. Dot was staring at her grandfather in a forlorn way. The sheriff was sitting nearby, smoking and drinking a cup of coffee, but also watching the old man.

"Ama," Jones said.

Maggie looked up at him.

"We must find Lily."

She shook her head no.

He watched her for a few moments longer, then said, "Alice can find me." He clucked to the gray and started into the darkness. Dot was sniffling.

"Please, let's go with him."

"No. Let's get our bedrolls."

"Samuel Jones," the marshal called.

Jones turned the gray around and sat looking back at the lawman.

The man didn't say anything for a moment. Then he cleared his throat and said, "You take care. Hear?"

Jones watched him through the wavering light of the campfire, and Dot thought that something invisible seemed to pass between them. Friendship, memories. Something. Then her grandfather nodded and turned the gray around.

The marshal and the men watched Jones and his little pony disappearing into the night. Nobody said anything for a while, most of them feeling a grudging respect for the old man and the way he'd coolly faced down his own death.

"He as tough as his talk?" a bald man asked.

The marshal poured his coffee onto the ground, nodding. "Pale around the gills now, but there was a time." He seemed to smile at some remembrance. "Those days I'd have thought long and hard before I'd have tapped him for a dance." He made another cigarette.

"If he's such holy-hell, how come we never heard of him?" the blond challenged.

Maggie and Dot returned to the firelight and sat down on the sand near the warmth of the flames.

Smoke from the marshal's cigarette was curling slowly in the cool night air. "He mostly stayed in Mexico. Clear of towns."

"Damnit, John," Red swore. "We were lynching the right sonofabitch."

Maggie and Dot both shot him mean glances. He kicked at a stone.

"He a breed?" the bald man asked.

"No," Maggie said. "He's white as you."

"But he's Indian in his heart," Dot said defiantly, then yawned. Maggie put her arm around her daughter's shoulders.

"I heard he went to college. That true?" the marshal asked, fanning a cloud of smoke away from his face.

Maggie nodded. "Boston. Afterwards, he taught school in

Connecticut, then came west to trade with the Indians for some St. Louis company." She paused. "After that, he farmed some." Her voice trailed off.

The marshal shook his head, amazed at the old man's changed circumstances. "When I knew him he was just a squaw man." The marshal poured himself fresh coffee. "Your mother?" he asked.

She turned red. "No. My mother was from St. Louis. I don't know who that woman was."

The marshal flicked the butt of his cigarette into the fire and took a sip of coffee. "White Mountain Apache. Cute gal—not much bigger than a deer tick."

Maggie felt hot behind her ears, hearing him talk about this woman who had destroyed her life. Nevertheless, she found herself waiting for him to continue. When he didn't say anything else, she cleared her throat and looked down at the sand beneath her feet. "Who was she?" She tried to make the question sound as nonchalant as possible, pulling her dozing daughter in close against her.

The marshal took his coffee cup in both hands and tipped his head back and looked up at the stars. Maggie liked him.

"Let me think about that," he said. "I was sheriff of Anthony near the border in the fifties. They'd come up from Mexico to trade two or three times a year. Those days an Apache could be in an American town without getting shot." He scratched the back of his neck and thought again. "One thing, she wasn't riffraff."

Curiosity was growing inside Maggie.

"Daughter to a head man of the White Mountain band. Royalty among Apaches. And she looked it. Pretty. Smart in her eyes. A certain pride. Always dressed in clean beaded buckskins. Had a nice way about her. I liked her. Liked her spunk. People in Anthony considered Apaches scum. She knew that, but she never let on. Always pleasant. She spoke a little English. I guess Jones had taught her."

The marshal looked at Maggie and smiled. "You would have been proud of her," he said, trying to be nice and not knowing the pain that his words caused her.

Maggie's immediate thoughts were confused. She might be a lot of things, but proud of this Indian woman wasn't one of them.

The marshal said, "That little gal loved your father. A rare thing in Apache women—loving a white man."

"Why?" Maggie found herself quietly asking.

"Straight-laced breed. Don't fool with whites or Mexicans. Don't marry outside their own kind. So I guess they had something rare." He laughed goodnaturedly again. "Your father listened to that little gal, no matter what the circumstances." He took another drink of coffee and gazed at the fire, thinking back to those years.

"Jesuspriest, John," Red growled. "He rode with the damn Apaches and we let him skip out of here like he was a Baptist minister."

The marshal took another sip of coffee, studying the man's heavy face over the rim of his cup. Finally he said, "You want him bad enough, Red, ride out after him. But go alone. Most of these men have wives and kids who need them."

Red thought a moment, then in a sullen voice, said, "Hell. He ain't that tough. But this isn't personal between him and me."

"I remember an August night," the marshal said, addressing Maggie, "when four Texas cowboys grabbed your stepmother on the sidewalk and started dancing with her. They were a bad bunch. Rumors were they'd killed a man up in Kansas, and I'd had trouble with them earlier in the day in one of the saloons. At first they were just dancing around with her on the street, holding her wrists so she couldn't get away. But they were drunk and they took to pulling at her clothes, until they got her top rigging opened up." He looked back into the flames, his eyes narrowing.

"Another Indian had gone for Jones, and when he got there things turned ugly. There was a law against guns in town. But not knives. And one of those boys pulled his and cut Jones. I guess they thought they'd scare him. You boys saw him tonight. He doesn't scare real fast," the marshal said. "Bad mistake. Before I got there, Jones had killed the one who'd cut him."

The marshal jammed his hands down hard into his pants pockets and stood gazing down into the fire.

"And?" the bald man asked.

"I ordered them to stop. Fired my pistol in the air. Shot at the ground near their feet. But Jones didn't know stopping. Some town women had hurried his wife away."

The marshal pulled on his lower lip and stared off into the night. He shook his head, grinning, as if the memory still surprised him. "I kept hollering at them, firing my pistol around them. Hell, I shot so many times I had to stop and reload twice."

The men were smiling and shaking their heads.

"I was looking like a donkey, shooting up my ammunition and yelling myself hoarse, and nobody paying attention. I even accidentally hit him in the foot, but he still wouldn't quit. He just kept hobbling around those cowboys."

The marshal stretched his arms to the sky and wiggled his fingers. The men and Maggie waited.

"All of them had their knives out. So I wasn't jumping in the middle to say howdy. But I had to conclude it." The marshal grinned sheepishly. "Sheriff was elected in that town."

The men roared.

"The Texans had had enough and were looking pasty. But not him," the lawman snickered, waving in the direction the old man had ridden. "Nope. He was determined to finish them. Never seen three sicker-looking cowboys in my life. I rather enjoyed that part."

"How'd you stop it?" somebody ventured.

"Shot him in the leg. Knocked him down like a poleaxed hog." The marshal stopped talking and looked like he was done for the night.

"That's it?" somebody asked.

"Hell no."

The men whistled and stomped their feet in appreciation of Jones's pluck.

"That man you were going to lynch—climbed out of the dirt and started after those boys again. Shot in the foot, shot in the leg and knifed, but still ready to fight." The marshal stopped and stretched his arms up again, as far as he could reach.

The bald man moaned. "Jesuspriest, John, you don't know story-telling from a bucket of piss. What the hell happened?"

The sheriff glanced at Maggie, who was watching him as intently as the others. "Your stepmother came running up." He paused. "Now I'm thinking this buffalo is crazy and going to have to be killed. When up comes your stepmother—a little itty-bitty gal—maybe she came up to here on me," he said, bringing his hand to a point just below his chest. "No taller."

Maggie figured the height at just under five foot.

"And in a voice I could barely hear, she says, 'Samuel.' "

The marshal's face broke up into a wide grin and he shook his head, like he'd just told a lie that he didn't expect anyone to believe. "That was it," he continued. "Just: 'Samuel.' Like she was calling him to supper. Nice as you please.

"And your father backs away—limps off up the street at her side. Like a big dog." He was chuckling. "Never seen anything like it before or since. Amazing as calling a bulldog out of a fight." He said, "That's love for you."

"Love. Stepmother. Smart. Pretty." Maggie couldn't get the words out of her head. They seemed to burn inside her like the lye she put into her washing soap. She stared at the fire for a long time.

"Mah-gee . . ."

Wet hair spilled across Maggie's damp forehead and her eyes darted wildly beneath their closed lids. Vague noises in her mind. The whispered voice again. . . .

"Mah-gee . . ."

She was squirming in her bedroll on the ground, the night cold, but her body covered in a sheen of perspiration.

"Mah-gee . . ." The voice seemed to plead with her.

She scissor-kicked, squealing in fright. Her eyes popped open. Maggie lay on her blankets in a pool of sweat, not moving. She was listening to the windy silence of the desert camp. Dot was asleep beside her. The marshal and the rest of the men were bedded down in various places around the campfire, the fire no more than glowing coals now. She wiped her face with the blanket and smiled. A dream. Nothing more. A crazy dream. She sat up trying to piece together its fragments.

Just a dream, she kept repeating. The familiar voice. Floating out of the night sky at her. The same dream-voice she'd heard for most of her life.

Whose? she wondered again. During all these years she'd never found the answer. Maggie rubbed her fingers gently over her lips and gazed blindly at the blanket, thinking about the strange whisperings. The voice of a child. An Indian child. The accent clear.

Thank God it wasn't like the first time. She could still recall that night, so many years ago, when she had been yanked into consciousness by the horrible screaming of her name . . . then a dark silence. She had never heard the scream again, as if the sound had floated away into the universe.

Now, only the little voice came to her.

Maggie shivered hard and pulled the blanket up to her neck. Tonight, the voice had said only one thing: "Leave."

Maggie fought the urge for as long as she could, then she pulled on her boots and got Dot up and hurried her along to the horses. It was crazy obeying a disembodied voice. But it had spooked her. It always did.

And, strangely, its whisperings were usually right. It had told her to marry Brake. Warned her the morning the Apaches had killed Thelma and Julia. She shivered again in the cool night air. She had learned to listen to this small voice in her head. It was the only Indian thing that she respected.

Dot stood wiping at the sleep in her eyes, then crawled up happily onto Alice and watched as her mother tightened the cinch on the roan.

"What made you change your mind?"

Maggie didn't turn around. "Just a little angel voice."

Dot smiled. Tired but happy.

They caught up with him as he and the gray trotted over a flat desert plain spotted with dark chunks of volcanic rock. Dot rode alongside her grandfather while Maggie brought up the rear. In between the rocks, the dusty plain was covered with creosote bushes and sloped gently down. The earth was cracked and dead-looking. Chaco was still unconscious and Jones was holding him in his arms. He barked weakly in his fitful sleep.

"How is he, Grandpa?"

"Hurt."

She studied the old man's odd face intensely from the side. Finally, annoyed by the attention, he asked, "What?"

Her eyes narrowed and she seemed to ponder something. "I

don't know what to think about those people at the wagons."

He stopped and put the red pigment back on her face and arms. Maggie cast him an angry look from the roan, but said nothing.

"Did you really do it?" Dot asked, standing and staring up at him.

They could see each other's faces in the dim light. He looked as though he were gazing through hers, then nodded.

Dot didn't respond, she just turned and crawled back up on Alice. They rode for a while without speaking, until she looked over at him again. "There's nothing. Nothing in the world should have made you."

He didn't respond.

They had put miles between them and the posse, when Dot next spoke. She could get angry at her grandfather, she just couldn't stay angry. It was an odd thing. "I'll pray God forgives you."

Maggie rode up alongside the old man and draped a flannel shirt over the little dog.

He didn't say anything.

The air was breezy and chilled and both Maggie and Dot wore sheepskin-lined jackets. Jones rode on in only his breechcloth and teguas, seemingly impervious to the cold. Alice had dropped back to her accustomed place behind the gray's rump, leaving Maggie alone alongside the old man. They rode on in silence. Dot had fallen asleep in the saddle and Maggie was afraid she would slip to the ground, and be lost in the dark.

"She needs rest," she said.

"You stop. I'll go on. Lily's time is short."

Maggie shook her head.

The horses were picking their way slowly through a stand of woody ocotillos when Jones next spoke. His eyes were focused on the dimness ahead of them. "Thank you for what you did back there."

Maggie looked at him, the gaunt profile barely visible in the night. "Please don't. I tried to keep them from hanging you so you wouldn't die a hero in Dotty's eyes. Nothing more."

She pulled the roan up and dropped back behind Alice.

They were climbing hard again as dawn broke, moving steadily up a series of rocky canyons, spooking bighorn sheep that were grazing on Mormon tea and wire lettuce on high ledges. The old man looked badly worn, exhaustion blanketing every emotion on his deeply lined face. The little dog had still not regained consciousness.

Maggie dismounted in a sandy clearing. They were surrounded by steep sandstone walls. She had stopped half in anger and half out of determination that they had to rest Dotty and the animals. She built a small stick fire and began making breakfast, her mind preoccupied with the marshal's story about the Indian woman and her father. But there was something else on her mind as well.

Her father had asked the marshal about another Indian. Asked whether or not he had jumped the reservation with the renegades. Maggie's worries focused on the question of whether he would try to find this man, perhaps leading them into the hands of the hostiles. He might. He just might.

Dot was sitting on the sand with her knees pulled up under her chin, watching Jones as he carefully dismounted with Chaco and stood next to the gray, getting his bearings against the hills. His movements were stiff and she could tell that his wounded shoulder was hurting.

Later, Maggie brought Dot a thin breakfast of boiled red beans and a little ham, then took a cup of coffee and leaned against a large rock a few feet away, staring blindly at the stone wall across the canyon. Dot ate and watched her.

"You thinking about Pa?"

Maggie half-smiled and nodded. "Yes. And James."

"Me, too. Maybe you should go home. We've got two people to worry about. Lily and Pa. We could split them up. You take Pa. I'll take Lily."

Maggie smiled. "That's just like you, Dorothy Baldwin, practical minded. Thanks but no. We'll go home when you're satisfied about Lily."

"That won't happen until we find her." Dot's voice implied more confidence than she felt.

Maggie sipped at her coffee, studying her daughter's thin face over the cup's rim, slowly resigning herself to the fact that after all her youngest daughter had been through, she could not abandon her sister. Even as the realization that Dot would struggle on no matter what the cost settled into Maggie's brain, frightening her in a way she didn't understand, she felt great love and admiration for the child. She pulled herself up straighter and poked at the sand with a stick.

"God," she prayed silently, her thoughts growing desperate. "Get us out of this. I'm losing Dotty. Please!" She closed her eyes and waited for some sign. There was none. Still, she was convinced that Jones was wrong, that there would be something. That God would not forsake her. She looked back at Dot and forced a smile.

"Just promise that when you finally face Lily's loss, you'll recognize it. Otherwise, you'll chase could-be's and maybe's for the rest of your life. Lily wouldn't want that."

"Yes, Ma."

Maggie looked off in the direction Jones had gone, watching him hobbling back toward them, Chaco cradled in his arms. From his slow, broken gait it appeared he was almost done for.

"He lives in dreams," she said sadly. "He'd love you to join him."

Jones squatted beside his granddaughter, laying the little dog carefully on the sand and pouring himself a swallow of coffee. He was gasping for breath, beads of sweat like tree sap covering his brow. Dot waited for him to say something, knowing he didn't like to be pressed into conversation. She watched the dog's labored breathing.

Finally, she cleared her throat. "Is he going to live, Grandpa?"

"I don't know."

Dot paused. "Which canyon do we take?"

"I don't know that either," he mumbled in a voice that sounded vague and uncertain.

He didn't look at her, just slowly swigged the coffee in his cup, tossing what remained onto the sand. Then he stood and carried Chaco over to a blanket, kneeling and laying him down and scratching the little dog's head.

When he looked up, his granddaughter was standing and talking to the gray, brushing deerflies from the old pony's head, then burying her face into her mane. A few minutes later, she turned and trudged slowly up the narrow canyon. He knew that her dreams drove her to save her sister, but he was losing any ability to help. He could hear the sharp scolding of a jay, uncertain as to whether the bird was angry with him. All he wanted was sleep. Confusion and doubt swamped him.

Samuel Jones was weak and feverish. His shoulder had been cut deeply by the whip; it was burning and he was lying on the ground, pressing his wound into the earth, using her to heal. He had done it this way since he had lived with the People of the shining mountains and been taught by their medicine men. He looked at Chaco, the little dog's head lying close to his own, remembering their times together. The child had not returned.

The workings of his mind drifted yet again to the Lame One. He could not stop thinking of the man. Uncertain why. Sensing only that he possessed power. Perhaps that was what drew him. No, there was something more. But he was too tired to grapple with it.

His thoughts drifted aimlessly, as if they were being blown helter-skelter over this desert by a hot wind. The marshal hadn't known whether Kayitah had jumped the reservation with the others. It was possible. He rubbed the back of his neck. He had not seen him in a couple of years. "Kayitah, be safe," he mumbled.

Maggie brought her medicine bag and squatted down next to him. She didn't look at him, she simply opened her kit and took out some things.

"Quit behaving stupidly—until you get that arm to the point it rots off."

He shook his head at her. "Ama. The earth heals."

"I've asked you to please not call me that. You don't have the right. And I'm not impressed by your Indian notions. Sit up."

He watched her for a few moments, then struggled until he was sitting up. Pulling the mud compress off the wound, she took a closer look. Her touch against his skin was a wonderful thing, he thought. She held his arm, examining the wound, beautiful hands, soft but strong, and a warm, almondlike smell in her hair. He could feel her trembling.

She opened the wound up some, then poured powdered alum over it that burned. He was surprised, looking at his own starved limb, at how far gone he was. It was almost over. He listened to her steady breathing, watching her work—efficient and gentle, determined to do the job, even if it hurt. She said nothing. He did not protest. When she slept, he would press the wound against the earth again to heal it.

Done, she closed the clasp of her bag with a small clicking noise that sounded sharp and final. He cleared his throat. "Ama." He paused. "I want to tell you why I left."

She stood quickly. "There's no reason good enough." She turned and walked off toward the horses.

Maggie gazed at the nearby cliffs and felt odd, a thin sheen of chilling sweat breaking over her skin. Ama. The name brought the memories flowing back. As she stood there, she remembered when he, too, had doctored. The plant medicine for the Mexican woman and her children had stirred the memories, but she had ignored them then.

But now, having worked over his wound, having touched his withered skin, felt the last of his energy and life in her hands, the memories seemed to flood over her and this time she felt as though she were drowning in them.

She stood straight and stiff and thought back more than thirty years. Her fists clenched involuntarily and she wanted to strike out with them or grab something and hold on tight. Her father had given medicine and care like she did on the ranch. She trembled, pushing the similarities out of her mind. Everyone had been welcome. Most had been poor. Some just desperate. Anyone who asked got care. Again, she thought of the similarities to her own work, and didn't feel comfortable.

She remembered her mother getting mad at him. He would never argue, but neither would he stop doing the work. The marshal was right, he was a stubborn creature. Only, she had admired him for it then. Now she just thought his stubbornness was stupidity. She turned and walked a few steps away, as if she could escape her thoughts by moving.

Over her mother's angry protests, he had used her as his nurse. Even now she couldn't help but smile at the memory—a regular nurse when she was just a kid, sparing her nothing in terms of what she saw or heard. He had treated her as if she were a grown woman. She hesitated, remembering how proud she had been. He called her "Ama," Mexican for a child's nurse. She had loved that name. No longer.

Susan had disapproved, saying that she was too young to be exposed to the human body. Too young for the pain and suffering; the dying. In response, he had always said, "Ama's soul is older than her life."

Standing there and thinking back in time, she remembered again the intense pride she had felt. An "old soul"—old enough to assist him, though the work be bloody or concluded by death. He had never wavered. And she had never failed him. His faith in her had been too great.

That was the reason she had never understood why he had left her, and never would. And why she hated the Indian woman. It didn't matter what the marshal said. She could never forgive—even if the woman was pretty and smart. It didn't change anything. Didn't make what she'd done right. The old familiar hurt returned. He was no longer heroic in her eyes . . . just pathetic, a broken alcoholic who had taken the easy road to damnation. In her heart she was fatherless, a fact she deeply mourned.

Fatherless. The Indian woman would never understand that. Would never know how much she had hurt. Maggie closed her eyes tight against the remembrances.

The day he walked out, she had waited up all night for him to return. Frightened and not knowing what to do. She baked the cookies he liked, the way her mother had taught her. And she waited. Waited at the kitchen table, listening to her mother crying . . . not believing he'd really left. Telling herself he couldn't leave. That he loved her. That she loved him.

He had once told her that love was the most powerful force in the world. And she had always believed everything he said. Until that night.

When the dawn came and the house was so silent that it hurt her to be inside it, she'd gone out to the barn and stood in front of his workbench. Just stood there. Stood and stared at his tools and talked to him; begged him to come home. To remember that she loved him. But he didn't come back. Ever. Even now, the thought brought a cold contraction to her heart. She shut her eyes.

They stayed on the farm for another year until they lost it. During that time, she never quit asking him to come home. Evenings, after she and her mother had cleaned up the kitchen, she would take a candle to the barn and stand in its wavering light before his workbench and plead with him. Sometimes she would pick up his tools and hold them the way he had. It made her feel close to him. But nothing she did—not her prayers or her pleading—ever brought him home.

The Indian woman would not understand what that was like. Nor would his excuses ever fill the void inside her.

Dot had climbed a small scrub oak and was sitting on a limb, closing her eyes and trying hard to believe, trying to get the same drifting, dreamlike feeling she had felt before. She held her breath. The sun was full in her face and hot. She tried breathing fast. Then slower. Chanting. Humming. Nothing. Her heart was beating harder. If she and her grandfather were right, this day or the next, at the latest, would be the last chance they had of reaching Lily before she disappeared across the border into the distant haze of haciendas, Mexican towns and cities; the last chance before she evaporated in the dry dust of that strange land. Dot was whimpering now. She loved Lily. She wanted her home.

She worried whether her mother was right about her vision

of the dragonfly and the cross not being real. The possibility frightened her. She looked back up the canyon, trying desperately to clear her mind. The unsettling thought came to her that if the vision was not real, if they were really lost, then so was Lily. Lost forever. She pleaded for the dragonfly to help her, knowing her mother wouldn't approve. But she had to. Lily was slipping away and it had brought them this far.

She studied the immediate problem that confronted them. There were four narrow openings in the canyon ahead. According to her grandfather, one would take them out, the other three were blind, but they wouldn't know which until they had traveled eight or nine hours through rugged, narrow canyon walls. If they were wrong and had to come back, it would be too late.

The possibility that they could be lost in this stone labyrinth and not find Lily began to penetrate slowly, cold and glasslike, into her consciousness.

It was late afternoon, the shadows of the rocks emerging from the canyon walls like living creatures, when Dot finally climbed down from the oak tree and returned to Jones and her mother. The old man was sitting cross-legged in the sand, gazing at his worn teguas and holding his arm in the new sling. He looked half-dead. Maggie was saddling Alice.

"I know which one," Dot said. "Or, at least, I know how to find out."

Looking at her, Maggie was taken by some sound in her voice. Dot was growing older, this tragedy speeding her along, aging her beyond her years. She hated to see it. Hated that this old man, her father, was doing to her child exactly what he had done to her. She went over and put her hand on the thin shoulder.

"Dot, there's no hocus-pocus Indian magic. There is nothing but life's chances. Search for her, but know that's all you're doing."

Jones had risen and was struggling to get the saddle on the gray with his good arm. When he finished, he swung a leg up and sat watching them, ready to ride. Maggie turned and looked up into his haggard face. Her eyes were pleading.

"Please," she said, looking first at her daughter, then back at him. "Tell her there's nothing to what she thinks she saw. Tell her Lily is lost. Please. For me."

Samuel Jones sat watching Maggie's face for a long time. She had finally asked him for something. After all these long years. He looked away to the distant hills and thought of Yopon and the children.

"I can't," he said slowly.

Dot clucked to Alice and started at a trot up the canyon. Jones followed. Maggie climbed slowly up onto her horse.

A few yards from where the four shadowy slashes split the granite wall, Dot dismounted and held Alice's head in her hands, leaning her own head into the warm coat, stroking the mule's flat cheeks. Alice nudged her. Jones sat on the gray, nodding off. Farther back, Maggie waited on the roan.

"You're a good mule," Dot whispered to her. "You found Grandpa. You know how it feels to search for someone you love." She looked deep into the jenny's brown eyes. "I need you to help me, Alice. Grandpa says the Power is with the young, so I can't ask the gray." Alice nibbled the edges of Dot's blouse. "Don't," she chided. "This is serious." The old mare had ambled up and stood next to them, as if she were listening. Jones was asleep on her back. Dot scratched idly at the old horse's head with one hand, while she studied the mule's eyes.

"Lily's in bad trouble. Alice, we've got to find her. Grandpa says animals can be spirits." The old man continued to sleep. "I think you are . . ." Alice snorted as if protesting the thought. "Which path do we take to Lily?"

The mule just stood staring blankly back to Dot. "Alice. Please. I need your help." Still she didn't move an inch. "Take your time," Dot added.

Minutes later, with Alice still staring back at Dot, the old mare moved off and entered the second cut in the wall. The child watched her, the mule pulling away and trying to follow. Dot grabbed Alice's reins and stopped her.

"Alice, wait," she said, peering into the mule's eyes again. "We can't make a mistake. Is this your choice, or are you just following the gray?" The mule swung her head and looked in the direction the mare had gone. "Alice?" Dot said. The mule swung her head back and looked at the girl, then turned and started off toward the place where the pony and Jones had disappeared. Dot didn't know what to think now. She looked back helplessly at her mother. The gray was old. Power waned in older creatures.

Dot hesitated a moment longer, then ran after the jenny and clambered up into her saddle, letting Alice have her head. If Jones understood what had happened, he never questioned the gray's choice. He merely rode, chanting softly to Chaco, looking glad to be on the move again, as if moving somehow kept him alive.

The gray's head was drooping permanently and Jones was concerned about her. He tried to walk as much as possible, sensing that her great heart was failing. He talked to her about her exploits, about the times when she had done great things. Remembering might not keep her alive, but she deserved, he felt, to hear tributes to her greatness.

"Grandpa, how much more can she take of this?" Dot asked sadly, as she watched the mare struggling gallantly up a thin rocky trail.

"As much as she needs to see it through."

Dot knew in her heart that the old man was correct. The gray was a fighter—Dot had been right about her the first time she'd seen her. Still, it pained her to watch the little horse fighting so hard. She started to suggest that they leave her behind and double up on Alice, then she realized that the gray would not stop even if they did this. She would follow. She was not doing this because they made her, but because she loved the old man and her courage was great, and everything was somehow tied to him. Their loyalty to one another was an amazing thing, Dot thought. They felt about each other the way she felt about Lily and her mother. That made her happy for a moment.

They rode through the evening and far into the dark night, climbing, struggling over rock slides, up narrow twisting trails that caused the animals to snort and paw nervously, over surging rapids where a small stream had become pooled by the narrowed walls, climbing higher and higher into the mountains. The gray went down twice and they had to wait a long time for her to regain her strength. The old horse's knees were raw and bleeding, and Dot cut a blanket into kneepads, tying them in place with cotton.

Finished, she put her arms around the pony's neck. "I pray you still have your power and that you chose the right canyon." Dot waited for some sign from the horse that might allay her growing fears. Dot's heart beat harder, she had heard some sound coming from the animal; then she realized that the mare was simply snoring.

Lily no longer had any sense of time, only that it was dark, and that she was starving. That's all she seemed to think about anymore. That, and water. She tried not to look at the body. Her mind drifted back to the question of how long it would take them to actually die of starvation. There were five other women huddled in the cave with her. None had eaten anything in two days, some perhaps longer. The hunger helped distract her from the small form lying in the dirt a few feet away.

Lily fought the trembling in her legs and arms, peering out the mouth of the cave at the Apaches huddled around the fire. The other women were asleep. All but the dead child's mother. She was sitting on the far side of the cave, staring blindly at her own hands, talking to them as if they were people.

She'd gone crazy, Lily figured. Glancing at the bloody nightshirt, she understood why. The Apaches were beasts. Dead or not, they shouldn't have dumped the body in the cave. One of them was sleeping in the back. Lily wished she could get to him. But she knew that was a lie. She was terrified of them. She wouldn't do anything, even if she had the chance. She was a coward.

She clutched the small penknife she'd found in Mannito's pants. She wanted to cry—but couldn't. Afraid. She shook her head back and forth hard, as if trying to dislodge something from her hair. She was even afraid to cry. Afraid that once she started she would never be able to stop, and they would kill her then. She moaned.

Lily forced herself to collect her thoughts, knowing it was her only chance at survival. She studied the Indians outside. Three were missing. Two of these had dragged the redheaded woman out into the night hours ago; the girl not much older than herself. She had begged them to leave her alone, telling them that she was married and had a child, begged until one of them had hit her hard in the face, breaking her nose. Lily felt unclean. She hadn't said a word, just pretended to sleep. None of them had. They were all cowards.

Some, like the red-haired woman, had been violated. She hadn't, but knew it would happen. All of them had been beaten—slapped and kicked or punched at the whim of their captors. Knocked down for trivial offenses. They begged constantly for water and food, and been given enough dirty water to keep them alive. Almost no food. She felt like an animal of some sort: a sniveling, dirty, hiding animal.

Lily gazed for a moment at the dead girl, then forced herself to look away, remembering the afternoon. She had been sitting in the sweltering heat outside the cave, watching nothing, just thinking of her family and the ranch—how much she missed them, how wonderful they were—when she'd seen a small white butterfly flutter down from the sandstone rocks and then float off across the parched sand. There was not a single flower to be seen.

It was a strange sight, this delicate creature adrift in the dry heat of the vast desert. She had watched it until it disappeared. It was as if the insect were all that was good and decent in her . . . fluttering away from her. The loss of her goodness. Her mother had once told her that people could lose the good that was inside them if they weren't careful. She believed her. Goodness. It was an elusive thing.

Her mind drifted to Mannito. He was good and brave. She groaned and pressed her eyes closed. Mannito. The little man had fought so desperately for her. He had died for her, refusing to leave her even when he had the chance. They had beaten him to his knees with clubs—wouldn't stop beating him. He had screamed, "The *viejo* will find you." For whatever reason, Mannito had liked the old man.

Sitting in the cave's darkness, desperate for food and water—desperate for help of any kind—she seethed, wondering where the "viejo" was. She knew all too well. Anger clogged her throat. She knew he was no good, a dangler looking for a free meal. Out only for himself. He wouldn't help her any more than he'd helped her mother.

She'd seen the posse that tried to rescue her. They'd passed within yards of where she had been held with a knife against her throat. She'd watched them. Seen her mother, neighbors, the sheriff . . . but not him. She had a right to hate Samuel Jones.

Lily stiffened. The Apache in the back of the cave had gotten up and was standing in front of her, stretching his arms over his head, his foot pressing down on the child's arm. Thank God she's dead, Lily thought, trembling at the nearness of the warrior. She averted her eyes, praying he would leave them alone. Then she saw it: the fingers on the small hand were moving. The child wasn't dead!

Lily looked at the woman sitting next to her. "She's not dead," she whispered frantically.

The warrior looked down at them.

The woman turned away and pretended to sleep. Lily looked back at the child's hand, the fingers clawing at the sand. Something broke inside her—broke as if a vessel holding her fear had shattered, the fear flooding away, replaced by rage.

"Get off of her!" Lily yelled, pushing herself up onto her bound feet and shoving the surprised Apache back. Off balance, she fell to her knees and pulled the child under her, bracing herself for the blows she knew were coming. But they didn't. The little girl stirred in her arms. She was still warm. Lily didn't move, waiting for the man to strike or kick her.

Cautiously, she raised her head, peering up at him. He wasn't looking at her. She waited a moment, then followed his gaze. The other one, the one she knew she'd see, was standing there. For a reason she didn't understand, this one, this grotesque, had been protective of her for days, keeping the rest of them at bay like so many mangy dogs. He was at the mouth of the cave, glaring at the warrior standing over her. Lily slid quickly back against the wall and into the darker shadows, tightly clutching the unconscious body of the wounded child.

Lily's attacker seemed to weigh the odds, then backed down and shuffled angrily out of the cave. "Good God!" whispered Lily, dragging herself and the child farther back into the cave. She kept glancing back at the freak of a man who stood watching her. "What do you want?" she mumbled to herself. "Thanks?" Looking at this pathetic creature, she couldn't feel anything but repulsion. His head, disproportionately large, the skin poxed, the features distorted, sat on a massive neck and shoulders. Below the waist, he was awkwardly bent, supported by one normal leg and another that was shriveled, so that he constantly looked as though he was about to take a bow.

Something in the man's features—the blackness around his small, wild eyes, and the sneering mouth—struck fear in her. A deep fear. His face marked him as mad. He watched her for a moment, then disappeared into the night.

Lily examined the girl. Maybe six or seven. She was gunshot through her stomach. Burning with fever and thirst. If she didn't get help soon, she'd die. Lily glanced across the dim light to the child's mother. The woman was still staring at her own hands. Lily clutched the girl closer, stroking her hair and talking to her. Then she reached out and picked up the doll and held both of them close. Promising the child promises she couldn't keep.

**D**ot wasn't certain when she first knew that something was wrong. The thought was just suddenly there in her mind. One moment they were riding through a narrowing place in the gorge; the next, she had this nagging feeling of fright sifting like sand through her. Then her grandfather and the gray stopped abruptly in front of her, the old man sitting still and rigid in his silver saddle, listening to the night and giving added rise to her sense of alarm.

The canyon was barren sand and stone, and this spot didn't seem different from the miles of ravine they had already passed through. But watching him, the way he held the Sharps high over the saddle horn in both hands, she knew he was expecting trouble. Even Alice was tense, her ears perked forward, listening hard. Then the gray snorted and started backing up. Jones put his heels softly to her flanks and she held steady.

Dot probed at the surrounding darkness with her eyes and ears, worried there might be a panther somewhere up the wind-chiseled bluffs. She was holding Chaco cradled in one arm and she quickly unbuttoned her blouse and slipped the little terrier inside against her skin. Then she pulled her shotgun from its scabbard and gripped it hard, letting her gaze move carefully over the boulders and jagged creases in the cliffs, searching for something—the flick of a tail, a glint of yellow cat's eye— anything to ease the bad feelings building inside her. Nothing. Things seemed normal enough. But things weren't normal. Alice sucked in air and held it, the way Dot knew mules will when they're frightened or angry. She could hear the faint calling of migrating geese overhead in the cloudless canopy of black, the sound lonely and strange in this desert land.

"Grandpa?"

He didn't say anything.

"Grandpa, what's wrong?"

"Men."

"Where?" she asked, her eyes darting quickly down the deeper darkness along the walls of the canyon. But she saw nothing unusual.

He didn't answer her.

"How do you know?"

Jones continued to ignore her, concentrating hard on the silence, then said, "The crickets, their rushes and lulls," as though talking to himself. He went back to listening.

That was crazy, she thought. Nobody could tell anything about anything by the sound of an insect, not even her grandfather. She turned and watched as her mother reached her hand slowly for her pistol grip, the act scary in a way Dot didn't want to think about. She glanced back quickly at her grandfather for some reassurance.

"That's sill—" she started to say.

Jones held up his hand, cutting her off. She caught her breath and tried to hear in the darkness that surrounded them whatever it was that was bothering him and his animals. But there was nothing. No wind. No voices. Just the chirking sound of the crickets and leather noises from their saddles. Then her mother's roan began to spin the metal roller in his bit and to turn nervously, Maggie reining him in hard. Dot shivered. The darkness was cavelike and smothering. She could hear the delicate lisping *tsit-tsit-tsit* of a scolding savannah sparrow somewhere in the nearby rocks.

Dot was busying her mind wondering what the little bird was doing in the cramped and rocky canyon when its kind usually lived in grassy fields. Then she noticed a large clump of shadow near the sandstone to her right that looked different from the rest, oddly shaped. Her eyes focused hard on it, and when it moved she realized with a sickening feeling in her stomach that it hadn't been a sparrow making the noise. Her grandpa had been right. It was a man. When she got them all spotted, there were four of them. Two in front and two behind. Mexicans. From their rough looks she knew that they were bandits, not Mannito's kind of Mexican. One of them lit a torch and the light from the flame reflected off the narrow canyon walls, illuminating the desolate place where they stood.

The bandit behind Maggie jumped up on the roan's rump, jamming the muzzle of his shotgun against the side of her head. Dot started to jerk Alice around so that she could bring her own shotgun to bear on the coarse-featured man, but Jones reached out and grabbed her reins.

"No play," he said firmly. "Drop it. Now. Slowly." He kept his eyes locked on the girl's face until he was certain she was going to do it. Then he looked back at the man in front of him and smiled his golden-tooth smile.

The Mexicans were staring through the darkness at the mean-faced old man's strange dress and Dot's red paint, looking confused. "*Fusil, señor,*" the one in front of Jones said, his Henry repeating rifle poking cautiously in the direction of the Sharps.

The bandit's voice was friendly and soft, but his eyes were hard and darting beneath a faded blue cavalry cap, and Dot sensed he wasn't right somehow. He had a muscle tic in his neck and every so often it caused his head to dip and his shoulder to rise until they slapped together, his face contorting in an odd grimace that made him look crazy.

Armitas, big flaps of tough Mexican leather, were held by a belt around his middle and tied to his legs, hanging down to the tops of his knee-tall boots, apronlike. Dirty-looking, the man was big and strong, his face chiseled, but without any dignity or refinement to it. He was pacing angrily in front of Jones now, the large rowels on his chihuahuas jaggling in the night air. Impatiently, he pushed the muzzle of his rifle at the Sharps again. "*Fusil.*" The word and gesture more threatening this time.

Jones leaned forward in his saddle and held the rifle out by the barrel toward him. Dot was stunned that he had given up his weapons so easily. She figured he was just too far gone. Frustration began to build inside her chest until it hurt. She looked back at the man behind her mother; he was pawing her, Maggie slapping at him.

"Leave her alone!" Dot shouted.

"Stay out of this," Jones said firmly. Dot stopped, not believing what she had heard.

The old man had swung down and was standing in front of the gray, naked except for his long clout and boots. His battered Colt revolver hung at his side. The big Mexican pointed the muzzle of the Henry at Jones again and said, *"Pistola."*

Again, the old man gave up his weapon without so much as a wink. Dot winced. They were at the mercy of these men now—and she sensed there would be precious little of that. Jones stood with only his war axe hanging from his side and a half bottle of whiskey. He took a drink. Dot felt shame for what her grandfather had done, something she never would have thought she would feel about anything he ever did. They were about to be robbed and probably worse by bandits, one was grabbing at Maggie, and he had surrendered his guns, ordered her to do the same, and was boozing. Dot turned back to the filthy-looking man behind her mother, glaring at him, trying to buck up her courage to fight the trembling in her body. Jones snapped his fingers at her and she turned back.

"What Indios are you?" the leader asked.

"Apache."

The man grinned. "No. Loco Indios." His friends laughed.

"Suit yourself, bean." Jones raised the bottle and took another drink.

The man's eyes were on the whiskey. *"Alto,"* he said, pointing at the bottle with the rifle.

Jones took one last pull on the mescal. The Mexican stepped up to take it away from him, reaching a thick hand and grabbing the bottle. The old man didn't resist.

"What do you want?" Jones asked, pulling his clout up and wiping his face.

*"Todo*—everything," the man smiled. *"Las señoritas."*

Jones nodded as though this were a perfectly normal request for the man to have made. He held the bunched-up material of his clout near his waist, then dropped it. Dot was watching him, not because she wanted to see him, but because she didn't want to see the others; then her eyes noticed something—a silvery flash in the flickering torchlight as if Jones had caught a creek minnow in his huge hand. Then it was gone.

Jones stood watching the man beside him, waiting as he tipped his head back to drink; the eyes of the outlaw's compadres were on the fluid inside the bottle. Jones raised his big hand, slowly, as though it pained him to have the man drinking his whiskey, as if he wanted the bottle back. Then he shifted the direction of his arm slightly, sticking his hand next to the man's temple. Dot jumped as lightning itself seemed to bolt from Jones's fingers. The Mexican's hair blew wildly, then she heard the explosion of the little hideout pistol, and saw the man's head recoil from the blast.

Without much wasted movement, Jones turned and shot the second man in the center of his forehead, just under the brim of his hat, a small spot of red that looked garnetlike suddenly appearing above his surprised eyes. A two-shot affair, Jones dropped the little pistol and pulled hard for his war axe. Sick and old aside, he could still move.

The man straddling the rump of the roan made one mistake: he misjudged Maggie, trying to push her out of the saddle with one hand while using the other to bring the muzzle of his shotgun around on the old man. She wasn't about to let this happen. She wasn't going anywhere, except after the bandit behind her, hitting at him and clinging stubbornly to the shotgun barrel until finally in desperation the man hit her with his fist, knocking her dazed to the ground. And even then she was still clawing at his leg.

Realizing he had lost precious time, his eyes wild and

showing white, the bandit twisted back hard toward Jones, yanking the gun's heavy muzzle around and taking the axe blade deep in his sternum with a *thunking* sound. The roan bucked, the gun boomed at the night sky, and the bandit rolled backward.

Maggie staggered over, wobbly and dazed, and pulled the shotgun from him, leveling it on the back of the last outlaw as the man scrambled frantically up the canyon. Dot winced and turned away, holding her breath and waiting. The blast never came. She was thankful.

The Mexican with the axe in him was making a horrible squealing noise like the one James's blue pig had made when it got run over by the freight wagon. It scared Dot badly. He looked too young to die. But she knew that was foolish. People died at all ages. He was trying desperately to breathe. Maggie was kneeling over him.

She stood and trotted quickly to her saddle and brought back her medicine bag, fumbling in it for cloth and scissors. Jones was beside her now, helping her cut the Mexican's shirt, blood spraying in fine droplets over their arms and faces. The man continued to make the squealing sound as they worked, his eyes locked on Maggie as though he would die if he stopped staring at her. He opened and shut his mouth without sound and Maggie leaned closer to him, still working desperately on his wound.

"*Manos*," he gasped. "Hands."

Maggie hesitated, then motioned with her head to Jones to take over, and reached out and grasped his hands in hers. The man squeezed hard, his eyes still fixed on her face, a horrible gurgling sound rising from the hole in his chest. Jones continued to fight the bleeding. Maggie watched him, then looked back at the Mexican.

"I've got to let go," she said softly in Spanish. The man just squeezed her hands harder. Maggie glanced at Jones. The old man shook his head slowly. Maggie looked back down at the frightened face. She watched him for a moment, then tried to smile reassuringly and cleared her throat and said, "Our Father who art in heaven—"

Dot was standing and holding the animals in the darkness of the canyon. When Maggie finished praying, the Mexican began to scream again. Jones reached and took his hands from her and held them.

"Son, listen." The Mexican stopped squealing and grabbed for breath, and looked at Jones. "Think of a place you liked as a boy . . . and go to it now. Go in your mind." The man's eyes moved slowly over Jones's old face. "Sit down in that place and hide. You'll be safe there. Be still and hide. Your gods will find you."

Jones looked up at Maggie. "Take Dot up the canyon."

She watched his face for a moment, then nodded. Maggie looked back down at the Mexican, sadness overwhelming her. So much death.

"Do you have a wife? A mother? A child? Anyone you want me to write?"

"I hurt—Mother of Jesus, I hurt," he cried, softly, blood bubbling on his chest now.

"Go," Jones said. Then he looked back down at the young man. "You are not trying. Find your secret place. Go now. You knew it as a child." The man quit struggling and seemed to be thinking back to another time.

They rode. The Mexican continued to moan and scream in his agony. He could not find his secret place, Dot thought. She looked around to see her grandfather still holding the man's hands and talking patiently to him in Spanish.

"Ma, can Grandpa help him?"

"He's dying."

Dot turned back and watched Alice's ears and tried to shut out the sound of the man's awful pleadings. They had traveled only a few hundred feet up the canyon when the report from the little pistol reached them. The screams stopped as if they'd been yanked from the night sky. Dot's eyes flew to her mother's face. Maggie stiffened but kept riding.

"Grandpa shot him," Dot said quietly.

"He was suffering. There was no hope."

Dot didn't respond, her thin shoulders just seemed to slump some. They rode through the silent canyon for a while longer, neither of them speaking when Jones rode slowly up to them. He made them stop and Maggie dismount, then he took a rag and water and cleaned the film of blood from her face and arms. Finished, he checked the bruise on the side of her head where she had been hit.

Slowly, she reached a hand up and put it on top of Jones's hand. "Thank you for saving Dot from them," she whispered.

She was standing with her eyes closed, holding his huge hand against her head. Then she pulled away and crawled back onto the roan.

Dot's mind was churning. Over the killings. Over Lily. Over the gray's choice. Wondering and worrying whether this was the rock passage that led to Lily or a dead end.

She got her answer a few hours later. Pitch dark, but near dawn, they were standing on top of a flat place, high in the mountains, at the end of the canyon. Both Jones and Dot believed they had made it to the place in the dragonfly dream—that the gray's power had worked.

Maggie felt they were crazy. Then she thought of the small voice that had come to her over the years, questioning whether or not they were following something similar. She shrugged the possibility off. It wasn't like God had spoken to her, not the way her father was pretending, with his mystic visions and things. Hers was just the kind of thought-voice—a kind of feeling in the bones—that people have when they get a hunch about something. She tightened up. Wondering why the voice in her head always sounded like an Indian child. She had no answer.

Dot hopped off and stood holding the gray's head. "Thank you," she whispered. The gentle-eyed horse nuzzled her. Without being able to see much in the darkness, Dot was nevertheless convinced they had finished the trek. She could hear water far below.

Maggie unsaddled all three of their mounts, then went and wrapped herself in a blanket and prayed, staring off into the night sky. She was still shaken by the ambush and the killings. But even more than that, by the fact that she and her father had nursed together again over a dying person—worked as they had so many times before—so many years before. It seemed a sacred ritual that they were committed to share. But Maggie wasn't certain she ever wanted to again.

She forced her thoughts to Lily, remembering everyday things about her daughter; gazing off into the void of darkness beyond the edge of the cliff, trying to see Lily in her mind.

Jones and Dot sat exhausted on the edge of the rocks that fell away beneath them for hundreds of feet. The gray was down on her knees, snoring peacefully. Alice was dragging one of Jones's blankets playfully across the small clearing. Maggie contemplated again the voice that had come to her over the years. Was there anything to it? No more than any woman's intuition, she figured. She slept.

The old man held Chaco in his arms, the little dog whining somewhere in his dreams. Dot studied the darkness below. The silence was full and deep. Her thoughts drifted to Lily, worrying that they had come too late, or that the band of Apaches would never cross here. The longer they sat and waited, the more questions and fears rose in her.

THE MISSING ★ 167

"Grandpa? Where's Mexico?"

"Where the birds are singing," he said, staring out into the darkness.

"Out there?" She listened to the chattering sound of birds she didn't recognize, and pointed out at the dark void beyond the cliff.

He nodded, shivering in the dawn air.

Relieved, she went and pulled a blanket off the back of her saddle and draped it over his wide, bony shoulders. He was sitting with his eyes closed. She jumped back. A wolf spider was crawling slowly over her grandfather's bare leg. She bent and picked up a switch.

The old man raised his hand and stopped her. "Don't," he said. "It has come to remind me of a promise. Nothing more." He made a circling motion in the air with his open hand over the creature. "I have not forgotten."

She watched as the spider moved off of her grandfather's thigh and scurried away over the rocks and sand into the shadowy night.

"What promise?" she asked.

He was silent for a while, then he said, "To a friend."

It must have been important, she thought, for a spider to search him out, way out here, to remind him. She hoped he would live long enough to do this thing for his friend. And to help her save Lily. But she doubted it. He looked too weak. And everything that was happening seemed so strange and farfetched. How could anything in her head have told her where Lily was going to be at any time in the future? And asking an old horse for help—a spider carrying a message. Her mother had a point. It was crazy.

She slept.

Dot woke slowly with the orange-colored dawn, rubbing her eyes. The blanket she had placed around her grandfather's shoulders was on the stone surface nearby, Chaco lying in the center of it. She was worried about the little dog. She didn't like him, she just worried about him. He had hardly moved since being kicked. Jones was gone. She could hear her mother humming softly behind her. She stretched. The morning sun had breached the far horizon with brilliant streams of light and these were shining warmly in her face.

She was fully awake now. "God, protect Lily," she said. She questioned anew whether God and the Power were one and the same thing. She knew her mother didn't believe that. It was confusing, but she thought they might be. But how could she be sure? Was believing in Indian things a sin? she wondered. Sin was a hard thing to figure. She stopped trying.

Dot stood and turned in a slow circle, her heart suddenly beating faster, her mind filled with wonder. She was looking out over the edge of the cliff. If she had any doubts about her vision, they vanished with that one glance. She had seen all this before. Seen it in her mind.

Perched some four hundred feet above the place where the two rivers intersected, she let her eyes move slowly over the waters and the surrounding rocks and the desert beyond. All these things had been at the place in her dream. The Power had worked. She went over and thanked the gray again, shivering as she stroked the mare's neck, happiness flooding over her. They would soon be with Lily. She was convinced of it.

Maggie was squatting before a small stick fire, frying bacon. Dot smiled and wrapped her coat tighter around herself and knelt in front of the fire. Her mother passed her a cup of coffee.

"Ma, this is the same place." Dot smiled over the cup's edge. Maggie ignored the remark.

Dot glanced up as the old man's head appeared over the edge of the slope. "Morning," she called happily across the rocks at him.

He put his hand in front of his mouth to tell her to lower her voice. She nodded. She was feeling genuine excitement for the first time since Lily had been kidnapped. Her grandfather laid a handful of desert flowers beside Maggie, then sat warming his huge hands over the fire. Maggie didn't look at the flowers. "Morning, Margaret," he said, formally polite. He was holding his injured arm.

"Good morning," she said, the words not friendly—but not hostile either.

Dot was smiling at him. "This is it, Grandpa. The place I saw."

He nodded.

Dot studied his face, her eyes narrowing, suddenly concerned. "Did we make it in time?"

"They haven't crossed," he said, pouring a cup of coffee.

Dot grinned at her mother. "Isn't that wonderful?"

"What? That there are no tracks down there?" She hesitated, then quietly said, "They aren't going to cross here. Ever."

"Ma, this is the place I dreamed of. Everything I saw in my dream is here."

"It just looks like a place of misery to me."

Jones built a low wall of dried mesquite brush near the edge of the high cliff for camouflage, then settled down to wait, steadily watching the river below, scarcely moving or seeming even to breathe. Periodically he thumbed through a couple of books, but his attention wasn't on reading. His plan, as he had roughly sketched it, was to wait until the kidnappers crossed the river, then to follow them into Mexico, stealing Lily back when the opportunity arose.

Dot moved closer to her grandfather, finding his presence, sick and unsteady as he was, strangely comforting. She thought about her father and brother for a while. Then Lily. Their life as a family had been wonderful. She doubted it would ever be again.

Chaco lay on the blanket between them. A few times during the day, Maggie had given water to the hurt dog. She seemed to like the little animal. Each time, Jones watched her caring for the dog—watched her as if she were a saint, as if everything she did, every movement she made, was of major importance in the scheme of things on earth. Dot also noticed that Maggie had placed the flowers on a small rock ledge near her blankets. That surprised her.

As evening approached, Dot was beginning to feel the sadness creeping up on her again, and she reached and put her hands on her grandfather's. Though she half expected it, he did not pull away. She felt secure, holding his old and battered hand in both of hers. Later that night, her mother did an odd thing that surprised her even more than the flowers. She brought two blankets, putting one across Dot's shoulders and the other on Jones's. It made Dot feel funny. Good, but funny.

The thin crescent moon was floating high over the desert and Maggie was sitting near the horses, watching the stars above, when Dot stood and stared down at her grandfather's ghostly visage. With his head so thin, his skin like fine, dry paper pasted over bone, it sometimes frightened her to look him square in the face. At these times, he appeared already dead to her. He looked like that now. She didn't like to talk to him when she felt like this, but she had to. Her nervousness was increasing. The Apaches should have been here. It was more than three days. Her dream had said three days. Something had gone wrong.

"Grandpa?" she whispered.

He didn't answer her, but he had been coughing quietly,

muffling the noise in a rag he carried, and she knew he was awake. "Where are they?" Doubt crept back into her thoughts. Jones didn't answer her. She was getting frustrated with him, he spoke so little, he rarely confided in her.

"I found my medicine."

"You were visited by your medicine spirit. That was all."

"That's the same thing."

"Until you can control the things in this life, you have found nothing."

She thought about this for a while, watching a thin cloud slide over the moon, then turned and looked at him.

"I don't get it."

"I told you once," he said impatiently.

"Tell me again."

He looked at her for a few moments, then turned back to stare into the dark void before them. "Control life through your beliefs, then—and only then—you possess it."

That's impossible, she thought, but didn't say it.

Dot went back to her blankets and slept.


Jones pulled his canvas journal out and searched its worn pages for a while, peering hard at it through his little glasses, squinting in the thin light of the moon. He seemed to be counting and calculating something. Finished, the old man rose and took his bottle and two cups and went and stood in front of Maggie.

She looked up at him.

"Let's drink to your mother."

"Why?"

"Because we must not forget her."

Maggie continued to study his features. "I never have."

Neither of them spoke for a while, then Jones said, "You were born on a night like this." He stood looking at the stars overhead. "Susan's mother was dying. We were trying to get there when your birthing came. We made a rough camp." He paused. "She bled a great deal and neither of us thought she would live. For days she drifted in and out of delirium. Each time she awoke she made me promise that I would tell you that she loved you more than life."

Maggie studied the sand.

He held the cup out toward her.

She shook her head.

"Ama, this week is her birthday, I think. I've lost count some. But it is close enough."

Maggie tensed, then calculated some on her own, her lips and fingers moving in the darkness. Slowly, she reached out and took a cup from him. He filled it with whiskey.

Jones put the bottle down and cleared his throat. "Do you mind? I say some Tennyson each year."

She shook her head.

He cleared his throat again and stood up straighter. Maggie watched a night hawk dart across the moon.

> "She is coming, my own, my sweet;
>> Were it ever so airy a tread,
> My heart would hear her and beat,
>> Were it earth in an earthy bed;
> My dust would hear her and beat,
> Had I lain for a century dead . . ."

Jones raised his cup to the starry sky. "Susan. To you, to our children and what we once had." He took a drink. Maggie turned away so he wouldn't see her eyes and took her own large gulp of mescal, nearly choking on the burning liquid, and pondering yet again about this old man—who he was and what he had done, and what she felt toward him. And she pondered something else: all the nights that she had heard her mother sobbing in her room in a hundred towns, talking to him as if he was there with her. Could it have been that he, too, was sitting somewhere in this vast desert talking to her? Perhaps. Perhaps her mother hadn't been crazy after all. That thought made her feel better.

He sat down on the sand next to her and they considered their separate remembrances, and drank in silence.

"There were reasons I left. Reasons for those people in the canyon."

Maggie didn't say anything for a while, the alcohol numbing her; then she said, "Just tell me about Mother."

"What do you want to know?"

"Who she was to you. What you talked about. Those things."

Jones turned and looked at her and nodded.

They stayed up most of the night talking and sharing the mescal. They became drunk. They laughed a little at old stories remembered, and told each other new things about Susan. They talked about her pandowdy and pepper pot stews; about her love of dancing quadrilles and sleighing over frozen rivers on moonlit winter nights. Her theories of life and happiness. Her courage and resourcefulness. Her quirks. The way she dressed and argued and laughed. Then Maggie told him how she had just given up life, lain down and died in her bed one day. She said this without bitterness. Neither of them spoke for a while. And somewhere in the deepest part of the night, Maggie felt something come alive again for Samuel Jones. Something that she had thought was dead forever.

Though they talked of many things, nothing was ever said about why he had left. For some reason Maggie was afraid to hear the reason, was afraid to listen to him tell her that he loved another woman—an Indian—more than her mother and her. She knew he sensed her fear. She also knew how important the explanation was to him. But he did not mention it again. It was good of him to spare her this, she thought.

Jones sighed heavily, his eyes focused on the sand beneath his feet. "Tell me about Thelma."

Maggie waited a moment, then talked about her little sister for a long time. Described her tallness, the dark coloring of her beautiful hair, her gentle, caring ways, and how she rushed her words when she was excited or happy. Her love of school and music. Her laughter and the goodness of her heart. And he listened carefully, examining every word and what they all said about this child of his that he had never known. He asked many questions. She tried to answer all of them.

There was something painfully beautiful in being able to describe her sister—this woman she had loved so deeply—to their father. It was as if she were introducing strangers who had seen each other from afar, and fallen in love, though they had never met. And for a moment, she was overwhelmed by a feeling of wonderful, replenishing love . . . a feeling that Thelma was hovering in the night air above them, listening to her talk and smiling down. But that was silly.

She looked up to find his small eyes studying her intently. He shifted quietly on the sand beside her.

"Did she know anything about me?"

Maggie cleared her throat. "Mother told her." She paused and looked into his face. "She kept you alive for us." She looked back down at the sand.

He twinged, something seemingly tearing loose inside him at the thought of this abandoned woman faithfully keeping his memory alive for his children. Waiting for him. Searching for him. "Susan," was all he whispered to the night sky.

If Maggie heard him, she didn't say anything. Her thoughts were confused by new emotions swirling inside her. She tipped her head back and watched the stars, swallowing hard a couple of times. "We deserved more. At least Mother did."

"I'm sorry." ·

"I don't want to hear sorry," she said sadly. "I just want to forget." Her hands were shaking badly.

"How did Thelma die?"

She didn't answer.

"Ama."

"You don't want to know."

"Yes, I do."

"Indians. Apaches," she said. "They killed Mannito's wife as well." She hesitated, staring at his craggy face. "They've killed most of the things I love—one way or another."

He began to chant softly.

He had not stopped his low chanting when Maggie drifted into sleep. She dreamed of her mother and Thelma and Lily. It was the first time in what seemed a lifetime that she felt whole again. Not quite, but almost. But when she woke in the morning, the wonderful sense of well-being was gone, replaced by a nagging guilt that somehow she had been unfaithful to her mother. And the old familiar feeling of stiffness toward her father and the Indian woman had returned.

Jones was showing subtle signs of tension by noontime, leaning forward some, scrutinizing the sand and trees below, as if determined to will Lily's kidnappers to appear, then rising in a stiff crouch and moving back to the gray, coughing hard and spitting up blood. He took the rag and clamped it over his mouth. When he had recovered, he said, "I'll check the river again, to see if they crossed during the night," the words gasping out of him.

Maggie contemplated the rock under her feet, shaking her head slowly, as if what he'd said was the dumbest thing she had ever heard. In some ways, Dot guessed, it probably was. Watching her mother, she caught a flicker of movement from the corner of her eye, and turned fast, studying the spot below. Her heart sank. Nothing.

Jones had seen the jerk of her head, and he moved quickly, squatting close to her so that he could fix the location. "What?"

"Nothing. I just thought I saw something move down there by that stump."

"Sit still." His tone was deadly serious.

They waited almost an hour before they saw the man. He rode slowly out of a thicket of locust trees that ribboned the far edge of the sandy bank, moving his horse forward a couple of yards onto the sand, and then stopped and sat and studied the river. He was Apache.

"Is he one of them, Grandpa?" Dot said in a hushed, anxious tone.

The old man didn't reply. Maggie had walked over and was standing behind them, a strange look on her face.

"Down," he said. She squatted.

"Is he one of them?" Dot asked again.

"He's nervous," Jones said quietly, as if to himself. "He knows something isn't right." He looked at Dot and Maggie. "Do not look directly at him. Think of something else. And don't move," he whispered. Then he looked back at the Indian. "Peace and serenity, traveler. Safety lies across the river. Lead them forward. Cross," he said softly, directing his words and thoughts at the motionless figure below.

"God," Maggie whispered. "This can't be true." Every few moments she would look away from the Indian, back to Jones, scrutinizing his face, as if she were seeing him for the first time, and didn't understand something. She was wringing her hands together.

The Indian sat motionless on his horse for half an hour. Dot couldn't see what he was doing, her vision blocked by brush, but she figured her grandfather was right, he was trying to understand what was bothering him. She listened to the old man coaxing the fear and doubt from the stranger's soul. Encouraging him to lead them across.

"Lily's down there," Dot said, the excitement too great to contain any longer.

"Where?" Maggie said, standing again.

"Down and quiet," Jones hissed.

"Where?" she repeated.

"I just feel her."

"Both of you, stop."

Minutes later, the Indian turned his horse and disappeared back into the trees. "He's getting away," Maggie groaned, standing once again. "We must go after him."

"Margaret." The old man watched her for a moment, then said, "Lily's life depends on you sitting down and being quiet."

She sat back down and reached into the saddlebag lying on the rock beside her, pulling out her Bible. Jones watched her to make certain she understood, then he turned back toward the river.

Maggie didn't know what to believe. She had seen the Indian. Was he one of Lily's abductors? It seemed incredible. What game was God allowing to be played? What strange powers did the old man possess? Or was he simply right? Right about Indian religions. Right about Christianity. Was God unwilling to help mankind? That thought numbed her, her hands trembled. She couldn't imagine her world without God.

She retraced the happenings of the past few days. They had ridden over three hundred miles from the ranch to this lonely spot on the Rio Grande, crossing dry, trackless desert, rugged stone mountains, following no roads, no tangible landmarks. They had come here because of Dot's dream. The old man had translated and unraveled it, claiming it a message from the Indian spirits. That was impossible. Yet, here they were.

She had seen the Apache. He was no spirit.

She rubbed her face. Could Jones and Dot have divined this place in their minds? What of her own prayers? They had brought nothing. She studied the old man. Wondering. She rethought things about him. If this was really happening—if they had truly found Lily—then she had been wrong. For the first time in thirty years, he might possibly have been there for her. She studied his bony profile, the high bridge of the nose, the heavy brows.

Near sundown, Dot glanced at her grandfather. "They aren't coming."

He turned and looked at her. "Is that what your medicine tells you?"

"Just what I think."

Jones was turning back when down below a line of riders rode slowly out onto the strip of sandy shore, heading for the water. Dot saw her sister's spirited bay dancing in the long line of horses.

"It's Lily!" she squealed.

"Where?" Maggie said, pulling a pair of binoculars out of her saddlebag.

"See her! She's carrying something in her arms."

"No!" Jones hissed. Too late. Maggie already had the binoculars to her eyes, the setting sun bouncing off the glass, the light flashing back over the sand and the riders.

The Apaches yanked their horses to a halt and Dot heard them cocking their weapons. But they didn't fire or run for it. They had guts—and something else: the women. It was a card they knew how to play and they sat calmly staring up at the rock ledge. For a moment, neither side moved. Then a heavy-bodied Indian with a deformed leg trotted his horse back along the line of women until he was next to a Mexican girl on a shaggy brown horse. He turned and looked up at the cliffs, glaring defiantly at them, then grabbed the reins of the girl's mount and led it away from the others. Even at a distance, there was something in his dark eyes that frightened Dot.

Maggie stood frozen, the reality of what she had done splashing over her, flooding her with cold guilt. And fear. Fear for Lily's life. Dot glanced at her grandfather. He hadn't moved. His eyes were locked on the heavy Apache. Maggie sank down slowly onto the rocks, looking ill. The cripple seemed to be daring them to shoot. Then he raised his pistol and fired into the base of the girl's neck, nearly decapitating her. For an instant she seemed to fly away from the Apache and the horses, landing facedown on the sand. The concussion of the explosion slapped at the cliff and Maggie blanched.

Still the rider didn't move, his eyes fixed on them. He sat this way for a long time, and Dot could tell that her grandfather was struggling to control the anger within him. Finally, the Indian turned and cantered slowly for the river; the others followed, trotting their horses single file, each man riding with a captive between him and the ledge. The riderless horse went with them, the sand darkening beneath the dead girl. Dot couldn't stop looking from her to her sister.

It was suddenly too much for Maggie. "Lily!" she screamed, lunging for her rifle. Jones beat her there, holding her and clamping his hand over her mouth. She bit him, but still he held his hand over her face.

Then a clear voice rose from the river below, the sound making all that they had struggled through worth it in Dot's mind. "Mother!" the voice called. It was Lily.

Maggie struggled harder but Jones held her down.

"If you keep this up," Jones said, "they'll kill another one. And this time, it could be Lily." He watched Maggie for a moment. She stopped struggling. "I'm going to let you go.

Don't say a word. For Lily's sake."

When he released her, Maggie stumbled to the ledge and looked through the glasses once more. "Lily, Lily, Lily," she cried softly. She watched until the riders disappeared in the mesquite on the far side of the river. She had seen her daughter. They had found her! But the relief was quickly swallowed by a sense of helplessness and shame. The girl lying on the sand below was dead because of her. And Lily might be lost. Forever.

The Lame One sat in the shadows of the trees and searched the cliffs across the river. He had seen the woman and the old giant. They'd come for the girl. He fingered the watch, opening the clasp. That was where he had seen her. The man beside her in the photograph was the one they had shot the day they killed the Mexican and took Li-Lee. He still didn't know how the old man fit into this. He didn't look white. It didn't matter. Somehow he fit. He glanced back down at the picture, the idea coming full-blown in his mind.

He had heard the girl pleading across the river to her mother. She had called her name: Mah-gee. He smiled. He possessed magical things of hers: How she was called. The time stealer. Her spirit-image. It was enough.

Jones waited until it was full dark, then he led them quickly down out of the hills, traveling west. He was pushing hard, cantering through deep sands, trotting in the river shallows until they were drenched and frozen, moving over jagged rocks, then cutting northwest across deep drifts, riding away from the Apaches. His mind was on the lame rider.

Dot couldn't figure it. He was behaving like a crazy man. She kicked Alice alongside the gray. The old horse had lathered early and was making a harsh breathing sound. Jones was cradling Chaco's still form in his arms. Maggie rode behind them, slumped over her saddle, looking back every few minutes as if she might still catch one last glimpse of Lily.

"We aren't following them," Dot called, her teeth chattering.

He shook his head. Though he continued to wear only his medicine shirt, breechcloth and teguas, his legs damp with river water, Jones didn't appear cold.

"Why?" she asked.

"They're following us. Least some of them."

"Why?"

"To find out who we are. Then, when they find we are only three, to finish us before we alert the Mexicans across the border."

"What do we do?" Dot asked nervously.

"Put distance between us—headed where they don't want to head."

"What about Lily?"

He stopped talking.

"Grandpa?"

He looked at her, annoyed at her continual pestering. "Hope we can pick up their trail."

"Can we?"

He didn't answer. He just held Chaco's little body tighter and clucked the gray into a hard trot, the old horse seeming to teeter on her legs, as if she might topple over, then she straightened out and settled into her familiar jolting shuffle. Dot looked behind her and felt suddenly frightened of the night. She dropped back until she was next to the roan. Maggie didn't look at her. Dot leaned over and grabbed her mother's reins and kicked Alice into a canter, the roan following.

Dot rode this way, leading the roan and forcing Alice to stay alongside the gray, for several hours, until Jones stopped and sat scrutinizing the vague shape of a sandy hill that rose from the desert pan like a small pyramid. The old man was squinting hard and looking uncomfortable. Even the gray seemed preoccupied with its odd conical shape, lifting her tired head and seeming to study it.

"Grandpa!" Dot yelled.

Jones turned to see Maggie vomiting over the neck of her horse. Dot wet a rag and tried to give it to her but Maggie ignored her. Then suddenly she began to babble. Jones rode alongside her and put a hand to her forehead. She was burning. He turned and looked at the small hill once more, the strange sensations stealing over him again. He put his heels to the gray.

"Bring her," he called to Dot.

A few miles later, Jones guided them down into a small gully, dismounting and walking back and looking up into Maggie's face. Dot looked scared.

He reached up and gently coaxed Maggie into his arms and off the horse, drool running from her mouth.

"Spread some blankets for her," Jones said, fighting a cough.

"What's wrong with her?"

"Just spread the blankets."

Maggie was babbling in a tongue that sounded Indian to Dot.

Jones stroked her hair. "Sleep, child," he whispered, as if she were still small. He touched a finger to her lips but she would not stop her incessant chattering.

"Grandpa, what language is that?"

"Apache."

Dot looked frightened. "She doesn't know Apache."

The old man didn't respond.

He was troubled by much more than the fact that Maggie was babbling in a strange tongue. The Apaches hadn't pursued them. He couldn't figure why. He had seen their horses at the river. They were fresh and well fed and he had fully expected a fight before they reached the gully. But nothing. Their backtrail was empty. Nor did he understand the unsettling feelings he was getting whenever he thought about the little sandy hill.

He knelt and studied the twitching muscles of Maggie's face, reaching out one of his hands and holding it tenderly to the side of her head. "What's wrong, child?" His skin tingled and he pulled it away. She did not move.

J ones rode through the night headed back toward the small hill, momentarily confused directionally. That rarely happened. But for some reason he couldn't remember where the cone-shaped hill was located. Confusion swamped him. It was as if someone or something had snatched the information from his mind. But the little gray seemed to know where they were going, picking her way determinedly through the cactus, over sand drifts, down long sloping plains. She moved at a steady gait, her walk chewing up the miles. Juncos were calling in the darkness around them. The old man rubbed fresh red pigment into his skin, and put red handprints on the horse's shoulders and rump.

They rode steadily for more than an hour. Then the gray stopped and the old man got down. He put a hand on the animal's thin neck and patted her, marveling at her powers. He was used to them, but still he marveled. How had she known to come back to this place in the vast desert night? He had no answers.

They were standing at the base of the small conical hill that rose some fifty feet from the desert floor like a sacred temple in this sprawling wasteland. The old man checked the cartridge in the Sharps and then started up the sandy slope.

The little ring had been drawn in the sand: the dark origin of his circle dreams. Jones chanted for a few minutes and then lit his calumet and blew smoke carefully over it. Only then did he squat down close to the circle and examine the things that lay within its magic realm. He made certain that he did not touch it.

The tiny photograph of Maggie and Brake was propped against an agave pad in the center near someone's withered eyes. The long hair of an animal's tail—the roan's it looked like—was curled around these things, everything sprinkled with mica dust and cattail pollen. Looking at the glazed and sightless orbs Jones knew fully what manner of man was the Lame One. His heart began to constrict, fear building in him for Maggie.

He burned the eyes, the hair and the photograph in a hot mesquite fire because the lame man had touched them and spoken over them. Then he ran stumbling down the hill to the sleeping gray.

Lily knew it had to be now. Help was close by. As close as it might ever get. And the child couldn't wait.

Slowly, she cut the rawhide with Mannito's knife, then waited for the Apaches to pass deeper into sleep. The little girl was whimpering again, sweat beading on her forehead, unconsciously clutching her rag doll in her arms. Lily stroked her hair and said a prayer for her, and thought of Dot. "I love you, Dotty Baldwin," she whispered in the darkness.

She squinted and counted six Apaches again. She had been counting them every few minutes. The cripple was missing. It was not unusual, he often disappeared, usually returning with another woman. She studied the child's mother where she lay sleeping on the sand. Still not right in her head. But she had to take the risk of bringing her. She stood slowly.

They'd gotten away clean, the woman smiling and following like a well-trained dog as Lily slipped past the sleeping Apaches. Fortunately, the Indians had been drinking hard and were sleeping it off.

Carrying the child and her doll, Lily led the woman quickly down the narrow arroyo, hurrying toward the place where the Indians had hobbled the horses.

The woman stopped.

Lily turned. "What's the matter?"

"My husband," she said softly. "He's calling me."

The woman was crazy, but she still might have heard something. Lily focused on the expanse of night around them. Nothing. Then a moment later, she heard it.

"It's just the horses."

Lily placed the injured girl gently in the woman's arms, watching her face to see if she would retreat. She didn't. She just turned and gazed at the darkness surrounding them, as if she were searching for someone in a crowd. It made Lily want to cry.

Lily was saddling the bay when the woman began to walk slowly up the trail. "Don't wander off," she hissed.

"I'm just going to pick those berries I promised you."

"We don't need any berries. Stay here."

But the woman had disappeared in the shadows. Lily started to go after her, then stopped and went back to the horses, figuring she'd just have to keep rounding her up until she got her into the saddle. Finished with the bay, Lily quickly saddled the best animal she could find for the woman, tightening both cinches hard. Done, she turned and looked for her.

"Let's go," she called softly.

Lily thought she heard something in the darkness ahead. But the sound was gone now and she wasn't certain she'd heard anything but her own fears. "Where are you?" she called.

Lily was trotting in the darkness, hunting frantically for them, when she tripped over the woman's lifeless body. She was sitting spread-legged on the sand, leaning back against a large boulder, holding her entrails and her dead daughter in her hands, and staring up at the night sky; smiling as if she'd finally found whoever it was she'd been searching for. The doll was in the dirt.

Maggie was muttering and cackling like an old hag. Her face swollen almost beyond recognition, no longer did she look like his child. Jones sat holding his calumet, smoke drifting slowly from its red bowl, watching her. Dot was nearing panic, eyeing the small red blotches forming on her mother's neck and face. Suddenly Maggie stopped babbling and lay staring up at the night sky.

"Dorothy?" she called through her puffy lips.

"Ma?"

Maggie's face grimaced. "Dorothy, help me up."

"No!" Jones said sharply. "Do not touch her."

"Ma, what's wrong?"

Maggie smiled weakly. "I'm just a little tired, that's all," she said in the strange falsetto. "And my eyes are blurring."

Maggie struggled into a sitting position, and Jones pulled a saddle behind her and she leaned into it. He squatted in front of her and studied her face.

Maggie closed her eyes as if she were going to sleep, a

tremor shaking her.

"Ama." His voice was firm.

Maggie looked blindly through him.

"Where are they?" he asked.

"What?" She cocked her head to the sound of his words.

"The necklace and the pollen that I asked you to carry."

She thought for a moment, then said, "I threw them away. They belonged to that woman." Maggie's eyes focused for a moment and darted fearfully to Jones. "What's happening to me?"

He stood quickly and went to his saddle and untied a small leather bag.

"What's wrong with her, Grandpa?"

"Ama," he called over his shoulder. "You must help me. Besides your vision. What else is wrong?"

Maggie was babbling again.

"Ama," he said louder. "Listen to my voice—what is wrong? Tell me." She didn't answer.

Jones rubbed red pigment onto the palms of his hands and pulled one of her boots off and took a pin and pricked the bottom of her foot, until he drew blood. She didn't move. Dot's eyes widened.

"Is she going to be okay, Grandpa?"

"Quiet, child." He sat thinking for a moment.

Suddenly Maggie sat up, her eyes open wide. "Dot," she said, turning her head, searching for her daughter. "My crucifix."

"No," Jones said, holding up his hand to stay the child and ignoring Maggie's rantings. "Do not get near her."

Dot trotted over and pulled the cross from her mother's saddlebag, returning quickly to stand beside her grandfather.

"Child. Sit near her feet. When I'm ready, follow the things I say. I will tell you when." He glanced at Dot. She looked scared, her eyes locked on Maggie's face. "Dorothy. Do you understand?"

She nodded and reached to put the crucifix in her mother's

hand.

"Do not touch her," he said firmly. "She is not clean at this moment."

"What do you mean?"

"Her spirit is being held. The Lame One is a pesh-chidin." That, Jones knew, was why the Apaches hadn't followed.

He was leaning over Maggie now, his fingertips covered in fresh red pigment, her eyes darting wildly over his face.

"Don't please," she said, struggling to move.

"What's a pesh-chidin?" Dot asked, trembling and watching her mother's angry face.

"I don't care," Maggie muttered.

Jones smeared the red pigment over Maggie while she twisted under his hand and recited the Lord's Prayer.

"What's a pesh-chidin?" Dot asked weakly, as though she didn't really want to know.

Jones smeared Dot's face in fresh pigment. Finished, he looked back at Maggie and said, "A witch."

"Witches don't exist," Dot said.

Jones stared at her until Dot looked down at her mother. "What's wrong with her?"

"Ghost sickness."

Maggie closed her eyes and seemed to drift suddenly away from them, her face contorting in a grimace.

"Ma?"

Jones grabbed Dot before she could move and held her for a moment, then placed her at Maggie's feet, pushing her down gently until she was sitting in the sand.

"Child, you must stay here and do only what I do. But you must not touch her. Do you understand? Repeat what I say. Do it to save your mother."

Dot planted the cross in the sand at Maggie's feet and began to rock back and forth in a nervous rhythm, reciting the Lord's Prayer.

The old man ignored his granddaughter. Maggie was slipping away. He grabbed frantically at his flat rawhide drum and began to pound it, chanting in a monotonous cadence: *Ugashe, ugashe, ugashe.*

Dot had heard the word from the Apache herders on the ranch. Whenever she would pester them with questions or interfere with their work, they would say it: *Ugashe.* "Go away." Now her grandfather was using it to try to drive an evil spirit from her mother's body. It seemed crazy to believe that simply repeating a word, and smearing red paint on someone's skin would cure anything. She started into the Lord's Prayer again, louder this time.

"Child," Jones said, handing her the small drum and standing. "This is not a time for you to hold a discussion with your god. We must reach the spirits and ask them to help us. The word is U-GA-SHE. Beat the drum slowly and repeat it. Think about the evil leaving your mother. Think pure thoughts. Drive it from her with the force of the word and your goodness. Call on your power. I will return."

Dot nodded and began to beat the drum, remembering her mother's warning that it would harm her soul. She didn't know who to listen to. She loved her mother and usually she was right about things. But she loved her grandfather, too, and he seemed to know about these things—and anyway her mother was sick, maybe dying. She beat the drum harder. *Ugashe, ugashe, ugashe.*

Maggie was in mortal danger, her life in his hands. He climbed back up on the gray and rode, searching for the things he needed, the little horse faithfully grinding out the miles, Jones's mind on the crippled Apache.

The old man and the pony rode into a harsh land, through

stands of ironwood trees and honey mesquite, searching for the palms of the gods and the spiritual things he needed to save Maggie. His breath was coming in ragged gasps. It would finish all his dreams to lose her this way.

**H**e had been lashing her back with the switch for so long that Lily could no longer feel its sting. She dug harder, her fingers split and bleeding, her heart determined that he would have to kill her to stop her. She would bury this woman and her child. No matter what.

The Lame One had gone through a number of branches, breaking each over Li-Lee's strong back; still she would not quit clawing at the earth. He was determined to teach her. She had run. She'd helped others run. And now, she was defying him. The branch in his hand snapped and he cursed her and kicked her hard in the buttocks. Still she dug. She was mad, he thought.

Panting hard, he stopped and watched as Li-Lee struggled to pull the bodies of the woman and child into the hole, placing the small one facedown on her mother. Then she frantically started to scrape sand in on them. Blood was seeping through the back of her shirt.

She was stubborn. He did not admire stubbornness in a woman. He would beat it out of her. No woman would defy him. Ever. He bent and picked the little rag doll out of the dirt, examining it, then tucking it into his clout and moving off to find another, stronger stick.

**J**ones had been gone long enough for the moon to pass completely from the night sky, when he finally returned to the small gully. He was scratched and dirty, as if he had been crawling through heavy brush. Dot was gazing in a dazed way at Maggie, the woman covered in the red blotches and drenched in sweat. Jones watched his daughter's swollen face for a moment, then took the drum from the child and began again his monotonous cadence.

Dot started in again, as well, then Jones began to dance slowly in place, his voice becoming incoherent gibberish, the intonations like a sedative. Hypnotic. Dot struggled to stay awake and to copy the sounds. On and on through the night went the singing and chanting, Dot mimicking, until she thought she could no longer stand it. Maggie was sweating badly, but otherwise looked unchanged. Dot swooned. Jones sang on as if his very life depended on it.

Then suddenly he stopped. The night was silent and seemingly poised, waiting for some moment of magic. He dropped to his knees beside Maggie and drew out his long knife, leaning over her.

"Grandpa—don't!"

He paid her no mind, cutting Maggie's pants from the thigh down and peeling them back to expose her legs, then he took the red pigment and made crosses on her thighs, covering these with sprinkles of sacred pollen. He sat talking over her for a few minutes, then tipped Maggie's head back on the sand. She looked dead, her eyes rolling to white. Dot was whimpering behind him. He put pollen on Maggie's tongue, then tied her mouth closed with cotton strips, so that she looked like she had a toothache.

They sang until dawn. Then Jones stopped singing again, the silence strange and foreboding, and produced a live snake from somewhere on his person. Dot jumped. Where had he hidden it? She hated snakes. At least it was small and harmless, a yellow gopher. Jones rubbed the writhing creature slowly over Maggie's thighs, up and down her arms, over her face, hissing all the while like a snake himself. When he was done, he spat into the fire and then turned and held the reptile out to Dot. She stepped back in fright.

"Take it. It will not hurt you—but it carries now the demon's spirit. Take it and let it go free so that it can vomit the evil into the earth."

Dot reached out trembling hands and took the glass-smooth body of the reptile, terrified of what it possessed.

The lame Apache had been shaken from his dreams by thoughts of the ancient one. He was sweating and concerned. The worry seeming to claw at him from out of the night. Something was happening. He thought of the girl, Li-Lee, and picked up the doll. He walked past the campfire and the other Apaches. They were like cur dogs, he thought, they watched but did nothing. It was always the same. Had been all his life. He stared boldly into their faces as he moved past, daring them to stop him. He knew they would not.

He stooped under the ledge where the women were being held, squatting in front of Li-Lee and studying her face. She returned his gaze with a repulsed look. He was used to this, but he was not used to the defiance that he saw in her eyes. He had the urge to reach out and grab her, but she was weak from the beating he'd already given her. She had to be able to ride.

He held the small doll out toward her, teasing. She studied it for a moment, gradually recognizing that it was the child's, her throat contracting until she was having a difficult time getting air, then her expression changed. Slowly at first, then more rapidly until it was one of absolute fury.

"You bastard!" she screamed, lunging at him, scratching at

his face and grabbing the doll.

The Lame One grabbed her by the neck, squeezing until she dropped the doll, crying out in pain. Raging himself now, he shoved her back onto the sand, straddling her, hitting her face with his heavy fists, then wrapping his hands around her neck and squeezing. Lily was kicking and gasping for air, turning a deep red, the fight slowly leaving her. Her arms slipped to the sand as she fainted. He continued to squeeze her soft throat, the Other urging him on, until he knew he was about to lose her, and let go.

Then the earlier feeling of concern was on him again. This time it felt like fear. He wasn't certain why—only that it had something to do with the woman, Mah-gee, and the ancient one. They wanted the girl. Perhaps he should kill her. Be rid of them.

Maggie did not recover that day. She looked stiff as if her body were frozen, her skin pale and translucent. She was barely breathing. Jones said nothing. He did not chant or drum or sing. There was nothing more to do, he felt. His power had failed.

Dot was frightened. "Grandpa, when will she get better?"

"She should have been by now."

"But she is going to—isn't she?"

"I have done all that I know."

"Then we've got to try something else!"

"Child, be still. There is nothing else. Do not disturb the spirits. If they are going to help her, they will do it. Nothing you or I can do now will change that."

Dot was suddenly scared that she had sinned as a heathen and that was why her mother had not recovered. Right there she determined to forsake her sinful ways and to become God-fearing again. She was desperate. "I don't believe that. We've got to try." She picked up the small Bible on the blanket beside her, clutching it in her shaking hands. Jones watched her but made no comment.

"God. Please help my mother. She's bad sick. I don't know why, only that she's dying. Please help her. If I made you angry by believing in Grandpa's magic, I'm sorry." Dot prayed hard for a long time, the old man studying her.

He was impressed by her fervent prayers as she knelt near Maggie, her small body swaying, sheets of sweat covering her. He listened to her pleadings, the plaintive cries for help that died slowly on the thin desert air. While he didn't know how to reach the Christian god, she deserved to do it. Her heart was pure. Still, her god did not intercede in the affairs of man. He felt badly for the child.

When the sun had reached the peak of its arc in the cornflower-blue sky, they rigged a travois and put Maggie on it and started off once again across the dry landscape. This did not stop Dot. She simply moved her prayers into her saddle, riding alongside her mother, talking to her. Pleading with God, and pleading with Maggie. She did this until she was so hoarse that she could barely speak.

She rode Alice up next to the gray. "Grandpa," she rasped, the words hurting her, "do you think God is mad at me?"

The old man shook his head. No god, he figured, could be mad at this child of courage. He felt sad for her. None of her dreams were coming to pass. It was sometimes so. It was a lesson she would have to learn.

That night when they camped, Jones began his chanting and drumming once more. But he had no hope left in him. This time, Dot refused to join him, kneeling instead beside her mother and praying, holding the small cross. The two of them seemed to tug back and forth over the woman's body—pagan chanting and Christian prayers floating and mingling in the night air.

Dot stopped and looked up at the old man with tears in her eyes. "Why doesn't anything ever stay the same, Grandpa?"

"I don't know. Perhaps to teach us things we must learn."

That was decidedly discouraging to her. She shook her head dolefully and went back to her prayers.

It was in the deepest part of night, when the air turns its coldest and the creatures—neither day nor night creatures—no longer stir, when the earth and all her inhabitants truly sleep, when Maggie finally moaned. It was a long, low painful sound that seemed to carry with it some of the prayers and chants, and it made Dot sit up straight and shiver.

Jones squatted near Maggie's feet and smiled his golden-tooth smile at her. She ignored him, upset about the red pigment. She could open her eyes and drink and sip broth, but mostly she was just upset. She wiped the crosses from her thighs—knowing they were not Christian—and had Dot help her change her pants.

All she could say to Samuel Jones was: "How could you?"

He did not respond. He just alternately watched her and then the child, wondering about his granddaughter's Christian prayers. He had no answer. He studied the silver crucifix that Dot had stuck in the sand beside her mother, questioning things he hadn't thought of in a long time. All he knew for certain was that he had not cured her.

Dot didn't know what to think. She had participated in both rituals. She was just thankful that somebody had saved her mother.

When the sky was lightening in the east and the prairie

wolves were trotting to their dens, Maggie felt strong enough to stand up. A while later, she could sit in her saddle, and they started off again on their journey, still traveling in a direction away from the Rio Grande and the Apaches. And Lily.

Maggie thought about the voice. It had come to her again during her illness, leading her out of despair. She could not remember the words. She knew only that it had spoken of life. The goodness of life.

They rode into the red dawn, moving through a land filled with catclaw brush and dry sand, the thorns tearing at their pant legs and flesh, the hot sand burning the hooves of the animals. Rough country. They rode, spooking coyotes, rabbits and ground owls. What little water they found was smelly with mud and minerals. Chaco had not awakened and Dot was beginning to believe that he wouldn't live. She had not liked him before, but watching the tiny terrier and holding him in his unconsciousness drew her a little closer to him. Maggie, when she was more aware of things, continued to care for Chaco, forcing him to take small sips of water and broth.

They were all exhausted, man and beast. All but Alice. The young mule still had a nice lively gait. Dot watched the gray struggling along and felt a great surge of love and admiration for her, marveling that the old pony and her grandfather could keep going. Seemingly impervious to the cold and heat, the thirst and fatigue, the old man and his horse were a perfectly matched pair in their determination and endurance. Every once in a while the ancient war pony would stumble, even fall, but always she would regain her footing, plodding onward. Then, whenever they stopped, she would drop down onto her torn knees, camel-like, and slip immediately into her deep sleep, each time looking as though she had finally died. But when they were ready to travel again, she was always up and trudging, head low, leading the way.

Dot loved them both—loved the way they shared this struggle together, the old man spelling her, trotting gamely beside her, holding the saddle horn in one bony hand, pushing her from behind when the climbing got steep. He watered her when there wasn't enough for both of them, rubbed her dry at night and doctored her sores and cuts. That he greatly loved and respected the old animal was obvious. She must have been a terror as a young horse, Dot thought. Now she just looked busted. But then, the roan looked badly used as well. Alice was the only animal showing little wear.

As the sun topped the distant mountains, the earth tilted some, and they began a slow climb up a rocky slope covered with prickly-pear, lechuguilla and cholla cactus. Jones and the gray seemed to pick up the pace. There was more spring in their steps. Cactus was everywhere. The worst of the lot was the lechuguilla. Second, the cholla. The lechuguilla made walking tricky because of the bunches of green spiked stems that wound over the ground. The cholla, known as "jumping cholla," got its name, Dot knew, because it seemed to almost jump on anything near it.

She was carefully picking some off Alice's shoulder and her own pant leg. Alice was trailing the gray again. The old pony was walking alone, Jones having slipped from the saddle a few minutes before, dropping behind them to study their backtrail. He had been doing this off and on for several hours. Dot wondered how the horse knew where to head, trudging along each time with seeming purpose.

Dot watched her grandfather trotting past and swinging back up into the saddle, the little horse swaying precariously with the weight. "Are they back there, Grandpa?"

He ignored her. Maggie was gazing blindly at the roan's neck, the sun sparkling in her lovely hair.

They continued to climb the slope toward the tall bluish

mountain that rose thousands of feet above the desert. Slowly, the terrain began to change. They drank from, then crossed, a wide stream of clear water. Agave and creosote gave way to sunflowers, Indian rice grass and wild rose. The air was sweet, high mountain, summer-cool. The land turned beautiful; the mountain was tall enough for rain. There were red-winged blackbirds and yellow sulphur butterflies, and little plants in cracks. Springs. Good forests.

They followed a pleasant stream into the hills. The banks were lined with tules and thick with willows and cottonwoods, and Dot could hear ducks pond-dabbling. She saw a night heron take off from the water and slowly flap its way downstream. There were beaver signs, and catfish, and deer and raccoon tracks. Mexican poppies provided rich colors in splashes throughout the canyon, and small green trees stood in clefts in the hills. It was truly a wondrous, sunny paradise. She thought it might be the prettiest place in the world.

The massive cave was cut into the canyon wall, rising perhaps seventy-five feet at its mouth, and reaching back a hundred more, a soaring cathedral in red sandstone. It was majestic and beautiful. Light and airy inside, it could easily shelter a hundred people beneath its vaulted rock roof, the floor covered with deep sand. There were dozens of rock circles with charred firepits in their center. Strange drawings covered the walls. Jones dismounted and walked slowly into the cool drifts of shadow, turning and looking at the walls and the cold black ashes of long-dead fires, seemingly wandering in a dream, as if seeing other times and other people.

"Grandpa, do you know this place?"

"The sacred place," he said. He was still turning in his slow circle studying the rocks and sand, remembering.

"Are we safe here?"

He looked at her, squinting at her face. Then he turned and

looked off into the shadows again, wandering deeper into the cavern. Maggie slid down and wrapped her arms around herself. She, too, was turning and looking. "I get a bad feeling here," she said.

"Grandpa says it's holy."

"It smells Indian."

Jones had squatted in the coarse sand and was chanting softly.

"Grandpa." Dot waited, then asked, "Lily?"

He chanted louder.

He had left them alone in the shadows of the huge cave. They had moved the horses and mule into the deepest part, then tried to sweep their tracks away. Finished, they'd checked their weapons, and nervously watched the shelter's mouth and the bright sunlight beyond. Chaco was in Maggie's lap, whimpering. She was stroking and talking quietly to him.

"Where do you think Grandpa is?"

"Trying to find his Indian friends."

"No, he's not. Even if he was, Indians aren't bad."

"Why do you believe so in Indians?"

"I've read—" Then, quickly, she added, "They're good."

"You can't read a book and think it's real life. And you shouldn't think of them as being the same as you."

Dot stared into the sunlight for a long time before she spoke. "Ma, Grandpa is Indian. Indians are good. At least as good as we are."

"Dotty, he's white. Born in Boston. To English parents. You know that."

"That doesn't mean everything. He learned to be Indian."

"True," Maggie said, clearing her throat. "But it's not a thing he or you should be proud of."

The conversation had taken something out of both of them and they just sat for a while, until Dot slipped slowly into sleep.

*     *     *

Maggie jumped when she saw Jones striding down to the stream to drink, then slipping up a trail that led into the mountains. She watched until he disappeared, curiosity rising in her, suddenly determined to learn what he was doing. If he had located his Indian friends, she wanted to know. Dot was in a deep sleep. Maggie laid Chaco on the blanket and followed him.

The thin rocky trail wound up the side of a granite cliff, rising quickly into harsh mountains, the air chilly and still. She could hear water somewhere ahead. She continued forward, stopping at the foot of a thin waterfall. Mist filmed her face and made her shiver. He was nowhere to be seen.

Maggie was turning to start back down when she heard voices. She froze, listening hard, the faint sound coming from a shadowy break in the rocks beside the falls. She edged forward, canting her head to catch the drifting sounds, hearing snippets of sentences, and though she couldn't decipher their meaning, she knew the language: Apache. She was trembling hard now, fighting the impulse to run.

He had led them as she suspected to his Indian friends. She moved closer. Someone was calling Indian names, repeating them, over and over again: the sound of one mourning. Maggie peered into the cleft in the stone, blinded by the shadows. The voice stopped. Slowly, her eyes adjusted.

Samuel Jones was on his knees, rocking back and forth, naked except for his clout and long Apache moccasins. The spot where he knelt was small and circular, a vertical shaft inside the massive granite wall. He began to wail.

Maggie fought the sense of compassion inside her, telling herself that he had earned the right to suffer—had given his soul away in order to live with an Indian whore. Had wasted his life among savages. He was consumed by their superstitions and fears, driven by their strange beliefs of witchcraft and magic, a world run amok with spirits and demons. She started to turn and leave, then stopped, the feelings stirring her thoughts again like wind through dry leaves. She couldn't rid herself of them. She was thinking about her childhood with him. He looked worn and sick, tears streaking his gaunt features.

"Thank you, Ama," he said, turning to look at her, his voice shaky. "I prayed someday it would happen."

"What?"

"Come closer."

Without knowing why she did it, Maggie turned sideways and slipped into the small enclosure. "What?" she asked again, trying to sound impatient, but just feeling the magnetic draw to the old man.

Jones struggled to stand and stepped forward, staring at a horizontal slit in the rock as if it contained precious treasure. The cut was some two feet high and six feet wide, and sealed with stones. Maggie watched as he pulled rocks from the cut, opening a small hole and peering into it. She stepped closer, her heart beating hard. He moved back so that she could look. There were Indian things inside: necklaces, pottery, clothing. Dusty and old. Then she saw them. Bones. Piles of them, and three skulls.

He was singing in Apache. Maggie was rubbing her hands together nervously when he finally stopped his singing and spoke. "It's where I buried them."

"Who?"

"Your brother and sister."

The sound of Maggie's breath being sucked in was audible. "That's a lie."

"They are what whites call half brother and half sister."

"I don't believe you."

Jones began to chant softly again, slowly refitting the

stones. Maggie could not take her eyes off the shadows within the grave. She had known only about the Apache woman. Never about any children. Her breath kept snagging in her throat. She bit at her lip and pressed her eyes shut. She'd never thought of her as anything but an Indian whore who had stolen her father. The marshal had told her that she was small and pretty and smart; that she'd loved her father; that he had loved her. Maggie's body stiffened. Now she'd learned the hardest thing to accept: she was the mother of his children. Offspring out of wedlock. Bastards. Mongrels. But nevertheless, her siblings.

"They were eight and ten."

Maggie didn't respond.

"Their mother, Yopon, is here with them. My wife."

Maggie looked angry. "You mean the Indian you abandoned Mother for."

He was silent.

In an anguished voice spoken only to herself, she said, "I don't care." Maggie was crying quietly now, not in sorrow or anger, simply in frustration of the immutable past. She stood studying the rock grave, seeing beyond it to the remains of her life.

"Your sister's name was Lozen. Your brother, Eskim."

"I don't care," she said out loud, her voice sounding helpless. Maggie sat on the stone floor and wrapped her arms around her knees, rocking slowly.

"I told them stories about you."

Maggie shut her eyes. "Why? Why would you mix us together like family? We weren't. And I don't want to be."

Jones ran his hand gently over the surface of the gravestones. "They were scared and hungry. We were being hunted, unable to find game or light fires. The springs were guarded, so we drank what we could find in the hills. Many died of the ague."

He stopped talking and studied the stones. His voice sounded distant when he next spoke. "It was terror for the children, watching their friends and families wasting away or being killed. That's why I told them the stories, Ama, so that they could leave their world and escape to you."

Maggie bit at her lower lip and nodded, unable to condemn him for that.

"You were a spirit-keeper to them. They believed you had the power to rescue them, to take them away from the horror. I never told them you couldn't. I didn't have the heart." He stopped talking and gazed at the rock wall before him as if he could see them moving in it. "They used to beg me to call your spirit. They wanted to see you, Ama. To watch you drive our enemies away. Lozen loved you without ever knowing you."

He began to chant and shake his rattle again. When he was finished, he turned and looked into her face. "At night when I was lonely for you, I would hold Lozen and pretend she was you. I would talk to you. She understood. She would sit still and serve as a tiny spirit medium, so that I could reach your heart and soul.

"Your sister loved you deeply. Near the end, when we were always hungry and cold, she made me talk more often about you. It eased the pain for her. She believed that as long as one of you lived, both of you lived." He looked at her. "Now she lives through you."

Maggie shook her head slowly.

He fumbled in a small leather pouch that Maggie had seen him remove from the stone grave. "The week before she died, she made this for you." He pulled a small acorn necklace from the rotting leather bag. Maggie held it in the palm of her hand, trying to imagine the little Indian girl, then slipped it into her pocket.

He watched her. "I promised that someday I would bring

They had built the campfire far back in the cave, but its glow could not be hidden and it danced warmly in the air like a living thing, splashing on the ceiling and over the sand, casting a faint, undulating wash of light over the entire cavern. After a lean dinner of beans and wild desert cabbage, they rested on their blankets, each with their own thoughts.

Jones had hobbled the stock in a stand of salt grass near the cave's entrance. Maggie could hear them grazing. The sound was peaceful. Her father was sitting and gazing into the flames of the hot little mesquite fire. She watched it herself for a few minutes, then looked back up at him and saw his eyes locked on the crucifix. He looked deep in thought. Troubled thought. The little cross stood on a small rock near the fire, throwing a large trembling shadow of itself out across the sand. Looking defiant in the night, in this place of heathen gods.

What was he thinking? she wondered. Redemption? Could a man like him ever find it? She doubted it. The thought troubled her deeply. She closed her eyes and said a prayer for him. For all of them.

Maggie thought of Lozen and Eskim, and the woman, Yopon, and felt sad and uncomfortable. But there was nothing she could do about it. About any of it. From the time she was eleven, she had mistrusted anything Indian. Her father had abandoned her for them. She and Brake had fought them. They had lost Thelma and Julia to them. Indians had killed Mannito, wounded Brake and stolen her Lily. And now, she had come to this lonely place to learn that she had a sister and brother who were half-Indian. None of it seemed fair or right, or to belong together.

Slowly, the thought came to her that even if they were her half brother and half sister, it didn't matter. She had never known them, would never meet them, would never have to face her feelings. Just because he had done what she'd have expected of him, fathered Indian children out of wedlock, that didn't affect her. This thought made her feel better. She was sorry they had died but relieved she wouldn't have to confront whatever they meant to her and her life. While she might someday grow to accept the knowledge of these illegitimate siblings in her mind, she knew that she would never accept the Indian woman, Yopon. She had destroyed her mother, and Maggie would never forget or forgive that fact. She couldn't—not and live with herself.

She looked at him across the drift of weak shadowy light, his lips soundlessly mouthing a chant. He had stopped staring at the crucifix, but not stopped his religious ceremonies. She put the little cross away in her coat pocket, watching him whispering his litany of pagan nonsense. He hadn't ceased since they'd arrived at the cavern. He truly believed it was sacred ground. She shook her head, remembering what he had told her about Indian spirits not leaving the place of their death—that Lozen, her half sister, was here, and would come to her. Maggie shifted nervously on her blankets, glancing at the shadows beyond the fire's light.

She shook off the thought of Lozen, understanding better how primitive people's fears fed on the night. She glanced back at him, questioning how he could have let this happen to himself. College educated, a schoolteacher. He had given it all away. Given away his birthright, his wife and children, his right to be her father. All so that he could take up with wandering nomads. Then at the end, he had panicked at death and come back needy and seeking forgiveness. This last thought made her shoulders tense.

She held her Bible tighter. Maggie considered herself a good Christian and knew she should forgive him, but search her soul as she might, she couldn't find it in her to let go completely of the past. Each time she tried, she recalled her mother's love of him, her struggles to survive, and whatever compassion she possessed shriveled. She looked back at him, thinking again of Lozen and Eskim.

He was gazing at her.

"What?" she asked.

"I am happy you were spared."

"You believe your Indian magic saved me."

He didn't respond.

"You had no right to involve me or my child in your heathen mummery. We are Christians." She paused. "You were one once yourself."

He nodded, watching the flames.

"Now you believe in feathers and smoke."

He turned and stared into her face for a moment, a hint of agitation in the lines around his mouth. "I believe in a creator of the earth and man. How is that so different from what you believe?" When she didn't respond, he continued in a firm voice. "Ama, tell me."

"Your gods scurry around lending power to men. You're obsessed by your heathen rituals and trappings . . . your chantings, your pipe smoke, your paints, your pollens, your beads—"

"—Your prayers, your angels," he interrupted, "your ashes, your incense, your holy water." He stood and put wood on the fire and watched the sparks ascending to the roof of the cave. Then he turned to her. "Your saints and disciples who performed magic."

"Miracles," she said quickly.

"Christ, who walked on water and raised the dead. Your crucifix."

"Blasphemy."

"No. I believe Christ was truly God. But the whites lost Him."

Neither of them spoke for a long time. Maggie read her Bible, while Jones cleaned the Sharps. The wind was moving through the cave rocks, murmuring voices. She shivered and closed the book and looked across the firelight at him. Maggie wasn't finished with the discussion.

"If you believe that, why aren't you still a Christian?"

"I told you, Ama. I don't know the name of what I am. I know only that the whites ruined the thing you call Christianity."

He pulled a cleaning rod out of the barrel of the old gun and peered inside it to see if it was clean. Still looking down the barrel, he said, "The whites lost their god."

"That's not true. I can talk to my God."

"Talk, but nothing more. He is lost somewhere." He studied her face. "My god helps, Ama. He can be reached. His good spirits help me."

"My God will help me."

"Then use Him to find Lily."

"I won't test Him."

"You don't know how to find Him, that is all. I didn't know either. That is why I am not a Christian. When I needed

Him, He was not there." He sat and thought about the fact that he wasn't certain whether or not Dot had reached Him. No, he wasn't certain. This possibility bothered him.

She reached for the crucifix in her pocket, touching instead the acorn medicine necklace Lozen had made for her. She jerked her hand free.

Jones continued to clean his Sharps and to think about what Dot had done: the unsettling possibility that she had used the Christian god to save her mother.

The fire had burned to coals and Chaco was barking softly in his dark dreams, when Maggie next spoke. Dot had slipped into a deep sleep and she stirred beside her mother and Maggie laid a hand on her. Looking at her child, Maggie's thoughts again flew to Eskim and Lozen.

"How did they die?"

Jones didn't answer for a while. "Mexicans and whites," he said finally. "They trapped the women and children here in this place. I had gone with the men to Sonora to sell mules." He paused and studied the coals of the fire. "When we returned, they were lost. Yopon and the others dead." He took a long drink of mescal and sat scrutinizing the fire as though trying to see something in it.

When he spoke again, his voice seemed drowned in pain. "Two women escaped with a boy to tell us the story. They violated the women and girls and then shot them, or clubbed them to death. Then they herded the younger children to a high cliff and made them jump," Jones said, fighting a cry in his breast. "Your brother Eskim was very brave. The women watched from the rocks as he held his big sister's hand and told the others not to be afraid, that they would join their ancestors. Then they jumped together."

He turned and looked into her face and took another drink. "Believe."

"Believe what?"

"That your sister still walks."

"That's foolishness."

"No, the truth. Spirits live in the place of their death. Lozen is here. You are not alone. She is glad of heart. She will come to you. You will believe. The dead are not without power." He stopped talking and studied her face. "The old women said that before she jumped, Lozen screamed a spirit's name: May-re-teet. But I knew. It was: Margaret. Your sister was calling you. She believed you would save her." He continued to gaze at Maggie. "Lozen loved you deeply. No matter what you feel towards me—return her love. She waits for you now."

Maggie could not stop staring at him, her eyes darting over his face in panic. She mouthed the words slowly. "What did you say?"

"That Lozen still loves you."

"No. Before that—what did the woman say?"

"That Lozen screamed your name before she jumped."

Maggie lowered her head into her trembling hands, her elbows braced on her knees, and began to rock back and forth on the sand.

"Ama, what's wrong?"

"Nothing," she said quickly. "I don't want to talk anymore." She was stunned by the possibility. "No," she said silently, over and over again. It wasn't true. But try as she might to reassure herself, she could not stop thinking about the possibility that it was the truth. Could not block the memory of the haunting shriek of her name that she had heard in her nightmare so many years ago. And now there was the chance that it might have been real. A cry for help. A death cry from her half sister that had traveled through a thousand miles of space . . . until it had reached her . . . a silent scream in her mind. Was it Lozen's voice that she had heard all these years? Had her sister been trying to protect and guide her? She shivered.

Jones sat and watched her struggling with her emotions. When she had collected herself, he cleared his throat and said, "After I buried them, I joined the other men and we traveled until we came to a rancheria of the Chiricahua. But our hearts had been left here. It was with the Chiricahua that we ambushed the emigrants. It seemed right until I saw the first of them fall—but it was too late then. I couldn't stop it." He turned and looked into her face with a haunted expression. "I went to the canyon believing their deaths would ease my hurting." He glanced into the coals, staring as if he was reliving that day. "It only made it worse."

She watched him without saying anything, then looked down at Chaco, the little dog trotting in her arms, crying in his sleep. She stroked the terrier's small head, and whispered a silent prayer for Lozen. Suddenly exhausted, she lay down, placing the dog beside her, and drifted into a troubled sleep.

Chaco was whining again. Dot stirred on her blanket and then sat up and looked at the dog, and said in a sleepy voice, "Grandpa, what's wrong with him?"

"Nothing. This is a sacred place. The Place of the Dreams. He is running with the spirits. We will all dream."

Dot looked nervous. "I don't want to dream."

"Don't be afraid. Wisdom comes from dreams."

"Grandpa," she yawned, "when will we start after Lily?"

"When it is time," he said quietly. He did not tell her that he was unable to go on, that Lily was lost.

Dot sat peering through the mellow light of the fire at this old, drunken man she loved. He was right. Life was strange, a changing thing, like the kaleidoscope at home. Constantly forming and reforming new patterns. Painful changes. But good ones, too.

Little Chaco at one moment had been boisterous and

angry, now he lived an odd gentle existence in a shadow world. Where? she wondered. Was he here with them? Was he still a dog?

She studied the dark, sooty patterns on the cave wall. None of it made any sense. Lily had been free, now she was a captive. Her father wounded. Where was Mannito? What was real for them and Chaco? Was real only what a person thought—so that there were different realities for everybody?

The possibility frightened her, causing her throat to tighten. She thought about her father, running her fingers absently over her medicine necklace, talking to him about what had happened, telling him it would be all right, that they would find Lily and come home. She promised this to him, promised it on the power of God. Then quickly, to be safe, she promised it on the power of the dragonfly. She wiped a tear from her eye and began to feel drowsy, as if drawn to sleep by an invisible hand. She drifted slowly along in its gentle grasp. The wind rose, and it seemed woven with children's voices.

Jones could not stop watching his daughter. But even as his eyes moved over her features he remembered her mother, Susan. He remembered Yopon, Eskim and Lozen as well, and the long nights they had spent huddled together around similar fires. His heart ached. Kayitah had been born in this cave. Suddenly, a pine branch flared into bright flames, sending sparks rushing toward the dark stone canopy. He watched the hot embers rising like angry bees in the air, then cooling, and dying to darkness, to nothingness. The sacred cave had spoken. It was so with human life. It was natural. It must be accepted.

He smiled. This sacred place still had the power to teach those willing to listen. He tried to hear the wind voices in the broken rocks. Nothing. He wondered where Kayitah was this night. He called to the spirits to make him safe, to tell him that Samuel Jones was thinking of him. Jones calculated that he was nearing thirty years.

Maggie tossed hard in her sleep. She was back in their bedroom at the ranch, gazing from the foot of the bed at Brake. She wrapped her arms around herself in her dream and smiled. He was still alive. Chaco stirred beside her on the blanket.

The door to the bedroom was opening slowly. Maggie watched it, concerned. Moments later, she saw her: a small Indian girl, standing with her arms at her sides, staring with large, soft eyes at her. Maggie waited but the child didn't move or speak. Then finally, the little girl reached her hands shyly out toward her, smiling. Lozen. She was lovely. The child was about to speak when, suddenly, Baldwin sat bolt upright in the bed, pointing a pistol at her.

"No!" Maggie screamed. "She's my sister."

Maggie shuddered awake and lay still in the smothering darkness of the cave, listening intently to the awful silence, wondering what her sister had been going to say to her. Then she felt foolish. It was only a dream—the dead do not speak. Maggie studied the shadows. The fire had burned to coals. She was trembling from the dream. Had he been right? Had Lozen come to her? She shook the thought off. Then she tensed. Something was wrong.

Dot woke to Chaco's growling, groggily figuring the little dog was still caught in the snare of his dream-world. She started to sit up but felt a hand touch her and jumped.

"Grandpa?"

Chaco hopped off the blanket and stood barking into the night. Dot wiped sleep from her eyes; then the muscles across her shoulders tightened and she focused hard on the shadows in front of her.

"Grandpa, Chaco is awake."

The dog continued barking.

"Chaco," Jones said quietly. The little terrier hushed. To Dot, the old man said, "Child, do not talk." The words were low and filled with danger.

She tried to see his face but could make out only his shape in the cave's darkness. She turned and looked out toward the entrance. Her heart sped. There were moving forms, shadows backlighted by the moon. Alice brayed somewhere in the night. Had the spirits come for them? Or had God sent avenging angels to punish her? She shuddered.

Dot heard her mother cock the hammer on her pistol.

Jones said, "Put the gun down and say nothing. Make no movements or you will be killed."

Suddenly, the shadowy shapes entered the cave and there were angry Apache voices around them. Not spirits. Jones said something in Mexican. There were sharp exchanges. Dot heard someone spit and felt the droplets.

"Pinda Lick-o-yi," a voice hissed in the darkness. Dot knew from her books that the words meant White Eyes.

Someone kicked sand on them. Jones did nothing.

"Do not move," he said quietly, his tone leaving no doubt that he was serious.

Dot trembled, desperate to be in her mother's arms, but afraid to move for fear she would be murdered. The desire to call out to her mother almost overpowered her fear. She pressed her lips together.

Jones tossed a handful of dry sticks onto the hot coals, and moments later, they burst into flame. Frightened as she had been by the dark, the dancing light of the fire, and what it illuminated, brought a worse fear. There were twelve or thirteen of them. Apache bucks with rags around their heads. Armed and angry. Somewhere in the darkness behind them, a child was crying.

"Lily?" she called weakly.

"Hush," Jones said.

The warriors stood in a half circle, glaring down at them. Jones sat with his hands folded in his lap, the Sharps lying across his thighs, not acknowledging them in any way.

Dot searched the faces, her heart pounding. The eyes were dark and hard, and penetrating: harshly weathered faces. Most wore a strip of pigment smeared in a line across their cheekbones and nose, the paint running just below their eyes, making them look as if they were sneaking—peering over something. None showed the least compassion. Only wild-eyed anger.

Dot searched a moment longer for Lily, then understanding came crashing down on her. The men in the posse had said that renegades had bolted the reservation. This must be them. Dot was numb. Chaco was sitting next to Jones, shivering and looking angrily at the Indians.

Dot glanced at her mother's stricken face. When she turned back, two Apaches were moving through the crowd. One was tall and wore a hat; the other was shorter, barrel-chested.

The warriors cleared away from the two. The tall one had a narrow, handsome face, with black hair hanging past his shoulders; a crisp-looking English bowler sat on his head, looking incredibly out of place in the dark cave. He wore a neat long-sleeved cotton shirt, buttoned at the wrists, and clean white cotton pants tucked into shiny cowboy boots, the look of the dandy about him. He was studying her mother. Dot looked away from him to the other man.

Something about the shorter man, something harsh and cruel, seemed to radiate beyond his physical body. His thick and dirty hair, the small eyes, puffy cheeks, the broad, toothless-looking mouth, gave him the look of a fierce, mannish woman. She had seen old Mexican women in Santa Fe who looked like this: haglike. She shuddered.

Jones struggled to his feet. The hag-Indian didn't move or change expression; he just stood holding a rifle in hands that looked too small for the rest of his body, staring rudely into Jones's face. The old man gazed back, gripping his battered Sharps with both hands. Sick as he was, Jones was ready to fight.

The night air was cold, and the hag-warrior wore a faded cotton shirt, a red scarf around his neck, and a new-looking suit jacket. Cinched around his waist was a heavy cartridge belt, and another that held a knife and a bone-handled pistol; a long, filthy-looking breechcloth hung well past his knees. His legs were dark and bare, his feet covered by worn-out teguas. Unlike his companion, he paid no attention to his dress. Clothes did not matter to him, she sensed. Life and death—these were what mattered.

Dot looked at his eyes: There was no sense of tomorrow in them, everything was now, today, this moment. Or had been already. And would never be again.

Maggie was similarly unnerved by the appearance of this warrior. She let her eyes move slowly over him, her gaze stopping on his coat. It looked out of place in this wilderness. The jacket was clean, its buttons made from mother-of-pearl. Her heart beat faster. She squinted. Yes, she could see the gold badge hanging on the inside lapel. The marshal's badge! Maggie's breath reversed in her throat in an audible way and Jones shot her a harsh glance.

The voice's warning in her dream had been right. The Apaches had ambushed the posse—just like they'd ambushed the sheriff and the men back home. Maggie was stunned. Sadness churned inside her. The marshal had been a good man. He had saved her father and she knew he had been trying to find Lily when he was killed. He was like a lot of lawmen on the frontier: mean-tough, but honorable and loyal. Maggie closed her eyes and wanted to forget all of this— everything that had happened or was going to happen. She could hear the hag-warrior muttering something harsh.

The Apache was talking and watching Jones with disdain when Maggie opened her eyes. The taller Indian nodded. Jones said something half Mexican, half Apache, the sentence short and sharp. The hag-warrior waved a hand over Dot and her mother and spoke in Apache. When Jones didn't respond, the man said it again in Mexican. Dot knew Mexican from Mannito. "Let me have them," he had said. "To show that you are still my friend."

"Nanata," Jones said to the hag-warrior, "does not need a gift from me to know we are friends."

There was movement in the crowd, and someone shoved a white man forward, tripping him so that he fell to his knees. The man's arms were bound behind him to a thick locust branch and they had wrapped rawhide around his mouth and head, bridlelike, and were holding him by a long leather lead. He was tall and lean and had been beaten, but still Maggie and Dot recognized him. It was the yellow-haired man who had lashed Jones with the whip and kicked Chaco unconscious. He stared at Maggie, pleading silently.

"Ma, that man."

"Let him go," Maggie said.

"Margaret," Jones said firmly.

Nanata glanced from Jones to Maggie and shook his head violently, spitting out another short sentence and half-lowering his rifle toward Maggie. Jones lowered his own weapon until the muzzle pointed at the Indian's chest, and said something slowly in Apache. Nanata studied Jones's face, not answering, then jerked the barrel of his rifle away from Maggie. Jones raised the Sharps.

Maggie hadn't taken her eyes off the captive. Dot looked back at him and wanted to cry, forcing herself to look away. Chaco was beside the old man, growling as though he were ready to tackle them all. Then there were voices deeper in the cave's darkness, and another warrior, thirty-some years and handsome, with a face that demanded attention, graceful and of medium build, stepped out from the crowd and took a stand beside Jones, carrying a long-barreled rifle.

He, too, looked outraged, seemingly mad at everyone. Suddenly he yelled at the Indian leader, then said something equally sharp to Jones, and made the same sweeping gesture with his hand toward Maggie and Dot, a sharp, cutting slice. Whatever it meant, Dot didn't care for it.

Nanata kicked sand toward them, and spit. Jones cocked his rifle. The noise had a frightening finality to it. Then the Indian who had joined Jones leaped between the two adversaries, roaring again at the warrior, and kicking sand in return. There was a catlike litheness to his movements. His rifle, like Jones's, was at the ready.

"Why kill these people?" he yelled in Mexican. "You have the captive. This is Fielito," he said, gesturing at Jones. "The husband of Yopon, daughter of the White Mountain Apache." He was talking Mexican, Dot figured, for Jones's sake.

Nanata looked at the bellowing man, seemingly not surprised that he had joined Jones, then he shook his head, muttering something Dot figured was an insult. The younger man tensed and started to move, but her grandfather reached out and stopped him. Nanata spit air toward them. Dot noticed her grandfather had stepped almost imperceptibly closer to the hag-warrior.

"I want the captive," he said in a low voice.

Maggie turned and looked at her father.

Nanata grunted in a disrespectful way.

"I am an old man. I want the captive as a slave. What will you take for him?"

Nanata studied his face for a moment, then said, "The woman and the child."

Dot's spine seemed to freeze, her hands shaking.

Then in a quiet voice, Jones said, "You insult me asking for my daughter and granddaughter. Do not do that. I am old and willing to exchange life for honor."

They watched each other like circling dogs.

"I want the captive," he repeated to Nanata, turning and walking back to the fire and pulling the gray's blanket off the beautiful saddle, its silver dancing in the firelight.

"I will trade this for him. He is worth less."

Nanata stood looking down at the sparkling saddle, and Dot thought she could tell he liked it, but when he turned back he looked uninterested. He started off across the cave, stopping to look back at Jones.

"I will not harm you, Fielito. This time," he said, smiling. "We have left San Carlos for the Mother Mountains in Mexico. Join us."

Nanata turned again and walked away. Someone yanked the yellow-haired man viciously to his feet and pulled him into the darkness. He was making a funny sound that scared Dot, and she could smell urine.

"I want the captive," Jones called.

The old warrior stopped and looked back. "Put the saddle here," he said, pointing to a place in the sand. "If I choose it, he will be outside waiting for you in the morning."

Jones did not take his eyes off the back of Nanata, as though he didn't trust him. Finally, he picked up the saddle and placed it in the open place indicated by the warrior.

When she could finally breathe again, Dot didn't want to. Her eyes went to the Apache next to Jones. The man cast a quick sideways glance at Maggie, reeling off a string of Apache words that didn't sound friendly. The old man made the now familiar sweep of his hand toward them.

Slowly, the remaining warriors drifted off, spreading out and starting their small fires throughout the cave.

Maggie looked at the side of Jones's face and said, "Thank you."

The young Indian glared at her. Jones held out his hand toward her but didn't look at Maggie. "Ama," he said, "don't talk."

Dot shook at this statement, wondering why the warrior had helped when it was obvious he didn't like them. Jones walked him away from their campsite, sitting with him in silence in a darker part of the cave. They sat for a long time without saying anything. Maggie was boiling soup for Chaco, the little dog watching her closely and whining.

"Yes—I'm glad you're back," Maggie reassured him. He wiggled.

Dot saw her grandfather gesture toward them again, then the other man shook his head. At times they seemed to be arguing, then laughing. She couldn't figure it. Finally, Jones clasped the man in a hug and returned slowly to them.

Maggie straightened on the sand and said, "I can't believe you brought us here." The words were loud.

"Talk softly," he cautioned. "As long as you are here, you must not behave rudely. It will not be tolerated. Neither I nor Kayitah will be able to save you." He watched her face, until she nodded.

"That man," she said, indicating the young warrior who was stalking out of the cave, "is angrier than the others. Why?"

"You are white. This place is sacred. I would not have done it if Yopon and the children were not here," he said, avoiding her question. Chaco finished eating and hopped into Jones's lap and licked his face. The old man patted him and let the little dog show his pleasure.

"Why didn't they just take us?"

He waited awhile before he spoke. "They may still. But

they have the white man, and they are tired and hungry. And even Nanata understands blood ties." The old man stopped talking and stretched out on his back, dozing in the firelight.

"Because you took an Apache woman, they didn't kill us?"

"Family means much to them," he said, opening an eye. "I am related through marriage to the wife of Taza, the warrior in the hat."

Maggie reflected on this, surprised when a number of women entered the cave. They were wearing long, bright skirts and blouses, their thick black hair hanging loose to their shoulders. Then fear for Dotty rose in her. Dotty couldn't live like this. She wouldn't let her.

Minutes later, the man called Kayitah returned, followed by a thin, gangly boy of nine or ten. They settled at a firepit a few yards away. The man didn't look at them, but the child peeked shyly.

Maggie studied the warrior. He was barechested, wearing full-length pants and the long Apache breechcloth, handsome and well proportioned, his arms seemingly sinewed with steel cords. She felt gratitude for what he had done and wondered about the tie between him and her father. He squatted with his back to them and began to work on his fire.

Maggie let her gaze drift over the camp, surprised by the happy sounds. She had expected that a band of hostiles on the run would be huddled in the shadows snarling and fighting. But the camp seemed peaceful, even industrious—piles of yucca flowers, cattails and wild potatoes spread on tarps, pots boiling. The smells mingled pleasantly in the air until her stomach began to grumble.

A small cluster of women was struggling to hoist the butchered hindquarters of a horse onto poles that had been lashed together. No men moved to help, confirming her suspicions about Indian males: good-for-nothings. It was the seeming contentment that surprised her. She had always thought of the Apaches as sullen and unpredictable. These people didn't appear like that at all.

Suddenly Maggie stiffened, her eyes darting back to the haunch of meat hanging from the poles. She recognized the hide markings: the roan.

"They killed my horse," she said loudly. The talk in the cave stopped, as Apaches turned to stare at her.

"Be quiet," Jones snapped.

But Dot couldn't. "Alice?" she asked.

Jones motioned Kayitah to him. The Indian came reluctantly and squatted. They spoke for a moment, then the young warrior left the cave.

Maggie watched him. "Why does he help us?"

"Loyalty."

Maggie thought about this as she watched him return and say something to Jones, then move back to his fire and the small boy.

"Nanata has promised that Alice won't be harmed."

Dot smiled. She hadn't done that, Maggie realized, in quite a while.

Maggie continued to watch Kayitah across the shimmering light.

"The others have gone about their business, but this one is still angry," she said.

"This night is difficult for him," Jones said softly.

"Why?"

Jones looked reluctant to speak. "He grew up hating whites. Now in this sacred place, he has been forced to defend them against his people." Jones hesitated. "Worse, he has learned things that he cannot accept."

Maggie squinted at his face, trying to comprehend. "What things?"

"Relationships." Jones studied her features. "He is Yopon's son." He stopped talking for a moment and stared blindly into the fire. "I did not want to tell you in this way."

"Tell me what?"

"Like Eskim, Kayitah, too, is your half brother. That is why he protected you. It is an Apache's way—to defend his clan." Jones paused. "He, like the rest of these people, distrusts whites, so you must be careful around him. Still, he is your half brother. And I believe that is more powerful than even his hatred. He is the boy the old women saved on the day of the massacre."

"No," was all she could manage to say.

The Lame One was haunted by his dreams. Something had gone wrong. What, he had no idea. Unable to sleep, he checked to see that Li-Lee was still there, and still alive. She was asleep, clutching the rag doll. Satisfied, he took whiskey and a button of peyote and climbed to a ledge overlooking the camp. The wind was moving slowly. He felt a gnawing urge to know what had happened.

He squatted on his heavy leg and drew a circle around him in the sand, and pulled on his mask. After he had adjusted it, he began to drink. When his head was whirling, he broke a piece of peyote off and ate it. It was sickening. He fought to hold it down. He groaned and called to the Other—his voice deep and penetrating in the stillness among the rocks. He sipped more whiskey and began to chant, the peyote burning with a glow inside him. He tried to visualize the dream that had awakened him, struggling to know what was wrong but unable to answer the question. Slowly, the peyote took possession of him.

He saw nothing. Instead, his thoughts drifted to that moment when he had learned who he was. He had always sensed it—felt it scratching wildly within him to be free—knew that the shamans eyed him cautiously, suspecting. But it was not until that spring morning in the rancheria that he understood. He thought of his parents.

He hated them both. They tolerated him, but nothing more. He was an outcast even among his own family. His birth had been hard. Too hard, some said. He had been ripped from his mother's womb by an old woman. When they saw that he was damaged, they had lain him in the dirt to die. The stories told around the night fires said that he had scurried between his mother's open legs like a demon trying to return to the darkness inside her. Some did not believe the tales, saying that the old woman had simply crippled him. But most did, convinced that he was a child of the witch people, that his lameness marked him. A changeling of the demons.

The peyote vision was growing clear inside his mind. He could see them as if they were standing in front of him now: his mother arguing that it was time for him to live on his own. He had been nine years old. Still a child.

He let his thoughts drift back. His father had been cleaning his rifle. Reloading, he had leaned it against his saddle. Sweat broke over the Lame One's brow as he remembered. Some of the recollection blurred, but he recalled focusing on the weapon, ordering the gun to respond to his will. His father had begun working on a pistol, ignoring his mother's carping. He recalled looking at her face, but she did not look at him. She never did.

His eyes had burned into the weapon, his thoughts commanding it again to rise from the saddle. That was the first time he had heard the Other. The voice clear and deep, seemingly coming from somewhere inside him. It was the only voice he had ever been afraid of in his life. It had caused him to freeze. "I will," was all it said. And with that, the rifle fired, blowing his mother's skull away. He recalled the sound of gentle laughter. He had heard that same laughter many times since.

Suddenly, his mind went blank. The wind rose to the ledge, casting sand over him. His thoughts were spinning in his peyote trance. Then he saw her face swimming out of the night, and knew the source of his dread: the woman at the river, Mah-gee. She was looking at him out of the blackness, smiling at him, mocking him. She was alive. His magic had failed to kill her.

How could this be? How could he have failed to destroy her when he knew her name, possessed her spirit-picture, had used the hair from one of their animals? Anxiously, he rethought the steps of the magic ritual, the drawing of the circle, the chants and the purifying pollens. Everything had been done correctly. But it had failed. His medicine had failed. That possibility stunned him. The Other had not defeated her—had not stolen her life spirit away. Why? Surely she was not as powerful as the Other.

His thoughts flew to the ancient one. The aged giant knew the old ways, he had watched him performing the rituals at the ranch . . . listened to his chanting, heard the sacred sound of his rattles and seen his medicine paints. But, no. The tall one had not saved her. He shook his head to give vent to his growing anxiety. The old man's medicine was fading even as his life faded. No, the old man had not saved the woman. Of that, he was certain. He sucked in a breath. Nor was his own power weak. There was only one answer: she had saved herself. The woman, Mah-gee, possessed her own great power.

Maggie could not take her eyes off of Kayitah. He looked to be asleep in a sitting position. He wore two strings of white beads tied tightly around his throat, and held his rifle across his lap, his thick dark hair caught neatly in place by a clean lavender-colored band of cloth. She shuddered to think where he had gotten it. His skin was smooth and a deep olive color. Even she saw him as handsome, even refined in his looks. Still, that wasn't proof of anything, she figured. The little boy was Kayitah's son, Jones had told her.

The old man was reading beside the fire, stopping every few minutes to gaze alternately from Maggie to Kayitah. Maggie leaned forward and placed the crucifix back on top of the rock near the fire as sort of a spiritual guardian against the heathens. As she settled back onto her blanket, she noticed that her father's eyes were on the cross again. Something in his stare, something lost and lonely, moved her and she knelt and picked it up and held it out across the shadowy light toward him.

He looked from the crucifix to her face for a moment as if he might reach out and take it, then he half-smiled and shook his head and looked back down at his book. The moment lost.

Dot was lying quietly beside her mother, her eyes shut, but too worried about the Apaches and Lily to sleep. Earlier, she had heard her grandfather talking about Kayitah and she rolled now onto her side and gazed at him. He had saved them, he was a hero in her eyes. She looked at the boy. He had edged closer to their campfire and sat playing in the sand, watching them shyly.

"That makes him my uncle," Dot said quietly, glancing at the man's back. "And the boy, my cousin."

Maggie didn't respond.

Dot watched a circle of warriors broiling the roan's guts on green sticks held over a fire. She looked away. He had been a good horse, and deserved a better fate. The Indian boy was sitting in the sand between the two camps, looking at Dot, and smiling. She walked over and sat down next to him. Kayitah paid them no mind.

"We are cousins," she said. *"Primo."*

The boy didn't understand.

"What's your name?"

He looked at her blankly.

"My name is Dot." She pointed at herself.

"Dot," he said slowly. "Dot, Dot, Dot . . ." liking the sound.

She nodded at him. "Yes, Dot. What's your name?" she asked, pointing at him. Then she remembered the Spanish words Mannito had taught her. *"Cómo se llama?"*

Instantly the boy's face broke into a smile. "Ho-nes-co," he said proudly.

"Honesco," Dot repeated.

The boy shook his head. "Ho-nes-co," he said again, giving pause at each point.

"Ho-nes-co," she said slowly.

The boy grinned. "Dot," he said, pointing at her. He was thin and wiry. Dot liked him immediately. She showed him her knife, and he was properly impressed, making a sucking sound through his teeth and growling. She giggled and liked him even more.

"Ho," she said.

He nodded enthusiastically. "Ho," he returned.

Dot knew something was wrong at the sound of Chaco's whining. The little dog was perched on her grandfather's stomach, his nose stuck skyward, howling. Maggie pushed him off and looked at the old man's ashen face. Blood was trickling from the side of his mouth. She pulled his eyelids up: only the whites were visible.

Kayitah watched as Maggie spread a horse blanket over her father, kneeling again and rubbing his hands, pumping his legs. She felt the faint pulsation at the side of his thin neck.

"Ma, when is he going to wake up?"

"He's old and very sick."

Maggie stared at Jones's face. She had seen death enough to know that he was about gone. The suns of more than seventy summers had burned deep into his harsh features until his skin looked like the earth itself. She suddenly felt sad. She couldn't change what had happened to her or to him. If she had any regret it was that she had not let him explain.

Now, with him lying near death, that seemed a cruel thing to have done. His book was on the sand and she picked it up: *Madame Bovary* by Gustave Flaubert. She shook her head, unable to get a good grasp of who this man was who had fathered her. She should have listened—that was all she knew.

She was putting the book into the saddlepack, when she

saw the canvas journal. She took it in her hands and paused, feeling odd prying into his private world, not knowing what to expect, not feeling right about it. But she suddenly had the urge to know more about him—who he was, where he belonged in her world.

His handwriting was strong. Expecting a book filled with scribbles, mindless pleadings and pointless rationales, she found instead something that stunned her as if she'd been kicked by a horse. Her hands were trembling and a muscle near her eye began to twitch. What she saw caused her sense of this old man and who he was to shift awkwardly inside her mind until she wasn't certain of many of the things she had believed for most of her life.

She ran her fingertips gently over the pages: letters. The journal was filled with them. Hundreds of them. Dated. Letters written over long years. Something caught in her throat. Letters written to her mother and Yopon. Letters to his wives. But also, farther back in the dates, letters written to her and the other children. Letters never sent. Never meant to be sent or read. Letters written to dead women and lost children. But the sentiments were there, carefully jotted down—personal and detailed as if he were carrying on old familiar conversations that hadn't been disrupted by decades of silence, sadness and loss.

Maggie closed her eyes and told herself she didn't want to read any of them, that nothing they said could change anything in her life: not what had already happened . . . and certainly not the future. She sat there with her eyes shut until she heard Dot clear her throat questioningly, and she opened them and looked at her young daughter, who sat gazing at her with a sad expression. Maggie smiled at her and knew that she had to read them; for herself, for her mother and Thelma, as well as for her own children. She looked back down at the page. It was dated May 5, 1870. Her eyes moved slowly over the first sentence, gingerly examining each word and the thoughts expressed, as if somewhere there was a hidden trip wire that if touched would spring a trap inside her.

She was shaking and perspiration was forming on her face. She wiped the back of her arm across her forehead and re-read the first few sentences, the words causing the muscles of her back to tense.

Ama:

    *I listened today for your voice in the wind. I used to hear you calling me, but now the sound is fading. I do not know why. Perhaps it is the years between us. Ama, I miss you, my child.*

    *I still think of you as a child. It is the way I see your face and hear your voice. But I know you are a woman, married I think and with children of your own.*

    *I doubt that you remember much about me. But we loved one another—so perhaps you still do. I like to think so. Ama, think about me so that I can hear your voice in the wind again. I need to hear your voice. I miss it so.*

    *It is spring. The geese and ducks gather on the rivers to start north. I have asked them to call down to you, to find you as they fly, and to tell you that I think of you always. To ask you to think of me. Think of me, Ama, and I will hear your voice again.*

Maggie closed her eyes and rocked back on her heels. She ran the tips of her fingers gently over the faded ink of the letter. She didn't move for a long time. Just sat and thought. Let the pain subside. Who was this man who cared so intensely for her and the other children . . . who cared so for her mother and the Indian woman? Something caught in her throat. Maggie's hands were shaking the pages badly as she fumbled to close the journal.

Maggie found five similar journals in his saddlebags. Thirty years of letters. The early ones had been written alternately to

Yopon and her mother and their children during those years when he was away from first one, and then the other. Thirty years of loneliness and sorrow. Thirty years of pain scrawled across these yellowing pages. Tears were falling on the books as she slipped them back into his saddlebags.

**D**ot's chest tightened with the thought of losing her grandfather. Then fear struck at her and she looked at her mother. Maggie was kneeling and putting books into her grandfather's saddlepack.

"If Grandpa doesn't get up tomorrow," Dot said, "we aren't going to ever find Lily."

Dot moved over beside the old man. "Grandpa," she said softly. "I know you're not well. But you've got to get up tomorrow. We have to get on the trail after Lily. Grandpa, we have to do it. Just get a good sleep." She paused, then said, "I believe."

"Dotty, he's dying."

"He can't," she sobbed. "He promised. He promised he would find Lily." Dot stared down at the old man as if angry at him.

Maggie studied his harsh, exaggerated features for a long while before she spoke. "He tried to do what he promised." She moved over beside him, kneeling and wiping his rough face with a rag. Then she turned to Dot. Ho-nes-co watched. "But whether he did or didn't doesn't matter. The result is the same. Dotty," she added, "you're old enough. These people, they won't let us go. They'll keep us, or sell us the way those men are going to sell Lily and those other girls."

"Ma, that isn't true. Kayitah is your brother. My uncle. Ho-nes-co is my cousin. They're Indian—they believe in family. Grandpa said that." The little boy smiled at the sound of his name.

"That may keep us from being killed. It won't set us free. It's best you understand and prepare your mind for it. There may come a time when we can escape. If you get the chance, take it. Don't worry about me. Just run and find your way back to the ranch. Promise me that."

"Ma, Grandpa is going to get up in the morning and we are going to leave here and find Lily. Just like we always planned."

"Dotty, promise me."

Dot nodded slowly, but in her heart she knew her grandfather would wake in the morning.

Kayitah returned silently, seemingly approaching from nowhere to kneel beside the old man. Maggie jumped, then moved out of his way. They ignored one another. He fastened a string of beads around the old man's neck.

Dot watched him for a moment, then looked at her mother. "Ma, tell him about Lily. Please. Tell him what we are trying to do."

Maggie watched her daughter for a moment, then looked at Kayitah. "The child's sister has been stolen," she said in Mexican. "We need your help. Will you help us?"

The man's expression did not change. He continued to stare down at Jones's stiff face.

"Ma, try again."

"Kayitah."

The man turned and looked at her.

"The child's sister has been stolen. Will you help us?"

Kayitah stood and looked down at Maggie, his eyes cold. "*Silencio*," he said, walking back to his own fire. Dot trotted after him. Maggie didn't move, her face turning red.

Kayitah settled himself by his fire, staring into the mix of flame and shadow. Dot knelt beside him, waiting for him to look at her. He didn't.

"I understand some Mexican, but I can't talk it," she said to him. "But Lily is my sister. You're my uncle. *Tío*," she said, remembering the Mexican word that Mannito had used. "My *tío* and Lily's *tío*."

Kayitah had turned at the sound of the word and was looking into Dot's face. Encouraged, she said, "Please! *Tío, por favor.* Help us find Lily!" The man looked back at the fire. Maggie was humming "Rock of Ages," the shadow of her small cross falling across the sand and over her father's still body.

Dot opened her eyes the next morning wondering what had awakened her. She had been dreaming about the dragonfly and knew she was in the cave, but something was different. She couldn't tell exactly what. Then suddenly she remembered her grandfather and turned and looked at him, her heart catching, knowing instantly her mother had been right: he wouldn't get up. "I love you, Grandpa," she whispered.

Dot stood and spun slowly around, gazing in surprise at the cave. There was no one here but her mother and grandfather. Chaco was sitting a few yards away from them watching the entrance as though he were on guard duty. The saddle was gone. Nanata had traded for the captive.

"Ma, where did they go?"

Maggie was cooking breakfast. "They aren't all gone."

"Who's left?"

"Kayitah and the child. I haven't seen that man from the posse."

"Kayitah will help us," Dot said.

Maggie didn't look up from the skillet. "My guess is he's waiting for your grandfather to die. Then he'll bury him and force us to catch up with the others."

"No. He is going to help us find Lily. I'm sure Grandpa told him everything."

"Dotty, our getting away from these people is Lily's only chance."

Dot shook her head and went to kneel beside her grandfather and touched his hand. "Grandfather. We need your help. Please wake up."

Kayitah came into the cave leading the gray pony harnessed to a travois. She looked as frail and wobbly as ever. The man stopped her beside Jones. She tried to nuzzle the old man and the Indian pushed her away. Dot walked over and held her heavy head, feeling her hot breath on her legs. She was a good old horse with a tremendous heart, and Dot knew she was worried about the old man.

"He'll be okay," she whispered into her ear. She checked the harness to make certain it wouldn't rub her sore, then brought her some hay and tried to feed her. She wouldn't take it. Dot pulled the old horse's head up so that she was looking her in the eyes. "You can't die on me. I need you. Please eat." As if obliging her, the gray nibbled at the hay. Dot smiled and fought her tears.

Maggie was kneeling beside her father, trying unsuccessfully to give him water. The Apache waited a moment, then motioned her out of the way with a rough brushing movement. He stooped and picked up the wizened body, reduced now to little more than desiccated skin and hard bone, adjusting the old man on the carrier; Maggie draped a blanket over him. Dot noticed that her mother held her grandfather's hand for a moment, talking quietly to him. Chaco jumped up and sat on the old man's stomach, barking for them to be off.

Kayitah made it clear he was leaving and that they were to follow him. They moved to pack. The warrior left and returned riding a horse into the cave. He sat glowering down at

Maggie as she packed, not happy about the arrangement that coupled him with this white woman. He obviously wanted no part of her or her child, and was apparently only controlling his anger because of his father.

"Faster," he said in Mexican.

"If you want me to hurry," Maggie snapped, "then get off your horse and help. Otherwise, wait." The day had already begun to heat and tiny sweat beads blistered her upper lip.

"Ma, don't," Dot said. "He's helping us."

"*Perezoso!*" she yelled, ignoring Dot's plea. "Lazy!" The man's features never wavered. He sat watching Maggie until she had stopped fuming and gone back to packing; then he turned and rode slowly out of the cave.

"Hurry, Ma. We've got to keep up. He's going after Lily."

Dot stopped talking and stared openmouthed as Kayitah returned leading two broken-down horses.

"Where's Alice?" she called to him. "*Tío*—Alice?"

He didn't answer.

"*Mula?*" Maggie questioned.

The man watched them for a few minutes, then said, "Nanata."

"But he said he wouldn't harm her—stealing her is harming her!" Dot yelled. She sat down hard in the sand and moaned, her world breaking up even more. Nothing lasted. Nothing worked. She felt an urgent need to cry, but refused. There was no God, she felt. No dragonfly power. Ho-nes-co came and sat next to her. Maggie left her alone, knowing how hard she took the loss of the mule.

After Maggie finished, they crawled up on the old horses and followed Kayitah and the gray out of the cave. Dot held her mount back and looked around at the shadows, feeling as if she had lost something here. Then she glanced up and saw Maggie sitting on her broken-down nag at the entrance, something in the way her shoulders slumped made her look frighteningly defeated. Dot tensed and rode up alongside her, following her mother's gaze, then fought the nausea rising in her throat. The yellow-haired head was stuck on a tall wooden pole near the cave's entrance. The hag-warrior had been true to his cruel word: he had left the captive for the saddle.

Maggie and Dot sat staring at the ghastly head in shocked silence until Kayitah rode up behind them and whipped their horses hard with a coiled rope.

"Now you understand Indians," Maggie said.

Dot didn't reply but she knew she could never look at Kayitah again without thinking about the yellow-haired man and the horrible thing they had done to him. The uncle she had so desperately wanted to be a hero now looked like nothing more than a murderer. She fought her tears.

Later, when Dot had regained some control over her emotions, she looked around and realized they had left the cave heading in the wrong direction. It was not the southerly heading they needed to find Lily. She rode alongside Kayitah and pointed vigorously behind them.

"Lily." The tone of her voice accusatory.

He ignored her. Dot pulled her horse to a stop and started to turn around, but Kayitah grabbed the reins and said, "*Alto.*" The word was spoken low and firm but left no doubt that he was deadly serious. Dot shivered, thinking about the yellow-haired man, and then got angry again.

"But this isn't the way!"

He glared at her.

"Go ahead—murder me," Dot cried. "But this isn't the way to my sister!"

Kayitah paid no attention to her, he just looped a rope over her horse's head and continued on, pulling hard on the animal whenever she tried to fall behind or turn out. The old gray struggled gamely with the travois, followed by Maggie and Ho-nes-co. Dot turned and looked at Maggie; she appeared lost in her thoughts, sighing every so often, riding as though alone in this vast desert landscape.

Later that morning, at a lonely place between two barren mountains, they crossed the ruts of a wagon road, and a sign pointing west that read: HOGANSVILLE: 40 MILES. Maggie stopped her horse in the middle of the road, the sun burning down harshly, and sat as though she would stay there forever. Kayitah waited for her to move; then he rode back and threw a rope over her animal's head, leading both of their mounts forward.

They rode steadily over a sprawling desert plain until evening, the shadows spilling blue-black pools over the cooling land. Dot had spent the entire day shouting at Kayitah about Lily and the fact that they were traveling in the wrong direction. She had cursed him a couple of times, glancing furtively at her mother; but Maggie, if she heard, didn't say anything. Nor did he. His expression neither softened nor did he appear to care what desperate things she was trying to convey to him. Dot was worn out from yelling and worrying. Maggie hadn't spoken since morning, seemingly resigned to something that Dot didn't understand.

Twice, when they had stopped to rest, Ho-nes-co had tried to crawl up behind Dot. Each time, a harsh word from Kayitah sent him scurrying back to his own pony. Dot thought she understood how the boy felt. She would have liked for him to ride with her as well. It was hot and lonely on the trail. The old man had cried out in his delirium once or twice, the sound agonized and desperately lonely, but he did not regain consciousness.

The evening sky was a bold mixture of oranges and pinks, anchored by a dark purplish horizon of distant mountains far across the waste of scrub desert. Kayitah had chosen a small arroyo for them to bed down in; and though Dot had tried pleading to get him moving again, calling him *tío* and begging for Lily, it was no use. He was determined to camp in this spot. Maggie crawled down slowly from her horse and sat on the sand, looking defeated. Dot squatted next to her and put her arms around her shoulders.

"It's okay, Ma. We'll find Lily. And we'll get back to Pa and James."

Maggie didn't respond.

"I've still got my power." Realizing what she had just said, Dot glanced quickly at her mother's face. Maggie was not listening.

A while later, Maggie pulled herself up and took a canteen and tried to give water to the old man. He took some, but most ran out of his mouth and onto the sandy ground. Maggie wiped his face dry and knelt and spoke quietly to him. Dot wondered what she was saying; was she scolding him or had she finally forgiven him? Kayitah watched Maggie for a while as well, then took his bow and arrows and climbed out of the small ravine. Dot went to gather grass for the gray.

Maggie was angry and ashamed of herself. She sat and studied the clefts of the old man's rugged face, her eyes moving over his features. She felt remorse. Bad as he was, she at least had owed him the chance to explain. But she had denied him that—denied a dying man a simple request. Denied her own father. She watched his still profile for a long time, feeling something hard breaking up inside her. She fought it.

She had waited too long, had left things buried too deeply. She and the old man had missed the moment when they could have talked. The blame was hers. Who was he really? What had he done with his life? What had he wanted to tell her? She knew so very little about him. Her mother had spoken of him after he left but only in positive, glowing, reverential ways. Never did they really talk about who he was. They both had played this game—Susan because of her love for him, Maggie because of her love for her mother.

She recalled the name she had heard Kayitah use for him: Fielito. The faithful one. How could that be? How could anyone—even Indians—think of Samuel Jones as faithful? She rubbed her face in her hands and fought the confusion in her mind. Maggie remained by his side for a time, thinking about her mother and him, how they had laughed and talked. They had been happy. But if that was true, then why had he left?

"Why?" she whispered to him, watching his features carefully. But there was no response, no recognition. "What do you remember? My room? The doll you bought me? The times I told you I loved you? Any of the things I said?" Maggie paused, staring blindly into the sandy wall of the gully. "You know nothing of how I suffered. The nights I cried for you to come home. You never came." Maggie was sobbing softly now and took the old man's hand in hers. "Don't you dare leave me again! You're not dead until I tell you you're dead. Do you understand?"

She forced herself to stop and looked down the arroyo at her daughter and the Indian boy. The hatred inside her was gone, but not the hollow hurting.

Ho-nes-co squatted beside Dot as she sat feeding green tidbits to the gray. He was holding a small bow and a fistful of arrows, and wearing a buckskin breechcloth and moccasin boots. He grinned a lot, and Dot liked him. He pointed down the arroyo and pulled the bow back and smiled. Dot nodded. She had been worrying about Lily and Alice and her grandfather and wanted to stop thinking about them for a while. They trotted off over the sands, hunting for rabbits and ground squirrels, or anything else that was edible. The boy let her try a couple of shots with the bow. Her aim was wild, and they had a hard time finding one of the small arrows. She handed the bow back to him and said, "Too hard."

He cocked his head like a curious dog and tried to understand her, intelligence dancing in his brown eyes. Then he gave up and shrugged his thin shoulders, and resumed the hunt, Dot following her cousin. Chaco trotted behind them.

Ho and Dot were laughing when they returned to camp. Kayitah was not. He was squatting with a dour expression on his lean face and poking with a stick in a large can of boiling water, clearly not happy about something. Dot looked for her mother.

"Ma," she called. She turned to Kayitah. "*Madre?*" He ignored her, staring at the pot and talking firmly to Ho-nes-co.

"*Tío—madre?*" she said, her voice betraying her fear.

He left the stick in the pot and held one hand out and straddled it with the thumb and forefinger of his other hand, the silent language for horse. Dot turned away from him. A piece of paper flapped in the breeze near the saddles. She opened it, her heart pounding.

Dotty:

   Gone for help. Give Grandfather water at each stop. Soup broth once a day. Should he die, bury him a Christian. I will come for you. I love you.

Mother

For a fleeting moment she felt a frightening sense of abandonment. Then Dot looked at her grandfather and felt better. Even unconscious he made her feel that things would somehow be okay. She picked up a canteen and tried to give him a drink. He looked dead. Her mother had wrapped a small chain and cross around one of his hands. Chaco hopped up on his stomach, and she had to shove him out of the way, snapping as he went, so she could listen to his heart. Then she sat down beside him and closed her eyes and held his huge gnarled hands.

"Grandpa. Take my power. Come back. You've got to do it. You've got to find Lily. You promised."

She stared at him for a long time. Nothing happened. She fought her tears and studied his hands and wondered what he had done with them during his life to hurt them so much.

"Grandpa. I believe." She wiped her nose on her sleeve.

**M**orning light was streaming over the distant mountains, producing a warm golden splash of color on the desert landscape. Maggie had been riding the old horse on the road to Hoganville for the past few hours and was exhausted. She urged the animal on.

She would telegraph the Army and the Mexican authorities, notifying them of Lily's location, and organize the citizens of Hoganville to rescue Dot and to capture Kayitah and Ho-nes-co. She felt sorry for the boy. Not the man.

She was convinced he was taking their father to Mexico to bury him in the mountains where the old man and the Indian woman had lived. He was as savage as the rest of them. Unfortunately, the boy was the same, already too old to be successfully civilized. It was a shame. She put her heels into her horse.

Maggie saw the edge of town first before she saw them. Hoganville was small, but still a town, and it was sitting no more than half a mile off on the dry horizon. She could see men roping horses in a corral in front of some shacks. She reined her horse in and sat looking at the buildings, then back at the cottonwoods, fighting the nauseating sensation in her stomach. The shadows dangled from the trees. Not one, but a group.

Maggie was heading into town, forcing herself to ignore them, when she saw, with a sideways glance, the last dark form: too small. She stopped again, studying the shapes more closely, her throat tightening, a muscle beneath her eye beginning to twitch uncontrollably. The ropes were making an awful straining sound in the wind. Everything in her told her to turn and ride on . . . everything but her heart. She couldn't do it. Badly scared, she clucked the horse toward the trees.

Maggie didn't move for a time. She just sat on the animal and looked at them. They hadn't been there all that long, the bodies still normal enough looking, the smell just starting in. She got down and lost her breakfast. There were four of them. Indians. At least, three looked Indian. The woman was Mexican. Four people, a family: father, mother, an old man like Jones, and a boy of eleven or twelve. A woman, an old man and a boy. Why? What could they possibly have done? They didn't look like dangerous renegades.

They weren't even Apache. From the beadwork and coloring of their outfits, she guessed they were Pueblos. They hadn't fought the whites in this century, but they had been hung nonetheless: a child and a woman. It made no sense, but then nothing made much sense anymore. There was a wooden sign nailed to the cottonwood: THE 100% SOLUTION. Anger began to swell inside her.

Maggie cut the limb with a small hand axe—the limb bending down, the rigid bodies falling in a ghastly pile. Then she hacked the ropes free, and scooped out graves in the loose sand with a tin pot. Her anger drove her. She prayed over them all.

"God, why would You let this happen? And why won't You help me?"

Maggie sat for a long time watching a black-throated sparrow hunting in dry leaves. After a while, she picked up two dried branches, and made a wooden cross with rawhide thong, pounding it into the ground in front of the graves with a rock.

Then she read a passage from her Bible, shouting the words out. She figured the Mexican woman was probably Catholic, and the child, too. Or close enough. It would be okay for the Indian men as well. God is God. That was her conclusion.

Finished, she climbed slowly back onto the horse and sat looking toward the town of Hoganville, remembering something her father had told her as a young girl: "You have to be born, and reborn, and reborn again, to live." She hadn't understood him. She thought she did now. One hour later, she turned her horse around and started slowly back up the road in the direction she had come. Whatever Hoganville contained, it didn't hold anything for her.

The desert sun was heating up the land, making it feel somehow different. Changed. She was thinking about the people at the cave, and what was happening to their world. Not innocents, but still humans. She swallowed hard, and kicked the old horse into a trot.

It was late evening when Maggie caught up. She saw the three of them and the river as she crested a tall hill and slid off her horse, standing stunned beside the exhausted animal. It was the same place. The spot where Lily had crossed three days before. She could see where they had dug a grave in the sand for the girl who had been murdered here and felt the guilt rush over her. "Forgive me," she mumbled. She closed her eyes and leaned into her horse's shoulder. She thought about the wonder of finding themselves back here.

Kayitah had accomplished it, had led them back to the exact spot where she had seen Lily. But how? The direction they'd taken from the cave had been so absolutely wrong. Was the cave truly sacred? She forced herself to stop thinking like that. More than likely her father had simply told him of the place, and he had taken his own route.

Maggie stood on the hilltop watching Dot and Ho-nes-co spinning wild, happy circles over the sand, their arms flung out, Chaco nipping angrily at their feet. Kayitah was squatting and watering the animals at the river's edge. She looked at her father lying motionless on the travois beside a small fire. She prayed he wasn't dead.

Maggie stood there in the twilight, watching the bats flitting through the darkening sky over the river, listening to the evening wind coming off the dry earth, and thinking of many things. Mostly about Lily and her father. There wasn't anything she wouldn't give to have Lily back, to have her safe. Now, thanks to Kayitah, maybe they had a chance. Her heart went out to the man—her half brother.

She looked beyond the ribbon of water toward the dusty land of twilight Mexico. "Lily, be safe," she said quietly. "We are coming."

The sound of the children's laughter drifted up the hill, washing gently over her. Then there was another sound. Sharper. Like a limb breaking in a winter forest. Harsh and unforgiving. For an instant in time, none of them moved. Then she saw Ho-nes-co crumple to the sand, and Dot running to the boy, Kayitah lunging for them both. Then the sharp sound came up the hill at her again, and Maggie realized it was rifle fire. Kayitah's horse went down. Then another animal squealed and fell writhing in the water.

Three men were charging on horseback down the beach toward Kayitah and Dot, firing and yelling, digging their heels hard into their horses' flanks. Maggie pulled her rifle and did not hesitate, settling the beaded sight into the V notch and leading the first rider. She knew they were still firing, but she heard nothing. Nothing but the small voice whispering once more deep inside her head.

Was it Lozen? She wasn't certain. All she knew was that it calmed her, helped her to block out all distractions, helped her to take careful aim on the first rider. She saw clearly that he was white. It made no difference. Dot was down there . . . and Kayitah and Ho-nes-co. He was trying to murder her child. She did not try to yell or wave, she just adjusted her lead, and squeezed the round off slowly.

She had always been a good shot. Samuel Jones had taught her. Somehow the man held on to his rifle, but Maggie could tell from the way he rolled backward over the rump of the running horse that he was dead before he hit the sand. The other two turned and galloped frantically toward the trees, firing wildly over their shoulders at Kayitah, crouched over Dot and Ho-nes-co. The whispering voice was gone.

The bullet had struck the boy in his neck. Dot and Kayitah were both holding his small, lifeless body, blood dripping in long rivulets down Dot's arms, the two of them making strange moaning sounds. Maggie joined them. She sat in the sand and put her arms around her daughter, and made the sound as well; it just seemed to emerge from some place inside her and mingle with their sounds.

Sitting there, listening to her daughter and her half brother mourning for the child, Maggie realized that she had never really looked closely at the boy before. She couldn't take her eyes off of him now. Her nephew. She knew him not—knew only that he had been happy and that he had taken instantly to his cousin. So he had risked his father's wrath to play with her, and Dot and he had bonded. Blood ties were instinctive and powerful. Tears filled her eyes. She turned and looked at Kayitah's handsome profile, grief exaggerating his features.

She reached out a hand and stroked Ho-nes-co's hair from his face, and hummed a church hymn.

Later she said, "*Hermano*." She waited for him to look at her. When he finally turned his head, she said, "I'm sorry," in Mexican.

He nodded with a solemn dignity, and returned to his moans and chanting. Again she joined him. Dot had curled into a tight ball on the sand and was bawling hard, pounding at the sand with her fists. Kayitah struggled to his knees, holding the boy in his arms, and looked at Maggie. Then he laid Ho-nes-co carefully in her lap, and walked slowly toward the camp where their father lay.

Maggie prepared the child for burial. When she finished, Kayitah sang Ho-nes-co's death song. Dot joined him. Maggie watched. Even Chaco was respectful of the moment, sitting quietly and watching, then trotting off to be with the old man again. He never left him for long.

# CHAPTER

# TEN

Dot selected the burial site. Kayitah had started to prepare a place among the rocks near the river, but Dot came to him and shook her head. Her uncle had stared at her for a long time, watching her point, then followed. She led them to a small clearing among the tamarisk trees. It was a beautiful, moonlit spot of sand with a view of the river.

They carried stones to the place. Then Kayitah sat down beside Ho-nes-co and talked to him in Apache. Maggie held Dot in her arms. When Kayitah was done, Dot pulled away from her mother and knelt next to the body. Untying the medicine necklace from her neck, she tied it around his small arm, and said, "Come with me, Ho. We will be together."

Maggie translated Dot's words into Mexican for Kayitah, and he nodded his head with feeling. He pointed an index finger in the air, wrapping his other hand around the finger. "Keep," the gesture meant. He seemed greatly touched.

"I promise," Dot said.

They left Kayitah sitting in the cool night air beside the grave and trudged back through the sand and the sounds of crickets to where Chaco sat guarding the old man. With the sun gone, the evening wind had died and a peaceful stillness had come on the river. It was a fitting place to bury the child, Maggie thought. Some small creature slipped into the water and she questioned whether this could be the child's spirit.

The gray was lying in the sand, sleeping. Dot held the old horse's head. Maggie gave her father a drink of water, marveling that he was still alive, and thanking God, then she and Dot bathed him with a wet rag, and put fresh clothes on him. Every once in a while, Dot would moan long and hard. Maggie understood. She thought of the little boy and Brake and Lily, and did the same.

Afterward, Dot and Chaco went down to the beach to catch the dead man's horse. Maggie watched her go, shotgun in her hands, the little terrier trotting importantly at her side, and realized with a catch in her throat that these collective tragedies had almost turned Dot into a grown woman. But this time, she was not sorry about it—not sorry because the young woman she had become was filled with strength and self-reliance, with love and courage. And, yes, compassion.

She looked down at the old man's face, the sound of Kayitah's prayers drifting sadly through the night air. As she examined his features, things in her mind began to slowly clear. He had abandoned her, but he had also taught her about life. The practical and the spiritual. To dream, to shoot, to doctor. Not to be afraid. And these had made a difference. Even his coming back to her had made a difference.

"Father," she said, then hesitated. "Maybe we were never meant to understand one another. We did once." She looked out over the river.

Later, while still watching the dark water, she said, "I used to try and think back to those times, try to understand, but the hurt and anger always stopped me. You left Mother and that killed her. But—" Her voice broke and she waited a moment. "But you left me, too. And that killed some of me as well. It isn't good enough to tell me you love me." Maggie stood up quickly. Dot was digging a grave down near the water for the dead man. Maggie looked back down at Jones and said, "I need to know. Need to know why you left me."

***

**M**aggie and Dot had finished burying the man by the time Kayitah returned to camp. He looked angry that they had honored his son's killer in this way, but he let it alone. They were down to the white man's horse and Maggie's old mount. The gray was nearly gone. Kayitah searched Maggie's face, his eyes probing deeply. He looked lost. She understood—had felt that same desperate feeling thirty years before when her father left, and now again with Lily. She wanted to cry for this man who could not cry for himself. He had come here to save her daughter, a child he didn't know, and had lost the only thing of worth in his life.

"Thank you," she said. "But go and find your people." She spoke in Mexican. "We will search for Lily. You owe us nothing more."

Kayitah motioned to the man's horse and said, "Yo *cabalgo.*" Maggie didn't understand, but nodded her head yes. He picked up his rifle and climbed onto the animal's back. Maggie pointed at Jones, and in Mexican said, "I will care for him. If he awakens, I'll tell him what you did for us. Your family." Kayitah formed a fist and stuck his index finger up in the air, his eyes wild with anger, then made a bounding motion, moving the hand forward. Maggie didn't understand this gesture either.

He disappeared into the night. She prayed for him and said farewell; then she sat and studied her father's face. After all these years, all the physical changes, she still saw him as he had looked the night he'd left so many years ago. Dot was sitting with her back to her, looking out into the expanse of night, lost in her own thoughts.

"Father," Maggie whispered. "I know you're almost gone. Find Lily, and watch over her." She lay down beside him and soon was asleep.

The darkness was chilled and still, filled only with the soft sounds of the river and night birds. Dot was not at the fire when Maggie awoke. She found her where she knew she would, sitting in the moonlight beside Ho-nes-co's grave. She knelt beside her and said nothing for a long while. The stars looked brilliant in the wash of darkness overhead. She put her arm around Dot's shoulders.

"What was he like?"

"Fun. Just fun. He liked me. I don't know why."

"He was of your blood," Maggie said softly.

Dot turned her head and searched her mother's face in the darkness, amazed that she had acknowledged kinship with Ho-nes-co.

"Are you saying goodbye?"

Dot shook her head. "I don't have to." She said the words matter-of-factly. "I'm just asking him to help me."

"To do what?"

Dot waited a moment before she spoke, poking the sand with a stick. She glanced at her mother. "You won't believe. And you'll just get mad."

"I won't get mad."

Dot watched her for a moment, then looked down at Ho-nes-co's grave and said, "Grandpa told me once that everyone has a special power inside them. And that as a person gets ready to die, they lose their power. That it must go to someone else."

Dot stopped and looked at her mother, expecting to see the anger. Maggie was just listening. "Well, Ho must have had a power, too. And I was asking him to send it to Grandpa. So that he will wake up and find Lily. Do you think that can happen? Do you think Ho can send his power to Grandpa?"

Maggie sat for a few moments before answering. "I don't know, honey. I don't know anything about these beliefs. But I know one thing."

"What?"

"That if you believe it . . . then I do, too."

Dot smiled at her and leaned in close to Maggie's warmth.

Maggie got up early, before the big brown bats had ceased their restless darting, to check on her father. There was the first tinge of light in the dawn sky. An immense stillness filled the land. She studied the old man's narrow face for a long time. Ho's power had not come to him. She caught herself feeling disappointed and was surprised. She laid an extra blanket over him against the morning chill, and gave him some water, then read from the Bible to him. Dot was still sleeping by the cold ashes of the night fire. Maggie felt as lost and frightened as she ever had in her life.

She was alone now in the wilderness with a dying man and his broken horse, her own poor animal, a young girl and a dog. There was no way, she knew, that they'd ever reach Lily. She didn't know what to do. Her choices were Mexico or Hoganville. She stood and opened her Bible at random and read: "Men ought always to pray." She felt anger building inside her. She had prayed—prayed without ceasing—and received nothing except pain and misery. Maggie shut the Bible. Then she turned and saw him.

Her brother was riding slowly across the sand toward her on the dead man's horse, leading the mounts of the other two men who had helped kill Ho-nes-co. The muscles of her back quivered. Why had he returned? There was nothing here for him. He belonged with whatever remained of his people. But he had come back to her, and the fear she'd been feeling all morning left her, replaced by new emotions for this man—this brother.

Kayitah reined in the horse and sat looking down at them, his eyes still burning with an intensity that frightened. Chaco barked angrily.

"Thank you," she said.

He watched her with an expressionless gaze, then waved his hand at the campsite in a gruff way, and Maggie knew he meant for them to pack. She nodded and began to stuff their belongings into the saddlebags.

It was before dawn of the next day and Maggie was shivering with hope. Dot had spotted the sign of Lily's kidnappers in the darkness, spying a broken cactus pad. Try as she might, she couldn't work it out, but Kayitah had unraveled it neatly. The man came and just sat near the place, seemingly melding his thoughts with the fading night and the morning stars, silently feeling the presence of those who had passed this way.

Slowly the stars disappeared and the eastern sky brightened, and the scaled quail started their happy little *pe-cos, pe-cos* call. Still, Kayitah sat studying the sign. Dot tried to see what he saw. Nothing. Then she watched as he reached out and touched a finger gently to a small stone that had been kicked out of its bed. She knew from what Mannito had taught her that he was gauging the distance between it and the hoofprint—that the single stone told her uncle the direction, the speed and the weight of the animal that had kicked it.

In the faint morning light, he moved slowly forward over the hard ground, reading dry cracked leaves, examining faint compressions in the dirt. He got down on his hands and knees and lowered his head close to the earth, scanning it sideways. Then he stood and ran his fingers over the dull vegetation nearby. He began to move a little faster, crouched and studying the sand and rocks.

When he was confident of their direction, he began a steady dogtrot, eating up the distance. They crossed and recrossed the tracks numerous times after that, the sign freshening. Maggie was deliriously happy. She couldn't believe it. The Indians should have been down deep in Mexico where they'd have been impossible to catch. But they weren't. They were close enough that Kayitah could read their tracks while trotting beside them.

The twilight had brought a deep purpled shading to the land and they were approaching a small grass valley shaped like the palm of a hand and ringed with sandstone hills. Dot could hear sand cranes near water. Her legs ached from having been in the saddle all day. But she was sensing from her uncle that they were close and closing, so she had stayed on her horse. Repeatedly, he stopped on the trail and listened hard, as if he could actually hear voices. She tried to as well but never heard anything. Only the silence of these desert lands.

Kayitah had halted his animal again and sat probing the stillness with his ears. She could glimpse the small valley through a cut in the hills and wanted to slip down and investigate. But Kayitah anticipated this and made a quick jerking motion with his hand, and Dot stayed put. She watched as he swung quietly off his mount and squatted, pushing his thumb into the dirt next to a hoofprint, carefully studying both indentations. Dot knew he was comparing the ages of the two prints. He stood, and for the first time since she had met him, he half-smiled. They had caught them!

"Where are they?" Maggie whispered.

There were no sounds. No visible sign. Kayitah held up his

hand and signed for them to be silent and to dismount. He led the horses back down the trail for a time, then hid the travois and picked Jones up in his arms and began to climb into the mountains.

The light was failing, the setting sun dusting the mountains pink. Kayitah had laid Jones on a blanket near a wall of sandstone. Dot was sitting out near the rim of rocks staring off toward the grass valley toward Lily. Maggie watched Kayitah.

He was sitting a few yards away, oblivious, staring at the rocks of the outcropping, as if he were watching some distant parade. A large desert tortoise was moving slowly past him in the shadowy night. He reached out a hand and touched its shell in a reverent way, and the old creature pulled in its head. Then Kayitah went back to thinking, and the tortoise crawled on. It wasn't a good sign. He looked to Maggie like a man about to surrender things. About to die. That notion scared her.

"We need a plan," she said in Mexican.

He said nothing in response. She watched him solemnly spreading his few possessions—a silver necklace, a beaded armband and a few other trinkets—on a blanket. Then they both sat thinking their own thoughts in the small place among the rocks. There was no fire, no moon rising yet, only growing blackness and evening stars. She sensed that he was preparing to go after Lily.

"Describe," he said.

Maggie, her heart racing, tried to describe Lily in Mexican. It was a struggle. Kayitah listened. Finally he stood.

"What can I do to thank you? What can I give you?"

Slowly, as if some vague recollection was dawning in his brain, Kayitah stared down at her through the deepening shadows. He looked angry again.

"Whites have stolen the stones and the earth. What can you give me?"

"Then why are you doing this?"

"For my father." He looked hard into her face. "And for the *niña*." He motioned harshly toward Dot. She was too far away to hear. "Ho-nes-co and her—" He made the sign for love.

"Cousins." She nodded.

"The boy will live in her. It is enough."

Kayitah had rubbed a fresh line of white pigment across his nose and cheekbones, the ornamentation making him appear threatening, his beautiful features demonized. He wore nothing but his clout, his deerskin boots, his knife and pistol. She could count only six cartridges. She pulled some from her own belt and held them out to him. He shook his head.

Kayitah squatted beside Jones for a long time, speaking in his own tongue. When he was done, he returned and stood looking down at her. "If I not return—give this to him." He held out a small leather poke. She took it, her fingers brushing slightly against his hand. She jumped, realizing it was the only time she had ever touched her brother. She sensed it was the only time she ever would.

"*Hermano*," she said to him, something squeezing in her chest.

He shook his head no in a rough way, as if the word annoyed him, then looked back at his father. "If I not return—" he said again, "give to him when the sun comes over the rocks."

Kayitah turned and left. Maggie couldn't stop watching him.

"Bring my child back. You are her *tío*." She trotted after him, pulling her ring from her finger. She handed it to him, putting it in his open palm and closing her hands around his. It was a wonderful feeling for her. He pulled out of her grasp as if her touch was distasteful to her.

"Show it to Lily and she will know you were sent by me."

Lily was tossing and turning on the sand where she slept, smiling and moving her hands as if to some faint music that only she could hear. She laughed quietly and rolled over. Then she began to stiffen, sensing something wrong.

Her eyes popped open and she stared at the dark roof of the small cave where she and the other captives were being held, clutching the rag doll to her. Fully awake now, she knew for certain that something was wrong. She listened hard. Nothing. Only the steady breathing of the other women. Every once in a while one of them would moan or cry out faintly, but nothing else. She listened again: a soft scuffling sound. She froze. Someone was moving in the cave.

Lily sat bolt upright and blinked into the night and found herself staring straight into the face of an Indian. The warrior was squatting in the darkness, studying her, as if looking for something. She had never seen him before. It took everything she had to keep from screaming. He made a cautioning sign with his hand over his mouth, looking behind him furtively at the others. They were sleeping around the fire.

Lily studied his face, trying to look calm. He was better-looking than the others, but still Apache. He was making silent signs toward her that made no sense. Then he inched forward. She pressed her back against the rock wall.

"Don't touch me," she said nervously.

He made the cautioning sign again and said in a fierce whisper, "Lily—*tío*."

She stiffened. How did he know her name? He moved closer.

"*Tío*," he whispered again.

Who was this savage? Why did he keep saying "uncle"?

He pointed at her, then turned the finger on himself, and

gave a long sweeping gesture with his hand which she took to mean that he wanted her to leave with him. She shook her head hard.

"Leave me alone," she hissed.

He glanced quickly to see if the other Indians had heard her. Finally, when he turned back, he looked agitated.

"Lily—*tío*," he said emphatically and made the sweeping gesture once more. Then he pulled something from a leather pouch and held it out to her. She stared at it until she finally recognized it and grabbed it from him: her mother's wedding ring.

"Where did you get this?" she shouted, lunging at him with her fists. The man tried to roll away and pull his pistol but the others were on him.

Lily pushed the knife she had grabbed from the man's belt quickly under the sand.

The moans were incessant, broken only periodically by his cries of: "Ho-nes-co," the scream shattering the still night air. But then always he would fall back into his ceaseless groaning. And when it was very late, when she thought she could take no more of it, when the night breezes had died over the dry land, she heard him yell, "Lily—*tío!*" the words ripping at soft places inside her. The Indians standing around him laughed. Maggie lowered the glasses and collapsed against a large rock. She had been hiding for hours in the foothills above the Apache camp, watching in helpless terror as they tortured Kayitah.

He did not scream much anymore—just emitted the awful, animal-like sound of the moaning. Maggie was rocking back and forth against the stone, slamming her body against the hard surface to distract her mind from the horror, pressing her lips together with all her might to suppress the scream building in her.

She tried again to block the terrible keening sound with her hands. It did no good. The noise seeped down into her like water through cracks in stone, eroding something hard inside her, flushing the residue from her soul.

Maggie had left Dot asleep at their camp and followed Kayitah, followed in case he and Lily needed help in their escape. But something had gone wrong. She pulled her knees up tight against her chest and pleaded again for help from God. None came.

"Damn Indians," she said bitterly, then shook her head. "No."

She would not blacken Kayitah's race. She might hate the cripple and the others, might damn her father's paramour. But not all of them. Not Kayitah. Not Ho. Not Lozen.

They had tied her brother by his wrists and ankles between two small trees, and were shooting arrows into him, carefully avoiding his vital parts. Maggie couldn't watch anymore. She fought the hysteria in her and started to turn away, then stopped. No. She wouldn't abandon him. Couldn't—her father had taught her loyalty. She turned back and looked through the glasses, sobbing. "Kayitah, leave this life. There is nothing here for you." She wiped at her eyes. Then made the sign of the cross over him. "I baptize you a child of God. May Jesus Christ have mercy on your soul." She watched him for a moment, then said, "Brother. Go. Find your boy."

Kayitah yanked at the ropes binding him and screamed, "Fielito!" Then it was quiet and she knew he had gone. "Thank You, God," she sobbed.

Morning was coming in the distance when she remembered. Maggie fumbled wildly for the small bag that her brother had given her and ran hard for their hidden camp in the hills. Crying as she ran.

A t the first spraying of sunlight over the rocks, Maggie placed the leather poke in Jones's hands as Kayitah had asked, squeezing until the gnarled fingers closed over the little leather bag, then she leaned forward and kissed his forehead.

"He's gone," she said sadly. "Kayitah is gone." She fought the tightening in her throat. "He wanted you to have this. I'm sorry."

Slowly, she stood and turned away, her thoughts on this lost brother who had loved and respected their father so much that he had died trying to do what the old man had asked. She sensed that Kayitah had known that he was going to die—that he wasn't going to be able to rescue Lily. And still he had tried. His last words had been "Lily—*tío*," and "*Fielito*." His family. His blood. Maggie continued to fight the tightening of her throat. Her brother was gone. Had died for her child.

As she stood there, her back to her father, she sensed an odd expectancy in the air and tensed her body without knowing why. Then she heard a noise behind her and whirled and faced him.

"Holy Mary, Mother of God," she whispered.

The old man was sitting up on the blanket, blinking into the morning sunrise.

"Are you alive?" she mumbled, stunned that Jones was conscious and moving.

The old man said nothing, just looked off into the distance of the awakening day as though he were listening to his name being called by the devil, his painfully starved body rigid.

"Grandpa!" Dot shouted happily. Chaco was darting around and over the old man, barking hard. Still, Samuel

Jones did not look at them or say anything. It was as if he were in a deep trance, lost in some netherworld that only he could sense.

"Dot," Maggie said quietly, "I think we'd better let him wake up slowly. He's been gone for quite a while."

They sat in the sand and watched the old man for most of the morning, marveling at his recuperative powers. He was still sitting up, leaning back against the mountain wall; but he had not spoken or moved. His ribs protruded sharply against his leathery skin like those on a starving cow, his already thin limbs, even thinner, a dried, crumbly leaf of a man. Scrawny and desiccated.

Once or twice, Maggie had offered him water. Each time, he acted as if he hadn't heard her or known she was nearby. He continued to look out from the shadows of the overhang toward the brightening morning sky, staring off in the direction of the Apache camp as if listening hard for something lost in the wind. Maggie felt she understood somehow.

"What's wrong with him?" Dot asked.

"He was pretty far gone. It takes a person time to come back from where he was."

Dot watched him, amazed.

"Ho's power worked."

Maggie hesitated then shook her head.

"What then?"

"Kayitah."

Dot turned sharply and looked at Maggie, absorbing what this meant. She shook her head hard.

"No. Kayitah is bringing Lily back."

Maggie didn't respond, staring at her hands.

"Ma? Kayitah went after Lily."

"Yes." She stood, dusting her pants.

Dot continued to watch her. "Ma?"

"He didn't make it."

"How do you know?" Dot's voice rose.

"He didn't make it." Maggie was watching her father.

"He could be late. Maybe they're hiding in the hills."

Maggie shook her head again.

"You don't know for sure. Kayitah went for Lily. He had to get her." Dot was beginning to make an odd heaving sound from within.

Maggie wrapped her arms around Dot's thin shoulders, holding her tight as if to trap the noise inside her.

"Ma, it's Lily's only chance. He's got to!"

"No, Dot. He's dead."

"You don't know that!" Dot shouted, turning and running to the edge of the clearing. She stood and screamed her sister's name into the morning.

Maggie followed and held her again. "Dot—stop. He's dead. I saw it." The child collapsed in her arms.

Dot had gone beyond tears when she next spoke, gone to a level of desperation that flayed her words. "We can't let them have Lily."

Dot was still crying as she watered the animals at the stone basin Kayitah had shown her. Then she heard a sound and stood, listening, the hair rising on her neck. Someone was slowly climbing the trail to the water. Too close for her to hide the horses. She couldn't even warn her mother. Whoever it was, they weren't much on being quiet, snapping branches and kicking rocks. Dot pushed herself deeper into the shadows of a manzanita bush, praying that it was Kayitah and Lily . . . praying that her mother had made a mistake about her uncle being dead.

Then Alice trudged over the crest of the ridge, looking as happy as ever, and nuzzled the old gray. Dot held the mule's head to hers, laughing and bawling.

The young jenny rubbed up and down against her chest for

a minute, before turning and starting up the trail toward their camp. Dot just shook her head. How did she always know where he was? Dot followed.

Maggie was gone. She'd left a note telling Dot to take her grandfather and start back to the ranch—that she'd gone for Lily and would catch up. Dot's body was shaking.

Maggie lay among the rocks above where the band was camped, the sun behind her, holding the glasses, knowing there would be no reflection this time. She could not stop looking at him.

"Kayitah," she mumbled, the words catching roughly in her throat. He had lost his son's life—then his own—for her child.

She looked away and scanned the camp. A group of Indians was sitting near a sandy hillside. She figured Lily and the other women were nearby. She went over her plan slowly, checking details, then slid the battered Sharps forward onto the rock ledge, sighting down the long blue barrel on the closest Indian. Old and beaten, the weapon still had a perfectly balanced feel to it and she understood why her father had carried it all these years. She snuffed and wiped at her eyes with the heel of her hand, then pulled cartridges from her pocket and lined them up on a small rock where she could get at them easily. She wouldn't use them all. Two, maybe three before they started after her. Enough. She wanted the cripple. If she got one or two others, fine. She took the small crucifix and laid it on the rock, her fingers moving over it.

"God. Forgive." She closed her eyes, thinking back over the years of their lives. Lily had always been bright and sassy. Knowing Brake and James had teased her about her clothes and her fancy airs, Maggie said, "Somebody has to appreciate fine things." She paused. "I love you. Your father, and your brother and sister love you. And your grandfather. If there was any other way—" Maggie stopped. "God, Lily—" She tore the words off as if they hurt, staring angrily at the cartridges. "This should not have happened to her."

Maggie wiped her eyes and prayed until sweat was beading on her forehead. Prayed that what she was about to do was right. There was no other way. Without Kayitah or her father, she and Dot would eventually lose the band; or be captured. She couldn't let that happen to Dot. No, she had to end this insanity here. She placed her pistol on the rock beside the shells. After she shot Lily and the cripple, she would use it on herself. Dot had the guts and stamina to make it back to the ranch. There was movement below. She chambered her first shell.

"Mother of Jesus," she whispered. "You watched Your Son suffer. You would have helped—" She couldn't say the words. "Help me." Her hands were trembling. "I know this is a sin. Forgive." She brought her hands together, unable to stop her steady shaking.

There was no way she was going to be able to fire the rifle accurately. Powerful as it was, it was extremely sensitive. Maggie's mind seemed to drift. Then she sat up straight. "Lozen, help—my hands." She paused. "You called to me for help once. But I didn't know you existed." She paused and took a deep breath. "I know now. I know you've spoken to me over the years since. I—"

Maggie waited for the sound of the calming voice in her head. Waited for her sister to steady her trembling hands. But neither happened.

The women stood in the evening light near the campfire. Maggie put the glasses on Lily, studying her carefully. She had never seen her look this unkempt—or this lovely. She had lost weight on her willowy frame and her eyes were swollen, but the gauntness, the strain and bruises only enhanced her beauty.

Maggie's hands were trembling so badly now that Lily's image in the glasses was bouncing. She was standing straight and tall, holding a small doll in one hand. There must be a child somewhere. Maggie smiled through the pain, knowing how much Lily loved children. She cleared her throat.

How could she harm her? Brake's child. Maggie was sobbing hard now. She talked to Lily for a long time. Talked to her as she always had when she was sick or afraid. Told her how much she meant to her. Slowly Maggie said her goodbyes to this child—spoke words to her that tore at her insides like nothing in life ever had. Or ever would again.

Maggie waited until the women began to eat, then she said goodbye to Lily one last time and cocked the Sharps. As she was squeezing the round off, the small voice came clearly into her head: "No," was all it said. But it was enough.

"Help me," Maggie pleaded. But even as she said the words, she sensed Lozen would not. Her sister had already spoken.

Then suddenly he was there—settling himself down beside her. She couldn't believe it. She had a hard time looking away from him, moisture blurring her vision. He was here—against all odds. Still, the chances that this dying old fool could save Lily were nothing. She settled the butt of the rifle against her shoulder and bit at her lip again.

"Ama," he rasped, his voice raw-sounding.

"There's no other way."

He shook his head.

She studied his gaunt features. "Where's Dot?"

He signed the word: riding.

"Promise?"

He nodded and went back to watching the camp, his body stiffening at the sight of Kayitah.

She let him mourn for a while, then said, "Ho-nes-co is gone as well." She could see his lips moving, his eyes blinking in the twilight. She stared down at the old rifle and agonized whether she could do it, then slid it toward him. "Do this for me. For Lily."

The old man took the weapon and looked away to Kayi-tah. Maggie watched him for a moment and knew he would not.

The gray pony strolled into the Indian camp looking as though she owned half the territory; stopping beside the fire while the Apaches pulled their rifles, and ordered the women back inside the cave, then dodged for cover. The camp was deserted now.

Jones smiled.

"All that does is destroy our chance to end this madness for Lily," Maggie said angrily.

He didn't respond.

"They'll just come looking to see who owns her."

He shook his head almost imperceptibly.

"They won't believe she walked from Santa Fe on a Sunday stroll."

Jones didn't move. "Kayitah's things." The words scratched out of his throat. "They'll believe his horse."

Maggie turned back. The Indians were examining the pack on the gray's back, holding up arrows and other things. She could see them pointing at Kayitah. Then they were dancing and laughing and holding bottles in the air.

"What are they so happy about?"

"Mescal."

Maggie swung her head around and stared in stunned admiration at his rugged old face, hope growing in her again. He was amazing—had come back from the dead and was still fighting. Kayitah's life-power: had it passed to him? Christians didn't believe such things, she told herself, then questioned whether that was right. Christ had infused the power of His mighty spirit into the dead Lazarus. She trembled, reaching and touching the crucifix lying on the rock before her.

The cave was dark, the only light the soft white rays of the moon shining in from the opening at the front, allowing almost nothing to be seen. Lily tensed. She had heard a scuffling sound at the entrance. She held her breath, listening hard and shivering. She thought she'd seen a piece of shadow move.

Had the cripple come back to beat her again? She clutched the doll and felt the clawing urge to huddle or hide, but knew it was hopeless. Lily fought the tremors that gripped her. Limbs of Satan, she'd heard the minister in Santa Fe once call the Apaches. Too grand—just brutes. Nothing more. And the cripple was the worst.

He'd assaulted her so many times she'd lost track—slapping and hitting her, ending each attack with the awful choking. She fought to control her emotions. The last time she remembered wishing that he wouldn't stop. She couldn't take any more. Her eyes were almost swollen shut and she could taste blood.

She formed the simple plan in her mind as she watched the dark shape moving toward her. She would kill him, then run. If they caught her she would take her own life. But could she? She didn't know. All she knew was that she couldn't take this. She closed her swollen eyes, pretending to sleep, her hand digging for the knife in the soft sand where she'd hidden it.

She could hear him breathing and smelled the alcohol and body grease, and knew that he was squatting directly in front of her. She hesitated for only a moment, then resolved that he would never again hit her, and brought the knife around in a wild arcing swing, plunging it with all her strength toward the shadow's side. But he saw it and was quick enough to deflect it downward so that it sank into his thigh. He shuddered from the shock of the penetration, moaning deep inside his body. Lily yanked the blade out and was raising it desperately over her shoulder, when she saw her grandfather's face contorting with agony.

The old man grabbed her wrist. "Child. Let go. It's over." He squeezed his mouth and eyes, fighting the searing pain, applying pressure to the bloody wound in his leg.

Lily could only stare at him, his presence incomprehensible. She had seen her mother at the river, but had figured that she was riding with a second posse. She would never have guessed that this old man would come. Not in her lifetime. It was beyond understanding.

He reached a hand and touched gently at the puffiness around her eyes. "You're okay now, child," he whispered.

"Take me home," she whimpered.

He made a cautioning sign with his hand. "I am. Tell these women they're to come with us. Make no noise."

She didn't respond, just searched his features as if he were the first human she'd ever seen.

"Lily."

He looked deathly thin and hollow-cheeked. She reached a trembling hand toward him. "Grandfather, take me home."

"We're going home."

There was a sound behind him, and Jones turned as Maggie entered. Then Lily was in her mother's arms, Jones clamping his big hands over both their mouths to silence them.

It was later that same night and every line of the hills, the trail, the brush, every rut and rock was illuminated to gray by the thin moon floating in a clear sky, a heaven washed with delicate white clouds and seeded with stars. Nothing moved but Jones and the line of women. The old man was limping badly. They were sneaking single file through the darkness toward the mouth of the small valley. He had already stolen the gray and the other horses and these were waiting a few hundred feet down the trail.

He stepped to the side and whispered to Maggie, "Get them on the horses. I'll be back in a moment."

Jones cut Kayitah free of the rawhide and laid him on the earth. He was stiff and hard like burned wood, and Jones couldn't get his legs or arms to move back into place, so that he looked like he was falling out of the sky. The body was screened by a stand of greasewood from the Apaches who lay sleeping off their drunk. Jones checked them from a distance. Fools. He would have killed them but the Lame One was missing and he couldn't take the chance that he'd return.

The old man sat beside Kayitah and held his hand, looking blindly into the night's darkness, seeing things in it. He was smiling through tears.

"Yopon. Be proud of your son. He has done all any man could. Gave his life—for his family.

"Kayitah." Jones was looking up at a bright star in the low southern sky. "Remember when I gave you that star? You were a boy. You said that if you died before me, you would go to your star and wait. Wait until I came to join you; wait so that I would not lose you in the vast heavens. Oooh, son." He paused, unable to go on. He patted Kayitah's stiff hand. "Go to your star. Wait for me. Take your mother, take Lozen, Eskim and Ho-nes-co and the others, go there and wait. I will come to find you. I have followed your sign over many a trail. Leave your sign for me. Mark the way well, so that I do not lose you on the last trail."

Jones rocked back on his haunches. "I love you, son. Tell your mother and sister, and your brothers, that I love them, too. I will soon be with them. And, Kayitah, if you see the woman, Susan, or my daughter Thelma, take them to the star as well." He hesitated. "But only if they wish to come."

"They will want to come," Maggie said quietly.

The old man jumped and looked at her. She untied the scarf around her neck. Lily was next to her, the doll in her hands, her bruised eyes almost swollen shut. She looked frightened by the body. Still, she found it in her to take hold of the corners of the cloth, when Maggie held it out to her. They moved around until they could place it over Kayitah's face. Lily gathered rocks and put them on the corners to hold it down.

"Do you believe so?" Jones asked. "That Susan and Thelma will want to come?"

Maggie knelt and pulled the crucifix from her pocket and placed it in the sand next to Kayitah's body. Lily watched the two of them, her mother and her grandfather, fighting something inside of her that she didn't understand.

"There is no doubt in my mind."

The old man looked deeply touched. Lily was kneeling beside Kayitah now as well. She raised the edge of the handkerchief carefully and stared down at the handsome face.

"He said he was my uncle."

Jones looked at Maggie.

"He was," she said. "He was good and brave. He cared for family."

Lily turned and looked into her mother's face, her own contorting in emotion. "I killed him."

"Child," Jones whispered.

Lily looked up at him.

"Tell him now that you know he is your uncle. That you are thankful he tried to save you." Jones waited a moment, composing himself. "This was my son. He was Apache. He believed in family. He would like that. Death has rubbed the whiteness from your skin for him. You are truly kin—bound by his death."

Maggie whispered prayers over Kayitah, then touched his hand and said, "Goodbye, my brother." She moved off into the shadows, leaving Lily alone with the body. Jones checked the Apaches near the fire again, then began searching for signs on the ground. He squatted and pulled his glasses on and studied a spot a few yards away. Maggie walked over and saw the moccasin prints in the sand.

"The Lame One," Jones said. "The one who killed the girl at the river. The one who sent the ghost sickness on you. He directed the killing of Mannito at the ranch. He did the same here with Kayitah. He tried to take Lily that night in the fog."

Maggie didn't say anything. She was convinced now that her father knew these things.

After Lily had walked away from Kayitah's body, Maggie saw that she had placed the small doll on her uncle's chest. Jones sat alone for a while with his son. Then they left the dead warrior in the stillness of the night, moving quickly toward the horses and the women. Jones saw to the saddles and then pulled the gray out of line, mounted and rode up alongside Maggie.

"I will be back. Follow the trail until you cross the river. Then head for the blue mountains to the north. Whatever you do, do not stop."

Maggie sat watching him, her eyes moving over his face. "You're too sick. He will kill you. It won't bring Kayitah back. We have Lily. Ride on with us. Please," she pleaded.

"I must."

"Why?"

"Mannito. And my son." He watched her face for a moment. "And so that you and the children can be safe."

"Please don't."

He turned the gray into the darkness and headed away from them. Maggie and Lily watched him until he disappeared.

"Will we see him again?" Lily asked.

"I don't know."

Maggie put her heels to her horse and started down the trail.

# CHAPTER

# ELEVEN

With a possum scurrying over the sand ahead of her, Maggie rode her horse out of the shallow waters of the Rio Grande, reining the animal in and trying to remember everything her father had told her to do. She tried to orient herself to the north and the blue mountains she couldn't see in the dark. She wondered how far off they were. Wondered whether the Apaches were on their trail.

She let her gaze drop to the sand beside the horse, her thoughts on Dot and the long, dangerous ride she faced in making it back to the ranch. "Be safe, child," she mumbled. Then she looked up and saw the old man riding out of the greasewood a hundred yards down the beach. She smiled. He came slowly, the gray's head down. He had given up the hunt. Thank God.

Maggie swung in beside him as he passed by.

"Did you find him?" she asked nervously.

"No." He rode for a moment, then said, "He will find us."

"Don't joke."

Jones looked at her in a way that said he was not joking. They continued on in silence for a while. Maggie tried not to think of the Lame One. Her thoughts were on God. She had not received a divine sign of any kind, no answered prayers. The old man had saved Lily. It was that simple. He had done it either through sheer luck—or . . . Or what? Could there be anything to his strange rituals, the odd chantings, the paint, the sacred smoke? Who were these gods of his? She studied the neck of the old horse she was riding and knew only that she knew nothing.

The sky was beginning to lighten in a thin line across the distant horizon. They had been trotting hard for the past two hours, the little gray wheezing as she moved.

"We need to rest," Maggie called. "These women and animals are ready to drop."

"We can't," Jones said.

"Why?"

He didn't answer.

"They're following us—aren't they?"

He nodded.

"They can't catch us." Her words were more a question than a statement.

Jones stopped the gray and set his bearings against the night skyline, then he started off again at a brisk trot.

Maggie caught up with him. "They can't catch us. We can't let that happen."

Jones rode into the breaking light of the morning like a man possessed, Chaco barking encouragement to the line of riders. All the horses were lathering white around their mouths and flanks. It was clear to Maggie that her father had carefully selected a single route of escape and was determined to make it. The gray was weaving a Virginia fence as she trotted close to collapse, gamely fighting on for the old man.

Maggie pulled up alongside him again. Chaco did a neat switch from the rump of the gray to her horse and back again, just for show. The land was caked and cracked. Cactus and little else. The sun's rays were knifing over it.

"Are they after us?"

Jones tipped his head back in the direction they had come.

Maggie turned in her saddle and looked. Straining her eyes, she could just barely make out a thin plume of dust rising from the desert perhaps five miles behind them in the dawn.

"Can they catch us?"

"Yes."

Near midday she spotted the object of their relentless drive: a massive chain of blue mountains, hazy and warping in the hot distance. The old man gazed intently at the craggy hills as though afraid that if he looked away, they would disappear. One of the women's horses gave out with a groan and sank to its knees. One look and Maggie knew it was gone. Jones turned in a big circle and swung the girl up behind him by her wrist—Maggie was certain the little gray would go down under the extra weight, but she staggered forward—then he slid to the ground and began to trot in a long limping gait, his wound oozing clear fluid down his leg. Lily kicked the bay up alongside him.

"Grab," she said, pointing at the saddle horn.

Their eyes met for a moment; then he nodded and took hold.

"Aim for that notch between the tall peaks," he told her. "Aim straight. They'll waver. We won't. That way we'll beat them."

Lily nodded.

Maggie was riding on the other side of him. He was coughing hard. She started to swing down off her horse. He waved her back in the saddle.

"My strides are longer. We have to make the hills."

"You'll kill yourself."

"If we don't make the hills, it won't matter," he rasped.

"The gray can't go much farther," Maggie said.

"She'll make the mountain. She has promised."

Lily and Maggie glanced at each other but said nothing. They rode in silence for a long time, then Maggie turned and looked down at the side of his face and said, "Where's Dot?" She sounded frightened.

Jones motioned toward the northeast. Maggie shaded her eyes and gazed off in the direction Jones had indicated, as if she might catch a glimpse of her daughter. Her thoughts were conjuring up the hundreds of miles of dry, desolate waste between her little girl and the ranch—and somewhere out there rode the lame Apache. Her heart beat harder. Then Maggie thought of Alice the mule and Dot's guts and felt better. If anyone could make it—it would be those two.

Pride surged inside her, briefly shoving the fear from her mind. Her girls were strong, like their grandmother. Maggie hesitated. Like Yopon and Lozen. Catching a quick glance at the side of Lily's bruised face, Maggie for the first time dared to believe they would see home. Be together again as a family.

She looked behind them. The plume of dust was larger. The Apaches were closing hard on them.

"Hurry," she said, kicking her horse into a gallop.

"No," Jones bellowed. "These animals will drop if you run them. We have to pace the distance." He was gasping for air.

"But they're catching us!"

Jones didn't respond. Lily rode with her eyes fixed on the notch in the blue hills, studying her grandfather with sideways glances, questioning how she should sort the mixed-up things in her head. She wanted to say something to him but couldn't find the words.

"They're heading us off!" Maggie yelled, pointing to the right of them at another, smaller dust plume.

"How did they do that?" Lily called down to him.

The old man just shook his head and kept trotting. Nothing seemed capable of deterring him from his intense focus on the blue mountains. A flock of Inca doves exploded beneath the hooves of Lily's bay, causing the horse to rear and dragging Jones off his feet. Lily grabbed the old man's arm and helped him hold on, his eyes never leaving the distant line of hills.

The dust plume off to their right continued to close, until some twenty minutes later Jones brought them to a halt and went to the gray and yanked his Sharps out. Maggie pulled her own rifle and handed Lily her pistol. Then the dust disappeared, and they knew whoever it was had stopped galloping and was walking them up.

There was a fair-sized arroyo nearby, and Jones slipped carefully into it with a grace that belied his years and health. Maggie turned and studied the horizon behind them; she could make out black specks beneath the tan cloud. Minutes later, she heard brush breaking and jerked her head back as Jones reappeared over the edge of the gully, followed quickly by Alice and Dot.

Jones gave them only a minute together, Dot laughing and dancing madly for joy with her sister, Maggie smiling and fighting tears. Dot ran to her grandfather and threw her arms around him and they both fell down. Dot yelled, "We did it!" The old man smiled his golden-tooth smile. Then they were off at their mad trot again.

Hours later they reined in at the foot of the blue mountains. Maggie could now make out the riders behind them, and the colors of the horses they rode, as Jones started them up into the wide mouth of a rocky ravine. Panic grew inside her until she felt it pressing against her lungs, making her gasp for air. The rest of them looked fear-stricken as well. Only Jones appeared calm, seemingly relieved by the fact that they had made it into the harsh stone walls of the hills.

Granite precipices—sharp ridges carved by the howling winds, thin ledges and soaring peaks—stood stark and unforgiving. Maggie couldn't understand why he felt good. It looked like the worst choice, a place to simply be trapped. But the old man continued stumbling and driving forward as though it were salvation itself. He had left Lily and was dogtrotting up a rocky trail, the line of riders struggling to follow, the women crying and worrying over the Apaches behind them.

The sun had begun its descent to earth, the sky going yellow and the canyons and rocks shading deep blue. The Apaches were off their horses now and climbing below them, no more than five or six hundred yards behind. Every once in a while they would send a shot up at them, but they were out of effective range and conserving their ammunition. It would be over soon, Maggie thought with dread.

She looked at her father's thin frame driving relentlessly forward, seemingly no end to his physical reserves. It was amazing: a man near death—now defying it magnificently. The steep trail was narrowing, threatening to give out as it ran into the blunt face of a massive wall of stone, the palisade shooting up in sheer vertical ramparts some six hundred feet. Where would he lead them now? Maggie questioned. Or had he finally miscalculated and simply led them unwittingly into a blind trap? She stumbled on. There was no alternative. Except one. She would use it if she had to. They would not take either of her girls. Not alive.

Maggie was ready to drop from the fear and exertion, when she saw why Jones had brought them here. Something caught in her throat. He had done it. Done it again. He was there when she desperately needed him.

In the shadows of the rock face was a narrow gap so tight

that horses would have to be forced through, riderless, one by one; then on the other side of the narrowing spot, the trail widened again, forming an hourglasslike effect. It was the perfect place to hold them back—the surrounding cliffs, sheer and defiant, were too steep for scaling. Maggie couldn't seem to take her eyes off his fierce old face as he worked each animal through the small opening.

Alice had been one of the first animals through the rift in the stone, and now she was braying wildly. Maggie looked at her and knew immediately that something was wrong; the young jenny was struggling through the other animals back down toward the gap, causing chaos on the trail. Jones grabbed her reins and turned her around and swatted her hard on the rump. She shivered, but didn't budge . . . just turned her head so that she could look past him down the trail again. They turned and saw the reason.

The old pony had collapsed on the stones below, the woman on her back scrambling off her and passing to safety through the gap. Jones started down toward the animal.

"Don't!" Maggie yelled.

He ignored her, lunging down the path and dropping to his knees in front of the old animal. Her tongue was out and she looked dead. Maggie followed after him in a crouch, rifle in her hands, searching the rocks below for Apaches. Then Dot bolted past her back down the trail, squatting beside her grandfather. She was coaxing and begging the old horse to get back onto her feet.

"Please!" Dot pleaded.

"Dotty, go back," Maggie said.

Bullets began to sound in the air. Maggie saw a dust puff on the trail near the horse and ran forward, dropping to her knees beside her daughter, scanning the boulders until she saw movement. She brought the rifle to her shoulder and fired. Then Lily darted down the trail and squatted behind the old pony, pushing hard on her rump. Dot joined her while Jones pulled on the animal's head. The gray was groaning.

Maggie cocked her rifle and threw it to her shoulder as another Apache moved over the rocks a couple hundred yards below. The shot cracked harshly in the still mountain air. While she hadn't hit him, it had been close and he sprawled hard out of sight.

"Hurry!" Maggie called back to them.

"Come on, horse!" Lily yelled frantically. "Get up."

Jones was talking softly to the gray in Apache. Then the other women joined them and soon the group of them had the little pony up and staggering toward the gap. She tried to go down to her knees again, but the group physically held her up. Then she was through the narrow place and Maggie took a final wild shot and ran. Jones stood at the neck of the trail with his Sharps until she was safely through, then he and Dot and Lily rolled a large, waist-tall rock down from the hillside, letting it settle into place like a stopper into the narrowest part. Maggie herded the women and Dot up the trail, collecting and sheltering their horses so they wouldn't be hit by stray bullets.

Jones turned and looked at Lily. She was standing beside him, gazing blindly through the narrow gap at the rocks below. He hadn't really looked at her in decent light since the ranch, and then she had always been so fancied up that he never noticed it before. Now, even with her swollen eyes, he was stunned at how much she resembled Susan, how much she possessed her grandmother's almost magical beauty. Her wonderful fight as well.

This young woman might like the finer things in life, he thought, but she would always give a good accounting of herself. He admired her for that. Little sister possessed the same qualities. So did Maggie. Susan had bred a line of warrior women. He smiled.

"Thanks for helping the gray," he said. Night was falling fast over the hills.

Lily was watching him closely and looked as if she wanted to say something, but didn't. He handed the Sharps to her and knelt beside the old horse, stroking her neck for a long time, talking to her again of her life and the heroic things she had done. The old pony looked finally played out. He told her of the great sweeping grasslands at the end of the last trail. He made the call of a meadowlark because he knew she liked the sound. Then Dot came hurrying and tried to give her water from her hat.

"Thank you, child, but it's no use. She's going now."

Dot began to shake her head hard. Alice had ambled down and stood with her nose close to the old horse, her soft breathing blowing gently against the gray coat.

"Why does she have to die now?"

"It's the right time. She has done a great thing. She knows, and she is proud. Only the mountains live forever."

"No. It's not time. It's never the right time." Dot leaned forward and buried her head against the shoulder of the horse.

"Child, don't disturb her. Let her go in peace and glory, proud of what she has done. She suffered for this; you must honor her now with dignity. She has given us all that was inside her heart." Jones began to chant in a low voice.

Chaco came and hopped onto the gray's rump as if doing it would infuse life into her again. But the old horse shook once, then was gone. Alice nuzzled her harder.

"Oooh, Ma," Dot cried.

"Think about the trail we rode together," the old man told her. "Remember it always, and she will live." He shook his small rattle over the horse.

Maggie uncinched the gray's saddle and pulled it off, draping the blanket over the horse's head. The old man motioned

Dot to him and sat down with her, pointing at the bright southern star. He was coughing hard, and Dot thought for a moment that he was going to slip back into unconsciousness. But then he stopped and caught his breath. "She and Ho-nes-co, and the others will wait there for us," he said, pointing at the sky. "All of us will meet there."

"Ma and the rest of us?"

"All. We are kin."

"But how will we find it?"

"Kayitah will mark a trail. You will know it."

Both Maggie and Lily were staring hard at the sparkling star, thinking separate thoughts. Then Maggie squatted beside the gray and put her hand on the pony's shoulder, thinking that they never would have reached Lily without her great courage. She had carried the old man over these hundreds of miles, had broken her heart. The little pony, Kayitah and her father had given her Lily back.

She leaned close to the blanketed head. "Thank you," she whispered.

Maggie helped Dot stand and walked with her back to where the women had built a fire and were cooking a meal. There was a drip hole with clear water nearby and Dot went and took a long drink. Afterward, she sat looking up into the night at the star in the southern sky. Maggie watched her for a while before she turned back toward the old horse and Jones. The old man was braiding the gray's hair and tying feathers and beads in it. Lily had squatted beside him and was doing the same. Watching the two of them together—her father and her oldest child—gave Maggie a wonderful feeling that heaven had at last shined its sweet light on her.

Later, the Apaches began to call and taunt from below. Jones picked up the Sharps and watched over the rocks, Lily joining him. Even at a distance, Maggie could sense the fear in her daughter. Jones must have felt it, too, and handed the weapon to her. She took it reluctantly, and Maggie could see the old giant talking to his granddaughter—talking the way he used to talk to her so long ago; a wonderfully warm, replenishing sense of family and kinship washed through her.

Lily fired the massive weapon, stepping backward from the shock of the heavy recoil. Jones chuckled. The laughter seemed to break the last of the hard knots inside Maggie. Lily reloaded, bracing, and fired again. They were both laughing now.

The Apaches were quiet. They would not attack at night, but Maggie knew they would not leave either. They were like wolves following a wounded beast. They would stay on the track until they brought them down. She thought of the Lame One and shuddered.

After darkness had descended, after the moon had lit the sky, and the night sounds had settled in, Maggie came slowly and sat down beside the old man. He was gazing at the dead horse, Chaco in his lap, Alice standing beside him. The dog growled at her. Jones snapped his fingers softly and Chaco quit. They did not talk for a while. Maggie watched a cactus wren in a nearby cholla. The bird was settling in for the night roost, moving slowly and deliberately among the spiny branches, its *chug, chug* breaking the silence.

Lily and Dot were sitting close together near the sparking embers of the fire, talking quietly. This was such a lovely sight, Maggie thought. Dot was laughing in the cool night air; her dream had come true—against the odds. Come true because of her grandfather. Maggie looked at his face. It looked like a death mask. He had truly been there for her. Listening to him struggling for breath, she knew now why the Apaches called him Fielito. He deserved it. He had fought to stay alive just to save his granddaughter. No, that wasn't all of it, she knew. He had fought to reach her as well. She looked up to the spray of stars overhead for a while and thought of Brake, Kayitah, Ho-nes-co and Mannito.

When she looked back at the old man, he was mouthing something silently in the night. She waited for him to finish, then said, "Tell me."

Jones cleared his throat. "Tell you what?"

"Why you left me."

He couldn't find the words for a while. A fool's hen called from somewhere up the canyon. The air was cold. He shifted on the sand against the pain that dug at his chest. "I didn't." He paused. "I just went back to them."

Maggie listened to the wind in the mountains, waiting for him to say more.

"As a young man I traded among the tribes—among the Lakota Sioux, the Crow, the Paiutes, the Cheyenne—lived among them in the years before they hated white men. I learned their languages and ways." He thought for a moment, then shifted on the sand again, trying to escape the relentless pain. "Perhaps I stayed too long. They became more my people than the whites. I believed what they taught me. I took meaningful things—for me—from each." He reached out a hand and stroked the little dog's back. "I put them together and made what you call my 'personal religion.' " He smiled at her.

There was a noise in the rocks above and they looked up to see the big sleepy eyes of a ringtailed cat looking down. Jones smiled. "Hunt well, brother," he said, softly, and the little cat with the dreamy face moved on.

"I traveled south in 1838 to trade with the Navajos and Zuni, establishing a post in the Mexican territory. I dealt fairly with them. Business was good. Then one day a band of White Mountain Apache came in to trade, and I saw her. Twenty, old for an unwed Apache. She was beautiful."

"Yopon?"

He nodded.

"She was intelligent and dignified, and she resisted my clumsy attempts to court her for a long time." He stopped and looked at Maggie, stroking her hair gently with his huge hand. She closed her eyes.

"But I was in love with her. Hopelessly so. When the band left, I sold my share in the post to my partner and went with them. They would not accept me. The young men fought me individually, then in groups to try and run me off." He smiled, remembering. "I guess I just outlasted them and they got tired of battling with me."

"Why didn't they just kill you?"

"Those days the Apaches treated the whites fair enough. It was the Mexicans they hated." He paused. "Later they came to hate the whites."

When he didn't continue, Maggie said, "What happened?"

"Something magical." He began to cough hard, his eyes tearing from the pain.

"How so?"

"Yopon fell for me," he said, smiling his golden-tooth smile and catching his breath. "We married." He wiped his eyes with the heel of his hand. "We had two children."

"Eskim and Lozen."

"No. Two boys, Nolo and Ishpia."

"Where are they?"

"Both dead. When they were small, the Mexicans began a campaign to rid their northern lands of Apaches. At the same time, Americans were moving across these lands, prospecting for gold and silver, and killing Indians." He stopped and looked down at the ground. "After an attack on our rancheria by Mexicans, I tried to get Yopon to leave with me and the boys, to live among the whites." He stopped talking and smiled. Maggie looked up at him and couldn't help smiling herself at the odd aspect the grin caused on the old man's ferocious face.

"What's funny?" she asked.

"Just how I've been surrounded by strong women."

She studied him for a moment, then said, "You chose them."

He didn't answer her, looking instead at his hands and remembering things in the past. His face began to cloud with dark thoughts. She waited.

"She would not leave. She feared what the whites would do to her children." He paused. "Times got worse. There was killing everywhere. Both sides. We could not be seen on Mexican land without being fired on. We became like the owl and the coyote, creatures of the night. Then what I had feared happened: our oldest son, Nolo, was killed by Mexicans. Still Yopon would not leave. And something in the world changed for me with Nolo's death. I no longer cared for the things of life.

"It was as if I, too, had died. I could travel over the land but my spirit would not come with me—it stayed behind with the child. If I relaxed my mind, he was in my thoughts. I could not escape this boy that I loved, who was no more. I began to drink. But it did not stop me from dreaming of Nolo's body beneath the earth, remembering the way he had been, the things he loved. His voice," the words trailing off in the darkness. "Once when I was drunk, I thought I heard him crying and I rode to his grave and dug him up. And now I cannot remember his face as it was . . . only the terrible face of death that I saw in the ground."

Jones struggled to his feet and seemed to shake off his memories and went to check the trail below, standing in the shadows for a long time before he returned to where she waited. He sat down hard, taking his breath in short gulps.

"Something had broken inside my head. Mescal was my only peace. Then one day I was captured by an American patrol at a water hole with two Apaches and put in an Arizona prison for two years. When I was finally released, I searched for Yopon and the boy for more than a year."

He stopped talking and thought for a moment. Then he looked up at her as if he'd just remembered she was sitting nearby. "I was told by other Apaches that the White Mountain bands had been destroyed, or put on the reservations. I spent another year searching the camps. But nothing. I tried to burn the memory of them out of my head with whiskey. I could no longer live here in these lands and I went east to St. Louis and bought our farm."

He sat and stared at the earth for a long time. Then he turned and looked at her. "Your mother lived a few miles away. I was drinking more." He listened to an owl calling in the darkness, tensing slightly. The bird stopped.

"I thought I had left the memories of Yopon and Ishpia behind. But I hadn't. Once, a year after I met Susan, I went back to search for them. I had to know if they were still alive. Again, the Apaches I spoke to told me the White Mountains had all been killed. I came back to the farm believing finally that they were dead."

"And you and Mother married."

"Yes." He stopped talking and looked at Maggie. "You must know: I never stopped loving Yopon." He thought for a moment. "I loved them both. Can you understand that?"

Maggie thought for a moment, then said, "Yes."

Chaco crawled into his lap.

She poked at the ground with a stick.

Jones studied her face for a time, marveling at the way of love, its amazing vulnerability, its stonelike durability. Pain suddenly spread her dark wings over him. He waited until she passed on, then said, "You were born. The years passed. Then one day I received a letter from my old partner saying things were going badly for the Apaches. That he had seen Yopon and Ishpia at the post. That Ishpia was sick. That the rancherias were in poor shape, starving and hunted constantly for scalp bounty by Mexicans and whites."

He cleared his throat and sat blinking up at the stars. "I had been reading to you in your room. You'd fallen asleep and I had taken the letter from my pocket where it had been unopened for a week. I knew it was from my old partner and hadn't wanted to revisit the painful memories." He shifted on the ground.

"After I finished reading it, I couldn't stop looking at your face. I sat there all night beside your bed. Just looking at you." He stopped talking and hacked hard for a while. "I loved you. I loved your mother."

He moved again with visible effort. "Life should never have such a choice. Love against love. Never," he muttered.

He stared into her face. "I thought Susan would remarry—the two of you have a new life." He stopped talking for a while.

"Ama. I left because they were fighting for their lives."

Maggie poked at the sand with her stick again. "What happened to Ishpia?"

"We never knew. He went hunting one day and never returned."

Maggie wrapped her arms around herself and said a prayer for these dead brothers she had never even known existed before this night. The old man was looking at her.

"I loved you. Every day. If you believe nothing else, believe that."

Maggie didn't speak. She stared at the muzzle of the dead pony and thought about this man and his wives and children. All gone except for her. Looking at his face and hands, she knew now why they were so battered. He had fought for all his wives and children, in different ways.

When she glanced back up, tears were coming and she said, "Dad—I'm cold. Will you hold me?"

Samuel Jones was making a strange sound in his throat as he reached out to put his arms around his daughter. They sat this way for hours, not talking. Maggie held her head softly against the old man's chest, listening to his heart beating, soaking up the thing she had craved since that night, so long ago. Then she slept.

This time when the little voice of her dreams spoke, she smiled. Lozen was leading her somewhere. Maggie recognized their old farm. They crawled over the pasture fence, running and laughing to the top of the hill behind the barn. It was sunny and warm, the bright sky filled with thin, drifting clouds. Maggie and Lozen had their arms around one another. Then Lozen stopped and pulled free and turned around. Maggie watched her face for a moment. Her half sister was smiling and Maggie followed her gaze down into the meadow below.

For a moment, she didn't believe what she saw. They were together. Walking hand in hand across the field. No anger or hurt. Just laughter and talk. Then Lozen was running down the hill toward them, and Maggie was suddenly filled with joy.

Watching them—her mother and Yopon—holding hands and walking together, and talking in that green field, healed something in her that had been hurt most of her life. Maggie couldn't take her eyes off them. They looked so happy together. She knew now that neither of them had harmed the other. There was no jealousy—no pain. They were not that kind of women.

They shared something beautiful and unspoken. Something wonderful and mysterious in this life: their love of the same man. It bound them for eternity. Lost children, pain and love. They shared these things as well.

Maggie woke up feeling a part of it.

Her father was smiling down at her.

"Do you have anything of Yopon's?" she asked.

"Yes."

"I would like something of hers."

Jones watched her face for a long time, unable to speak. Then he nodded and reached for his saddlebag, sorting through it, and finally bringing out a small wooden frame with a brass clasp. He opened it. Inside was a lock of black hair, and two photographs. Maggie looked at the pictures. It was the same woman that Maggie had seen with her mother in the dream. Yopon. As beautiful and delicate as the marshal had said. Her smile made Maggie smile.

Jones cleared his throat. "Take this," he said, removing one of the photographs.

"No."

"Please. She would want you to have it." He studied the picture for a moment, then passed it to Maggie. "You would have liked each other."

Maggie cradled the small photograph in her hands for a while, then stood slowly and walked off toward the campfire. When she returned, she was holding the silver frame that Jones had given her the day he left the ranch. She opened it and looked at the old picture of the three of them, and then slipped the photograph of Yopon into the empty glass on the other side.

Jones ran the tips of his fingers over the little wisp of hair. "This also," he said, handing her half of the black strands.

Maggie held them in the palm of her hand, touching them gently. "She had soft hair."

"It's not Yopon's."

"Whose then?"

"Lozen's."

Maggie's hands were shaking as she stroked the soft black hair of this little girl she'd known only in her dreams. She held it for a long time, then placed it in between the photos and closed the frame.

After she had composed herself, she turned and looked up at him and said, "I'd begun to believe you were right."

"About?"

"God not answering my prayers." She paused. "But he did."

"How?"

"He sent me you."

The old man smiled his golden-tooth smile. "You don't give up."

Maggie returned his smile for a moment, then her expression turned serious. "I fear for your soul."

He shook his head softly. "Don't."

Maggie leaned against him and shut her eyes.

Jones squatted in the darkness on the wide shelf of granite jutting out over the precipice. He inched forward, peering down into the dark abyss. Some seven hundred feet down. He breathed deeply and listened to the night sounds, not certain what impulses had brought him here, aware only that this was where he and the Lame One would meet. Destiny? He didn't know. It didn't matter. All that mattered was that he destroy the pesh-chidin. If he failed, nothing would matter.

Jones wore only his clout, carrying his war axe and his knife in its beaded sheath. Guns would not work. Not against the pesh-chidin. He had to be defeated according to the old ways. Otherwise, Jones's people—Yopon, Susan, Ama, Kayi-tah, Thelma and the others—were lost. Lost for all eternity.

He adjusted his little glasses, shivering in the cool air and taking a deep breath, ignoring the searing pain in his lungs, and listening once more to the night. He had called on his power, but felt weak. Still, something had guided him to this lonely place.

His ears strained at a faint sound. He tensed. Something or someone was near him. He could feel the presence. He turned slowly in a small circle, his grip tightening on the handle of the axe. Nothing but the darkness.

An owl called and Jones thought he could detect someone; an intruder, in the sound. Then the mosquito that had been hovering around him, searching in vain for a greaseless spot on his skin, moved off to his new prey . . . and Jones knew for certain that the man-being was somewhere nearby in the darkness.

He saw him out of the side of his eye, a heavy shadow moving in a strange rocking gait, moving faster than Jones had imagined and whirled too late, the stone club snapping his collarbone and driving him to his knees. Pain spurted up Jones's neck and he dropped the axe, his right arm suddenly heavy and useless. He wavered in the air, fighting to stay upright and conscious.

For whatever reason, perhaps simply to savor his victory, the man-being did not finish him, but hobbled backward a few steps and stood staring at him. Jones was aware of a sense of weightlessness and knew that he was fainting. He blinked himself awake.

The Lame One watched him from beneath a black hood, the man far heavier than Jones had guessed, massive from his grotesquely shaped head to his thick waist. Ill-proportioned and freaklike. Bull-strong. Jones felt a chill seep through him: aware there was little chance he could defeat this grim creature.

Like Jones, he carried only a club and knife. Of the face, only the eyes were visible, darting wildly behind the small slits of the hood. Mannito and Kayitah had stared into those eyes. Seen the reflection of their days in them.

Jones remained calm. He tried to move his right arm. No response. He saw the eyes dart to the flopping movement he'd made trying to swing his useless limb.

Sensing that he could toy with him, the Apache stepped sideways, circling slowly in his rocking hobble toward the useless arm, forcing Jones to turn on his knees with him. Neither spoke. There was no need. Both knew why they had come here. What they must do. Theirs was a ritual as old as the People. He pulled himself up straighter and picked up his axe with his left hand. He would get on with it. If destiny— then what would be had already been written in the winds and on the sand and stones. Nothing would change it. And he must play his part in it.

Suddenly, Jones was racked with convulsions, coughing uncontrollably, his glasses falling from his face. The hacking did not stop. He went down on his hands and knees, dropping his axe again. The Apache edged forward. Then with the warrior standing directly in front of him, Jones's coughing stopped as abruptly as it had begun, and he pivoted hard on his left hand, lashing out one of his long legs. The vicious kick catching the hooded warrior on the side of his good leg, sprawling him out of control onto the granite and toward the cliff.

Jones grabbed his axe and rolled into the darker shadows. He waited, breathing hard, and searching the night. The ledge was empty. He knew he had surprised him and they'd been close enough. But had he gone over? Jones waited, searching the night. No clumps of shadows. Slowly, he struggled onto his feet, moving cautiously. He leaned forward, peering into the deep darkness below. He couldn't see anything. He was straightening up when the club crashed hard into his ribs, bones snapping, pain searing his chest. He rolled left, dangerously close to the cliff. The pesh-chidin grunting and hobbling along after him, awkward and vicious like a bird of prey on the ground.

The man was over him now. Another strike with the club. Then another deflected. Jones scrambled desperately to the wall, falling back against the stones. He dodged a crushing shot aimed at his head. The pesh-chidin was breathing hard. The man-being kicked him in the side. Almost over. Jones was no longer able to avoid the blows. He saw the knife and sensed the end.

"Kayitah . . . go to the star," he whispered.

The man was on him. Jones looked down and saw blood spurting from his shoulder, the blade of the knife red. He felt nothing.

"Sweet Jesus, I tried." The words seemed oddly comforting to him and he said them again . . . "Sweet Jesus."

Jones tried to move. No use. He looked up at the hooded face. "Pesh-chidin," he said, waiting for the knife. Then he heard a sound like nothing he had ever heard in his life. The Lame One whirled and faced the darkness. It was silent now.

Then out of the shadows came a pistol sliding harmlessly over the flat stone and out into empty space, followed by Maggie herself sprawling onto the granite surface. The pesh-chidin was quivering, his back to Jones.

He stood slowly—distracted by this woman. The woman in the spirit-picture. The woman that not even the Other could destroy. He was trembling. He raised his club. She would be faster than the old one. Dangerous. He knew that she possessed a medicine as powerful as his own.

Jones took a breath against the pain and pushed himself up into a sitting position, then jammed his knife with all his strength deep into the back of the pesh-chidin's good knee, shoving it around hard, trying desperately to cut a ligament or an artery. The man roared, yanking the blade out and stumbling away. His eyes still on the woman.

Maggie had stopped screaming and silence seemed to fall hard over the place. She was on her feet now, her eyes darting wildly over the granite surface for a weapon, a rock, a stick, anything. There was nothing. Her father raised his head and watched her, dazed. She could see the blood and sensed it was over. He was mumbling something. She wanted to go to him, to be with him at the end. But the Apache stood between them. Jones was talking again. She strained to hear him.

"Sweet Jesus . . ." he said, his head falling back.

Maggie stared at the old man, shocked: the words an answered prayer. She felt a mixture of hope and gnawing fear. Hope that her father was reaching out to God, and an unearthly fear that this heathen would destroy their souls. She knew now that her father had been right—there was something terribly wrong with this man.

She reached and pulled her crucifix over her head and held it out toward her father. He had pushed himself back up on his elbows and was gazing through the moonlight toward her. She searched his face, but realized that he wasn't looking at her—he was staring at the cross. Frightened as she was, this calmed her and brought some measure of good to evil. She looked back at the hooded creature. He had leaped back when she pulled the crucifix, and now he was eyeing her and the cross cautiously.

She took a tentative step forward. The Apache hopped back again, raising his club at her in a threatening way, oddly more frightened of her than she of him. Then she saw it: Brake's watch. This evil man had Brake's watch hanging around his neck.

"Give it to me," she said calmly, shoving a hand at him. He inched back from her.

"Give it to me!"

She could see him watching her nervously through the slits in the hood, could sense his fear. She didn't understand it. Didn't care. He reached behind him and pulled something and held it out toward her as if offering it in appeasement. Maggie's eyes moved to this object, staring at it for a moment, anger building slowly inside her.

She squinted hard in the moonlight. Yes. She was certain. It was the same one. The anger Maggie had felt at seeing Brake's watch was multiplied manyfold when she recognized the little doll. The doll that Lily had placed in Kayitah's hands. The doll that had belonged to the little murdered girl. Lily had asked Kayitah to take it to her. And this thing standing before her—this thing that had tortured her brother and Mannito—had stolen it.

Whatever fear Maggie had felt before dissipated as she glared at this corrupt being who stood offering a bloody rag doll as recompense for all his wretchedness. She clutched harder at the crucifix and shoved it out at him.

"How dare you!" she yelled. She was shaking badly.

"You tortured my brother! You killed Mannito! And you tried to kill my husband!" Maggie was shrieking. The man backed up another step. She was fully facing him now.

"You stole my child. You beat her. You beat my little girl. And you would have sold her into slavery. And you hurt my father!" Maggie's rage exploded in the night.

The Indian backed up again, his eyes darting for a way out, some escape from this woman-demon. He had never in his life faced a human who screamed defiance at him.

"Look at you!" she yelled, stepping forward again. "Hiding behind a mask. You're afraid."

Maggie suddenly stopped screaming and stood trembling and breathing hard, her glare fixed on the nervous eyes behind the hood. The man was half-crouched as if he might run or charge. She didn't know which. Didn't care. She knew only that the rage still burned in her, fueled by something she had no control over.

She felt funny—was breathing deeply, as if gathering the winds from the corners of the earth. Getting herself ready. She'd never felt like this before in her life.

Maggie took another step. She was now within striking range of the stone club. It didn't bother her. She shoved the crucifix at him as if it were a weapon. Again, he backed away, eyes darting. Maggie hesitated, then with a yell that felt like it came from a hidden place within her, cried, "In the name of God! Leave!"

The scream seemed to pierce the man, driving him backward, his wounded leg giving way, awkwardly back, as if he had suddenly lost all sense of balance, all control over his arms and legs . . . his deformed foot reaching for rock but finding only dark space. His body pitching away wildly, tumbling out into the night.

Jones closed his eyes and lay back on the stone ledge.

Destiny.

Jones allowed Maggie to stop the bleeding in his shoulder, but he would not return to their camp until he had struggled down to the bottom of the ravine and found the peshchidin's broken body. He and Maggie covered it with dry mesquite brush and then lit it on fire. It was the only way to finish it.

Back safely behind the narrow place, Jones built another fire of sagebrush and made Maggie join him in its purifying smoke. She held on to him so that he would not fall, and cried. They did not move for a long time. Maggie was trembling hard, the smoke burning her eyes. Finally, she turned her face up to his. "Do you believe now? Will you pray with me?"

Jones didn't answer for a while. Then he looked down at her and said, "I am not ready. But I will hold the cross and listen to you pray: let your prayers be for Susan and Yopon, and your sisters and brothers. And I will feel your words. And I will believe that they are heard beyond this world."

Maggie pulled the crucifix out and placed it into her father's hands, clamping hers over his. She looked up into his face.

"But do you believe He is the one God?"

"I have sought the Creator of the earth all my life. Surely that is not wrong." Jones smiled his golden-tooth smile at her and gently brushed the hair from her face.

She nodded and leaned her head softly against his chest. It was close enough. "God is God," she muttered. Night birds called. Maggie settled him down on his blanket near the dead pony and doctored his wounds. He had broken bones and punctures, but none bad enough to kill him, and she figured he could still ride. When she was done, she noticed that a large wolf spider was sitting on his leg. She pulled a glove from her pocket to flick it off, but he shook his head and smiled.

"Mannito," was all he said.

Samuel Jones was asleep in the light of the morning, leaning against the rocks, when Maggie and Dot rode up, leading a saddled horse. Dot was on Alice. Chaco was sitting in the old man's lap. Lily was standing with the Sharps watching the trail below. "What's it look like?" Maggie asked.

"I saw one a while ago. They aren't quitting."

Maggie was holding a cup of coffee, and she handed it down to Dot who took it over to her grandfather. The old man was squinting at them.

"Time to ride," Maggie said. "We can get a good jump on them. Lily and Dot will double up on this animal." She pointed at a sturdy-looking buckskin.

Jones tried to stand but was too weak and settled back down in the sand. He took the coffee and sipped. He looked around.

"Beautiful morning."

Maggie didn't like the way he said it, for a reason she didn't comprehend. "Father, we need to get moving."

"Yes. Take your girls, and the women, and ride."

Lily said it first. "No."

"Grandpa, you've got to come," Dot said, fear in her voice.

"You children mind your mother."

"No," Lily said emphatically.

Maggie didn't say anything, just sat on her horse watching him. She blinked hard a couple of times and seemed to have trouble swallowing. Then she turned in the saddle and looked up toward the sky, shaking her head slowly.

Finally, she said, "We just found you, Father."

"I know. But you must ride now. Or they'll follow and catch up. This way, I can make certain you make it. Kayitah, Ho-nes-co, the little Mexican, and the gray, they died so you could live. You have to do it. For them. For me."

Dot had her head buried in Alice's shoulder and was crying hard, the young mule turning and nibbling at her shirt.

"No," Lily said again.

"Yes. Like the gray, it is time for me. It is a wonderful thing—to be able to do this. You must understand. And be glad."

Dot was wailing loudly now. Lily just shook her head and kept repeating "No."

Maggie stared at him for a long time, then said, "Girls, get on the animals."

"No, Mom, I can't leave him," Lily protested.

"Get on," Maggie said firmly.

Lily helped push Dot up onto Alice, then mounted the buckskin. They were both crying quietly now. Alice turned and walked over to the old man and nudged him with her nose, Chaco hopping out of the way and nipping at her heels. The old man leaned forward and held the mule's head against his chest for a moment, then patted her.

Dot was off Alice first and into her grandfather's arms, followed by Lily and Maggie. The four of them sat holding one another for a while, stopping only when a bullet whined through the narrow gap, sparking against the rocks behind them. The old man pushed them gently toward their mounts. Maggie hesitated, then she took the crucifix and slipped it into his hands. She tied Lozen's acorn necklace around her neck. He smiled at her, his eyes glistening.

Samuel Jones squeezed each of them and then watched as they climbed into the saddles. The old man looked down at his little dog and said something to him in Apache, then he held him up to his face. Chaco licked him. He set him down on the sand and looked up at Maggie.

"Turn your toe out a bit and lean to the side."

When she had done this, Jones looked at the little dog sitting next to him and shivering in the morning sunlight, and nodded. Chaco didn't hesitate. He took two bounds, touched lightly on Maggie's boot, hit her thigh and then landed in his accustomed place on the horse's rump. He stood balancing himself and barking harshly at the old man. Jones signed something to him that none of them understood, and the little dog sat and whined.

Maggie couldn't stop looking at the old man's face.

"Ride," he said, gruffly.

"I dreamed about you every day. I thought about you. I

prayed for you to come home. I loved you." She wiped at her eyes. "I love you now, Father."

"And I love you. Remember the southern star. We will know each other when we meet."

Alice turned without any coaxing and started up the trail. Dot twisted in the saddle and looked back at him.

"Look for me when the moon is over the corn," he called to her. "I will be there in the wind and the shadows."

Dot made the sign for "bad." Jones made the signs for "love" and "you." She signed back the same and turned away.

Maggie rode alongside Lily and put her hand on her daughter's shoulder and they started up the trail. Chaco was whining again.

The horses of the other women fell quietly into line. Near the rim rock, Maggie heard the wail and knew he had begun his own death song. No—his song of life.

Chaco barked back to him.